W. E. B. GRIFFIN
THE DEVIL'S WEAPONS

ALSO BY W. E. B. GRIFFIN

W. E. B. GRIFFIN

THE DEVIL'S WEAPONS

PETER KIRSANOW

G. P. PUTNAM'S SONS
NEW YORK

PUTNAM
— EST. 1838 —

G. P. Putnam's Sons
Publishers Since 1838
An imprint of Penguin Random House LLC
penguinrandomhouse.com

Hardcover ISBN: 9780593422281
Ebook ISBN: 9780593422298

Printed in the United States of America
1 3 5 7 9 10 8 6 4 2

W. E. B. GRIFFIN
THE DEVIL'S WEAPONS

CHAPTER 1

It was the peculiar smell that he remembered most.

Not the hideous scenes, the horrific sounds, or the paralyzing cold. Not the terrified faces, or even the bodies mangled beyond recognition.

It was the smell. Utterly unlike anything he'd experienced in his nearly forty-one years on Earth. It was almost a tactile sensation, damp and suffocating. The product of blood and urine and intestines; rotting flesh and pulverized organs. It seemed to have lined his nostrils, penetrated his skin.

As he trod carefully through the woods, trying to orient himself while remaining alert for patrols, he recited the names of his four contacts and the three passwords assigned for each. The passwords had been given to him just once, hurriedly and in a hushed tone. He hoped he'd heard correctly. If he hadn't, he'd be dead within seconds of uttering the error.

There was little risk of his forgetting the names and passwords, no matter how tense the circumstances. Dr. Sebastian Kapsky had a prodigious memory capable of retaining and retrieving the most complex equations ever generated by the human brain. Equations that could *affect or alter history. Memory wasn't the issue. Rather it was whether what his brain retrieved when he spoke to the contacts was actually what was spoken to him by his seatmate, Bronislaw Haller.*

Katyn, Soviet Union
1430, 23 April 1940

Bronislaw Haller was a jeweler from Białystok. He and Kapsky had been rounded up by Red Army soldiers within days of the Soviet invasion of Poland, ostensibly for "administrative processing"—at least that's what they'd gleaned from the statements from the *praporshchiks* taking their names before herding them onto transports. A lumbering open-bed lorry transferred them to the Ostashkov Camp in Katyn Forest, where they would be funneled into concrete bunkers along with thousands of other men—mainly soldiers and policemen—but also a fair number of municipal officials, clergy, and academics.

From the moment they clambered aboard the lorry and sat next to each other, Haller had been anxious. More than anxious; his face was covered with a look that ranged between apprehension and dread. Within seconds of sitting next to Kapsky, Haller leaned near and whispered, "Find your opportunity, friend, and run. Don't hesitate. You'll only get one chance. Run and run fast."

Kapsky was startled. None of the detainees had spoken a word since they'd been marched toward the transports. Haller recognized the indecision on Kapsky's face. "Listen to me, friend. This isn't going to be random questioning, temporary detainment." Haller nodded toward two Russians dressed in civilian clothes standing apart from the Red Army soldiers. "That is NKVD. They do not send NKVD to verify names and addresses. They send NKVD for one thing: to kill."

Kapsky glanced toward the two civilians. Each wore dismissive, contemptuous expressions as they surveyed the Poles arrayed on the lorries. It was as if they were looking at something that would soon be irrelevant, like spoiled food being hauled to a dumpster. Kapsky leaned toward Haller. "Run where?"

"Anywhere. Just run. You'll know where to go later, but you must go."

Kapsky looked back at the NKVD officers, then leaned closer to Haller. "You lead. I'll follow."

A sardonic look came over Haller's face. "Obviously, you were not paying attention when I came aboard." He moved his long coat aside and gestured toward his legs. They were encased in a latticework of metal braces. "I've not run since I was eighteen years old." He shook his head. "I have no chance. But you may have one. And I can help."

A Soviet soldier closed the lorry's tailgate. One of the NKVD officers motioned for the driver to drive. As he waved his arm, the seams of his overcoat parted, revealing a Tokarev semiautomatic. The lorry lurched forward slowly.

Kapsky asked, "What do you mean you can help?"

Haller said, "You don't have much time, and few opportunities." He glanced about the bed of the vehicle and reached into his pocket. Most of the passengers were watching the Soviet troops lining the lorry's path. He withdrew a small cloth purse and pressed it into Kapsky's hand. Kapsky inspected it quizzically before opening it. Inside were several dozen *złoty*.

Kapsky snorted. "What am I supposed to do with this?"

"Train fare."

Kapsky handed the purse back. "No disrespect, but that is no help. I will get nowhere near a train." He waved at the scores of troops escorting the caravan of lorries. "They will seize the purse as soon as we get to our destination."

"No. They will not."

Kapsky squinted. "Why not?"

"Because you will give them something much more valuable. Something that will make them ignore your train fare."

"I have nothing of value."

"But I do. And I will give it to you in return for an oath."

Kapsky struggled not to appear impatient. "Oath? Is this a child's game? No riddles, please. Tell me what you want from me."

"Go to my family. Keep them safe."

Kapsky inspected Haller's face. It was a practical face. The face of a man with few illusions. A man who assessed Kapsky in scant minutes and judged him up to the task. Or perhaps the only one who would consider performing it.

Nonetheless, Kapsky gestured toward the escort vehicles on either side of the convoy carrying scores of Red Army troops. "Seriously? You ask the impossible."

Haller drew closer. "I did not say it would be easy, but it *is* possible. With money all things are possible. Indeed, probable."

"A few *złoty*?"

"More than a few. More than train fare. Much more."

"Show me."

"I cannot at this time."

Kapsky turned away sharply and scanned the muddy road ahead. It was lined on each side by tall pine, the tops enshrouded in depressing gray mist. It produced a sense of foreboding. Haller was silent for several seconds, then leaned forward. "I have several grams of uncut precious stones. Their value is considerable. Very considerable. You may use some to secure your release, the remainder to see to my family's safety."

Kapsky returned his gaze to Haller's face. He scanned it skeptically for several seconds. "Show them to me."

A sheepish look came over Haller's face. "I cannot." He paused, then added hurriedly, "But understand, I do have them with me."

Kapsky continued examining Haller's face. It looked as if it were imploring him to understand what Haller was saying. After a few seconds, Kapsky blinked and sat erect. "You have them with you . . ."

"In a manner of speaking, yes."

". . . *Within* you."

Haller nodded. "Undetectable, yet retrievable."

Kapsky gazed toward the tops of the pines, then at the guards brandishing Soviet submachine guns. "How do you know that I won't simply abscond with the remaining stones after bribing the guards?"

"I do not."

Kapsky said, "We have no options . . ."

"We always have options, friend, always."

Kapsky stared at the floor of the lorry for nearly a minute. "How do I find them, your family?"

"They're in a hamlet outside Białystok. The address is in the purse."

Kapsky nodded and said nothing. They rode in silence for several minutes. Then Kapsky asked, "And when I find them, your family, what should I tell them about you?"

Haller smiled. "Tell them I escaped but had to take a different route, a longer route. It will take a while for me to arrive. Tell them I will join them when circumstances permit."

Kapsky understood. It was the response of a man who believed he was doomed.

CHAPTER 2

Washington, D.C.
1330, 24 April 1940

The humidity in Washington, D.C., was oppressive even in late
April. It was compounded by Professor Aubrey Sloane's unfortunate
choice in clothing. Originally from New Hampshire and now a lec-
turer at Cornell, his wardrobe consisted primarily of clothing suitable for New England. For his meeting today with Secretary of
War Henry Stimson he'd worn his best suit—pure wool. Though it
breathed well, it nonetheless caused him to perspire, which in turn
caused him to itch. Consequently, he was about to enter the most
important meeting of his life miserable and distracted.

He was astounded that he'd even secured the meeting. Obscure
associate professors of physics didn't score meetings with the secretary of war—especially one as formidable as Stimson—unless the
secretary had collected information validating the purpose of the
meeting.

Sloane's purpose was to warn Stimson that the United States of
America, and much of the world, might soon be in peril.

Sloane walked slowly up the steps of the Munitions Building trying not to exert himself and precipitate a flood of perspiration. His footfalls echoed throughout the cavernous halls until he came to the tall wooden door of the Office of the Secretary of War.

Upon his entry, the sternly efficient receptionist sitting behind a massive oak desk startled him by immediately addressing him by name. "Please have a seat, Professor Sloane." She gestured to the wooden chairs arranged along the wall of the anteroom. "The secretary will receive you presently."

Sloane proceeded to the chair closest to the entrance. But before he could sit, a buzzer sounded on the receptionist's desk and she said, "The secretary is ready for you."

Sloane straightened and walked through the wooden gate next to the desk and knocked twice on the door to the office before entering. Secretary of War Henry Stimson, seated at the desk, was sifting through a sheaf of documents. Another man Sloane didn't recognize was seated in one of the two chairs opposite Stimson's desk. He had the countenance of a bulldog, a taciturn expression. He said nothing.

Stimson glanced at Sloane, tilted his head toward a seat, and returned his attention to the papers. Sloane sat in the chair for a full minute before Stimson placed the papers neatly on the corner of the desk and said, "Thank you for coming to see me, Professor."

"Thank *you*, sir."

"There have been a few scientists and mathematicians who advised us that there have been some rather profound developments in certain academic quarters of Europe. No one provided much by way of specifics, other than the developments could be rather transformative." Stimson nodded toward the bulldog. "Professor, this is

Colonel Donovan. He, in fact, is the person who first alerted me to these transformative issues. When I related your message, he advised that I should, indeed, meet you face-to-face. And he insisted on being present."

Sloane nodded at Donovan, who was dressed in civilian clothes. Donovan remained expressionless.

"I gather the purpose of your visit has something to do with these developments."

"Yes, it does. It relates to an individual who is integral to what you referred to as 'transformative' scientific developments. He is one of a small group of kindred spirits. These are rather gifted physicists who I met two years ago at a conference in London. They had common, in fact parallel, pursuits in a field known as quantum mechanics. Since that conference we've been collaborating by correspondence, occasionally with Fermi of the University of Chicago, Niels Bohr of the University of Copenhagen, and Robert Goddard. They are the most renowned—"

"I know who they are, Professor. They are rather well known. Please continue."

"Yes, well, the individual of whom I speak was the key, the most integral, member of the collaboration. He was the man who initiated the joint correspondence among the group, developed the foundational theories, and produced the 'transformative' applications . . ."

". . . and?"

". . . and we haven't heard from him in nearly a month. Nothing. No cables. No letters. Even after the invasion of his country last September by the Red Army, he kept up regular correspondence without interruption—two, three times per week. He was prodigious. Then, suddenly, nothing."

The man introduced as Colonel Donovan had an intense expression on his face. Sloane could see muscles protruding like cables beneath his jawline.

"What do you think happened?"

"*I don't know,*" Sloane whispered. "But with the Nazis to the west and the Soviets to the east . . ."

"You're concerned, obviously, that some harm has come to him," Stimson said. "But it's more than that, isn't it? This isn't just about looking out for a friend or colleague."

Sloane appeared anguished. "Mr. Secretary, I know nearly nothing of international affairs, war, or diplomacy, but I'm wholly capable of making reasonable deductions.

"I read the newspapers and see the Movietone reels in the theaters like everyone else, and it seems only a matter of time before we're drawn into the war in Europe. Heck, we're already assisting Great Britain logistically and with matériel." Sloane halted abruptly, raising his palms plaintively. "I don't mean to be speaking out of school, I just . . ."

"No apologies necessary, Professor. I think I understand where you're going with this." Stimson looked at Donovan.

"The Germans are quite proud of their array of modern weaponry—superweapons, they call them. We've been watching the development keenly. Although they pose no threat to us at the moment, Mr. Churchill is obsessed with them." Donovan paused and withdrew a cigar from his breast pocket. "Your colleague . . . I assume his work would be of utmost interest to the Germans?"

"Not just to Hitler, but to Stalin as well."

"And to America, I suppose?"

"The potential strategic value of his work is unparalleled. Not only did he work with the likes of Bohr and Goddard, but before the war he also worked with Walter Riedel and Wernher von Braun. He is intimately familiar with the science behind the German rocket programs. Clearly, they would not want those revealed. But it goes even beyond that. I do not say this lightly. Bohr, Fermi, and the rest of us are knowledgeable about discrete components, but this individual is the glue. He is knowledgeable about *all*. Moreover, he has multidisciplinary proficiency. He is gifted, and not just in one subject. Although it remains hypothetical, the matters upon which we've been working have extraordinary implications, and he is the one among our cohort who is most capable of turning theory into reality."

Donovan exchanged a knowing look with Stimson, leaving Sloane to suspect that the two may have heard something similar from other sources. Donovan shook his head as if he were hoping Sloane would have dispelled or downplayed what these sources had said.

"What do you propose be done, Professor Sloane?"

"Keep him out of the hands of the Russians and Germans. If we're too late for that, *rescue* him from the Russians and Germans."

Donovan glanced at Stimson, who nodded almost imperceptibly.

"What's your colleague's name?"

"Sebastian Kapsky."

"You know what I think of these kinds of operations, Bill. The kind MI6 performs," Stimson said after Sloane had left to take the train back to New York. "This isn't what civilized nations do."

Colonel William "Wild Bill" Donovan didn't need a reminder. Stimson was old-school. Civilized nations, *gentlemen*, didn't engage in clandestine operations on another nation's soil unless they were at war. And even then, there were rules, conventions.

"Henry, we *are* at war. Maybe not formally. But we're assisting the Brits, we've got aviators in Indochina. The professor's right, it's inevitable and you know it. Churchill's been hounding the President for months, and you know that the President won't be able to withstand that man's relentlessness."

"I cannot go to the President and ask that he send troops to Poland, even if it's a small tactical force. Both the Nazis and the Soviets would declare war," Stimson said.

Donovan inclined his massive bulldog head forward, a fullback about to plunge into a defensive line. "You've seen the reports, Henry. Hell, you have access to more reports than I do. Britain can't hold out much longer, even without the Germans deploying these 'superweapons' Hitler keeps going on about." Donovan jabbed his meaty index finger on Stimson's desktop. "That's a strategic disaster for us, even if we're not at war. And that's even without whatever superweapon Sloane's talking about. If either Hitler or Stalin get the type of capability Sloane implies, we won't have a chance in hell. The mere *threat* of its deployment will cause us to cave. We'd have to."

Stimson was taken aback. He'd never imagined Donovan was capable of even entertaining any result other than success, victory.

"You don't know that, Bill. This is all theoretical. Sloane even said so. Even if it got off the drawing board, it would be several years—as much as a decade or two—before it would become a reality. By then, the war in Europe will be long over."

Donovan remained adamant. Stabbing the desk again, he said, "You cannot take that chance. Right now it might be just a bunch of numbers and hieroglyphs on a chalkboard, but what if Hitler's math wizzes can turn those equations into reality a lot faster than we think? You heard Sloane. Hell, you heard that white-haired guy from Princeton, Eisenstein . . ."

"Einstein."

". . . You heard him, too. What if Hitler's people—or Stalin's—get it off the chalkboard with this Kapsky's help?"

Stimson, who'd been secretary of war under Presidents William Howard Taft and Franklin Delano Roosevelt, struck a pose familiar only to his closest friends. It was a pose of deliberation and concern, a patrician pose. Nearly a full minute passed. He nodded to himself, then looked at Donovan. "What do you propose?"

"We don't need a large force, just one or two men. With adequate support, as needed."

Stimson shook his head. "That codicil is what worries me. 'Support, as needed.' That almost inevitably means an escalation."

"No, it wouldn't. I'm not talking about military support. Not artillery, not aircraft. Just logistical support."

Stimson shook his head again. "One or two men—with some undefined logistical support—to find one man somewhere in Europe? In the middle of a two-front war?"

"Put that way, it *does* sound absurd. But it can be done." Donovan's bulldog head remained inclined toward Stimson. His eyes, though plaintive, were locked in.

A rare, wan smile creased Stimson's face. "And who is the remarkable man who would achieve this? You must already have someone in mind."

"I do."

"Who, then?"

"You don't know him."

"I sure as hell will if you expect me to approve this."

Donovan straightened from his incline. "I haven't really decided yet. But I'm thinking of some Rangers."

"Why these particular fellows? What qualifies them for a task like this?"

"They're somewhat reckless, yet deliberate."

As he spoke he was considering another option. Someone who didn't stay in the lanes. Borderline reckless, even brazen, but dependable and effective. A young major by the name of Dick Canidy.

CHAPTER 3

Katyn Forest
1930, 24 April 1940

They first brought the doomed, one by one, into a dark concrete chamber the size of a large conference room. Two guards armed with PPSh-41 submachine guns would stand next to the exit as a *praporshchik* conducted a perfunctory final interrogation of the prisoner. The questions were anodyne: name, place of birth, current residence, occupation, immediate relatives. Any valuables that hadn't already been confiscated would be placed in a large bin near the entrance.

Due to the noise from massive exhaust fans in the adjacent room, both the interrogator and the prisoner had to shout their questions and answers. Accordingly, the interrogators would change every hour so that their voices wouldn't become hoarse.

The questioning lasted little more than a minute; the answers were not recorded in a journal or ledger. When done, one of the guards would escort the prisoner through a door opposite the entrance and into a larger concrete chamber for execution.

And so it was that Sebastian Kapsky was led by two guards into the antechamber, where he stood under a caged lightbulb, blinking against its harsh light at the *praporshchik* who would pose the last questions Kapsky would ever hear. One of the guards retreated to the side of the entrance while the other patted Kapsky down, retrieving a brown leather billfold from his right back pocket. Opening it, the guard found several *złoty*, and a University of Lviv identification card bearing a photo of the smiling professor of theoretical physics, room 201, Galician Sejm. Grinning, the guard held up the billfold, opening it to display the currency that they would momentarily distribute among themselves after the prisoner was questioned.

The interrogator nodded, then examined the clipboard that he held in his left hand, tracking his right index finger to the next name on the list.

"Name?"

"Sebastian Kapsky."

"Date and place of birth?"

"January 7, 1902, Kraków."

"Current address?"

"Hell."

The interrogator looked up sharply, unamused.

"Immediate family?"

"All deceased. Your compatriots saw to that."

"Occupation?"

"Professor. Lviv University."

"Do you have anything to declare?"

"You are a horse's ass."

The interrogator looked at the guard standing next to Kapsky, who winced as the guard delivered a blow to Kapsky's left kidney.

The interrogator's eyes narrowed as he studied the clipboard. Kapsky noticed his finger sliding back and forth as if he were checking Kapsky's name against a second list. After several moments he looked up, his head tilted slightly to the side.

"Your name again?"

"Sebastian Kapsky."

A glimmer of excitement shone in the interrogator's eyes. "Professor Sebastian Andrejz Kapsky?"

"Yes."

The interrogator spun on his heel, hurriedly proceeded to the door to the larger chamber, and disappeared. Kapsky heard him speaking rapidly to someone inside, his tone subservient. He reappeared momentarily and beckoned Kapsky to the larger chamber. The guard standing next to Kapsky flipped Kapsky's billfold to the other guard, grabbed Kapsky's right arm, and pushed him past the interrogator into the larger chamber and withdrew, closing the door behind him.

The larger chamber had a concrete floor that sloped toward a drain over which hung a water hose. The room smelled of gunpowder, blood, and disinfectant. As in the antechamber, a single lightbulb encaged in steel wire provided illumination. Standing beneath the bulb was a hulking figure built like a heavyweight prizefighter. He looked as if he could absorb multiple powerful blows to the face without flinching. He was encased from head to toe in rubberized gear: overalls, a trench coat, boots, and goggles. A sleek Walther .25 ACP was in his right hand.

He was NKVD Commandant Vasily Mikhailovich Blokhin, the most prolific executioner in the history of mankind. Stalin's chief assassin. Everyone in Ostashkov, including Kapsky, knew his reputation. It was tattooed on their minds. To this point, he had killed more than 5,500 prisoners—each with a single shot from the Walther to the back of the head. It was a seemingly incomprehensible figure, one not remotely approached by many whole armies.

Blokhin's prodigious kills preceded his arrival at Katyn Forest. They included the famous as well as the obscure. Among his victims were many of those convicted during the Moscow Show Trials, even Mikhail Tukhachevsy, marshal of the Soviet Union, and Genrikh Yagoda, former head of the NKVD itself. It was said that when Blokhin died, half the population of hell would pursue him throughout eternity and half the population of heaven would be cheering for his capture.

Blokhin stared impassively at Kapsky for several seconds before speaking—his voice impossibly deep and guttural.

"You are Sebastian Kapsky." It wasn't a question.

"I am."

"Professor Sebastian Kapsky, the mathematician."

"Indeed, I am."

"From Lviv University."

Kapsky nodded.

Something resembling a smile crossed Blokhin's face. It projected greed and success.

"You are most fortunate, Professor. You will not be sharing the fate of your comrades this day. A very important figure wishes to see you. Apparently, you have significant value."

Kapsky permitted himself a smile. "May I ask who this important person to whom I owe my life is?"

"Lavrentiy Beria, Professor Kapsky. My superior. The head of the NKVD."

Kapsky nodded. His smile disappeared. "The most feared man in the Soviet Union, perhaps the world."

"He *may* be the most feared man in the world. But he is the *second* most feared man in the Soviet Union, Professor. He reports, after all, to Joseph Vissarionovich Stalin."

"What, may I ask, would someone like Beria want with me?" Kapsky asked.

Blokhin shrugged. "I do not have the details, only that you are of extreme importance. And apparently not just to Comrade Beria. I was told finding you was of some urgency. We are in a competition. It seems Admiral Canaris also has instructed his people that locating you is of prime importance."

"I'm afraid I'm unfamiliar with this Mr. Canaris," Kapsky said.

"Chief of the Abwehr-German military intelligence. The genius spy."

Kapsky nodded, impressed with his own apparent fame. "A competition? Between the signatories to Molotov-Ribbentrop? I confess I do not understand."

Blokhin waved him off. "We will leave for Moscow in the morning. I am to deliver you to Beria personally. In the meantime, you may spend the night in the officer's quarters."

Kapsky smiled appreciatively. "I am very hungry also."

"Of course, Professor. You will be fed, provided a change of clothes, and will be—"

The interrogator burst into the chamber, a panicked expression on his face. He strode rapidly toward a startled Blokhin and without a word displayed Kapsky's open billfold to his superior. An irritated Blokhin blinked as he adjusted his focus upon the billfold's contents, the task made more difficult by the interrogator's trembling hand. Blokhin grasped the interrogator's hand to steady it and a moment later a look of terror covered the executioner's face. Blokhin recognized the professor's photo ID. He knew the face; he'd seen it yesterday, as the lorries brought in the prisoners. He remembered it because of the owner's distinctive shock of jet-black hair that combined with deep green eyes that made him appear almost spectral. He remembered thinking that the face belonged to an uncommonly inquisitive individual because the eyes darted about, scanning the surroundings as if he were calculating multiple probabilities—the best odds for escape. A futile calculation.

But the face was not that of the stooped man standing before him.

Blokhin looked up abruptly. "You are not Kapsky?" Alarmed, he looked down at the photo ID and then back up again. "You are *not* Kapsky."

Sebastian Kapsky was long gone. Bronislaw Haller, meticulous, nervous jeweler from the outskirts of Białystok, smiled and began to shake his head just as a single 6.35-millimeter round, fired in rage by the most prolific killer in creation, penetrated his forehead.

CHAPTER 4

Lakehurst, New Jersey
1612, 27 April 1940

He behaved as if they weren't watching him, inspecting him: Nonchalant. Indifferent.

His eyesight was good, but peripheral vision could be deceptive. Nonetheless, he determined that the tall blonde on the left was the most attractive—and most interested—of the four women huddled together on the periphery of the field.

Each was subtle. No staring, only furtive, coy glances and whispered assessments, probably of his physique.

Lieutenant (junior grade) Richard Canidy had attended MIT on a Navy scholarship, graduating with honors in 1938 with a B.S. in aeronautical engineering. He'd already logged 350 hours of flying time by then and was approached by General Claire Chennault to fly P-40B fighters, defending Burma Road supply lines against the Japanese in China.

He hated exercise for the sake of exercise. Physical exertion, he believed, should be directed toward a purpose other than improving one's physique. Otherwise, it was mere vanity. Vanity wasn't manly. It wasn't productive. It was the indulgence of those who otherwise were failures.

Canidy knew that he had a naturally superior build. It was primarily a matter of heredity. The males on both sides of his family were tall, lean, and naturally well muscled. He'd inherited all of those characteristics. He appreciated all of those characteristics. He would never, however, concede vanity because of those characteristics.

Canidy, nonetheless, was competitive to the point of irrationality. Although he disdained exercise, he hated being second best even more, and despite being blessed with a splendid physique he determined that his friend Eric Fulmar's was even better. Not much more, and perhaps not even discernible to the casual observer, but enough to ignite Canidy's competitive instincts.

So three weeks ago he'd embarked on a punishing regime of running, calisthenics, and weight training. He'd performed the latter in strict privacy; *normal* people didn't indulge in such pursuits. It was the province of wrestlers and circus performers. But he'd experimented with it at the suggestion of a friend—a former Annapolis football player—and was impressed at the results after just a few sessions.

So he persisted.

The women ostensibly were watching the baseball game on the diamond next to the football field on which Canidy was finishing up a set of fifty-yard sprints. There were no items on his agenda for the rest of the day or evening. He'd given some thought to meeting Fulmar at the St. Regis Hotel for a drink and taking advantage of whatever opportunities presented themselves. But he decided to explore the more immediate opportunities that had presented themselves on the bleachers along the first base line.

While catching his breath from the sprints, he considered what approach to use. Separating one woman from a group was not a task for amateurs. And while Canidy certainly was no amateur, even skilled players often floundered.

He'd already taken the first step—determining which one to separate. The blonde. Although it was a close call, really a matter of personal preference. She was tied with the raven-haired one for most attractive. Although something about the raven-haired girl suggested greater long-term erotic potential, the blonde had already displayed the most interest. Canidy didn't want to work at it. He preferred to go with the best short-term odds.

His calculus, however, was momentarily scrambled when he noticed the brunette casually stroke her left thigh while giving him a sidelong glance. The gesture was crafted to look innocent rather than purposeful, but a man like Canidy knew better. Still, after a slight hesitation, he decided to stick with the blonde.

Severing the blonde from the group would require finesse and tact so as not to alienate the rest. In these circumstances, females were more loyal to one another than males were. Males understood it was every man for himself; let the best man win and no hard feelings. Women, however, were far less likely to break off from the group if the pursuing male had offended or hurt the feelings of one of its members.

The scoreboard noted that it was the bottom of the eighth inning, one out. The game would be over soon. Canidy didn't have the luxury of finesse and tact. He'd ratchet the Canidy charm machine to ten and employ a full-on frontal assault.

Canidy began striding toward the group. It was a relaxed stride, projecting confidence. He was the big dog.

Before he got to where the women were seated, he noticed a man with a bulldog countenance standing in the parking lot behind the bleachers. He wore a suit with no tie. Next to him was an Army major in uniform.

Canidy recognized the man in the suit immediately. He was Colonel William "Wild Bill" Donovan, winner of the Medal of Honor, the DSM, and DSC, among other awards. He was without question the most remarkable man Canidy had ever known. The fact that Donovan even knew him amazed Canidy.

The sight of Donovan caused Canidy to forget the women in the stands. He immediately changed course and approached the legend. Canidy saluted the major and turned to Donovan and said, "Sir."

Donovan, whose seemingly limitless achievements included being a star athlete, looked Canidy's physique up and down and remarked, "Impressive as far as it goes, Dick. But it's what you can do with it that counts."

"No argument there, sir."

"I'm here because I think you *can* do something with it. And, far more important, do something with your mind."

"Yes, sir."

"You're not my first choice." Donovan's reputation for bluntness was well deserved. "But you are, at least, my second choice." Donovan put up his hand to signal he meant no insult. "I'm in the process of selecting a team for an operation in Europe. It's a risky operation. Very risky. Extraordinarily difficult. Men will die. And the likelihood of success is, well, quite limited."

Canidy glanced at the colonel, who looked as if he were gazing upon a dead man.

"You're my second choice because the first choice consists of a group of highly proficient men who've seen extensive ground combat and have proven themselves uniquely gifted and resourceful.

Nonetheless, the odds are that this group of men will all be killed before completing the operation."

"And as always, sir, you have a backup plan."

"Yes."

"And I'm that backup plan."

"Precisely."

"Sir, why me?"

"Because you're an unconventional, reckless SOB."

Canidy could barely suppress a smile. He'd never felt more flattered than at that moment. Wild Bill Donovan had called *him* a reckless SOB.

Canidy straightened. "Sir, with permission, what's the operation?"

"Too soon, Canidy. Need-to-know only."

"Respectfully, then why tell me anything at all?"

"Because we need to begin training now, regardless of whether you're ever needed. If the primary team fails, we'll need you to go at a moment's notice. Planning and training need to be done beforehand. That training will necessarily be rigorous. More intensive and demanding than anything you've been through."

Canidy nodded pensively. "Who else will be on my team?"

"So far, just you. And it may end up being *only* you. Although I have someone in mind to assist, I may leave *that* selection to you."

"Just one other person?"

"Perhaps."

"*My* choice?"

"Not entirely. He'll need to meet my approval. But I have a feeling we'd both choose the same man."

Canidy grinned. He suspected they would. "When do we get at it, sir?"

"Right now."

CHAPTER 5

Northern Poland
0812, 22 May 1940

Professor Sebastian Kapsky was trapped between the two largest armies in the world. And the deadliest elements of those armies were aggressively searching for him.

He'd narrowly evaded capture by the Soviets twice and the Germans once. In each instance, the cost of such evasion was the lives of Polish patriots and even some Russian peasants who had provided him shelter and sustenance. They included the four Home Army guides toward whom Haller had directed him. He'd never have gotten more than two or three kilometers from Katyn without them. They'd adroitly guided him from just outside Katyn to Hrodna by train and foot.

Kapsky had secreted himself among the corpses conveyed in large flatbed trucks to the outlying trenches of Katyn Forest. He lay inert, feigning death as best he could. Although the ride was short in time and distance, it felt interminable. The suffocating stench of rotting flesh and congealed blood permeated his clothing and made him nauseated, but he'd willed himself not to react, to remain absolutely still until an opportunity to jump off and sprint to the woods presented itself.

He waited for a dense growth of shrubs in which he could conceal himself. But none appeared. The closer they drew to the burial site the more anxious he grew. He imagined being dumped with the other bodies into a trench and being covered with earth by a bulldozer.

He knew he couldn't wait for optimal cover to present itself. It might never come. So when the truck slowed to round a bend, he rolled off the other corpses into a ditch and remained prone until all of the trucks disappeared from view. Then he sprang to his feet and ran due west as fast and as long as he could. When he could run no more he hunched over, hands on knees, and gulped air until he could run some more. He repeated the pattern until nightfall, when he reached Varniken Forest. He then followed Haller's instructions meticulously and walked northwest until he came to Svetly, where he encountered the four *Armia Krajowa* who guided him toward the northernmost part of the old border between Poland and the Soviet Union.

The patriots understood the risk when they volunteered to assist him. They'd lost friends and family members in similar pursuits. But the price was invariably brutal. Women, children, even grand-children were slaughtered during interrogation or to coerce cooper-ation. A tiny hamlet of twenty-three, consisting of just four families, was machine-gunned by a Soviet platoon because their lieutenant believed the residents were hiding Kapsky. They were not. The *bur-mister* of the village of Grajewo was disemboweled in the public square because the SS Totenkopf-Standarte believed he had har-bored Kapsky. He had, but months before the arrival of the Wehr-macht, and Kapsky had long since fled.

Scores of patriots had assisted Kapsky in ways large and small. They didn't know the specific reason why the Germans and Soviets were looking for him, they simply knew that if evil was searching for Kapsky, it was important to keep him alive and away from such evil. It was the Sikorski standard.

A few patriots had an inkling of his importance to the enemy. He was a scholar, a mathematician. It didn't take much imagination to deduce that he possessed knowledge that could provide a military advantage—possibly a strategic one—to whomever captured him. But the urgency of the search was breathtaking. It was almost as if Poland's conquest and occupation were secondary.

Ever since escaping from Ostashkov in Katyn Forest by bribing two guards with a few of Bronislaw Haller's gems, Kapsky stayed on the move, never remaining in one place for more than a few days. He kept part of his promise and delivered the remainder of the jewels to Haller's family. He did not, however, tell Anna, Haller's widow, that he'd be rejoining them. The moment Kapsky gave Anna Haller the jewels, he could tell from her face that she knew her husband of twenty-two years was dead.

She remained stoic and offered him lodging in a small flat above the jewelry shop. Exhausted and needing to orient himself, Kapsky accepted, stating that she'd be rid of him as soon as he was capable of traveling more than a short distance.

The next morning, he was awakened by the sound of voices from the shop. He crept carefully down the steps and observed Anna huddling with another woman who looked remarkably similar. He detected urgency in their voices.

Turning to see him at the bottom of the stairs, Anna dispensed with greetings and introductions and simply said, "You should go. It is not safe."

Kapsky nodded that he understood. Although he didn't need an explanation, Anna provided one. Gesturing toward the other woman, she said, "My sister says the Russians have been asking questions in Mikołajki in the way only Russians can do, if you understand my meaning. They are looking for a Sebastian Kapsky. Mikołajki is only thirty kilometers away. Go north to Ryn. My sister says word is that there are Americans nearby looking for someone."

Americans.

Kapsky nodded thanks and left, but not before Anna gave him a sack filled with sausage, bread, and cheese. As he made his way out of the city, he heard machine-gun fire far in the distance.

He did not hear any return fire.

CHAPTER 6

Washington, D.C.
1012, 3 June 1940

Canidy sighted the target ten yards away with the Colt M1911 and fired six .45 ACP rounds in rapid succession. He straightened and considered his aim, tilting his head slightly to the right. Three shots had hit the bull's-eye and the three others were grouped in a tight semicircle slightly to the right. Not bad. Indeed, pretty good. But he was still dropping his shoulder and pulling off to the right.

The M1911 was his personal weapon. He'd bought it from Ithaca Gun during a trip to visit two Tri-Delt sorority sisters at Cornell, neither of whom knew about the other.

The weapon's weight and balance suited him. More important, he had grown to rely on it. Over the last several months, he'd trained with a variety of weapons, several hours per day: on stationary targets and moving targets; on firing ranges and in combat simulations. He estimated that during that span of time he'd fired more than fifty thousand rounds—most from the M1911, but also from a Smith & Wesson M1917 revolver, an M1 Garand, and a Winchester

90 sniper rifle. That didn't include the Thompson submachine gun that he enjoyed firing just for the hell of it.

But the M1911 was his weapon of choice.

Canidy raised his pistol and fired the last two rounds. He straightened again to consider the results.

"Still pulling off."

Canidy turned to see Colonel Donovan standing behind him. Canidy waited expectantly for a few seconds and then asked, "Well, sir, aren't you going to tell me to slap in another magazine and go again?"

Donovan said nothing. He merely pursed his lips and stared as if contemplating what to say and how to say it. Donovan had devised the training regimen that Canidy had endured for the last few months. It was part preparation and part torture. Donovan had adapted it from the innovative regimen developed by Lieutenant Colonel Robert Laycock of the British No. 8 Commando Unit. Donovan had been clandestinely provided the details of the training by Lieutenant Commander Ian Fleming. It was unlike any military training that preceded it, premised on an expectation that the individual soldier would at some point be required to perform as a self-contained one-man unit—as a guerrilla, a saboteur, a spy— fully capable of creating havoc in any theater under any conditions. Speed, stealth, adaptability, and sheer ruthlessness were the primary and essential qualities of such men.

The concept was abhorred by most in the traditional military hierarchy. Some, including civilian oversight, had gone so far as to lobby against the creation of any such force. Civilized nations, they maintained, didn't employ such tactics. Stimson was one such man. He'd been appalled when Donovan broached the concept with him.

"The United States," Stimson responded indignantly, "does not employ pirates and assassins."

Donovan was undaunted. He embarked on an intense campaign to persuade both Stimson and Roosevelt that such a force was not just necessary, but imperative. The world was changing. *Warfare* was changing. The United States owed its very existence, in part, to similar tactical innovations. Now it was the Brits, those that had been defeated by such innovations, who were at the cutting edge.

To achieve the objective of standing up such a unit, Donovan attacked Stimson's flank. First, working through Laycock, Archibald Stirling, known as the Phantom Major, and Fleming, they'd prevailed upon PM Churchill to broach the concept with President Roosevelt.

Donovan knew Churchill could convince Roosevelt of almost anything. It didn't take long before Roosevelt raised the idea of a "commando" force with Stimson. Stimson, as expected, resisted at first. But also, as expected, after a few nominal protestations, he conceded.

Donovan, with occasional guidance from Fleming—who had a penchant for cloak, dagger, and dramatics—devised the tortuous training program Canidy had been going through for several weeks. Fifteen hours a day, seven days a week. In the field and in the classroom. Physical and mental. Canidy was drilled in every form of weapons combat imaginable: knives, guns, explosives, even poisons. Hours of hand-to-hand techniques, mental agility drills, sleep deprivation, and interrogation/torture resistance. Donovan fully expected the exhaustive regimen to purge Canidy of his conceit and impertinence, to sober his daredevil rebelliousness.

It had the opposite effect.

Canidy increasingly behaved as if he were invincible. He developed more of a swagger, an even bigger ego than before. By pushing Canidy's limits appreciably beyond that of other fighting men, Donovan had produced an elite, albeit somewhat overconfident, warrior.

And, though Donovan hadn't expected it, it was precisely what Donovan intended. But now all of the effort may have been wasted, at least that's what Stimson thought. The patrician was logical to a fault. Donovan, however, thought it was only a temporary setback, a delay.

Though Donovan was blunt and without pretense, he hesitated before giving Canidy the news. Canidy, after all, had put himself through weeks of hell in preparation for an operation that now would be scrubbed.

"Dick, you've performed admirably, done everything I've asked," Donovan began.

Canidy, nobody's fool, anticipated what Donovan hesitated to say before he said it. ". . . But the mission is off. Over."

Donovan, never at a loss for words, couldn't summon even a word of affirmation. He nodded almost imperceptibly. A dejected Canidy lowered the M1911, his arm hanging limply at his side. He forced a rakish smile. "The women of America thank you, sir. I'll now be returning to the playing field."

Though Donovan returned a fleeting smile, his expression quickly turned grave. "Just learned that a squad led by Staff Sergeant McTear was shredded by machine-gun fire from Soviet T-34. 7.62-millimeter DT machine guns. Not the easiest way to go."

A rare look of seriousness covered Canidy's face. "The entire squad?"

Donovan nodded. "Signals picked up a transmission from the *Armia Krajowa* confirming same." He nodded again. "That's a nasty weapon."

Canidy straightened, jocularity gone. "Sir, what do you need me to do?"

"The secretary has told us to stand down. The *Armia Krajowa* intercepted a message sent by the Soviet tank commander identifying—misidentifying—our men as Polish guerrillas—Home Army."

Canidy said, "So the Russians . . ."

". . . and probably the Germans . . ."

"Don't know we're involved."

"Right," Donovan said. "If they knew it, surely Hitler would declare war. Probably Stalin, too."

"Jesus . . ."

". . . had nothing to do with it.

"We got lucky." Donovan stopped himself. "What I mean is . . ."

"I understand what you mean, sir," Canidy offered. "It sure wasn't lucky for McTear and his men, *but* it was lucky for us Adolf and Uncle Joe don't know it was us."

Donovan looked down and kicked the dirt. He appeared hesitant at first. At least, the first time Canidy had seen it.

Donovan looked up, his face a mixture of frustration and contrition. "The President has ordered us to stand down. He thinks we dodged a bullet and doesn't want to tempt fate right now. Churchill's been pressing him to go beyond lend-lease, to commit troops. He's resisted thus far, but this could have thrown us in with both feet. We'll probably get in eventually, but the President doesn't want to be forced into it. If we get in, it has to be on our timetable."

Canidy's jaw tightened. "Hell, sir." He caught himself. "Sir, we're knee-deep already. What was I doing in Indochina?"

"A full-fledged war against the Nazis and Soviets is a whole 'nother ball game, Dick."

Canidy shook his head. Months of pain and discipline and nothing to show for it. He didn't even know what he'd been trained for, other than an operation in Europe. An important mission, unquestionably. He could tell simply by Donovan's behavior. Nonetheless . . .

Canidy transferred the M1911 to his left hand and extended his right hand to Donovan. "All things considered, sir, it's been an honor just to be considered for—whatever this was going to be."

Donovan shook Canidy's hand. "This isn't over, Dick. The original mission remains incomplete. And it can't stay that way. If what I've learned about the objective is accurate, it simply *can't* remain incomplete. Not for long." Donovan kept pumping Canidy's hand absentmindedly before releasing it. "Stay close. We may need you."

"You know where I'll be, sir."

Donovan smiled. "Where you headed, Dick?"

"With permission, sir, I plan on getting drunk and getting laid. The order of those occurrences doesn't particularly matter."

Donovan turned to walk back to his vehicle. Canidy took a few steps in the opposite direction before turning around and calling after the legend. "Sir, can you at least tell me what the hell this is all about?"

Donovan turned, a somber expression on his face. "Even if I could, you'd never believe it."

At precisely the same moment Donovan was entering his vehicle, SS Obersturmführer Konrad Maurer was entering 76 Tirpitzufer, headquarters of the Wehrmacht. He did so with a mixture of curiosity and trepidation, for he was going to see the genius, Vice Admiral Wilhelm Franz Canaris, chief of the Abwehr. Hitler's inner circle sported a number of formidable men, but none more so than the head of all German military intelligence.

Not that Maurer was easily intimidated. At six six, 240 pounds, with ice-blue eyes and hair so blond it was almost white, the well-muscled veteran of Fall Gelb and the Battle of Sedan was a menacing figure to most everyone he encountered. Among the badges decorating his chest were the Knight's Cross, Iron Cross (2nd Class), and the Infantry Assault Badge.

But no medal could shield him from Canaris's penetrating gaze. It was unnerving. Even Guderian, legendary commander of the Panzertruppe bearing his name, was said to look askance.

The Oberstleutnant in the antechamber to Canaris's office looked up from his paperwork and glanced at the wall clock to his right as Maurer entered at 4:57 p.m., only three minutes before his meeting with the chief. Unacceptable. All visitors were to arrive precisely five minutes before their respective appointments. No exceptions. The Oberstleutnant pointedly recorded Maurer's name and arrival time in a ledger. Ten seconds before 5:00, the Oberstleutnant pressed a buzzer to alert Canaris of the visitor's arrival, then rose from his chair and opened the office door at exactly 5:00.

Maurer entered and stood at attention in front of Canaris's desk. Without looking up from his papers, the chief gestured for Maurer to take a seat in one of the three high-backed leather chairs that formed a semicircle around the desk. After a moment Canaris raised his gaze to Maurer. His thick white eyebrows formed a canopy over his eyes that appeared to look through and beyond whatever they were directed at.

"What have you got?"

"A report from Eighth Army staff under Generaloberst Blaskowitz, if accurate, is very unusual, Herr Admiral. It appears a patrol near Mikołajki captured several members of the Polskie Państwo Podziemne."

"Of what possible interest could this be to me?"

"Herr Admiral, it appears the Soviet tank group killed several members of the Resistance. But on closer inspection, it's doubtful they actually were members of the Resistance."

Canaris slapped the top of his desk sharply in disgust. "SS. Again, the SS. They continue to bring dishonor upon us. They do not act as soldiers. They act as terrorists. I've expressed my concerns to OKW Keitel numerous times."

Maurer paused to ensure Canaris was finished before responding somewhat defensively. "Herr Admiral, it does not appear that it was the SS. This occurred in an area occupied by the Soviets. All indications are that it was indeed fire from a T-34 tank that killed these men . . ."

Canaris frowned. "I assume there is a reason I should be interested in this minor skirmish in Soviet-occupied territory?"

"The initial assumption was, indeed, that the dead were Polish underground. They were dressed accordingly and were carrying weapons that appeared to have been salvaged from battles with the Red Army. But they carried no identification whatsoever."

Canaris shrugged. "That's standard practice for the Resistance. Accordingly, when captured there are no identifying documents or other indices allowing the captors to trace back to the guerrillas' relatives."

Maurer nodded respectfully. "True, Mein Herr. But the appearances of these men were PPP to a fault. Nothing was amiss that would arouse suspicion."

"And that was what was suspicious," Canaris said flatly.

"Yes, Herr Admiral. So, therefore, the Russians examined the bodies in minute detail—more out of curiosity than suspicion. Until they came upon a faint discoloration on one of the dead men. Really, it was serendipitous. A *starshina* with tinea noticed what he believed was the same condition on the forearm of one of the bodies. It was faded, barely detectable, but he advised the others not to touch it.

"When he looked more closely he determined that it wasn't, in fact, tinea, but a tattoo of an eagle, barely discernible, as if the owner had done his best to scrub it, hide it."

Canaris's eyes narrowed. "And what did the Russians deduce from this?"

"Herr Admiral, we do not believe the Russians deduced anything. But one of the troops in question made casual mention of it and it eventually made its way to Blaskowitz's people.

"*They* gave it considerable deliberation. And they concluded the deceased was an American."

Canaris nodded slowly. "American." He rose from his chair, lost in thought. "*American,*" he repeated. He looked at Maurer. "And our intelligence suggests the Soviets have not yet concluded this man is American?"

"Herr Admiral, the Russians are brutes. There is no evidence they have come to that conclusion."

"The Soviets may be brutes, but they are extremely clever brutes."

"Clever, Herr Admiral? Respectfully, we got the better of them with Molotov-Ribbentrop, by far."

Canaris shook his head sharply. "That's what the politicians and the newspapers and the scholars say. We took all of the major cities— Warsaw, Kraków, Łódź, Danzig. But look at what problems they cause. We are tied down in every one of the great cities, battling constant resistance, committing massacres by the day. Whereas the brutes, as you call them, immediately consolidated their position. Staging elections and granting Soviet citizenship to legitimize their gains. We, on the other hand, have engaged in extermination. Look at Warsaw. The Soviets will hold on to their gains long after the war. Mark my words."

Maurer listened, but said nothing. He heard whispers that Canaris was at odds with much of the Führer's agenda. A less prudent man might utter some concurrence to ingratiate himself with his superior. But such a man could easily find himself in prison or before a firing squad, the subject an entrapment to smoke out those disloyal to the Führer.

"If these men were Americans, Maurer, why do you think they were there?"

"Herr Admiral, I suspect they were there to foment or help the Resistance. Perhaps they are Polish Americans?"

"Sensible conclusion, but no, Maurer. They were there to find someone. To extract him."

"Who, Herr Admiral?"

"A man I need you to find before anyone else does."

CHAPTER 7

Northern Poland
0447, 7 August 1940

The hayloft in the barn made it tolerable. In fact, borderline comfortable. It was dry, clean, and it wasn't infested with rodents.

Kapsky was nearing his limit. He'd been constantly on the move, trying to evade Red Army patrols. When he could, he slept in barns, sheds, and abandoned buildings. More often, he slept in the woods.

Fortunately, he had plenty of provisions. The gems that Haller had given him for his own use had yielded a generous sum of currency. He frequently was tempted to use the money to purchase lodging for a night or two, but he thought that might alert those who were searching for him.

Originally, he planned to move northward toward Danzig, eight to ten kilometers per day, reasoning that with a slow, deliberate pace he'd be less likely to make mistakes leading to detection. But even that pace proved difficult to sustain. Soviets seemed to be everywhere, and he had yet to encounter many Home Army personnel.

He never used rail or any form of motorized transportation. Red Army checkpoints were ubiquitous, and NKVD, posing as ordinary citizens, were known to ride buses, trollies, and trains looking for members of the underground and their collaborators.

Kapsky rose from a bed of hay he'd crafted for himself and gathered the bag that carried the few possessions—necessities—he'd acquired. It was almost dawn. He wanted to get moving before the owner of the barn began his day.

He oriented himself as he peeked out the barn door at the surrounding countryside. Other than the farmhouse and a copse of trees to the north, nothing but fields in every direction. It was completely silent. The stars were receding in brightness as the eastern horizon began to glow. He walked northward at a casual pace, hoping as he did every morning that this would be the day someone would deliver him from purgatory. Someone who could provide passage to the coast, perhaps even to England. Although he conceded it was mere fantasy, he used it to motivate himself and to ward off feelings of despair. But what if someone *could* actually help him? What if he encountered someone from the Home Army, Sikorski's tourists? Why *couldn't* it happen? And why stop at England? After all, it was under siege. Why not America?

Engrossed in escapism as he approached the copse of trees, he almost didn't discern the movement in its periphery a few meters away. Startled, the professor, who had never struck anyone in his life, seized a knife from the outer pocket of his bag and ran toward a figure emerging from the copse. *Strike before being struck. Take no chances. Eliminate the threat, silence the spy.*

Kapsky was on the figure in seconds. They crashed to the ground, Kapsky on top, knife raised.

And in the twilight before dawn, he saw that the person he was about to kill was a girl—probably eleven or twelve years old—her face contorted in terror. Her mouth was agape as if she were attempting to scream, but no sounds emerged. Her body was rigid, anticipating the thrust of the knife, the piercing pain from the blade.

Kapsky rolled off her in horror. His chest heaved as he tried to suck air into his lungs and compose himself, but his heart continued beating so rapidly it felt as if it would burst from his chest. It was several seconds before he gathered himself to speak. To his astonishment, the girl, already more composed than he, spoke first.

"You are the professor?" Fear remained in her voice.

"Who are you?"

"It is not important."

"It is to me. Who are you?"

"My name is Lara. I saw you enter the barn yesterday."

Kapsky stared at her in bewilderment. He'd been extraordinarily careful that no one would see him enter the barn. He hadn't seen the girl, but she'd seen *him*. As if she read his mind, she assured, "No one else saw you. So do not worry."

"Why did you ask if I'm the professor?"

"My uncles, Bogdan and Janusz, said the Russians were looking for someone—a professor. I have never seen you before. You are not from here. And you slept in the barn. It makes sense."

Kapsky blinked in bewilderment. The girl had regained her composure more quickly than he. "What are you doing here at this ungodly hour? Why aren't you at home?"

"This is my duty. I keep watch from four to eight."

"Watch for what? For whom?"

"For Home Army. Uncle Bogdan is the commander. Uncle Janusz is intelligence. Everyone does something. We all have a job."

"And your job was to look for me?"

"No. It is to watch for the Russians. But when I saw you I could tell you are hiding. You are not from here. Since the Russians are looking for a professor, I figured you must be that person."

Lara is going to go far, Kapsky thought, *provided she survives the war.* "Lara, I am going in the direction of Danzig," he said, pointing northward. "Do you know if there are Russians there?"

Lara shook her head. "If you do not know the area, they will get you. You do not *look* like you are from here. You will die. I am sure of it. But my uncles can help you. They are smarter and stronger than the Russians. You must come with me."

Lara rose and began walking. Kapsky got up and found himself obeying her command. She was not even as old as the shoes he was wearing, but she carried herself like a field marshal. And, just maybe, she could keep him alive.

CHAPTER 8

Washington, D.C.
1435, 3 March 1942

Every time Canidy entered the ornate lobby of the Willard Hotel he imagined himself as Errol Flynn or Basil Rathbone. He suspected most men who entered did the same and most women imagined they were Vivien Leigh. It wasn't merely the hotel's ornateness, it was also its proximity to the White House and the fact that there was a fair probability that on any given occasion a Flynn, Rathbone, or other star would be lounging in the foyer with a Macallan or Dewar's just presented by a number of the waitstaff.

Unbeknownst to Canidy—although it would have delighted him—was that several of the people in the lobby *had* suspected he might be a star of the silver screen, though they couldn't quite recall the motion picture in which he'd appeared. Nonetheless, they were relatively certain that he was a hero of some sort. Someone daring and dashing who had recently saved the day.

No one in the lobby, including Canidy, noticed the man who *was* one of the most daring individuals in American history. A man who had saved the day on multiple occasions and for which his country had awarded him its highest honors for heroism. As opposed to Canidy, he didn't look the part. He appeared unremarkable, save for a face that suggested unshakable tenacity, a suggestion that was, if anything, understated.

Donovan sensed Canidy possessed many of the same qualities. His swagger was partially that of a young man who hadn't yet suffered many setbacks or defeats, but it was mostly that of a man who had a realistic appreciation that his gifts and abilities were well above those of most. Donovan sensed Canidy's potential in the way a champion boxer senses that the upstart ducking into the ring might just be the heir apparent, but not before he had his face rearranged a few more times.

Canidy hadn't noticed Donovan sitting in the far corner opposite the reception desk. Donovan, however, had noticed the likely purpose for Canidy's visit to the hotel—an attractive brunette of about thirty-five who had deftly removed her wedding ring and deposited it into the side pocket of her handbag a few moments after Canidy had appeared at the entrance. Donovan suspected it wasn't the first time she'd practiced the maneuver.

Donovan watched as Canidy kissed the woman on the left cheek at the same time her right hand momentarily disappeared behind Canidy's back somewhere below the waist. Clearly, not their first or even their second encounter.

Canidy was no neophyte. Donovan suspected Canidy knew the woman was married. Donovan disapproved, but understood better than most that men who were inclined to take the greatest risks the nation asked of its citizens didn't limit such risks to death and dismemberment. Donovan was, however, disappointed in Canidy's lack of judgment. Donovan recognized the woman as the wife of a member of the House Appropriations Committee—a preening jackass who had fought any increases in the armed services budget after Neville Chamberlain had summarily declared "peace in our time." Although the cuckold was no longer in a position to affect military appropriations, he retained several influential connections on Capitol Hill and was just the type of jackass who would seek retribution against Canidy by sticking it to the military as a whole.

Nonetheless, Donovan believed Canidy's attributes made him the optimal spy, especially because the requirements of the occupation were evolving. Donovan believed traditional spycraft was gradually becoming much more physical: intelligence plus direct action. The Brits incorporated both in its MI6 and SAS operations. Donovan was fast doing the same with OSS. And Canidy was his prototype.

Canidy noticed Donovan sitting to the right in a plush high-backed chair. Donovan saw a look on Canidy's face that ranged between embarrassment and contrition—a child disappointing a parent. Canidy immediately, albeit smoothly, disengaged from the woman and approached Donovan, stopping a few feet in front of his chair.

"Sir. I didn't see you there."

"Obviously," Donovan said. "Don't let me interrupt, son. Clearly, you have business to which you should attend."

Canidy wore a rare, flustered look. "Sir . . ."

"I'm not your priest or your father. Nor am I your immediate commanding officer, son."

Canidy became even more chagrined. He felt like an undisciplined flake standing before one of the most serious men in the country. He looked at his watch: 2:44 p.m. "Sir, I just got your message to meet here at five o'clock as soon as I got back from—"

"Son, I said no explanations, please. Take care of your business.

Meet me here in . . ." Donovan glanced at his watch. "Two hours and fifteen minutes."

Canidy glanced back at the woman, who wore a look between impatience and irritation. She was a married woman with a schedule that didn't accommodate interruptions. "Sir, I'll be back in thirty seconds."

Canidy crossed the lobby and spoke to the woman briefly. She appeared alarmed and walked briskly out of the hotel. Canidy returned, swaggering once again.

Donovan asked, "Everything buttoned up?"

Canidy nodded. "Apologies, sir, but I told her you were a private detective hired by her husband and that I promised to double your fee if you agreed to tell your client that his wife was as pure as Caesar's."

Not bad, Donovan thought. He gestured to the seat next to him and signaled to the waiter by raising his glass of Macallan. The waiter approached expectantly.

Donovan looked to Canidy. "What are you drinking?"

"Thank you, but nothing for me, sir."

"Feigned abstemiousness is a wasted effort on me, Canidy." Donovan nodded to the waiter, who retreated.

"Dick, we're in a real fix," Donovan said. "I asked you here because we need to move on a critical matter immediately. No time whatsoever to waste. If you volunteer for this, you will leave immediately."

"Whatever you need, sir. You know that."

"I do. But you don't know what I need."

"Respectfully, sir, but I do. You just told me you need me immediately on a critical matter. Not to sound like a kid whose coach just told him he's the starting quarterback in the title game, but being picked for a critical job by a man awarded the MOH makes it a no-brainer. I'm in, whatever it is."

Donovan took a sip of his whisky. "We put you through some godawful training a while back, mental and physical. We've never done anything like that before. Running, push-ups, chin-ups, and sit-ups for hours. Hand-to-hand combat, incessant marksmanship drills . . ."

"Brutal, but it took. I keep it up when I can."

"Good, because you'll need all of it and more. What we're asking of you is the closest thing to a death sentence the War Department can issue. No margin for error. Even if you commit *no* errors it's still likely you won't come back. You need to understand that."

Canidy said nothing.

"We decided that because of the nature of this run, we'll only use volunteers."

"There's someone else besides me?"

"Possibly."

"How many more?"

"Only one. Logistics precludes more than two."

"You say that neither of us is coming back?" Canidy asked.

"That's not what *I'm* saying. That's what *math* says. I chose you because I think you have the best chance of beating the math and getting the results we need."

Canidy smiled sardonically. "Sir, you're not making this very appealing."

"I'm not trying to. If I'm going to ask you to do this, you need to go in with your eyes open. No illusions."

"What are you asking me to do?"

Donovan placed his glass on the table next to him and rose from his chair. "Let's go for a walk." Canidy thought to remind Donovan of the order he'd just placed with the waiter, but said nothing and followed Donovan as he preceded out of the main entrance of the Willard, past the bell stand, and left onto Pennsylvania Avenue. Donovan said nothing until they reached the intersection of 14th Street.

"The Abwehr has ears and eyes in the damnedest places. Beria, too. We're not nearly as sophisticated as they, but we're catching up. Slowly."

Donovan paused as two men walked past. When they were outside earshot, he resumed. "Do you remember the operation for which you were trained about a year and a half ago?"

"You may recall, sir, I was never told what the operation was."

"The President initially opposed that operation because he didn't want any complications that could drag us into war. That concern is, obviously, moot now. So the operation is back on—with even greater urgency." Donovan paused again to permit a woman to pass. "Frankly, with due respect to the President, it was a mistake to cancel it. In the meantime, the conditions for its execution have become exponentially worse."

"Eight men were killed the last time the operation was attempted," Canidy observed. "How, then, sir, are two men supposed to execute under much worse conditions?"

"War is not easy. War is not fair."

Canidy simply shrugged. "What do you need me to do?"

"Extract someone trapped somewhere between the Germans and the Russians."

"*Somewhere* between the Russians and the Germans?" Canidy asked incredulously.

"Maybe even *among* them. In Poland. But where in Poland . . . we have no idea."

"Well, that certainly narrows it down." Canidy exhaled. "Do we know who we are extracting?"

"Professor Sebastian Kapsky. He had been rounded up by the Soviets shortly after they invaded and transported eastward. He was in one of the internment facilities in Katyn Forest. There had been reports he escaped and is still alive, but we haven't gotten anything definitive. We assume—hope—he made it to Poland and he's being sheltered by Polish Resistance. Sikorski's tourists are known to operate in the eastern Soviet Union. But just before Molotov-Ribbentrop fell apart, the NKVD and Gestapo held a conference in which it was decided they'd jointly eradicate all resistance fighters. That didn't change after the pact was dissolved. Now they're trying to eradicate all resistance fighters *and* each other. It's possible that Kapsky may be in the middle of it. Both the Germans and Russians are scouring the area for him.

"Now, with Operation Barbarossa, the Germans bombed the hell out of Soviet-occupied Poland, followed by an artillery barrage beyond the scope of anything seen in warfare. And *then* millions of German troops swarmed Soviet positions. The scale of the fighting is downright biblical.

"The Germans have pushed the Russians back toward their border and now control most of the area from which we last received reports—more accurately, rumors—that Kapsky was last seen. The area is still the subject of ferocious fighting between the Nazis and Soviets, though the Germans are advancing incrementally. It's an area where before Barbarossa, the *Armia Krajowa*—Home Army— was very active."

"*Was* very active? Not anymore?" Canidy asked.

"Once Barbarossa began, reliable reports have been few and far between. The *Armia* is tenacious and clever, but they are overwhelmed by the sheer firepower of the Wehrmacht. Plus, the Germans are plenty clever themselves—and vicious.

"When the Soviets controlled the area they got information from partisans by interrogating them with a gun to their heads. Literally. Make no mistake, that produced results. But the toughest partisans still held out. So the Soviets then would point their weapons at the wives, sons, daughters—even grandchildren—of the partisans. That produced even greater compliance—maybe up to ninety-five percent. Outstanding for any intelligence operation.

"The Germans were no less vicious, but they got nearly one hundred percent compliance because they were just a bit cleverer."

Canidy understood. "Not just the stick. Carrot and stick."

Donovan nodded. "When German interrogators identified a high-level member of the Resistance who possessed lots of information, they'd first try to bribe him—provide him with promises that he and his family would be unharmed. As you might expect, few patriots would betray their country for an executory deal. The interrogator would then offer things of value—currency, jewelry, paintings, or even land seized from other Poles, often Jews. Again, a few would take it, but a substantial number would not.

"The Germans then would threaten the lives of family members of resistance fighters. The Germans, you see, understood the psychology of choice of graduated alternatives. When presented with a binary choice—betrayal or death—two bad choices, a sizable number chose death. Even if it meant family also."

"But when presented with multiple choices," Canidy said, "including one that's ostensibly good—at least materially good—a certain percentage will yield."

"Unfortunately, it only takes one."

The pair stopped at F Street, waiting for vehicular traffic to pass.

Both shielded their eyes against the sun reflecting off the windows of the office building across the street.

Candy asked, "So, we think somebody gave the Nazis information as to Kapsky's whereabouts, or general whereabouts?"

"We really don't know jack," Donovan responded. "We think, we hope, Kapsky's still alive, and preferably under the protection of the *Armia*," he said as they crossed New York Avenue. "The operating assumption is that Kapsky's in an area formerly held by the Soviets exclusively and now the subject of contention between the Wehrmacht and the Red Army. It's a race and we're behind. Every hour that passes vastly increases the probability that either the Nazis or the Soviets will capture him. They've had a head start and they control the area. Hell, one of them may have captured him while we've been talking."

Donovan's response produced a look on Candy's face between skepticism and disbelief. "Sir, hundreds of thousands have been killed in that area. Poles, Germans, Russians, Ukrainians, hell— sheep, cows, and pigs, too. Now, I'd like to think I'm as optimistic as the next guy, but it doesn't sound like an environment conducive to a mathematician's survival."

The pair crossed H Street. Donovan stopped and turned to Candy. The bulldog face that had seen and cheated death countless times looked even more sober than usual. "Look, Dick, here's the operation in broad strokes: You go to Sweden. From there a vessel will take you and several British Commandos from Lieutenant Colonel Robert Laycock's special service brigade across the Baltic to the Elblag vicinity. The Commandos have some experience at this type of operation and the *Armia* know the territory. Your insertion point will be in the no-man's-land between the Wehrmacht and the Red Army somewhere east of Danzig, hopefully during a lull in fighting. From there you'll make your way to wherever our sources say Kapsky may be. After you find him, you extract him by going to the same extraction point and returning by boat to Sweden."

Canidy gazed at Donovan for several seconds without expression. Donovan returned the look, aware of the implausibility of the operation he'd just described. Implausibility invited, at a minimum, a skeptical eye roll, an ironic chuckle. But no one, not even the President and definitely not an irreverent Dick Canidy, dared laugh at any utterance by Wild Bill Donovan. No one recognized that better than Donovan himself. After a moment, Canidy rubbed his forehead, exhaled, and said, "Two questions, sir."

"Fire away."

"When do I leave?"

"Immediately. There's a Lodestar 18 waiting at Langley Field. Everything you need will be on board."

"Sir, when we first spoke about this more than a year ago you said there might be someone else on the operation, someone we'd both choose."

Donovan nodded curtly. "I did."

"Is that still operative?"

Donovan stopped walking and squared against Canidy, who did the same. Wild Bill's enormous right hand grasped Canidy's and pumped it once. "Fulmar's waiting for you at the plane."

CHAPTER 9

Giżycko, Poland
1429, 4 March 1942

The building was made of twelve-foot-thick concrete walls, with a flat roof consisting of six-inch steel beams, all painted black. The engineers claimed it could sustain a direct hit from a Schwerer Gustav. A typical Russian exaggeration, but not by much: it had been strafed by Jagdgeschwader 77s on multiple occasions without suffering more than a few pockmarks; it had even been struck by a fifty-kilogram iron bomb with little effect. It was likely the safest place in eastern Poland, which was saying very much.

The interior consisted of a four-hundred-square-foot room containing a ten-foot-by-ten-foot iron table with two cushionless iron chairs on either side. Illumination was provided by a dozen painfully bright lights. The only other feature in the room was a single gunmetal-gray filing cabinet.

Major Taras Gromov, the sole occupant of the room, sat impassively on the chair facing the entrance. The two NKVD guards who had ushered him in a short time ago remained unsettled by his appearance. Physically, he wasn't particularly remarkable. He appeared to be a fit male in his early thirties, above-average height. But he appeared . . . predatory. Both in his eyes and in his carriage. As if his only purpose in life was to locate prey and kill it, quickly, unceremoniously, without any increase in his heart rate. Then onto the next victim.

The guards' instincts were accurate. Gromov was uncommonly proficient at killing, both in war and otherwise. He killed with guns, knives, and his hands. He was a soldier and an assassin. He was relentless. And he would kill again.

And that was why he was sitting in a concrete tomb. He'd been directed by Moscow, the fourth floor of the Lubyanka itself. He'd arrived thirty minutes before the appointed time. Even a killer as formidable as Gromov didn't dare be late.

At precisely 3:00 p.m. he heard the metallic groan of the metal door opening, and a stocky guard wielding a PPSh-41 submachine gun entered tentatively, scanned the room, and withdrew. Seconds later he heard several footsteps—someone moving at a casual, indifferent pace; someone unconcerned with punctuality. Yet he was precisely on time.

Gromov rose as Aleksander Belyanov, chief of the Otdel Kontr-Razvedki, the dread OKRNKVD, entered and stood tall and regal for several seconds, examining Gromov as if evaluating a racehorse for a wager. Gromov stood instantly and saluted. The guard withdrew and shut the iron door.

Belyanov regarded Gromov coolly for several seconds before approaching the iron table and gesturing for Gromov to sit. Gromov nodded deferentially. No one would presume to take a seat before a man who reported only to Lavrentiy Beria took his.

Belyanov sat, leaned back, and crossed his legs—hands folded in his lap. Gromov sat inclined forward.

"Your number of kills?" Belyanov's voice was cool and indifferent.

"I have not kept a tally."

"Of course you have."

"Several," Gromov replied.

"Precision, Comrade Gromov."

"Eighty-eight."

"Dyachenko has 179. Ilyin has 212."

"They are snipers. They kill from afar."

"And you kill with your hands. So what is the difference?"

"In my case, the target can fight back."

"Maybe you are just not as smart as Dyachenko and Ilyin. Maybe your brain is not as big."

"Maybe, Comrade Belyanov, their balls aren't as big."

Belyanov's face remained expressionless. "The kills were all during war?"

"Mostly."

"Any children?"

"No."

"Women?"

"Not yet."

Belyanov examined Gromov. The killer was surprisingly urbane. Yet the file in the Lubyanka said he had no formal education. Before the war he'd been a railyard worker, a common laborer from Novosibirsk Oblast, albeit with uncommon physical strength and endurance. His commander during the Ukrainian famine reported that Gromov had killed two kulaks with no more than a single blow to the head of each.

"What is your opinion of the war, Gromov?"

Belyanov saw a familiar flicker of suspicion in Gromov's eyes.

Like everyone in the Soviet Union who valued his life, he gave the proper response. "We will defend the Motherland with our dying honor and prevail against the Nazi regime."

Belyanov waved his hand dismissively. "Speak plainly, Gromov. This is not a loyalty test and you will not end up in a camp or in the bowels of the Lubyanka."

Gromov looked skeptically at Belyanov for a second or two, but no more. "We will defeat the Nazis because no army can overcome our natural defenses: land and cold. But it will not end there. At some point soon we will have to confront our ultimate enemy—the Americans."

Belyanov didn't try to disguise his surprise. The brute Gromov was more perceptive than ninety percent of the general staff. No wonder his reputation had reached Cathedral Square.

"Explain, Gromov."

Another look of caution flashed across Gromov's face, but he replied without reservation. "Germany is our present enemy because of Hitler's treachery. They have the most powerful fighting force in history. But history proves no fighting force can vanquish the Motherland. America, however . . ."

". . . is our ally," Belyanov interjected.

". . . is our long-term enemy. Our natural enemy. They're capitalists and exploiters of the proletariat, oppressors of the people. Inevitably, we will be at war with them. And that war will be cataclysmic."

Belyanov stared for several seconds as if Gromov was Rasputin reincarnated. This was no ordinary killer. He was calculating; more than that, he seemed uncommonly knowledgeable.

"That is an interesting observation, Gromov. I believe, therefore, the task I am about to describe will make perfect sense to you. It involves a mathematician . . ."

Gromov scowled. "Killing a mathematician will not be particularly difficult. Literally any soldier could—"

"You're not to kill him, Gromov, although it is likely you will need to kill several people along the way. Our last report is that the mathematician is in an area straddling our front line and that of the Wehrmacht. Our information is very good."

"Where does it come from?"

"Multiple sources."

"Specifically . . . ?"

Belyanov scowled. "Be careful, Gromov. Do not test me. Be assured that the sources are real and that some are in places that would astonish you. Indeed, they would astonish both our allies as well as our adversaries."

Gromov responded respectfully, but wasn't cowed. "The probability of apprehending this mathematician is dependent on the speed and accuracy of these sources."

"That is not your concern, Gromov. Your task is to first find the mathematician, secure him, and bring him to Moscow."

"He must be an uncommonly important mathematician."

Belyanov said, "Important enough that if we fail to find him, we may not just lose the war, we will lose the future. It is imperative we find him."

Gromov sat silently for a few moments. "I can do that."

Belyanov leaned forward. "Do that, Gromov, and the Order of Lenin is yours."

CHAPTER 10

Northern Poland
0923, 30 June 1943

The Polish partisan was a small, wiry man with intelligent gray eyes. Maurer would translate that intelligence into deceitfulness.

The partisan wore a ragged cloth coat and baggy pants that smelled of manure. The panzer group had captured him after surrounding his band of nine or ten *Armia*—a number uncertain because a few of them had managed to escape into the thick underbrush on the opposite bank of the shallow Nogat River. Despite being cornered by several panzers and a dozen soldiers on foot, the wily partisan had tried to conceal himself in the marsh into which the runoff from a nearby farm drained—a runoff composed in large part of cow dung.

The partisan sat on a rickety wooden chair on the other side of a small table within the small farmhouse where he'd been captured. He provided no resistance to the German troops, dropping his rifle and raising his arms immediately upon being told he had no means of escape and he'd be ripped to shreds by panzer machine-gun fire if he attempted to flee across the river.

Two German soldiers had escorted the partisan to the farmhouse at Maurer's direction several hours earlier. The man had been denied food and drink and use of the outhouse toilet. He sat nervously at the kitchen table waiting, likely for something bad. He wasn't a pessimist by nature. Experience had made him so. Everything seemed to go wrong for him in the war. First, the Germans had destroyed his village, then they'd slaughtered most of his family, and the previous evening they'd killed every member of his unit save for the two who had escaped into the river and—he assessed—had made it to the opposite bank to blend into the thick forest cover.

He expected to die, but hoped he wouldn't. The two soldiers flanking him betrayed nothing. No hint of what was to come, no clue as to his fate. Strangely, they, too, seemed anxious, apprehensive, as if whomever they were waiting for was as likely to kill them as the partisan. Their anxiousness frightened him.

The partisan glanced furtively about the room, hoping the guards didn't notice. He looked for items that could be used as a weapon and any means by which he could escape. It was largely an exercise to occupy his mind, to distract his imagination from whatever was to come. He saw nothing that might be employed as a weapon, and he was certain any escape attempt would be futile.

There came a barely audible footfall from the front porch, followed by the creak of the battered wooden front door. Then clearly audible footfalls and an intake of breath from the guards as they straightened to attention. Seconds later, the partisan saw a man nearly twice his size appear in the doorframe of the entrance to the room. He was a full head taller than the two guards, with boulder-like shoulders tapering to a small waist. His hair appeared white, but not from age. He appeared no older than his late twenties, perhaps thirty. But his arctic blue eyes projected the cynicism of someone much older. They were skeptical eyes, exceptionally intelligent. Eyes that couldn't be fooled.

SS Obersturmführer Konrad Maurer pulled a small wooden chair from the corner of the room and placed it a few feet from the partisan. It appeared it might not bear the giant's weight, but he descended into it without concern—as if he expected the chair wouldn't dare fail—and leaned forward until his face was no more than a foot from the partisan's.

The partisan withdrew his head sharply, an involuntary reaction. He looked askance, not wanting to provoke the giant with what might be perceived as an insolent look.

Maurer stared calmly at the partisan for several moments, saying nothing. Then, still staring, he softly said to the guards, "Get him."

The guard to the partisan's right immediately left the room and walked out the front door and disappeared. Barely twenty seconds later he reappeared holding a frightened man by the arm. He was Janusz, the partisan's only brother, who he'd assumed had escaped into the woods across the river. He was only a year older than the partisan, but appeared haggard and emaciated from the months of battling the Wehrmacht under unforgiving conditions. The guard pushed Janusz to within two meters of Maurer, who, without uttering a word, casually withdrew his Walther and fired three rounds into Janusz's left temple, causing him to pitch and collapse onto the floor.

The partisan's chest heaved in terror and he soiled himself. Maurer calmly slid his chair back several inches and resumed staring at the Pole. For nearly a half minute the only sounds in the room were the partisan's rapid breathing accompanied by a reedy wailing sound.

Maurer watched dispassionately, then turned to the guard, nodded, and the guard disappeared through the door once again. Maurer continued staring at the Pole, whose hands were shaking violently. Moments later the guard returned with a terrified young man in his late teens. He was tall, handsome, and robust, with more than a slight resemblance to the partisan.

Upon seeing the young man, the partisan's intake of breath was so sharp and abrupt that he began choking for several seconds. Maurer waited patiently as the Pole labored to catch his breath. His eyes wide with terror, he struggled to speak, but the only sounds he produced were a strangled wail.

Maurer leaned forward slightly. "What did you say?"

The partisan's chest continued to heave rapidly as he struggled to make intelligible sounds. Blood that had sprayed on his face from his brother's gunshot wounds formed bubbles around his mouth as he exhaled. "Please . . ." Terror rendered the word nearly unintelligible.

Maurer nodded. "You are eager to tell me everything I need to know. Yes?"

The partisan nodded frantically.

"You will do so truthfully and withhold nothing?"

Again the partisan nodded, so vigorously that his skull appeared as if it might become detached from his neck. "What do you want to know? If I have information, it is yours. Please. What do you want to know? Tell me."

"Very simple. I am looking for a man."

"Who?"

"His name is Sebastian Kapsky."

The partisan appeared confused. His eyes darted about the room as his mind desperately tried to recall anyone by that name.

"I do not know the name. I do not know anyone with this name."

"I am certain that you do," Maurer said evenly. "I am certain that he is under the protection of the *Armia*."

"I do not know the name. Please. I am being truthful. Who is he? Where is he from?"

"Think harder."

"I am telling you, I do not know anyone with that name. Who is he? Where is he supposed to be?"

"Think *much* harder."

Tears welled in the partisan's eyes, which grew wider when Maurer began to raise the Walther resting on his right thigh.

"I do not know the name. I do not know anyone by that name. You cannot punish me—punish my family—because I do not know someone."

"In fact, I can and will." Maurer shifted slightly in the direction of the young man. "Strong and fit," Maurer said and nodded. "He looks able to kill many Germans in the coming months. Who knows? Perhaps he will kill me or someone close to me."

"Where was this Kapsky last? What did he do?"

Maurer turned back to the partisan. "You see, that is the problem. Despite our prodigious intelligence apparatus, I confess I have no idea where he may be, other than somewhere between Katyn and Danzig. Many of your countrymen have died because they refused to give us a location." Maurer cocked his head slightly to his left. "Perhaps they did not know where he was. Like you."

"I tell you I do not know. Though I do not want to betray anyone, I would tell you his location to spare a life, especially that of a friend or family member." The partisan's voice cracked. "Tell me, what can I do to help you?"

Maurer shook his head in resignation. "Apparently nothing."

"Wait," the man pleaded. "Wait. Tell me something about this Kapsky. What does he look like? What did he do?"

Maurer shook his head again. "I've never seen the man. I do not have a photograph or sketch. I am told only that he is tall and lean, with black hair and green eyes. For what it is worth, the eyes are said to somehow make him appear exceptionally intelligent."

The partisan waited for Maurer to continue, but he did not. The description didn't register with the partisan, making him even more nervous. He feared if he provided nothing of value the young man would be shot. He temporized. "What did he do?"

"To my knowledge, he has not done anything yet. The concern is what he may do sometime in the future."

A genuine look of puzzlement covered the partisan's face. Maurer noticed.

"I am told he is, in fact, very bright. Accordingly, his eyes are not lying. He has the ability, apparently, to cause great harm with his intelligence."

Maurer noticed the partisan's eyes dart about as if trying to retrieve something from the recesses of his brain. He was connecting pieces of information, drawing inferences. He looked up at Maurer.

"He is very smart? Such as an academic? A professor?"

"That is correct."

The partisan's eyes grew wide and bright. Maurer saw a flicker of recognition and then excitement. "I know such a man," the partisan said rapidly. "Rather, I do not *know* him, but I know *of* him. He was a professor before the war—maybe even since it has begun." The partisan nodded as if affirming to himself the accuracy of his recollection. "Yes, he was an academic at the University of Lviv. A mathematician, I think . . ."

Maurer watched as the partisan dredged every piece of information he could recall about the mathematician from the depths of his brain. He held nothing back. The information was his son's—and his—salvation. The more he could provide, the greater his interrogator's appreciation. "He is tall and lanky. He came to the *Armia* in 1940 or 1941, late spring, I believe. A child brought him. It was said he came from Katyn. No one believed him. Rather, I did not believe him. *No one* came from Katyn. Katyn is a furnace. Katyn is a pit.

"I believe I even saw this person myself south of Pinsk." He paused again to refresh his memory. "Yes, I *did* see him. I remember now. He said he had been hiding, he needed to go to Danzig. Commander Matuszek gave orders to assist. Matuszek clearly thought the man was important. We could not readily spare men to escort someone to Danzig unless that person was very important."

A flicker of relief played on the partisan's face. He was providing value. *He* was valuable. By extension, his *loved ones* were valuable. He scoured his memory for anything he could provide regarding the professor.

Maurer nodded. "Go on. What else?"

"Several men volunteered to escort the man as far as Bydgoszcz, along the Vistula," the partisan continued. "We could not spare men to escort him all the way to Danzig. That was a journey of some distance. There and back would take too long. But, as I recall, four of our men were to accompany the mathematician about sixty kilometers southeast of Bydgoszcz. There, he would be handed off to others that would take him to Danzig."

"Very good. Helpful." Maurer nodded. "If you know, how long ago did this happen?"

"It was several days ago."

"Do you know whether they have reached Bydgoszcz yet?"

"I have not been told. Bydgoszcz is approximately one hundred fifty kilometers north of where *Armia* first encountered this professor. Wehrmacht controls much of the area. Patrols are everywhere. Travel is difficult. If they have not been killed or captured, they may reach Toruń in a few days. They are probably near Włocławek now. Maybe a kilometer or two north of there."

"To be clear, how many escorts?"

"I understand that there are three. Maybe no more than two." The partisan took a deep breath. "Is that helpful?"

Maurer nodded. "Very much so. I am grateful beyond measure." He leaned forward slightly and patted the partisan's knee. "Thank you."

The partisan exhaled.

Maurer rose from his chair. He shot the partisan twice in the head and the young man once in the chest.

CHAPTER 11

The flight was long, loud, and bumpy. Within two hours of takeoff both Major Richard Canidy and Lieutenant Eric Fulmar were beginning to get hoarse over the noise of the engines.

Lean, energetic, and exuding boundless confidence, First Lieutenant Eric Fulmar, Army Infantry, spoke German fluently and five other languages at least passably. As far as Canidy was concerned, there was no one better with whom to infiltrate German-held territory. With his blond hair and blue eyes he *looked* quintessentially German; not difficult, given that his father was, in fact, German.

When not ribbing each other, both Canidy and Fulmar wore skeptical expressions, not uncommon for men in their position. It was the ribbing common among siblings, although they weren't biologically related. Indeed, Fulmar, with his Germanic blond hair and blue eyes, was an Aryan contrast to Canidy—they'd known each other ever since Fulmar's mother had sent him to St. Paul's School in Cedar Rapids, Iowa, over which a Reverend George Crater Canidy,

Ph.D., D.D., presided. Fulmar's father was a German citizen and his mother an American actress. When his father returned to Germany, his mother sent him to St. Paul's, where he and Canidy engaged in all manner of youthful escapades. Those escapades formed the foundation of both friendship and the daredevil temperaments that Donovan prized in his operatives.

It was a full three hours into the flight before either of them spoke of the mission. Fulmar spoke first.

"Who the hell did we piss off to draw this assignment?"

"You're looking at this the wrong way," Canidy said. "We're the best and the brightest, the United States military's prime weapons. No one else has a rat's chance of pulling this off. You should be flattered."

"Well, I suppose that's one way of looking at it," Fulmar conceded. "A slightly more realistic way of looking at it is that we're the most expendable specimens in the U.S. military. And probably the dumbest, too." He took a sip of water from a canteen to lubricate his throat before continuing. "You know me, Dick. I generally look at the bright side. I'm an optimist about most things. But no matter how many times I turn this around, I come to the conclusion that this is a major train wreck. Someone must really have it in for us, because we're cooked, my friend. We're not coming back."

Canidy shrugged. "I'm not so sure."

"Not so sure? Were you paying the slightest bit of attention when Donovan gave you the particulars? Or did your ego get in the way? Wild Bill comes to you with all those medals flapping on his chest and tells you he has an operation that only you and the idiot Fulmar can execute. And with your trademark humility, you say, 'You're right, sir, only Fulmar and I can vanquish the Hun and save the damsel in distress. Where do I sign?'"

"It's not a damsel."

"And how is that relevant? Just so I'm clear, did he explain to you exactly *where* we're going?"

"He did."

"He told you about the Germans and the Russians and how we'll be right in the middle, looking for one man among hundreds of thousands of men trying to tear each other to pieces?"

"He did."

"And he told you that the highly specialized troops who he'd sent in before haven't been seen or heard from since?"

"He did."

"Yet you saluted and said, 'I can't wait to die, sir.'"

"I did. And you did, too."

"Hell, *someone* needs to make sure you don't lose this war for us."

"You came because of the layover in Sweden. You thought you might get a chance to bag a Teutonic goddess."

"Nordic."

"There's a difference?"

Fulmar smiled.

The plane began pitching violently for thirty seconds that seemed like thirty minutes as it approached the Scandinavian landmass. Fulmar waited until the noise of the turbulence subsided before speaking again.

"What do you know about our escorts?"

"Not much," Canidy said. "They're Swedish, or something, and have been helping the Brits infiltrate into Poland and Germany. We'll be accompanied by some of those Brits, who will help us get into Poland. That's the easy part. Once in Poland we'll be in the maw of the Wehrmacht, as well as the Red Army, and on our own."

"Right in the middle of the heaviest expenditure of firepower in human history," Fulmar noted. "Should be quite a show. If we live to see even five seconds of it."

Candidy smiled sardonically and nodded. "I confess I'm a little nervous about this. But you're right. When Donovan asks, what the *hell* are you supposed to say? The man has been in situations like the one we're about to go into and came out of them with a rack of hardware. Not just *any* medals. Hell, even if you didn't know about the medals, that face is a face you don't say no to. You feel like a coward for hesitating even a second before responding in the affirmative."

"I was awed that he even thought about someone like me." Fulmar chuckled. "But you know what really went through my mind? Sure, his medals and all. But what kept going through my head was this picture of him sitting in some damn room in the White House drinking brandy with the President, tobacco smoke swirling around his head, saying, 'You know, that Fulmar's a pussy. He rejected the mission.' The President of the United States is told by the toughest SOB in North America that I'm a pussy."

"Well, you are."

"And I had this thought that somehow that description would make it into the history books because there would be a stenographer there taking down everything they were saying because, well, it's the *White House* . . . it's history. And then that transcript would leak to the press and the headlines would say 'Donovan Declares Fulmar a Pussy.'"

Candidy looked askance at Fulmar. "Right. That's *exactly* what would have happened. So much for your Teutonic rationalism."

"*And* that I'm half Kraut. Shouldn't have been trusted in the first place."

Candidy and Fulmar felt the aircraft begin its descent. Reality intruded. The operation would begin shortly.

Fulmar said, "They're going in steep. Maybe Luftwaffe in the area."

The craft broke the cloud deck and Canidy and Fulmar could see the coastline of Sweden as they crossed the North Sea.

"Not maybe. Definitely. We're coming in over the southern tier of Norway, just northwest of Denmark. We're lucky that most of the Luftwaffe is occupied with bombing the hell out of Mr. Churchill six hundred miles southwest of here. We're supposed to be landing at a club airfield east of Visby on Gotland Island. Probably no more than an old cow pasture. So it'll be a little bumpy."

The aircraft banked to the south. Farmland appeared below—a few random edifices dotted the landscape. Not a landing strip in sight.

"This should be fun," Canidy said. "Hold on."

The aircraft descended abruptly, touching down on what appeared to Canidy to be nothing more than a strip of grass without any markings whatsoever. Nonetheless, it was surprisingly smooth.

The plane taxied to a stop a half kilometer from touchdown. Canidy and Fulmar saw three vehicles speeding toward them across the pasture. The pair deplaned, the door closing behind them just as the vehicles came to a halt thirty meters away. Canidy waved to the cockpit and the plane resumed taxiing.

The three vehicles stopped a few feet from the two Americans. A large man sporting a beret and a bushy handlebar mustache emerged from the lead vehicle and strode toward the pair with his hand extended.

"Sergeant Conor McDermott," he said with a Highland brogue as he pumped Canidy's hand, then Fulmar's. "We best get going into the vehicles and out of the open. Damn Gerry planes appear at the damnedest times."

Canidy and Fulmar climbed into the back of the lead vehicle, McDermott seated in the front passenger seat next to a freckled redheaded driver whose face resembled that of a greyhound. McDermott gestured toward the greyhound. "This is Corporal Colin Spivey. We and the lads in the trail cars, Corporal Mark Trent and Corporal Alain Colby, are your escorts to northern Poland—well, some say Prussia. Have you been briefed on the itinerary?"

"The basic outlines," Canidy replied. "I'm Canidy and this is Eric Fulmar."

"Where is the remainder of your gear?" McDermott said.

"What are you talking about?" Canidy asked.

"Your gear. Those devices the famous Research and Development branch of your OSS keeps cooking up—silent pistols, K&L pills—all manner of gadgets that Mr. Donovan has your laboratory people create."

"I suppose he thinks this assignment is different than the others. No occasion for gadgets. We do, however, have our most valuable weapons—the most effective devices in the OSS lab."

"And what would those be, or can't you say?"

"Cigarettes, my friend. Wild Bill says they're the most important item OSS operatives can carry. Universal currency. And of the highest denomination."

McDermott again shook Canidy's hand and then Fulmar's. "We'll take these vehicles until we get within a kilometer or so of the Baltic coastline. The terrain becomes a little rough in vehicles like this, so we'll go by foot until we reach the shore. A boat is tied off at a small dock there. Our skipper—quite experienced at these matters—will take us across the Strait to northern Poland."

"That's consistent with our brief," Canidy said and nodded.

"Unlikely that we'll encounter any Gerries between here and the

Polish coast, but those bastards don't exactly announce their intentions, so keep your eyes open. They're downright hateful bastards, but very clever."

"How many times have you done this?" Fulmar asked.

McDermott grinned. "A little nervous, are we? No worries, mate. So are we, despite the fact that we've made this trip about a half-dozen times. It helps to be nervous. Keeps you alert and alive. Never *ever* let your guard down or underestimate the Germans. They don't miss anything, believe me. One small error in judgment—only one—and you're dead."

Canidy said, "We were told you'd be providing our supplies."

"Quite right." McDermott nodded. "Weapons and such are on the boat. The quartermaster acquired them from your people in London. I must say I was a bit surprised at your choices."

"I don't understand," Canidy said. "M1911 is a good weapon, by my lights, the best of its kind. Why would you be surprised?"

"I don't fault the quality of your choice, old man. Splendid weapon. Just the model. I would think that for an operation in enemy-held territory, you might want to 'blend in,' as it were. Use German weapons—perhaps a Luger or Walther."

"If it gets to the point where we're close enough to the Germans that they notice the make of our weapons, we're dead anyway. I don't speak German, and"—Canidy jabbed his thumb toward Fulmar—"I doubt even his German would fool them for long."

They drove in silence on dirt and gravel roads for half an hour. Canidy could smell the salt water in the air twenty minutes before they reached the ocean. McDermott raised his voice over the din of the vehicles.

"The owner of the vessel has conveyed us across the Baltic several times, sometimes from Gotland, other occasions from the mainland.

Knows the best routes to avoid the Germans and will be our guide for the first ten kilometers or so after we make landfall."

Canidy raised his head abruptly. "Whoa. Hold it right there. That wasn't part of the brief. I don't like last-minute changes and I don't want some sailor guiding me on land. That was supposed to be your job. Besides, I don't want anyone who can't consistently hit a target from at least thirty yards anywhere near us."

"Sorry, mate," McDermott said with a tone of finality. "The captain calls the shots. If you want to go to Poland, you've got to obey the captain. End of discussion."

"Great," Canidy said. "We're not even in the water and already this is turning into a cock-up."

"Look, mate," McDermott responded in a sympathetic tone, "I had the same reaction the first time the captain conveyed us across the Strait. But no one is better at navigating the Strait, avoiding the Germans, or, for that matter, killing the Gerries. Bloody deadeye. Never seen a better shot."

They rode in silence for several minutes before cresting a hill, the Baltic appearing before them no more than a kilometer away. The caravan maneuvered another three-quarters of a kilometer around a series of large boulders toward a cove hidden within a thick grove of silver birches. A thirty-foot vessel was moored next to a pinewood dock where a tall figure stood, fists on hips, scanning the sea. The captain wore a battered cap, baggy gray trousers, and a yellow slicker.

McDermott looked at his watch. "Damn, twenty minutes late. The captain is notoriously punctual. Insanely so. We're going to catch hell."

They walked the remaining quarter kilometer, came to a halt

adjacent to the dock, and the occupants gathered their gear and proceeded toward the vessel, McDermott and Canidy in the lead.

"Apologies, Captain," McDermott called out over the sound of the waves lapping against the dock. "The plane was a few minutes late."

The tall figure turned and stood imperiously, fists still on hips. As Canidy drew near, he was struck by the mesmerizing quality of the piercing pale blue eyes staring at him from beneath the cap's visor. They conveyed an almost regal aloofness. He thrust his hand toward the captain, more a peace offering than a salutation.

The captain grasped Canidy's hand and respectfully removed the cap, releasing an avalanche of blond hair that fell in cascades to the small of her back.

"Kristin Thorisdottir."

Both Canidy and Fulmar came to a complete halt—their British escorts looked on, grinning broadly at their comrades, gauging whether they were more stunned by the fact that the captain was female or that her looks were otherworldly. Each had had similar experiences upon first meeting their skipper.

Canidy's brain, although not unacquainted with such female beauty, took several seconds to absorb the vision. Captain Thorisdottir was at least his height. Although the contours of her figure were hidden under the baggy pants and slicker, it was obvious she was slender and fit. Canidy concluded she had the longest hair, longest neck, and longest legs he'd ever seen on a woman.

Realizing he hadn't responded, Canidy said, "Major Dick Canidy, U.S. Army Air Force." Canidy turned vacantly to his right to introduce Fulmar, who had appeared on Canidy's left and introduced himself instead.

"Lieutenant Eric Fulmar. Sergeant McDermott informed us that you'd be taking us across the sea to Poland and then escorting us into the interior. Thank you." Fulmar winced at his imitation of a lovestruck thirteen-year-old boy.

Thorisdottir turned to the sea and pointed southwest. "Admiral Donitz's wolfpack has been sinking many Liberty ships. There have been reports of U-boat patrols there. Approximately thirty kilometers offshore. Primarily in the afternoon and evening."

"Is that unusual?" Fulmar asked.

"Reports, no. Fishermen report mermaids also." Thorisdottir squinted at the sea. "*Reports* are as plentiful as mosquitoes. U-boats are more like mermaids. I'm skeptical, but of course we must be vigilant."

"I understand. But if there are, indeed, mermaids, how do you evade them?"

"Pray." Thorisdottir waved them toward her boat. "It is best to depart sooner rather than later. Please board now."

As they boarded with their weapons and gear, Thorisdottir walked along the pier conducting one last inspection. Fulmar turned to McDermott. "Now I know why you Brits invaded Iceland. It had nothing to do with sea-lanes and shipping. I'm impressed at your initiative and strategic vision."

"Thanks, mate. But strategic vision won't count for much if one of those German mermaids happens along."

Thorisdottir was the last to board, casting off the line and settling into the cabin. The motor rumbled to life and they pushed from the dock.

Candy and the Brits sat aft while Fulmar sat on a bench next to the captain. "How long will it take to reach the Polish coast?"

"If the weather cooperates, approximately five hours. Provided, of course, we encounter no hostile vessels requiring evasive maneuvers."

"How many times have you made this trip?"

"At least once a week over the last year and a half," Thorisdottir replied, her gaze fixed on the horizon.

"*Why* do you make the trip?"

"I have my reasons, Lieutenant Fulmar."

There was a brief silence. Thorisdottir asked, "Why are *you* making the trip? This is not an ordinary exercise, especially for an American."

"All I can say is that I was asked to make the trip and I agreed," Fulmar responded.

"You had options?"

Fulmar chuckled. "I'm not sure that under the circumstances I truly had options. But I suppose, theoretically, I could have chosen not to do this."

Thorisdottir considered Fulmar's reply for several moments. "Your superiors chose you because you possess certain unique skills or you are particularly talented and trustworthy, or, perhaps, both."

Fulmar didn't respond. He could think of no good reason to disabuse her of the notion he was an exceptional individual.

The wind picked up, as did the waves, although both remained relatively modest. Fulmar scanned the cabin. It was unremarkable save for the absence of any charts or maps. "Do you usually take the same route?" he asked.

"The route depends on the circumstances, Lieutenant Fulmar."

"I ask because I don't see any navigational guides."

"They're not much use to me, Lieutenant Fulmar." Thorisdottir shrugged. "My father taught me to sail. He fished the North Atlantic, the Norwegian Sea, and the Greenland Sea for nearly thirty years. You're not a true seaman until you master waters such as those. He had little use for charts. He said one must sail by instinct."

Fulmar considered that for a moment. "No disrespect, but that seems a little imprecise for this operation. Especially when we're near shore. If we're sailing by instinct, how do we know there won't be German troops where we make landfall?"

Thorisdottir smiled. The effect was electric. "I have several locations for docking that have proven relatively secure. There are no guarantees, of course. But for this occasion, the best option is a narrow channel east of the Gulf of Danzig. It was a canal that once connected to the Vistula before being abandoned half a century ago. No one goes there now. It is overgrown and infested with flies and mosquitoes. There is still a small dock around a bend approximately four hundred meters inside the mouth. It's a bit tricky sometimes, but it's a good place for our purposes."

Fulmar nodded. "And from there?"

"I will guide you to a small place a few kilometers from there. Southeast. It is near the place the man you are seeking was last reported to be. Rumors, actually."

"Why you?" Fulmar asked. "McDermott has done this before. Why not leave it to him?"

Thorisdottir nodded. "Perhaps, but the problem is that the geography changes constantly. By that I mean who controls the area, Wehrmacht or *Armia*, the number of troops, so on and so forth.

"I make the trip regularly. Sergeant McDermott and his men last made the trip over a month ago. I do not have to tell you that may as well be millennia when it comes to troop deployment. A satisfactory infiltration point a week ago may now be overrun with German infantry."

"Still, why accompany us into the interior? Once you've safely gotten us into the country, we can take it from there."

Thorisdottir remained silent for several seconds. Then, "I have my reasons, Lieutenant."

They sailed in silence for a few minutes, then Canidy called out, "Lieutenant Fulmar, would you join us aft?"

Fulmar nodded to Thorisdottir and proceeded to the rear, taking a seat between McDermott and Canidy.

"You look to be making a fair amount of progress up there with our Viking princess," Canidy observed. "I should note, however, that I haven't yet thrown my hat in the ring, at which point you don't have a prayer."

"Go ahead, Dick." Fulmar grinned. "Give it your best shot. She's not easily impressed, as opposed to your usual collection of desperate housewives and widows."

"It's not a fair competition. Look at you and look at me. No comparison. Ask McDermott."

McDermott laughed, waving his hands. "Leave me out of it, lads. If you want my opinion, neither of you have a chance in hell. If you don't want to be shot down, leave the woman alone and just focus on the operation."

"You're saying *I* don't have a chance?" Canidy scoffed. "Look at Fulmar. Now look at me. It's no contest."

McDermott nodded with mock earnestness. "Fine specimens indeed. The both of you. Handsome as fairy-tale princes."

Canidy shook his head. "I'm not sure that description applies to Fulmar."

"It doesn't really matter, my friend. She doesn't care."

"What are you talking about?" Fulmar asked.

"She doesn't really care what you look like, lads."

Canidy and Fulmar appeared puzzled. "What the hell are you talking about?" Canidy asked.

"She only cares about the operation," McDermott said. "She's obsessed with defeating the Nazis. Wouldn't be surprised if she swore an oath of celibacy until they're beaten. Most important, she's a damn fine sailor. This is our fifth trip with her, Canidy. I wouldn't put my men in jeopardy if I had the slightest doubt about her."

As if for emphasis, McDermott rubbed his bushy mustache. "And let me tell you, she's pretty nifty with a carbine, too. I saw her plug an Oberstleutnant straight in the center of his chest at forty meters."

"We all get lucky," Canidy said.

McDermott raised an eyebrow. "Every soldier I've served with would rather have someone beside him who can't shoot very well but is lucky as opposed to someone who can shoot the eye of a hawk but has bad luck."

"Speaking of lucky"—Canidy waved his hand at Fulmar—"that would be this guy. Not only does he know how beautiful she is, she doesn't care how ugly *he* is. He wouldn't stand a chance otherwise."

The men were startled by a loud voice from the bow. "Gentlemen," Thorisdottir shouted over her shoulder. "In fairness, you should know that God often blesses those who have bad eyesight with the gift of exceptional hearing." She paused so they'd be appropriately mortified. "You should also know that we're only a short distance from waters that contain the occasional German vessel. I suggest you cover yourself with the canvas in the rear of the ship until further notice."

CHAPTER 12

Białowieża Forest, Poland
2123, 30 June 1943

The chilled night air seared Jan Kalinowski's lungs as he ran as hard as he could through the forest. His legs faltered every few steps as he drew closer to his limits of endurance.

Tymon was already dead. Or at the very least, severely incapacitated. He hadn't been able to keep up and had been overtaken before they'd reached the stream over half a kilometer back. Kalinowski hadn't seen Tymon go down. He hadn't dared lose a step by glancing back. But he'd heard it: the sound of an impact on flesh, then a piercing shriek.

Kalinowski tried to listen for pursuing footsteps, but the sound of his own on the twigs and pine needles of the forest floor prevented distinguishing quarry from predator. So he kept running, hoping to put distance between himself and his pursuer.

He struggled up a small ridge, slipping and stumbling as he ascended. Just as he reached the crest, a half-moon emerged briefly from behind a cloud, revealing a dense tree line approximately three hundred meters down the opposite slope. If he could reach the tree line before being overtaken, he'd have a chance. He could see another bank of clouds moving swiftly toward the moon, and he'd soon be enveloped in the safety of near complete darkness.

Just two hundred meters.

He scrambled down the sheer slope toward the tree line. He lost control of his acceleration down the hill and fell—tumbling and rolling—but regained his footing, barely losing a step.

As he continued to sprint as fast as he could, he now heard sounds behind him. Footfalls. Panting. The sound of the Russian. *Gaining* on him.

When he approached to within one hundred meters of the tree line, the sounds behind him seemed to drift to his right—still to his rear but veering away at a slant. The moonlight continued to illuminate the landscape, but the clouds were approaching and would provide cover within seconds. When he was within fifty meters of the forest the sounds of pursuit faded to silence, but Kalinowski continued to run toward the trees as fast as he could. The moonlight faded almost simultaneously with his entry into the woods, causing him to slow his pace slightly in order to gain his bearings in the gloom.

His breathing was shallow and ragged, mixing once again with the sound of twigs and pine needles snapping underfoot.

Moments later Jan Kalinowski came to an abrupt stop. A few meters in front of him was his pursuer. He'd passed Kalinowski on his right flank and, improbably, had circled in front of him.

Kalinowski fixed on him with an expression of disbelief. He estimated that the pursuer was approximately five eleven, maybe 170 pounds. Not a particularly imposing physical presence. But he had wolf eyes. Predatory. He wasn't even breathing very hard. And he held an NR-40 combat knife at his side, likely covered with Tymon's blood. Kalinowski held his hands chest high, palms facing his pursuer.

"Please, I don't know any more than what we told you," Kalinowski said between strangled gasps for air. "It's the truth."

"Then why did you run?" Taras Gromov asked.

"The Germans killed many of us looking for the same man. They executed several men outside Hajnówka to make us talk."

"I am not German," Gromov said.

"But you are looking for Sebastian Kapsky?"

"I am," Gromov confirmed. "I am not, however, looking to kill anyone. I require only information."

"Believe me, if I had any information about Sebastian Kapsky, I would give it to you. But I have none. That is the truth. I have no reason to lie."

"Perhaps," Gromov conceded. "Tell me, where are you from?"

Kalinowski looked perplexed. "I am a Pole."

Gromov shook his head. "What region?"

"Near Danzig, east of the Vistula."

"And you have family, yes?"

Kalinowski nodded.

"Then, clearly, you would lie to protect your family. Because you know the Germans are also searching for Kapsky. And if the Germans suspect you are withholding information, your family would be executed."

Kalinowski said nothing.

"I believe you know nothing about Kapsky." Gromov approached Kalinowski slowly. "Tell me what you *do* know."

Kalinowski's eyes darted about as he scoured his brain for anything that Gromov might deem useful. Gromov took a few steps closer, causing Kalinowski's anxiety to spike.

"The SS officer looking for Kapsky. He has been in several places looking for him. I know wherever he goes he leaves corpses. Is that of use?"

Gromov recognized that Kalinowski had no information directly pertaining to Kapsky. He was desperately trying to placate Gromov. Nonetheless, information about Germans searching for Kapsky was not without value. They had more extensive networks in western and northern Poland than the Soviets. If they were searching in a particular area, it might be because their informants had relayed Kapsky's probable whereabouts, areas in which Gromov might concentrate his own efforts.

Gromov pointed the blade at Kalinowski. "Go on."

"The name of the officer asking the questions is Maurer, Obersturmführer Maurer. Earlier this week he was in Kazubski interrogating villagers and captured *Armia*. When he does not get satisfactory answers, he kills. I understand he has killed many."

"What questions was he asking, specifically?" Gromov asked.

"That I do not know, but he was asking for the whereabouts of Sebastian—"

"Yes. I know. Do you know where Maurer is?"

"No. But I understand that he's been moving in an easterly direction. As the Wehrmacht pushes eastward, he follows. But there are rumors that he does not confine himself to German-held territory."

"Tell me about the rumors."

"I have not heard much," Kalinowski said. "But it has been reported to Commander Matuszek that he occasionally infiltrated behind Red Army lines."

"Do you know how he does this?" Gromov asked.

"No. But he is said not to be the kind of man who simply blends in. He's said to be quite large and distinguishable."

"You are suggesting he has assistance from Soviet troops or officers?"

"I am not suggesting anything," Kalinowski said wearily. "I am simply repeating what I have heard, to tell you all that I know about Kapsky."

"And since then?" Gromov asked.

"I do not know. He was, however, traveling in a southeast direction."

Gromov closed to within two feet of the Pole, who flinched. "You have been helpful. I can use the information you have provided," Gromov said to a relieved Kalinowski. "But I believe, however, that you would be similarly helpful to the Germans." Gromov thrust the NR-40 under the Pole's jaw, through his tongue, and into the roof of his mouth.

CHAPTER 13

Thorisdottir guided her boat expertly around a sandbar and into a narrow channel filled with muddy water and moss. Canidy stood slightly behind her. He could see smoke rising approximately thirty-five kilometers to the west.

"I thought we were landing near Danzig," he said to Thorisdottir.

"This is as close to Danzig as we dare go. The Nazis have been executing non-Germans there. Hundreds. Maybe thousands. German troops saturate the area within a ten-kilometer radius of the city. In fact, this may be too close. But this is the only place where we have a chance of going undetected."

"I understand you to say we are going to an area to the east of Danzig?"

"Correct," Thorisdottir acknowledged. "I know McDermott. I don't know who you are. I am not going to tell you anything until I know I can trust you."

They traveled nearly a quarter kilometer down the channel, the banks of which were lined with thick rows of trees and shrubs, until it began to bend westward. A small wooden pier extended from the eastern bank. Thorisdottir cut off the motor and allowed the vessel to drift slowly toward the pier.

Fulmar, McDermott, and his men slung their gear over their shoulders and climbed onto the dock. Canidy watched Thorisdottir tie off the boat and sling a Gevarm 1938 over her shoulder.

"What's the weapon for?" Canidy asked.

"What do you think? I am taking you inland to the last place the person you are seeking was reported to be. Jan, an *Armia* partisan, should be there. He may have information, he may have Kapsky, but he may also be dead. And there is more than a remote possibility we'll encounter German troops on the way. The area is infested with them."

"Look," Canidy said, "you've already done more than enough. McDermott can get us there. That's why he's here. You've done everything you were asked."

"Not nearly," Thorisdottir said. "Besides, McDermott has been here four times, yes. But I've been here dozens. And more recently. The battlefield is, how you say? Fluid. It changes weekly, if not daily. It is not the same as it was last time McDermott was here."

Canidy pointed to the rifle. "All due respect, what do you plan to do with this?"

"Kill Germans if it becomes necessary," Thorisdottir said matter-of-factly. She cocked her head to the right. "I sense you are restraining yourself from laughing. An understandable reaction. But I will wager that if we encounter a German patrol, I will be much more effective than you in eliminating the threat."

Canidy replied, "The idea is to *avoid* Germans. How effective are you at that, given—"

"Given that I am a mere sailor? Again, I suspect more effective than you." Thorisdottir turned to face him directly. "How many German patrols have you evaded in the last year, Mr. Canidy?"

Canidy smiled. "Lead the way, ma'am."

Thorisdottir motioned to get everyone's attention and beckoned them toward her. The six men formed a semicircle before her.

"My understanding is that the latest information from the *Armia* is that the person you are looking for was last twenty kilometers southeast of Danzig. It is also my understanding that you recognize that the information may not be timely or otherwise reliable."

Canidy and McDermott nodded their concurrence.

"Before we proceed further, it is imperative that we all understand certain matters. I have been briefed by Sergeant McDermott on the essential timing and logistics of your operation, but it's important to acknowledge that the timing contained in the plans may not conform to reality. First, it is probable that this individual . . . I am sorry, what is the person's name?"

McDermott looked at Canidy, unsure whether the information should be disclosed to Thorisdottir. Canidy nodded assurance.

"Sebastian Kapsky," McDermott said.

"It is probable—very probable—that Mr. Kapsky has been killed or captured by the Germans. Second, if he is alive, it is very probable he is not remotely near the area last reported. Not only is information in this area notoriously unreliable, even reliable information remains so only briefly. Circumstances shift with a blink of an eye—and not merely from day to day, but hour to hour and minute to minute."

Thorisdottir swept her left hand in an arc. "This area is not just *occupied* by the Germans, they have taken a unique interest in it. By virtue of the large ethnic German population that inhabited this region before the war, Hitler believes this to be not merely occupied territory, but German territory and Germany itself. It is, after all, Prussia.

"I will guide you near Koszwały, which is ten kilometers south. From there, you are on your own. Although my boat is well concealed, the probability of its discovery increases with the passage of every hour, so I will take the vessel back to the sea and return in twenty-four hours after I leave you at Koszwały."

"How long will you wait for us?" Canidy asked.

"Not long."

"The plan was that the extraction vessel would not leave sooner than seventy-two hours after our initial insertion," Canidy said. "You were informed of this, right?"

"I'm afraid, Major Canidy, that such precision works only on chalkboards," Thorisdottir replied. "I will wait as long as I deem it prudent. But it is likely to be very brief—a few hours at best. That is simply acknowledging reality. So endeavor to return to the insertion point in a timely fashion."

Canidy glanced at McDermott and nodded.

Thorisdottir continued. "Please discard any German weaponry you are presently carrying. It marks you for immediate execution if you are captured." She looked disapprovingly and pointed at Sergeant McDermott. "*You* should know better."

McDermott gestured toward Canidy. "He doesn't speak German. I thought if he was carrying German armaments, he'd be presumed German."

"Anyone wearing civilian clothing bearing German arms will be presumed to have taken said arms from dead Germans. You'll be shot on sight. If you are fortunate. Besides, if the Germans don't shoot you, *Armia* snipers will unquestionably do so, then gut you and feed your intestines to swine."

Canidy nodded agreement and turned to the others. "I'm carrying only my M1911." He turned toward Thorisdottir. "Okay if I stick it into my belt and cover it with my shirt?"

"It would be much more satisfactory, Major Canidy, if you carried no firearms whatsoever."

"Not going to happen," Canidy said with a shake of his head.

"I thought not," Thorisdottir conceded.

Canidy said to the other men, "Put all weapons other than pistols back on the boat." He turned toward Thorisdottir. "Okay?"

Thorisdottir nodded. "I can conceal them if I am stopped—there is a compartment below."

Canidy examined his M1911. "Men, sidearms only. Place all other weapons back on the boat." As they complied, he turned to Thorisdottir and pointed to the Gevarm. "What about you?"

"Probabilities and captain's privilege, Major Canidy. I will be accompanying you only a short distance, in which we are unlikely to encounter Germans. But if we do, I'm going to kill them."

Canidy inspected her face and concluded that was precisely what she would do. "Let's get moving," Thorisdottir said. "If Kapsky is as important as they say, we're not going to be the only ones looking for him. And whoever else *is* looking for him probably has gotten a pretty good head start on us. We need to play catch-up and fast. Otherwise, we'll lose the war, and if by chance we were to win this war, we'll lose the future."

Thorisdottir walked wearily but briskly through the woods. Canidy, Fulmar, McDermott, and McDermott's men falling into a single line behind her.

CHAPTER 14

Donovan studied the desk in the Oval Office as he waited silently for the President to sign several documents that his aide, Harry Hopkins, handed him.

Donovan liked the desk. It was large, heavy, and practical. It lacked the pompous ornateness of the desks favored by many cabinet secretaries and bureaucrats. Much of Franklin Delano Roosevelt's New Deal agenda was signed into law on the desk. Although Donovan strenuously opposed much of the legislation, he understood that history demanded ceremonial signings, and the desk was perfectly suited for ceremony. Nonetheless, Donovan thought the *Resolute* desk was probably better suited for ceremony. It had a backstory fit for Presidential furniture. Located in the President's office on the second floor of the White House residence, it was an ornately carved gift from Britain's Queen Victoria in 1880. It had been crafted from oak taken from the HMS *Resolute*, a British research ship that had been locked in ice in the Arctic until rescued by an American whaler and returned to England. It was a symbol of the enduring bond between the two countries.

The President seemed forever to be signing something at the desk, and this occasion was no different. Donovan had grown accustomed to waiting patiently for Roosevelt to scan the documents placed before him by Hopkins or Hopkins's aide, Laurence Duggan, sign them with a flourish, and expel a stream of blue smoke from his cigarette. Donovan would know the President had signed the final document when he tapped it with his pen after signing it with the flourish—as he'd just done. He handed the stack of documents to his aide, who nodded to Donovan and left the room.

Roosevelt removed the cigarette holder from his mouth and asked, "What do we know so far, Bill?"

"Very little," Donovan replied. "The last concrete information we have is that our two men arrived in Sweden and immediately departed the airport in the company of Churchill's men. They were to travel to the southern coast of Gotland, where they were to be conveyed by boat across the Baltic to the northeast coast of Poland. If all is preceding without any hitches, we can assume they've made landfall by now."

A blue haze surrounded the President's head. "Just so you know, I informed Marshall," he said. "He thinks the probabilities of success are near zero. And the odds of our men's survival even less."

Donovan shifted in his seat. "Mr. President . . ."

Roosevelt waved him off. "Yes, I know, Bill. You object to my telling him anything about the operation. But for God's sake, he's the U.S. Army chief of staff. I can't possibly leave him ignorant about something like this. In his position, he'd find out eventually, whether the mission was a failure or success. And then I'd have an

Army chief of staff who would no longer trust a single thing I say or do. That is, if he didn't resign."

"No argument there, sir. It's simply a matter of timing, that's all."

"Don't you think I know that, Bill? How would you react if I told you about an operation only at its conclusion that it was a success or failure? An operation over which you have ostensibly command authority?" Roosevelt held up his hand to forestall Donovan's reply. "You wouldn't simply tender your resignation on parchment in a dignified, soldierly fashion. You'd storm in here, smash the coffee table, and throw the pieces through the window. And rightly so."

"*Marshall* wouldn't do that," Donovan replied.

"The effect would be the same. I'd lose the confidence of half my staff," Roosevelt said. "In fact, Bill, you and I need to consider how we tell Eisenhower, Gerow, and MacArthur."

Donovan raised his eyebrows. "Eisenhower and Gerow I understand. But why the hell MacArthur? He's on the other side of the world, for God's sake."

Roosevelt looked at his old friend with mock incredulity. "Are you suggesting I leave that immense ego in the dark? Hell, immediately upon finding out about the operation he'd declare his candidacy for President." Roosevelt pointed his cigarette holder at Donovan. "And you, you son of a bitch—you'd vote for him. You share the exact same politics."

Donovan remained taciturn save for a slight crinkling of his eyes that betrayed his amusement. "The odds of success of the operation are not good. This is the biggest test of the OSS thus far. A unique operation combining intelligence and direct action. This will be a template for Special Operations going forward. The fewer that know, the better. And not merely from the standpoint of security. Failure will have its own effect on morale," Donovan observed.

Roosevelt grunted. "Hell, Bill, morale will be the least of our concerns if we don't succeed. If Hitler or our good friend Uncle Joe wins this race—"

"Mr. President . . ." Donovan interrupted. "We'll make sure no matter what happens, neither Hitler nor Stalin gain access to that information."

Roosevelt looked askance at Donovan. "I don't like the sound of that, Bill. I understand what you're saying, but I just don't like the sound of it."

"Believe me, sir, neither do I. I'm not advocating anything other than preventing those two from acquiring strategic superiority."

Donovan noticed Roosevelt looking past him to the entrance to the Oval Office. Glancing over his left shoulder, Donovan saw Harry Hopkins standing in the doorway, pointing at his watch.

"Yes, Harry, in a moment," Roosevelt said. Hopkins turned and left. Roosevelt looked at Donovan. "I'm scheduled to spend more of your money in ways you won't approve." He smiled. "But before I do, tell me where we are with this."

"The short answer, Mr. President, is that we don't know. And we likely won't know for several days. Any information we get before our team is extracted will come from Commander Ian Fleming, who is in sporadic communication with the British Special Operations executive.

"What we know right now, Mr. President, is this: Our two men and four Brits made contact with a boat captain who is to convey them to the Polish coast—"

Roosevelt interrupted. "A boat captain," he repeated.

"Yes, sir," Donovan replied. "A civilian boat. Anything else would have been detected and blown out of the water."

"Who is this captain? Who would volunteer for something this risky?" Roosevelt smiled. "Are we sure he's sane?"

"She, Mr. President."

"She?"

"Yes, sir. She was recommended by Ian Fleming as being highly competent and reliable. And as a woman, Fleming believes she may be given a pass if interdicted by the Germans."

"What do *we* believe?" Roosevelt asked.

"Frankly, Mr. President, we have little upon which to base a belief. We're new to this and do not have assets readily available, so we must rely on the Brit's judgment."

"Do we know anything about this person?"

"According to Fleming, she's done several runs for British secret service. All successful."

"She's British?"

"She's from Iceland, sir."

"I don't know, Bill," Roosevelt said skeptically. "Why would she have a dog in this fight?"

"Fleming vouches for her. It seems her father, also a fisherman, was killed early on by the Germans."

Roosevelt nodded. "What about her mother? Siblings?"

Donovan hesitated. "She has one sibling, sir. Our information is that her mother is still alive. She's German. More precisely, she's German on one side and Russian on the other, but born in Germany."

Roosevelt removed the cigarette holder from his mouth. "My lord, Bill, you approved this?"

"The mother left Germany shortly after the Great War. Fleming reports that she was appalled by Hitler's ascent to power. That hatred of Hitler was conveyed to the daughter even before the father was killed."

Roosevelt motioned with the cigarette holder. "Go on."

"They were scheduled to land in Poland a short time ago. They should be on their way south to make contact with *Armia* near Kapsky's last reported location. Once they make contact with Kapsky, they will return to the vessel and take him to Gotland."

"Rather straightforward."

"I wish, sir. We estimate that there are over two hundred thousand German troops in the immediate area. And we have to presume they consider Kapsky to be as valuable as we do . . ."

"Splendid," Roosevelt said sarcastically.

". . . and Uncle Joe has large members of troops nearby also. Query whether Stalin is fighting for Polish land, or fighting to get Kapsky."

Roosevelt sat silently for nearly thirty seconds. "Bill, what percentage do you place on our team's getting out alive?"

Donovan rubbed the back of his neck. "Optimistically? Twenty-five percent."

Roosevelt closed his eyes. "What about extracting Kapsky alive?"

"Half that."

CHAPTER 15

Canidy was impressed with the speed with which they traveled. More impressive was the fact that they'd encountered no German troops. Thorisdottir had guided them expertly through brush, across streams, and around open fields to the sparsely wooded highland area that overlooked a small village consisting of approximately twenty edifices approximately a third of a kilometer away. Two Kübelwagens were parked next to what appeared to be a mechanic's garage. No German soldiers were in sight. No villagers, either.

Thorisdottir knelt on the grass and motioned for the others to do the same. Canidy took a position next to Thorisdottir, who pointed toward the village. "The last time I made this journey this was an *Armia* waystation. Armaments are hidden in the cellars of several of the buildings. Residents provide whatever other supplies they can."

"Would Kapsky be here?"

"Clearly not at the moment. Otherwise, I'd expect some commotion with the Kübelwagens next to the garage. But it's likely the Resistance would eventually bring him here on the way to the coast. Our last information was that he wasn't far from here."

Canidy saw at least a dozen figures dressed in what appeared to be German military uniforms emerge from the garage. Each of them was carrying a firearm.

"They look serious."

A civilian emerged from the garage, followed by two more Germans holding rifles trained at his back. Canidy could hear angry shouts that sounded German. They came from a German soldier who appeared to be an officer. He was jabbing a finger into the civilian's chest as he shouted. Remarkably, the civilian appeared to shout back.

Canidy turned to Thorisdottir. "*Armia*?"

"I don't know, but he's either crazy or incredibly brave."

"Maybe both," Canidy said. "Do you think they're asking about our friend?"

"I can't distinguish the words," Thorisdottir replied. "It could be they're asking about the location of *Armia* or accusing him of harboring *Armia*. The person doing the questioning is SS."

Fulmar and McDermott crept next to Canidy. The shouting seemed to increase in volume and intensity. The civilian continued to give as good as he got.

Fulmar said, "This is not good. He's looking for our guy. Something's about to happen."

"That's not our man, not our fight," Canidy observed.

"How can you be so certain from this distance?" McDermott asked, squinting toward the scene.

"If it were our guy, they wouldn't be shouting at him. They'd treat him like precious cargo, bundle him up in one of those vehicles, and be happily off to see the Führer. Besides, from here it looks like the guy's hair is thinning. It sure doesn't look like a—what is it? 'A thick shock of black hair.'"

The shouting below only seemed to grow louder with each passing second. The Pole's gestures grew increasingly agitated as well. The officer appeared to throw up his hands in exasperation and turned to his men to issue commands. Several broke off from the rest and trotted toward the dwellings, where, moments later, they ushered the inhabitants outside.

Fulmar pointed at the scene. "What's going on here?" It was less a question than a statement of trepidation.

Roughly two dozen civilians were herded into the square, where the Pole was shouting guttural Polish phrases that were unmistakably profanity. The officer issued another command and one of the German soldiers raised his rifle and shot a male villager in the chest. Anguished screams wafted through the valley as a female member knelt next to the body, sobbing.

The officer turned sharply toward the Pole and angrily asked another question. More unmistakable profanity issued in torrents from the Pole's mouth. Again, the officer turned and shouted commands. And, again, one of his men shot another male villager in the chest.

"Jesus," McDermott whispered.

"Stay calm," Canidy said.

Before the officer turned to face the Pole again, the man leapt forward, seized the sidearm holstered at the officer's hip, and shot him twice in the back. The Pole pivoted and managed to squeeze off several more rounds, felling two Germans before being riddled with fire from the other troops. When the echoes of the gunfire subsided, they were replaced by the sobbing and wailing of the village citizens.

Canidy glanced at Thorisdottir, whose gaze was riveted to the scene below, the muscles in her jaws tensing and contracting.

"What do you think that was about," Fulmar said. It was not a question.

"Yep," Canidy acknowledged. "It's pretty clear we're not the only ones looking for the good professor."

"No one can be that important," McDermott said.

Canidy noticed a wispy swirl of dust approaching the village rapidly from the south. As it drew near the square, Canidy could see that it was a German Horch 108 convertible staff car with two soldiers in the front and a single officer to the rear. As it came to a halt in the square, the soldiers in the square stood at attention and saluted. The officer stood and returned the salute before stepping from the vehicle. Even from a distance, he cut an impressive figure. He towered over the troops. His peaked visor cap added to the disparity. As the officer moved imperiously among the troops, Canidy instinctively sensed that he was searching for something of exceptional importance.

Canidy's concentration on the German officer was broken by Thorisdottir's voice. He had caught only the word "now." He turned toward her. "I'm sorry," Canidy said. "What were you saying?"

"I said the show is over. This is where I leave you. Apparently, Jan is either late or dead. Either way, he is not here. Continue proceeding south and you will encounter *Armia* near Pszczółki. McDermott should be able to take it from there."

Canidy nodded, reluctant to see her go for more reasons than one.

Thorisdottir examined her watch. "It is now 1312 hours. I will return to where we docked in twenty-four hours."

"And you won't wait long if we're late," Canidy added.

Thorisdottir nodded.

"Thank you," Canidy said. He couldn't think of anything clever to say. "Good luck."

"Luck is for gnomes and idiots," Thorisdottir said dismissively before descending the slope and vanishing into the forest.

Canidy turned to McDermott. "You're the tour guide now. Take it from here."

McDermott pointed southwest. "We'll take a wide westerly arc around the village before proceeding south again. It's mainly farmland and woods. We have fairly decent cover if we need it all the way to south of Pszczółki."

"How long do you estimate it will take before we get there?"

McDermott cocked his head to the side as he performed a mental calculation. "Ten to eleven hours, maybe less if we get going right away."

Canidy said, "Ten hours, then, because we're not going until we're fairly certain the Germans won't detect our movement. This will be tight."

Canidy watched the activity in the village. The troops had lined up the residents, including children, in a single row. The attitude of their bodies conveyed obedience and fear. The tall officer, flanked by two troops, walked down the line, stopping to question each resident. Most remained absolutely still. A few shook their heads, presumably in response to a question posed by the giant. Canidy watched the officer closely. He wasn't conducting a perfunctory interrogation. He appeared to pose multiple questions to each resident. Even the children.

Canidy understood that he was watching his rival in the hunt for Sebastian Kapsky.

CHAPTER 16

Northern Poland
1321, 1 July 1943

Taras Gromov peered through the 6x30 binoculars at the towering German officer as he strode down the line of civilians, questioning each. Gromov had witnessed scenes like this before. They rarely had a pleasant ending, and something about the officer suggested that the ending in this case could be horrific.

The assassin raised his binoculars to the surrounding country-side and conducted a slow sweep of the hills on the opposite side of the valley. Nothing but tall grass punctuated by an occasional tree. His sweep was interrupted by an anguished cry from the village. He returned his gaze to the square and saw one of the villagers on his knees in front of the tall officer. It was unclear whether he had been struck or was simply begging for mercy.

Less than an hour ago Gromov had received information from his contact in Pszczółki that Kapsky was in the vicinity. The contact emphasized that he couldn't vouch for the timeliness of the information, but all indications were that it was fairly recent. More important, the contact conveyed two messages from Belyanov. First, the Americans had dispatched a team to secure Kapsky. The contact didn't know how many were on the team, but NKVD concluded that by now they should have entered Poland from the north coast after crossing the Baltic from Sweden. Gromov didn't doubt the accuracy of the information, but wondered about its provenance. He knew the NKVD had placed informants within Allied governments, but this information was unusually detailed.

The second message was unequivocal. Acquire Kapsky, or, failing that, be sure that neither the Germans nor the Americans acquire Kapsky.

Gromov understood the latter message to be quite plain. Belyanov was not suggesting Gromov simply thwart the German and American efforts to acquire Kapsky. Rather, Belyanov would rather that Gromov kill Kapsky than allow him to fall into the hands of anyone else. Gromov had few illusions as to why he was chosen for this assignment. He was a proficient killer, and that is what Belyanov—and Beria—expected him to be. If, however, he could secure Kapsky and return him to the Kremlin—so much the better. But doing so was not the imperative.

Gromov watched the German officer methodically go down the line of villagers, conducting examinations. The Russian concluded the officer was likely among those that would have to be eliminated. It was clear he was exacting and would leave no stone unturned in his efforts to secure Kapsky.

Gromov studied his appearance as well as his movements and methods. Had Gromov raised his binoculars across the valley and slightly to the north he would have seen Canidy, directed by McDermott, lead his team in a wide westerly arc around the village, on their way south.

CHAPTER 17

Northern Poland
1545, 1 July 1943

They'd traveled for the last two hours in near silence, not uttering more than a few words among them. Each was stunned by the horrific scenes from the village. The sheer brutality was beyond anything any of them had ever witnessed. Gratuitous cruelty such as that demanded retribution. And each member of Canidy's team silently vowed that when the opportunity presented itself, he'd exact that retribution.

It was a slow slog. Not because of the terrain, which was relatively manageable despite brush and mud, but because the area was saturated with Germans. They were in panzers and trucks and cars and planes. They were in the tiny villages that dotted the landscape as well as on the roads and in the fields. Canidy's team seemed to be dropping to the ground or hiding behind foliage every few minutes.

Nonetheless, they were making progress, moving in a general southeast direction, even with the many detours occasioned by German presence.

Canidy calculated that they were proceeding at roughly two to three kilometers an hour. While the Germans seemed omnipresent, there had been no signs of *Armia*. McDermott assured them that was to be expected. The last time he had been in the region, *Armia* had not been operating in the area, and it was likely that since then the Germans had further consolidated their positions. Moreover, the Resistance was not likely to announce their presence. After all, the Germans were forever laying traps for them. But McDermott assured Canidy that they would be in contact soon.

Canidy glanced frequently at his watch. It had been several hours since they'd left the boat, and he had no doubt that Thorisdottir would be as precise as possible in her departure, Kapsky on board or not. His team had been moving almost without pause, no stops for rest or sleep, eating small bites of food from their rucksacks while walking through brush and tall grass.

When they came to another shallow stream—there seemed to be one every half kilometer—Canidy motioned for his team to stop and gather around. They dropped to one knee in a semicircle.

Canidy looked to McDermott. "How much farther?"

"No more than a couple of kilometers."

"Okay, we barely have time at our present pace to go another two kilometers and return to the dock on time. In fact, we're at about the halfway point now. We can't afford to pause for any distractions, like the scene at the village, or any detours whatsoever. We're all a little tired, but we have to be careful our pace doesn't slow. Otherwise we won't make it back on time. And let's hope we don't run into any Germans."

Fulmar asked, "What happens if we *do* run into Germans?"

"We can't. Simple as that. We can't afford any delays. We have to do whatever we can to avoid them, not be detected. If we get pinned down by fire or have to remain concealed or immobile for more than thirty minutes, we're going to have a very hard time meeting Thorisdottir's time frame. And I don't think any of us doubts that she means it."

"Hell, if we encounter German fire we're done for anyway," Fulmar said, holding up his M1911. "Their Kar98k rifles against these? We're done for."

"We can't let it get to that," Canidy said. "Let's be disciplined. Let's be smart."

"Even so, all of this assumes that Kapsky is waiting for us wrapped up in a big red ribbon, ready to go," Fulmar said. "Like you said, we can't really afford *any* slowdowns and expect to be back at the dock on time. I don't know what Thorisdottir means by 'not long,' but my guess is it's measured in minutes, not hours."

Canidy nodded. "Right. We're going to have to pick up the pace. But be smart. No mistakes."

Canidy began to rise when he was startled to see a figure dressed in loose gray cotton clothing carrying a carbine standing behind McDermott. The figure held a finger to his lips and smiled. Seeing Canidy's expression, the other members of the team turned in the direction of his gaze and saw the figure also. He was a boy. No more than fifteen or sixteen, but with the face of someone who had lived a lifetime.

"American?" he asked.

Canidy nodded. "American and British."

"We were expecting you. Well, maybe not *you*, but someone."

"*Armia*?" Canidy asked.

The boy nodded. "Commander Matuszek has been expecting Americans to arrive for some time. He received word from your OSS through Czech Resistance. We've been watching you for the last two hours. You are very fortunate to have avoided German patrols. One such patrol almost intercepted you an hour ago. We could not warn you without alerting them to your presence. That was—how you say?—a close shave."

"Where is your Commander Matuszek?" Canidy asked.

"Not far. Do not worry. I heard your discussion—we will be there in less than fifteen minutes."

Canidy inspected the boy for a moment. "What's your name?"

"Emil."

"How the hell old are you?"

"Twelve years. I will be thirteen in a few weeks."

"Emil, how the hell do you know we aren't Germans dressed as civilians?"

Emil smiled. "Because I would be dead by now."

Canidy shook his head. "You've been watching us how long?"

"At least two hours, maybe more. Since you crossed the creek just before the railroad tracks, and"—he pointed to McDermott—"the one with the big mustache fell on his face."

Canidy grinned. "Emil, after you take us to Commander Matuszek, I may have a job for you."

"You must make your request to the commander," Emil informed him. "What kind of job is it?"

"Get us back to our boat before it leaves without us. Otherwise, based on what we've seen so far, we're dead."

CHAPTER 18

Northern Poland
1630, 1 July 1943

Gromov's contact was a small, thin man with wiry hair and teeth stained brown from nearly incessant smoking. His eyes were rheumy and his skin was sallow. He was standing, as directed, next to a barn with faded red paint and had the look of someone resigned to a miserable fate. He did not have the look of someone who should be entrusted with highly sensitive information audaciously procured for the NKVD by its mole within the White House from a source trusted by the United States President himself. When he saw Gromov emerge from the woods at precisely the time he was told, he began to twitch noticeably.

Gromov approached slowly so as not to frighten the man any further. "You know who I am?"

"Yes."

"What do you have for me?"

"Americans are looking for a professor. The professor is nearby."

The man stared with rheumy eyes bulging, as if he expected to be struck for his statement.

Gromov asked, "Is there nothing else? I know that already."

"Americans are here now. They will leave by boat."

Gromov shook his head in disgust. Having a source in the highest levels of the United States government was of scant value if the information gleaned was so unremarkable.

"You must be sure the Americans do not leave," the man added.

Gromov was skeptical the man was conveying the directive accurately. "Do you mean the Americans must not leave with a certain individual?"

The man stared blankly.

Irritated, Gromov restated the question. "I'm to kill the Americans *regardless* of whether they have located the person they're seeking? Is that what Belyanov said?"

The man continued to stare, now with a look of panic and confusion. Gromov turned sharply In disgust and began walking away, when he heard the man make an indiscernible croaking noise. Gromov spun toward the man again.

"Did you say something?"

The man nodded and said, "Before they return to the coast. You are to kill them before they reach water."

"No matter what?"

"That is my understanding. They are not to reach the sea."

Gromov, having scant confidence in the man, pressed. "Is this directive from Belyanov?"

Again, the infuriating vacant stare.

"Belyanov," Gromov repeated. "The directive is from Belyanov himself?"

"I do not know what you are saying."

"*Aleksandr Belyanov*, you idiot," Gromov snapped. "Is that who told you this?"

"I don't know."

Gromov restrained himself from seizing the man's throat and crushing his trachea. It wasn't his fault he was stupid. And it wasn't his fault NKVD had entrusted a simpleton to convey instructions. Belyanov had a reputation for intelligence and precision. He left little room for misapprehension. Clearly, he'd entrusted the message to this simpleton because the message was unambiguous. The message, Gromov concluded, was the Americans were to be eliminated with all deliberate speed.

"When did you receive the message?" Gromov asked.

"Today, I believe."

"You believe?" Gromov shook his head. "Who gave it to you?"

"I do not know him."

"Describe him."

"He was short and thin. A sharp nose." The man paused to refresh his recollection.

Gromov placed a few *złoty* in the man's breast pocket to aid his recollection. "With a beard and round spectacles?" Gromov asked.

"Yes!" the man replied excitedly, as if relieved to know he hadn't hallucinated the encounter. "He was as you described. He was very short. He would come barely to your shoulder and he had a very sharp and straight nose. A very thin nose. And a beard—very, very neat; very neat. His spectacles had gold-wired rims like a watchmaker might wear. He spoke very slowly and quietly, and he gave me a goral and"—the man rifled through his pockets, retrieved two photographs, and thrust them toward Gromov—"these photographs, I believe, of the Americans." The man squinted to jog the last morsel of information from his brain, unsuccessfully. "I do not know the man's name, the one who gave me the directive."

"I do," Gromov said flatly.

He was Colonel Yevgeni Goncharov, former battalion political officer and NKVD assassin, without a unique portfolio. He was there to ensure that no witnesses remained alive who could confirm that someone connected to the Soviet military had anything to do with the assassination of American and British troops. No witnesses whatsoever.

CHAPTER 19

Northern Poland
1647, 1 July 1943

Emil's estimate of their arrival time at Commander Matuszek's encampment was disrupted by a column of panzers and troop carriers. Although the procession seemed interminable, in fact, it passed in less than ten minutes.

When the last panzer had passed, Emil motioned for the others to remain concealed in the tall grass. No more than five minutes later several German infantry troops passed by them—a common German tactic to intercept enemy troops who would emerge from concealment after a German column had passed.

Shortly thereafter, they arrived at the *Armia* encampment—located at a deserted farmhouse and barn obscured by an overgrowth of trees, wheat, and weeds. There was no sign of Commander Matuszek or any *Armia* as they approached the rotting edifices.

Emil held up his hand to signal Canidy and the others to stop approximately fifty meters from the front porch of the farmhouse. Several seconds later, several score of ghostlike figures brandishing firearms rose out of the tall grass like corpses from a graveyard, their weapons trained on the Americans and Brits.

A man who Canidy immediately identified as Commander Matuszek emerged from the front door of the farmhouse. He didn't look like someone who was commanding an outgunned, outmanned, untrained group of civilians fighting the most powerful military force in history. Instead, he looked as if he had stepped out of a painting of a sixteenth-century pirate captain, and he had the swagger of a Viking raider.

He was missing his right eye, gnarled flesh surrounding the uncovered cavity where it had once been. His left eye regarded them with disdain bordering on contempt for a full ten seconds before he strode forward, stopping several feet away with his fists on his hips.

"It's clear God loves Americans and British because you are too stupid to survive long without his favor." Matuszek turned to his right and spat. "It is your choice if you wish to commit suicide by exposing yourself as you have, almost completely oblivious to the multitude of German convoys and patrols in this area. If you wish to operate so recklessly that *your* discovery and death are assured, I have no quarrel with you. But where your idiocy threatens brave Poles, that is a matter altogether different. Irresponsible. Inexcusable."

Matuszek strode even closer, his proximity to Canidy and McDermott making them both uncomfortable. He pointed his finger at McDermott's chest. "You in particular have no excuse for your carelessness. This is not, as the frivolous Americans like to say, 'Your first dance.' We have seen you here before. You may be an outstanding operative by British standards, but by our standards, you are a liability. Churchill may think he's helping us, but all you are doing is alerting the Germans to our presence. My troops have saved your life at least twice. Yes, *twice*. Not that you would know."

Matuszek shifted his ire to Canidy. "So the Americans have arrived, finally. The cowboys. The saviors. Do you expect us to be impressed? Genuflect at your feet? I'm not sure what is worse, the evil of the Nazis and Soviets, or the ineptitude of the British and Americans. All of you contribute in your own way to Polish death and suffering."

"Commander Matuszek," Canidy said, his tone contrite, "we didn't mean—"

A young man jogged up to Matuszek, addressed him in a low voice, and then backed away. Matuszek said, "I'm advised that the Germans once again have snipers in the area. They are quite clever. Their sights may be obstructed by the trees and tall grass, but it is not advisable to afford them a stationary target." He turned toward the farmhouse and said, "Follow me."

As they followed Matuszek toward the dwelling, Emil sidled up to Canidy. "Commander Matuszek lost nearly two dozen men in the last day, including his father," he said, to explain the commander's belligerence. "We killed many Germans, but that will not bring back our dead."

Matuszek pointed to the steps and the warped wood of the porch. "Be careful."

The commander entered the farmhouse door with Canidy and his men. The front room was a large kitchen with a long wooden table surrounded by enough chairs to accommodate the group. Everyone remained standing, Matuszek once again with his fists on his hips.

"You are looking for a professor, am I correct?"

"We are," Canidy answered. "His name is Sebastian Kapsky."

"Why are you looking for him?"

"Because I was asked to look for him. *Find* him," Canidy said.

"Asked?" Matuszek scoffed. "Do American superior officers no longer issue orders?"

Canidy felt strangely defensive, as if the integrity of the U.S. military was being questioned. "The operation was deemed extremely high-risk, with a high probability that the personnel charged with executing it wouldn't be coming back. So our government looked for volunteers. We were given the option of taking it or rejecting it."

Matuszek shook his head disdainfully. "Only the very, very stupid volunteer."

"Guilty," Canidy conceded.

"Your governments must have a great deal of confidence in you to select you for something so risky. You must have a demonstrated competence."

Canidy shrugged. "I don't know about that. But we're the ones they asked. Maybe they thought we're the only ones dumb enough to accept this assignment."

"Maybe it is a mixture of both," Matuszek said.

"Look, Commander," Canidy said. "No disrespect. I'd like nothing better than to engage in idle banter with you all day, but we're on the clock. We need to secure Kapsky and then find our way back to the extraction point as fast as possible. We don't have any margin for error. In fact, we're probably a little behind schedule if you factor in one or two surprises or delays on our return trip. We need Kapsky and we need him now. Do you have him or do you know where we can find him?"

Matuszek stroked his chin. "Why are your governments so keen on securing him? Of the millions of Poles under the thumb of the Nazis, why is he so important that they'd send their best to possibly die in order to find him?"

Canidy was becoming impatient and irritated. "Hell if I know. He's important, okay? That's all I know. I don't give a damn about anything else."

"Poles are being massacred by the thousands every day. No one is coming to save *them*. No secret expeditionary forces. No armies. You only came to get Kapsky. Because he is useful to *your* governments. Not because he could help save his own countrymen."

"Commander, all due respect—I don't have time to discuss national interest or political motivation. We need Kapsky now. *Right now*. And then we need to sprint the hell out of here. Are you going to help or be a pain in the ass?"

"I can't help you," Matuszek replied.

"Jesus!" Fulmar erupted. "Why are you wasting our time?"

Matuszek turned to Fulmar. "Wasting *your* time? You are wasting *my* time. *I* have a war to fight. *You* are playing hide-and-seek."

Canidy spoke calmly, trying to lower the temperature. "Commander, look, I understand you've had a rough time with the Germans. We aren't trying to make things any rougher. We just want to complete our assignment, okay?"

"If I could help you, I would," Matuszek responded. "But that is not within my control."

"Whose control is it?"

"God's," Matuszek informed them dryly. "Kapsky is dead."

Canidy blinked several times before staring at Matuszek for several seconds. "Dead? You're sure?"

Matuszek nodded slowly.

"You're sure," Canidy repeated. "Sebastian Kapsky is dead. Sebastian Kapsky, professor of theoretical physics at the University of Lviv."

"Yes. He is dead. Single shot to the chest."

"How can you be so sure?"

"Unfortunately," Matuszek said, "I have seen the body."

Fulmar pressed, unwilling to believe the expedition was for nothing. "How do you know it was Kapsky's body? Did you know him? Did he tell you he was Kapsky before he died?"

Matuszek asked, "Have you ever seen him? A photo?"

Canidy said, "I have seen a drawing of him. We weren't allowed to bring it with us for operational security, but I memorized it. He was recognizable. I'd know him on sight. He had a distinctive shock of hair. I was told it was black. I was also told he had distinctive green eyes."

Matuszek walked to the door. "Come with me."

They followed Matuszek, along with Emil, out of the farmhouse and to the right. They were escorted immediately by four rough-looking *Armia*, each carrying a Poln M29.

They walked silently and alertly through the tall grass for approximately half a kilometer before coming to a shallow, muddy stream bisected by a cluster of large, smooth boulders. Canidy could see someone sitting in the stream with his back resting against the rocks. Two corpses were lying nearby on the bank. Matuszek stepped into the water—it was no more than a foot high—and approached the person resting against the boulders. The others followed.

When he closed to within a few feet of the body, Matuszek gestured as if displaying a piece of fine art. The others gathered around the scene as if at a wake.

Canidy examined the corpse closely for a full minute. There was an entry wound in the chest—fairly large-caliber. Rimless spectacles—the type in fashion among academics—stuck out of the breast pocket of the tweed waistcoat.

Atop the corpse's skull was a thick shock of black hair, the most distinctive feature from the drawing shown to him by Donovan. And the eyes—though lifeless—were vivid green, just as described. Unmistakable. Professor Sebastian Kapsky was, indeed, dead. But at least he'd killed the two who had killed him.

Canidy turned to Matuszek and said, "That's him. That's Kapsky. Jesus."

Canidy raised his voice slightly and confirmed it to the rest. "The operation is over. All that's left is getting back to the boat."

There was a round of sighs and expletives from the squad. Fulmar said, "We should at least check his pockets. See if there's anything useful."

Canidy nodded and did as Fulmar suggested. He found nothing in Kapsky's pants pockets except a small tin containing four L&M cigarettes. Canidy ran his hands over the corpse's torso and inserted his fingers into an inside breast pocket that contained the rimless spectacles, retrieving a slim 3x5 leather notebook. He thumbed through the pages, then handed it to Fulmar. "What do you make of that?"

Fulmar scanned the contents, his brow furrowed. "Equations of some kind, I guess. Way beyond me." Fulmar turned to McDermott and the rest of the squad. "Any of you go beyond long division in school?" Fulmar glanced at the contents again and then passed the notebook to the other members. Not expecting to decipher its contents, each examined it perfunctorily before handing it to Canidy, who handed it to Matuszek. "Any ideas?"

"I suggest you take it with you and have your mathematicians examine it. Perhaps it is what your governments sent you here for."

Canidy asked, "How long has he been here?"

"At least a few hours. We couldn't move or bury the corpse because there were still lots of Germans around. We think they propped him up like this as bait, a common trick to lure us into the open. So we watched and waited until they left. We'll make sure he has a proper burial in due time."

Canidy put the notebook in his shirt pocket, looked at his watch, and curtly announced to the squad, "Time to go."

Canidy turned to Matuszek and said, "We need a favor. Can we borrow Emil? He offered to guide us back to our boat if you approved."

"Yes. Frankly, if I let you go without a guide, the Germans will have you within an hour. It was only by sheer luck that you arrived here without encountering them."

Canidy extended his hand to Matuszek, who grasped it. "You should know that there has been an SS officer and his detail in this area the last several days," Matuszek said. "Based upon what we've heard from villagers, I suspect he was searching for Kapsky also. He was in the vicinity in the last twenty-four hours."

"A big man? Tall?" Canidy asked.

"That's him. With white hair."

"I couldn't really see his hair, but we saw an SS officer terrifying villagers several kilometers from here. Seems like a real sweetheart."

"He's a monster—mentally as well as physically. He's established quite a reputation here recently."

"Do you think he was responsible for killing Kapsky?"

"I do not know, but I would be surprised if it was without his knowledge and approval."

"Why would he *kill* Kapsky?" Fulmar asked.

"Because the professor is so important to his enemies that the Americans and the British would dispatch soldiers on a suicide mission to secure him," Matuszek replied. "Plainly, to keep him out of your hands."

"Maybe," Fulmar said skeptically. "But if they know the professor was that important to us, he must be equally as valuable to them—"

Canidy interrupted. "We can speculate later. Right now, we need to move."

Matuszek gestured for Emil to escort the squad, and Canidy grasped Matuszek's hand once more. "Thanks for your help. Good luck to you and your men."

"Luck is better spent on you. My men and I are unlikely to survive the war, no matter how much luck we have."

Canidy motioned the squad forward. He took a last look at Matuszek. He wanted to remember the face. And then he directed Emil to the point.

Emil led the squad so deftly through the forest and tall grass that McDermott was pleased to have been demoted. The boy had memorized the recent locations of German sniper teams as well as the usual routes for German convoys and patrols. Although they couldn't afford to stop more than a few times for breaks and orientation, at their present pace they would arrive at the dock with about thirty minutes to spare.

Fulmar, walking alongside Canidy, nodded ahead to Emil and asked in a low voice, "What were you doing at that age?"

"Riding my bike, collecting bottle caps and baseball cards."

Fulmar shook his head. "What do you think he'll be like—after all he's experienced—when he becomes a man?"

"He *is* a man. Tell me there isn't a part of you that isn't a little in awe of him."

"Good-looking kid, too. Hell, Canidy, in a couple more years you'll have stiff competition for the ladies."

"If he makes it," Canidy said soberly. "Care to give odds as to whether he sees fifteen?"

Emil held up his left hand, signaling for the squad to halt. He listened for a few moments and then made downward movements with the same hand as he dropped through the knee-high grass onto the ground. The squad did the same.

They remained motionless and listened for nearly a minute. They heard nothing but sporadic bird chirps until there was a barely perceptible sound of a cautious footfall on vegetation. A scant five seconds later they saw an infantry squad pass through the tall grass less than twenty meters from their position. The squad leader carried an MP 40 submachine gun. Several feet behind him was a Stabsgefreiter carrying an MG 42 machine gun. An assistant gunner carrying a light load of ammunition trailed him. He was followed by several riflemen armed with Karabiner 98s. All wore black uniforms. They looked experienced, competent, and lethal.

The Germans moved slowly past them, training their weapons from left to right as they scanned their surroundings. They disappeared from view in less than a minute, but the squad remained prone for several minutes thereafter just to be sure the patrol wasn't trailed or didn't double back. Emil was the first to rise and gave the others a signal to do the same.

"It is best we move more quickly to place distance between us and that patrol," Emil advised. "They are quite smart. They run patterns to entrap hidden *Armia*. We are fortunate we heard them before we saw them or we would be dead."

Emil began walking silently but swiftly north, followed by the squad. They didn't have much time.

CHAPTER 20

Northern Poland
1812, 1 July 1943

Taras Gromov saw the same German patrol five minutes later. He was even more fortunate to evade them than the squad, for he hadn't been alerted by a stray noise. Rather, he saw a momentary glint of light reflected off the barrel of the squad leader's MP 40 when he briefly emerged from the shade. Gromov reacted the same way as the squad, waiting a sufficient interval for the German patrol to pass before he resumed tracking his quarry.

Gromov's primary target was no more. He'd surveilled the Americans and British as they first met with the *Armia* commander. He followed at a distance when they went to the stream and watched as they inspected the corpse resting against the boulder. He'd instantly recognized it as Professor Kapsky. As opposed to Canidy, he hadn't needed to assess the corpse against his memory or an oral description given by his superiors. Rather, Gromov simply withdrew the photo of the professor given to him by way of Belyanov, a photo forwarded by Vasily Blokhin from Katyn to the Lubyanka.

It wasn't difficult for Gromov to surmise that Blokhin didn't come into possession of the photo due to his intelligence or cleverness, but because he'd been outwitted. Kapsky must have switched identities with someone at Katyn, given that person his papers, and somehow escaped. Quite simply, Blokhin had been tricked. But this wasn't any ordinary error. This error was on a titanic scale. Judging simply from the fact that the Americans, British, Germans, and Soviets all had been searching for this professor in the midst of one of the biggest military engagements in history, the escape of Sebastian Kapsky clearly was of extreme strategic significance.

For any other Soviet citizen, errors of far less significance would result in summary execution. Not so Vasily Blokhin. He had been Lavrentiy Beria's most prolific and reliable executioner. In Joseph Stalin's Union of Soviet Socialist Republics, an individual such as Blokhin had a unique and nearly indispensable status. He wasn't merely an assassin, a surgical instrument like Gromov; Blokhin was an executioner on an industrial scale. As such, he was too valuable to Beria—and to Stalin—to suffer permanently for the blunder.

Belyanov, on the other hand, wouldn't give Gromov similar latitude; his errors wouldn't lightly be forgiven. He needed to execute his assignment without a flaw: the American and British soldiers must be killed. Gromov estimated he had no more than two or three hours to complete the task, more than enough time if it weren't for the presence of Germans in the area.

Gromov observed that the squad was moving quite briskly. The boy leading them clearly knew what paths were quickest and what areas to avoid. Nonetheless, Gromov was closing on them incrementally. He needed to find a spot that afforded a view of the entire squad and permitted a quick series of shots. An interval of even a second between shots would provide one or more of them the ability to disperse and seek cover. He'd given some thought to closing the distance completely and killing them with his NR-40, but concluded that seven were too many, especially since the tall one who seemed to be in command appeared as if he might be a challenge.

Gromov pulled from the scope and gauged their distance. He estimated that it would take him approximately five to seven seconds to shoot all of them. The boy was farthest from cover. Gromov determined he should shoot the man farthest to the rear who was closest to cover and then proceed forward. By doing so he should be able to hit them all—with the possible exception of the boy—before they could get to cover. It was immaterial whether he hit the boy; Belyanov hadn't known of his existence before he directed all of the squad be eliminated anyway, so there was no need to waste precious rounds on him.

Gromov steadied himself, sighted the man to the rear, exhaled, and squeezed the trigger. Corporals Spivey and Trent collapsed to the ground before the rest of the squad even heard the report from Gromov's weapon.

Candidy glanced to the rear just in time to see Corporal Colby's skull explode into fragments. The corpses of Spivey and Trent had already fallen to the ground before his mind registered that they were under attack. He turned forward and instinctively fired several rounds in the general direction of the report. Simultaneously, Fulmar and Emil began firing several rounds in the same direction as they dropped to the ground for cover.

McDermott was a fraction of a second too late. A round skimmed his left shoulder, inches from his heart, propelling a jet of red mist into the air above his head just before a second round struck his right arm. He dropped to the ground grimacing in agony, but held on to his Enfield.

Canidy raised his head slightly to see where the fire was coming from but saw nothing but tall grass. He ducked when he heard the air snap inches above his heard. "Stay down. He's somewhere in the grass. On my signal . . ." Canidy's voice was drowned out by the sound of machine-gun fire coming from somewhere at the bottom of the slope to their left. It was directed not at them, but toward the sniper. Two panzers emerged from the woods to the left, firing devastating bursts of 7.92-millimeter rounds in the sniper's direction and scything all of the vegetation and saplings in a five-thousand-square-foot swath at the base of the hill. Hundreds of jets of dirt erupted into the air as a haze of blue smoke wafted over the devastation.

"I don't think they see us," Fulmar shouted over the echoes of machine-gun fire. "They're directing their fire at the sniper, who must be a pile of ground beef right now."

Canidy looked back at McDermott. "Can you move?"

Still grimacing, McDermott nodded. "Sniper got my boys."

A sustained burst of panzer machine-gun fire began ascending the slope. "They know we're somewhere on the slope," Canidy shouted over the din. "They'll just saturate it with fire. We have a better chance if we spread out and move over there." He pointed toward the woods to their right. "On my signal sprint like hell—McDermott on the right, then Fulmar, me, and Emil." Everyone nodded concurrence.

Canidy seized a momentary lull in the fire to shout, "Move!"

The squad immediately sprinted for the woods, spreading from one another as they did so. The panzer machine-gun fire roared back to life, strafing the ground thirty meters to their rear and closing rapidly. Fulmar was the first to reach the woods, followed by Emil, and then McDermott. Canidy reached the tree line last. The machine-gun fire ceased seconds after they disappeared into the woods. All kept running for another thirty to forty meters before slowing to a jog, shoulders hunched as they panted from exertion and adrenaline.

"Keep moving," Canidy commanded. "Anyone hit?"

Before anyone could answer, Canidy saw that McDermott's right sleeve was shredded and soaked in blood. McDermott caught Canidy's gaze. "It's okay. I caught one on my upper arm. It looks worse than it is. It's really just a nick."

"Like hell," Canidy said. "Look at your shoulder. The blood's dripping from your wrist. Once we clear some distance between us and the panzers, we're going to need to take care of that."

They moved rapidly through the woods, Emil taking the lead. Even though the sniper must have been atomized by the panzer fire, they kept their heads on swivels, looking for other sources of danger.

A half kilometer later the woods became denser, but Emil seemed well familiar with the area. He motioned in a northwesterly direction and minutes later they encountered what appeared to be a dried-up creekbed that allowed them to move without being hindered by the dense, thorny undergrowth covering the forest floor. They traveled along the creekbed for another kilometer before Canidy raised his hand.

"We'll stop here for a few minutes, orient, rest, and take care of McDermott's arm."

Canidy looked to Emil. Anticipating the question, Emil said, "At best, another nineteen, twenty hours."

Canidy nodded and turned to Fulmar. "This has turned out to be a class A screwup. No professor. Three Brits dead and one who will be out of commission for a long time."

"If you're expecting an argument or reassurance from me, Dick, you'll be disappointed. When he was trying to convince me to volunteer for this, Donovan told me this would be a 'low-probability' operation. I didn't know if he meant there was a low probability we'd accomplish our objective or a low probability we'd survive. Turns out it wasn't either/or. It was both."

Canidy leaned close to Fulmar. "Look at McDermott," he whispered. "He's seen his last action. That arm's shot. He won't be able to even lift a weapon with it. Oh, sure, he'll give 'em hell for suggesting he handle logistics or some such, but you can already see it in his eyes."

Fulmar looked at McDermott, whose arm was being dressed by Emil. His face betrayed not the slightest bit of pain, but he couldn't mask the resignation. The unmistakable millennia-old look of a warrior who knew that, for him, the war was over.

McDermott glared at the two. "Don't give me those pitiful looks, you shits," he hissed. "I know what you're thinking and I'm telling you right now, you don't know anything about it. You Yanks can afford to put someone like me to pasture. You've got a dozen more to take his place. We Brits don't have that luxury."

Canidy smiled. "All that assumes we meet the lovely Miss Thorisdottir's timetable. If we don't, all of us will be *buried* in a pasture."

Emil secured a bandage made from cloth torn from the leg of his trousers around McDermott's arm.

"Done," Emil said.

Canidy looked at his watch. "Absolutely no time to waste. Let's move. *Now*."

CHAPTER 21

Northern Poland

1940, 1 July 1943

Four kilometers southeast, Gromov finished wrapping his left thigh
with cloth from his left sleeve. He hadn't realized he was bleeding
until he'd run more than a kilometer from the site of the panzer attack. Adrenaline had obscured the pain until he was out of immediate danger from machine-gun fire.

The wound was minor, at least by his standards. He hadn't found
any shrapnel lodged in the tissue. Nothing like his last wound, a
six-inch-long gash inflicted by a kulak with a rusted sickle.

Gromov was more concerned about any wounds that might be
inflicted by order of Belyanov.

Gromov had killed three of the squad; of that he was certain.
But unless the panzers had struck the rest, they had escaped, including their apparent commander. He'd reasoned, however, that
there was a fair probability that the barrage from the 7.92-millimeter
guns had finished the job. He could plausibly report to Belyanov
that the squad had been eliminated. Besides, in the context of a

massive, sprawling, chaotic war, there would be no way of disproving the assertion.

But his failure to secure the professor was another matter. Realistically, there was nothing he could have done to affect the outcome. He'd been dispatched too late. And neither the Germans, British, nor Americans had secured him, either.

Gromov concluded that the assignment, while not a success, also wasn't a failure. A rationalization to be sure, but when dealing with men such as Belyanov, the quality of rationalizations often was the difference between life and death. *Belyanov* might accept the rationalization, but *he* had to report to Beria. If Beria wasn't satisfied with the rationalization, Gromov would be summoned to the Lubyanka and, like countless others, wouldn't emerge. At least not in any recognizable form.

Gromov had, however, a more immediate concern. He was a lone Red Army soldier deep within German-occupied Poland in the midst of a raging battle involving hundreds of thousands of combatants. He'd have plenty of time to perfect his excuses for Belyanov. Right now, he needed to find his way back to relative safety. As was common, the NKVD had provided only for his entry into Poland, not for his exit. He was on his own, his only resources the M91 slung over his right shoulder, the NR-40 strapped to his left hip, and his wits.

CHAPTER 22

Danzig, Poland
0917, 2 July 1943

Maurer was reasonably pleased with himself.

Canaris had charged him with finding Professor Sebastian Kapsky before anyone else. Maurer had done just that. More precisely, soldiers under his command had discovered a body fitting his description and had advised Maurer, who had gone to the site and had seen the corpse sitting peculiarly against a boulder in the midst of a stream, two dead soldiers lying nearby. True, Kapsky was dead when he found him. But Maurer had found him before the Russians, Americans, and British.

The whole matter was as inconsequential as it was peculiar. Yet another corpse in the woods. Maurer had matched the corpse against the meticulously detailed description given to him by the genius Canaris and then, before returning to his Schutzstaffel, gave orders to have all three bodies carried to a field hospital south of Danzig.

He expected to be recalled to Berlin and given an assignment more relevant to the war effort. Something befitting his talents. He'd operated long enough in Poland. He'd been efficient—bordering on brilliant—and that brilliance was best suited for strategy, not mere tactics. Berlin, not Danzig. Although Berlin appreciated his talents, until now he'd been used as a laborer wielding a sledgehammer, not a surgeon wielding a scalpel. But he'd demonstrated over the last several months that he was meant to lead, not merely execute.

Sitting in this cramped, makeshift office in a converted railroad depot on the outskirts of the godforsaken city of Danzig, he was scanning a stack of communiques from Berlin when his Unteroffizier knocked twice on the open door and saluted.

"Herr Maurer, Oberbannführer Frantz to see you."

The Unteroffizier stepped outside, and a small, thin, severe-looking man appeared in the doorway. He was a contrast to Maurer in nearly every way. Whereas Maurer was large and muscular, Frantz was short and slim. While Maurer had the handsome features of a stage actor, Frantz had the face of a bookkeeper; and while Maurer was direct, Frantz was duplicitous.

Maurer hated him. But Canaris respected him, so Maurer feigned the same.

Maurer motioned to the chair opposite his desk. "Please sit, Herr Frantz."

Frantz took a few steps into the room but remained standing, his hands clasped behind his back. He looked disapprovingly about the cramped office for several seconds before addressing Maurer.

"I am to provide a full report to Admiral Canaris regarding your assignment involving the professor." Frantz tilted his chin upward. "What do you have?"

Maurer was both irritated and puzzled. He'd immediately conveyed a thorough report to Berlin upon returning from the forest where the professor's body had been found. He'd described the body, location, and time of discovery. There was nothing more to report. Frantz was purposefully trying to aggravate Maurer.

"It is, Herr Frantz, as set forth in my report." Maurer's tone was both deferential and inquisitive. He sensed that Frantz was somehow baiting him to make a misstep or error that could be reported, with the requisite amount of disdain, to Canaris.

"Your report is noticeably deficient in several aspects, Maurer. That is why I am here." Frantz gazed slowly about the cramped quarters. "That you do not recognize its manifest deficiencies is somewhat concerning."

You little shit, thought Maurer. *Without that badge of rank and Canaris's protection, you'd be pissing in your boots if you addressed me like that. I've got ten times more accomplishments than you in this war and you know it. You owe your position to your impressive proficiency in licking boots.*

"Apologies," Maurer said respectfully. "What deficiencies would those be?"

Frantz's upper lip curled in disdain. "Most glaringly, Maurer, you failed to explain why you did not capture the professor *alive*."

"Herr Frantz, Admiral Canaris commanded that I find Professor Sebastian Kapsky before anyone else. I did so. He was dead when I found him."

"Then, obviously, you were not the first to find him. Someone else must have gotten to him first and killed him."

Maurer was slightly thrown off balance. Yes, someone had killed Kapsky. But there was no evidence that Kapsky had yielded anything of value to that person.

"Herr Frantz, we found the professor in the stream, dead. Judging by the condition of the corpse, he had expired a short time before we discovered him. Clearly, if someone desired that he provide information, they would have *captured*, not killed, him."

"Do you know what killed him?"

"A chest wound."

"Do you know *who* killed him?"

Maurer hesitated. "Clearly it was either our troops or *Armia*. Stray fire."

"You do not *know* that," Frantz hissed.

"Herr Frantz, I am well familiar with this area. It is an area of heavy conflict and often intense fire. The only plausible explanations are stray fire from our troops or *Armia*." Regaining his footing, Maurer paused for emphasis. "Given that Kapsky was a professor, it is plain that whatever value he possessed was the provision of information, unique information, likely complex, that could not be conveyed in mere minutes or seconds. And definitely not information that could be comprehended and conveyed by a mere foot soldier."

Maurer knew that what he was saying made perfect sense. More important, Frantz knew it also.

But Frantz remained unplacated, nonetheless. "All assumptions," he said. "Your job is not to make assumptions. Your job is to execute. This is not acceptable."

Although Maurer nodded deferentially, he doubted Canaris felt the same way as Frantz. In the first instance, Canaris understood the remote probability of locating a lone individual during an ongoing conflict, especially one as large and intense as the current one. He would also appreciate the possibility, if not the probability, that such an individual might become a casualty. And he would know that an individual who possessed information so valuable that Admiral

Canaris himself believed the Americans were searching for him—well, such information could not be conveyed in mere minutes, or even hours.

The look on Frantz's face told Maurer he'd scored. But someone like Frantz didn't easily concede.

"Admiral Canaris dispatched you to acquire and deliver Kapsky. You did not deliver Kapsky. You failed."

Maurer's face remained passive as he scrutinized every detail on Frantz's face. He wanted to sear it into his memory so that when he eventually rearranged that face he'd be able to measure the damage inflicted.

The two saluted before Frantz spun curtly and walked out of the office.

Soon, you little shit, thought the big man. *Very soon.*

CHAPTER 23

Northern Poland, Baltic Coast
1308, 2 July 1943

They moved at a surprisingly brisk pace considering McDermott's pain. Emil had led them along the dry creekbed for at least a kilometer before veering northeast through dense brush that slowed them a bit. But even so, their pace was much faster than their trip from the boat. The last hour of their journey was uneventful, save for an encounter with a massive herd of deer that became confused when startled and nearly stampeded them before changing direction. Other than that, and the occasional chirp of a bird, or snap of dry twig underfoot, there was barely a sound.

Canidy saw the boat first. He could tell by the barely perceptible ripple in the surrounding water that it had just arrived. Seconds later Fulmar let out a muted cheer. McDermott simply smiled in relief.

Thorisdottir gave a curt wave from the foredeck, which they all returned, including Emil, who was instantly enraptured. "A woman," he said with a note of surprise. "From here, she appears quite attractive."

"Just wait until you get closer," Canidy said. "You sure you don't want to come along? The war is going to go on with or without you."

"Once again, thank you for the offer. But it will go on *with* me." He grinned expansively. "Perhaps one day you will read about me. Like Sikorski, or perhaps even Kościuszko."

Canidy grasped Emil's hand. "I'll be reading the papers." He shook Emil's hand once. "Stay smart."

Fulmar and McDermott each clapped Emil on a shoulder. "Give 'em hell, kid," Fulmar said.

Emil gave a slight nod of acknowledgment, turned, and within seconds disappeared into the brush. Canidy turned back to the boat, where Thorisdottir was standing imperiously with fists on hips. "Been waiting long?" he asked.

"Actually, no," she replied with an inflection conveying mild astonishment. "You're several minutes ahead of schedule. Come aboard." As Canidy, Fulmar, and McDermott climbed onto the dock, a second figure emerged from the cabin and stood next to Thorisdottir, causing a stutter in the gait of each of the men. The two figures were identical in every respect but clothing. Each was approximately six feet tall with ice-blue eyes and blond hair to the waist. But while Kristin was clothed in formless weather gear, the second figure wore shorts that displayed toned legs that caused Fulmar to mutter, "Incredible."

"This is Katla," Kristin informed. "She is my twin sister," she added superfluously.

The effect on the warriors was electric, causing each to take extra care in boarding, lest their distraction cause them to plummet into the canal. Once they were securely on deck, Katla extended her hand to each, in the case of McDermott with considerable gentleness. Her broad smile was an inviting contrast to the taciturn Kristin.

"Katla is an able seaman. I asked her to join me because there was an increased number of Admiral Dönitz's vessels in, and Reichsmarschall Göring's planes over, the Baltic on my return to Gotland after dropping you off. This ordinarily does not pose a problem, but given your presence on the vessel, I determined it best to have assistance."

"Makes sense to me," Fulmar said and nodded appreciatively. "Good decision."

Kristin added, "Endeavor not to stare, gentlemen. Katla has perfect vision and can perceive leers from one hundred meters. In addition, she is quite strong."

Despite their fatigue all the men laughed, albeit a bit self-consciously. Canidy noticed Fulmar's enraptured look and nudged him back to reality. "We're ready to shove off whenever you are," he informed Kristin.

Kristin scanned the bank. "Where are the rest? You're three mates?" She suspected she knew the answer, but wanted confirmation before departing.

Canidy replied simply, "They won't be making the return trip."

Kristin nodded and said to Katla, "Let's go." Then she said to the men, "Until we're clear of the canal and at least a kilometer offshore, it is best if you go below."

Canidy didn't argue, although he thought two stunning women sailing a boat on the Baltic might generate at least as much attention as a crew of three men and a couple of women.

They reached the sea in less than ten minutes without event. Canidy knew they'd done so because of the pitch and swale of the boat, the water choppy if not rough. He could hear the wind whistling above deck.

He felt anxious. Not so much because of the rough sea or the increased German patrols, but because of the failure of the operation. Nothing he could have done would have changed the outcome. He had made no mistakes, but Wild Bill Donovan had chosen him out of hundreds of thousands of other candidates to execute the rendition of Sebastian Kapsky to the government of the United States of America, and that wouldn't happen. The reasons it wouldn't happen were immaterial. Canidy was coming home empty-handed. Worse, Kapsky was dead. Whatever made him important to the U.S. government, it was now unattainable and there would be a notation in his file—if he was fortunate, it would be a mere footnote or asterisk—that said, in essence, "Failed Operation." It was not a notation seen in the files of those who had advanced from obscurity to respect or even notoriety. History was being written. The world was at war and Canidy wouldn't even be a footnote, or, if he was, it would say "Failed."

Fulmar had similar thoughts. "What do you put the odds that we get debriefed by Donovan himself?" he asked Canidy.

"Zero to none. Maybe less," Canidy replied. "No one likes to be around failure. You don't want the stench to rub off on you—seep into your clothes."

"To be fair," Fulmar noted, "it wasn't our fault. It wasn't really a failure."

"You're welcome to tell that to Wild Bill," Canidy said. "Personally, I'm determined to say as little about this operation as possible. I just hope we get another opportunity to distinguish ourselves."

"Based on the German firepower we saw on display, this war isn't ending anytime soon, Dick. There will be other opportunities," Fulmar assured. "Right now I'm contemplating the opportunities presented by the lovely and talented Thorisdottir sisters. Not so much Kristin—she's a hard case. But Katla . . ."

Canidy said, "We're in the middle of the Baltic, infested with German ships and probably U-boats, and you're thinking about some damn women?"

"Hell, why do you think I'm thinking about some 'damn women'? Better than thinking about a torpedo from a German U-boat or strafing from a Messerschmitt."

Canidy looked to McDermott. "How does it feel?" he asked.

"A bit of pain, to be sure. I'll manage."

"Stiff upper lip and all that," Fulmar said.

"I'll ask the Thorisdottir twins if they might have something to ease the journey," Canidy said and winked. Canidy began to climb the stairs to the deck, stopping when he saw Kristin standing at the top with her fists on her hips. Again.

"You'll find some spirits in the chest next to the bunk," she informed. "I recommend Luksusowa vodka applied to the wound and Mortlach whisky for consumption."

Canidy grinned appreciatively. "Splendid recommendation, Captain Thorisdottir. You seem to have a passing familiarity with the medical arts."

"More than a passing familiarity, Major. One cannot sail the Baltic and the North Sea without intimate knowledge of salves, potions, and medicinal applications."

Kristin turned and disappeared. Canidy winked at Fulmar, who had already retrieved the Luksusowa vodka and the Mortlach whisky. He removed the cork from the Mortlach and took a healthy slug before handing it to McDermott, who did the same. "Our captain has excellent taste," he said. Then he took two more long swallows, belched ceremoniously, and offered the bottle to Canidy, who declined.

"You need more painkillers than I do," Canidy said.

McDermott returned the bottle to his lips, gulped, and belched again. "Already feeling no pain," he said. "How much more satisfying it would be if we had the professor—simply to celebrate?"

Canidy pulled the small notebook from his pocket and held it in front of him. "We don't have the professor, but we didn't come away completely empty-handed."

"Hate to be the pessimist," Fulmar said. "But I doubt that whatever caused the President of the United States to send us into German-occupied territory could be captured in a small notebook like that. Besides, what's to say the Germans didn't already take a much bigger notebook off the corpse?"

Canidy thumbed through the pages of the notebook. Nothing but hieroglyphics. He retrieved the bottle of Mortlach from McDermott and took a healthy gulp.

It did little to stem his growing sense of foreboding.

CHAPTER 24

As he approached the stream from the north with a team of six men, Maurer could see Sebastian Kapsky's corpse still resting against the boulder. From fifty meters, it truly appeared to be a naturalist in repose, taking a break from a hike. A slender ray of sunshine shown directly over his head, as if blessed from above.

As he drew nearer, Maurer saw signs of spreading decay not apparent during the previous inspection. Exposed flesh was flecked with brown and gray splotches. The eyes were essentially gone—probably consumed by birds and insects, leaving hollow sockets that appeared to stare intently at Maurer and his detail.

As they closed to within a few feet, the stench of decaying flesh prompted Maurer to withdraw a kerchief from his pocket and place it over his nose and mouth while he inspected the remains. Save for that decay, the corpse was not appreciably different than it was when he had first seen it.

Maurer had returned before the detail he'd dispatched had

retrieved the corpse because Frantz had angered him. He'd insisted that Maurer had been negligent in handling Kapsky's remains. The little man made it abundantly plain his disdain at Maurer was personal and that he would emphasize said negligence to Canaris. Men like Frantz, thought Maurer, took pleasure in destroying men like Maurer. Little men who needed to redress some childhood injury sustained from superior specimens such as him.

Maurer had also returned because he feared he had, indeed, been negligent. His initial examination of the corpse had been standard. After confirming cause of death, his men had rifled through the clothing, doing a perfunctory pat-down. Since the directive had been to return a live Professor Sebastian Kapsky to Canaris, and since that wouldn't be feasible, Maurer reasonably assumed that nothing remained of his mission. Maurer was a soldier, not a detective.

The stench of decaying flesh caused Maurer to retreat a few steps and wave two of his men forward. "Search his clothing thoroughly. Pockets, sleeves, socks, undergarments."

The men held their breath as they rifled through Kapsky's clothing, pausing every fifteen to twenty seconds to turn away and catch their breath.

Nothing.

"Remove the clothing," Maurer commanded.

Less than a minute later, Maurer examined Kapsky's mottled flesh, the extremities covered with scores of slugs. The chest wound was a garish multicolored cavity infested with small flies and maggots. No tattoos. No diagrams or codes written on the flesh.

"Search all cavities."

One of the two unfortunates signaled to the other to turn the corpse onto its stomach. As they examined the alimentary canal, both retched. They then turned the body over and examined the nose, mouth, and throat, yielding nothing. Both turned to Maurer and shrugged.

"Hold the mouth open once more," Maurer directed.

One of the soldiers grasped Kapsky's head and pulled the jaw downward as far as he could. Maurer held his breath and leaned toward the corpse. The oral cavity was dark, but he could see that the decomposition of the tongue was more advanced than the rest of the body and the gums appeared to be receding from the teeth. He picked up a twig from the bank and used it as a probe, pushing the tongue from side to side, then lifting it to inspect underneath.

Maurer withdrew so he could exhale and catch his breath. He motioned for the soldier holding Kapsky's head to open the mouth wider.

Maurer took another deep breath and leaned inward.

Using the twig, he depressed the tongue to the floor of the mouth. "Flashlight," he said to no one in particular. One of the men dutifully provided a flashlight that Maurer turned on and shined inside the oral cavity. He could barely see what appeared to be a foreign object lodged in the throat, protruding slightly above the floor of the mouth. Maurer attempted to snag the object by inserting the twig inside the mouth and scraping it forward along the floor of the mouth without success. After three attempts to pull the object upward and outward, Maurer adjusted his tactics, using the twig to push the object deeper down Kapsky's throat. When the object disappeared from view, he turned to his men. "Knife."

One of the men handed Maurer a bayonet.

"Hold the skull firmly," he instructed. Maurer made a deep incision just above Kapsky's sternum and sliced upward to the chin, releasing an overpowering stench in the process. He rose and stepped

back to inhale a lungful of clean air before bending over once again
and pulling the sides of Kapsky's throat open to remove what appeared to be a slender scroll of waxy paper. Maurer seized it between his thumb and forefinger and carefully withdrew it from the
cavity.

Maurer took several steps back from the corpse and exhaled before holding the scroll before his face and turning it at several angles
in order to examine it thoroughly. It was surprisingly large and appeared to be sealed with some type of gummy substance. The wax
paper exhibited little, if any, corrosion or damage, but Maurer rolled
it gently between his fingers to ensure that it wouldn't flake or tear
if he removed the gum and unrolled it. As he did so, he glanced at
his men. They were watching him with a mixture of curiosity and
apprehension, feelings Maurer shared, although he'd never before
projected anything but supreme confidence to his men. Accordingly, they were somewhat surprised when he asked, "What do you
think this is?" and "Why was it in Kapsky's throat?"

No one responded.

"Quite peculiar," Maurer observed. "Did he attempt to swallow
this or was it shoved down his throat?"

Unteroffizier Becker, who nearly matched Maurer in size, observed, "Herr Maurer, he was shot in the chest with a medium- to
large-caliber weapon at range. It strikes me as unlikely that whoever
shot him shoved the scroll in his mouth after he was dead. It seems
more likely Kapsky was attempting to swallow it in order to hide it."

"Yes." Maurer nodded slowly. "My thought also. But quite large
to swallow. Either way, most peculiar, don't you think?" He continued to slowly roll the cylinder between his thumb and forefinger,
considering whether he should open it or present it to Canaris's fo-
rensics team to reduce the chances it might be damaged upon in-

spection. Curiosity prevailed over caution. Holding the scroll in his left hand, he used the nail of his right index finger to gently slice and scrape the gummy substance from the scroll.

It took nearly a minute to peel the substance off the waxy paper without damaging it. He unwrapped the scroll gingerly and held it with one hand at the top and the other at the bottom as if he were a page or town crier reading a proclamation.

The scroll was covered with small, densely packed symbols that appeared to Maurer's untrained eye to be mathematical equations or formulae. The multiple lines were in black ink save for the last two, which were in red and underscored.

Maurer studied the document for more than a minute and then looked up, his expression pensive. After several seconds, Becker asked timidly, "Herr Maurer, do you understand it? What is it?"

Maurer didn't reply, his gaze remaining intense.

Becker repeated the question. Maurer looked past him into the woods. "I cannot say for certain. I am a soldier, not a mathematician. But as a soldier, considering the obsessive pursuit by the major powers, my instincts say it is an instrument for civilizational dominance," he replied. "Or civilizational destruction."

CHAPTER 25

London, England
1806, 7 August 1943

The carnage was almost incomprehensible. Hundreds of thousands had perished in Europe from enemy fire, disease, or starvation. More than even in the Great War.

The reports across his desk were horrific, but he didn't have need of the reports. He could tell from the mangled bodies stacked on the lorries that the world, let alone Britain, was witnessing human suffering on a scale once unimaginable even to the most alarmist members of Parliament.

Churchill knew, however, that the British people were resolute. They would fight the Nazis until the last man perished in the Highlands of Scotland. Hitler's Wehrmacht had inflicted grievous wounds on the island and its people. And yet Great Britain remained standing, and aside from a few backbenchers who wet their trousers every time they heard the drone of an airplane engine, the people were

steeled for the fight. Churchill's primary concern was with his allies. In the east, Stalin was treacherous, a man never to be trusted.
But he could be relied upon to send millions of his countrymen into
the Eastern Front meat grinder without flinching. The worst mistake Hitler had made thus far wasn't declaring war on the United
States, it was breaching Molotov-Ribbentrop and engaging the Soviet Union in war on their land. Was the man that ignorant of history? Of simple geography?

Stalin wasn't Churchill's problem. It was his English-speaking
cousin to the west. Roosevelt was smart and savvy, but he was also
political. Perhaps more so than anyone Churchill had ever met.
More Machiavelli than Disraeli. FDR calculated the political implications of everything from the Allied invasion of the European continent to the cost of lanyards for MacArthur's binoculars. That
made him more difficult to manipulate than Stalin, who was wholly
unconstrained by politics. In the Soviet Union Stalin *was* politics.
Nothing distracted him from concentrating on Hitler.

Churchill exerted enormous effort to keep Roosevelt's concentration on Hitler as opposed to Hirohito or domestic political opposition. One of the more successful techniques in maintaining
FDR's concentration on Hitler was to remind the President of not
just the consequences of defeat in discrete battles in the European
theater, but the consequences of a postwar Europe with *either* a
German *or* Soviet hegemony.

Intelligence from MI9 often proved to persuade Roosevelt better
than almost anything else. It had to be deployed deftly and not
overplayed, but after Roosevelt devoured the information, he usually came to the same policy conclusions as Churchill. The latest
piece of information came from Commander Ian Fleming, who

sometimes trafficked in hyperbole, but more often than not possessed nuggets of intelligence that were not only useful but valuable.

Churchill enjoyed listening to Fleming's briefings, which occasionally sounded like mystery novels reaching a climax.

Last night, Stewart Menzies, chief of the Security Intelligence Service, lately referred to as MI6, sent a message to Whitehall requesting a meeting to discuss certain information Fleming had obtained from British OSS operations in Berlin. According to Menzies's boss, the information was potentially of strategic significance. A source alleged to be in the office of Chief of German Intelligence Wilhelm Canaris claimed that the Germans were in possession of information that could tilt the strategic balance of the war, as well as the postwar world, decidedly in Hitler's favor.

The claim sounded fantastic to Churchill. He had a difficult time believing that *anything* of value could be pried loose from the office of the Genius, let alone anything of strategic significance. But Churchill knew history better than any other world leader. And he knew that entire empires had vanished because leaders had discounted certain information as implausible.

Moreover, despite Fleming's theatrics and occasional hyperbole, his intel was usually spot-on. And Churchill valued both theatrics and accuracy. So Churchill had summoned MI6 and Fleming to Whitehall.

There was a perfunctory knock—two raps—and Churchill's security opened the door to the War Room to announce the arrival of Stewart Menzies and Naval Intelligence Officer Fleming. Churchill, sitting in a high-backed leather chair at the head of the horseshoe-shaped table, a massive color map of continental Europe directly behind him, opened his mouth slightly in surprise. He hadn't been expecting Menzies, whose appearance signaled something of great importance was afoot. Moreover, Churchill hadn't known Menzies to work with Commander Fleming in the past. The combination caused Churchill's expression to shift from mild surprise to consternation.

Menzies entered the room with his usual Eton aplomb, followed by Fleming, who sported civilian clothing with his trademark bow tie. Menzies nodded toward the prime minister. "Good day, sir. My sincerest apologies for the intrusion on my part. I hope you'll forgive me, but I'd learnt from Rear Admiral Godfrey that Commander Fleming had secured an appointment with you. And since MI6 was integral to obtaining the information Commander Fleming wishes to share, I insisted on coming along."

Churchill's jowls quaked. The rivalries within British military and military intelligence were almost as pitched as the animosity between Britain and its enemies. Churchill, however, did little to quell the rivalries. He believed competition produced better outcomes. Churchill waved an unlit cigar toward the chairs to his left on the horseshoe. Menzies sat nearest to Churchill, Fleming to Menzies's left.

"This must be a matter of some importance for you to be pried from your codebreaking, Stewart," Churchill observed. "I don't think I've seen you concerned with anything else in more than a year. *I'm* concerned that you're going to inform me that Hitler and Stalin have kissed and made up."

Menzies flashed a patrician smile. "We've been making splendid progress on the Gerry codes, sir. Some of our finest chaps are on them. Including Gaither—you may recall his father at Sandhurst."

Churchill nodded. "I am just as interested in the Germans'

capabilities in deciphering *our* conversations, Stewart. Please remember that. If Hitler catches wind of our plans for one General Bernard Law Montgomery, we'll have quite a problem on our hands."

Menzies smiled again. "We may have a greater problem with Ike."

"True." Churchill turned to Fleming, who appeared somewhat agitated, unusual for a man who normally appeared unflappable, even serene. "Well, Commander, I've been told very little about the matter, but I gather you believe this is of some grave importance. Please do not tell me those infernal engineers Hitler keeps entombed in those tunnels in Bavaria have developed a better panzer."

Fleming pointed to the cigarette holder peeking from his breast pocket. "May I, sir?"

"Hell, why don't we all?" Churchill proffered the tip of his cigar to Fleming, who produced a match, lit it, and placed it under Churchill's cigar until it glowed. He then lit a cigar withdrawn by Menzies from the inside of his suit coat. Fleming then retrieved the cigarette holder from his pocket and lit the cigarette. The entire stoking ceremony consumed nearly a full minute, then each of the three men leaned back in their respective chairs simultaneously.

Fleming said, "Sir, we've obtained information which, I'm afraid, may compel the mounting of an operation in German-held territory to confirm."

"Why must we *confirm* the information?" Churchill asked. "That sounds like the information is mere rumor. I'm quite disinclined to authorize an operation in German-held territory to confirm a mere rumor."

"Sir, to be more precise, the existence of the information needn't be confirmed," Fleming explained. "Rather, it is more to confirm that the information is what it purports to be."

Churchill scowled. "Well, *that* clears it up."

"It is a matter of whether the information may plausibly be what our informant claims it is, sir," Menzies explained. "If it is what he thinks it is, it would be worth moving heaven and Earth to obtain it—which is nearly what we would be required to do, given that it is presently in the custody of Canaris."

"What does he think the information is?"

Menzies said, "As I understand it, he's unsure but believes it may be a blueprint for a new superweapon. One that would be two to three generations beyond anything the Germans or anyone else presently have. Something that, if developed, would provide Hitler with an insuperable advantage."

Fleming nodded in agreement. Churchill puffed his cigar while examining the faces of the two intelligence officers. "Let's start from the beginning, shall we, Commander Fleming? Perhaps with an explanation of who the informant is and why we should consider him credible?"

"He is a clerk in Canaris's office, sir."

Churchill removed the cigar from his mouth, incredulous. "A clerk in Canaris's office? The office of the Genius has been so compromised? Why haven't I heard of this before and why aren't we three steps ahead of Guderian, Rommel, and Keitel at all times?"

"Sir, the term 'informant' may be somewhat misleading," Fleming explained. "He is not a regular asset. Indeed, this is the first time we have ever gotten information from him. As we understand it, he works in cartography now, but before the war he was some sort of engineer for Krupp, and from what we gather, a fairly adept one.

"A short time ago, information came into the Abwehr that created a bit of a stir. Not immediately, mind you, but after some analysis. It seems as if some SS officer had obtained a document containing certain formulae—equations and such. Seventy-six Tirpitzufer, normally so tight the air within is the same as it was last year, was buzzing at first, primarily because of internal politics. One of Canaris's closest lieutenants, a chap by the name of Frantz, seems to have rapidly lost favor at the same time the SS officer became a Canaris favorite—precisely because of something to do with the information.

"The information was on a document obtained by the SS officer. The document purportedly came from Professor Sebastian Kapsky."

Churchill straightened slightly and turned to Fleming. "Kapsky? The chap you identified as the target for extraction?"

"That's correct, sir," Fleming replied. "The mathematician. You and President Roosevelt authorized a mission to extract him from occupied Poland. He was killed before the team could acquire him."

"What makes them think it came from Kapsky?"

"Frankly, sir, we can't answer that specifically. But circumstances strongly indicate it came from him."

"I need specifics, Commander," Churchill said.

"The informant says the SS officer who acquired the document is a bit of a climber—a self-promoter. He said nothing directly, mind you, but gave a hint about his involvement in highly consequential matters—as if the fate of the Fatherland hinged upon his deeds. The matter of the document was one of those consequential matters to which he alluded, however vaguely. Rumor had it in headquarters that this SS officer had been charged with finding Kapsky and that the document came from Kapsky himself."

Churchill waved his cigar dismissively. "Rumors."

"Yes, sir, rumors. But more than that. The informant relates that immediately after the Obersturmführer presented the document to

Canaris, several mathematicians and physicists were immediately summoned to Tirpitzufer to decipher the document. They determined it was produced by Kapsky, although they were unclear about its conclusions."

Churchill appeared surprised. "They don't know what it means?"

"Sir, our people—that is, our scientists—concede that Kapsky was of a different order," Menzies interjected. "In the category of a Newton, or a Tesla, or Einstein. Without him, his theories and equations could take a generation or two to confirm and put into use. They know that Kapsky was working on the matters contained on the document and they have familiarity with it, but it will take them time to understand it completely. That said, the informant says they were acting like toddlers unwrapping presents at Christmas, even though part, or even most, of it was encrypted."

Churchill's brow furrowed with worry. "I've never seen scientists or mathematicians excited."

"Precisely, Prime Minister," Fleming said.

Fleming and Menzies watched Churchill's face turn dark as he puffed on his cigar, contemplating the implications and options. "How voluminous is the Kapsky document?"

"Our understanding—the informant's understanding—is that the entire document consists of one scroll of paper," Fleming responded.

"A scroll of paper?" Churchill asked. "How could something so purportedly consequential be contained on one scroll of paper?"

"The handwriting is said to be rather small," Menzies explained.

"Still," Churchill scoffed. "The Germans think the fate of the world may be decided by the contents of a scroll of paper?"

"More than the outcome of the war, sir. Hegemony for the foreseeable future," Menzies said.

"Even if we were to acquire the document, it's been in the possession of the Germans for some time. Even if we dispatched agents in the next five minutes to acquire it, they've had an insuperable head start."

"True," Menzies conceded. "Unavoidable, sir."

"Could this informant get it for us, or make a copy? A transcription?"

"He is not trained for such things, Prime Minister. Not remotely. And it is impossible to leave the Tirpitzufer without being thoroughly searched each and every time you do so."

"Could he memorize portions and record them after he leaves the building?"

"Much too complex. The problem is that we can't afford even the slightest error, and this is a supremely complicated formula or equation, as we understand it. Quite long."

"Who is this individual?" Churchill asked.

"Kurt Bauer," Menzies replied. "Thirty-five. From just south of Mainz."

"How did we recruit him?"

"We didn't, sir," Fleming answered. "He made contact with a Czech Resistance fighter and began transmitting information through him nearly a year ago, sporadically. Nothing of much use to us, until now."

"Do we have any idea why he would take the risk of contacting us? Could this be a German misdirection operation?"

"Although we never discount that possibility, sir, we've assessed it as unlikely. The Czechs tell us that Bauer's maternal grandmother and several of his cousins were taken into custody by the Geheime Staatspolizei before the Anschluss. They haven't been seen or heard from since then. It's believed they've been killed, sir."

"Why were they arrested?" Churchill asked. "What was their offense?"

"We understand his grandmother and the cousins in question were Jews," Menzies said. "We understand Bauer was quite close to his grandmother. We suspect that may have some bearing on his motivation."

"I see," Churchill said. "Nonetheless, quite curious that Bauer would be permitted anywhere near Canaris's office. They never miss such matters."

Fleming grinned. "Ah, yes, Mr. Prime Minister. We conducted a thorough amount of research on this chap to ascertain his bona fides to determine whether we were being set up for some form of disinformation operation. And as you know, there exists in Germany a remarkably vibrant black market in false identities, manufactured personal histories. These operations are enormously sophisticated, given both the consequences if a true identity is revealed, as well as the fact that the Nazis are astonishingly proficient at rooting out such frauds.

"It seems Bauer did not attempt to hide the fact that his grandmother and cousins were Jewish. One Czech told us that what he did was kill both the person that had reported them to the Gestapo as well as the Gestapo Kriminaldirektor to whom he had made such a report. Then he went to the Gestapo Kriminaldirektor's superior to confirm that his relatives had been taken into custody, claiming that it was *he* who had turned in his relatives. The Gestapo Kriminaldirektor's superior was sufficiently impressed with Bauer's fealty to the Reich that a year later he recommended him to a position with the Abwehr, where he's performed with proficiency ever since."

"Quite clever," Churchill said.

The room fell silent for several seconds while Churchill puffed on his cigar.

"Gentlemen, you've come to me for approval of this operation rather than simply execute it on your own authority, not because this promises to be an unusually difficult operation behind enemy lines, but because you have prudently concluded that this is the type of operation that suggests consultation with the American President."

"That is your prerogative, sir," Menzies said superfluously.

"It would be politic for me to do so, obviously, and I shall. But am I correct that some functionary in cubicle 14A of your establishment has concluded that certain American assistance is advisable?"

"That is correct, sir," Menzies and Fleming said in unison. "The assistance, if I may," Fleming added, "consists not of matériel or logistics, but of personnel." Fleming glanced collegially at Menzies, who nodded. Fleming continued. "Any logistical assistance Mr. Roosevelt—through Messrs. Eisenhower and Donovan—may choose to provide, is, naturally, very much appreciated. But after some deliberation with our Lieutenant Colonel Laycock, as well as Major Stirling, we've concluded that the odds of success of any operation along the lines contemplated would be enhanced by the participation of two Americans in particular—a Major Canidy and a Lieutenant Fulmar, who come fairly recommended by one of our best and most experienced men."

"I see," Churchill said. "Is it expected that we will command the operation?"

Fleming and Menzies glanced at each other. As senior, Menzies spoke.

"Sir, we understand the trials you've had managing a certain general—indisputably a talented general—in both North Africa and Italy. We do not wish to replicate that trial for you. However, whomever is leading the operation is less important, we believe, than the talent of the individuals taking part in such operations. And we've identified, sir, Canidy and Fulmar as two highly talented— and might I say—somewhat daring individuals of the sort that would improve the probability of the operation's success considerably."

Churchill smiled. "Given that the Special Air Service commends them and based on the description of the objective, I gather they must be quite mad also."

Menzies and Fleming chuckled. "A prerequisite, I'm afraid." Fleming nodded agreement.

Churchill looked pensively toward the ceiling, his jowls quaking as he did so. "Remind me, are they the chaps who accompanied McDermott to Danzig or some such?"

"They are, Mr. Prime Minister," Fleming confirmed. "To be sure, McDermott was accompanying *them*."

Churchill pointed his cigar at Menzies. "Didn't you say we lost men on that operation?"

"True, sir, but it is our opinion that, but for Canidy, we would have lost them all. They faced overwhelming firepower deep in hostile territory, yet managed to evade Gerry patrols across difficult terrain."

Churchill fell silent contemplating the next steps.

"Very well, gentlemen. I shall consult with the Yanks and leave it to you to plan this operation. I confess that in all of my years I've rarely, if ever, encountered one that presented so many self-evident and steep barriers to success; inserting a team into Germany itself and retrieving a document that, based on what I've just heard, must be one of the most tenaciously guarded items in one of the most securely protected environments in all of Europe, if not the world."

Churchill pointed his cigar at Fleming. "I suspect you've already taken the liberty of planning the operation?"

"We have, indeed, developed a series of plans in consultation with the SAS, sir. Quite challenging, as you've just suggested. The one with the greatest promise replicates in large measure the operation McDermott and Canidy ran a while ago to retrieve Professor Kapsky."

"Remind me a bit of the particulars," Churchill said.

"Well, sir, it involved the insertion of the team into Poland by way of the Baltic. We still maintain contact, however sporadic, with elements of the Polish Home Army, who continue to prove quite resourceful. In that operation we had the good fortune of encountering members of the Home Army who provided assistance, primarily in extraction. In the present case, rather than moving southward, we will be moving westward into Germany until reaching the outskirts of Berlin."

"Forgive me, Commander, but this already appears to be a suicide mission," Churchill said.

"Clearly not a holiday jaunt," Fleming agreed. "Nonetheless, we've done a bit of this before—admittedly, with increasing difficulty, but that's the job. We've continued to develop and expand a network of ethnic Poles and Polish émigrés in Germany to guide us to Seventy-six Tirpitzufer. They are even more extensive now than they were during our previous operations."

Churchill smiled at the mention of the audacious operation that resulted in the airlifting of an entire intact V-2 rocket out of Poland. "I confess, that was one of the few delights of this godforsaken war."

Menzies said, "The nightmare, sir, will be the extraction. More so than the insertion. If we can succeed in obtaining the document, the Germans will be on high alert. Every depot and every terminal will be crawling with Gestapo and SS. German civilians will have their heads on a swivel looking for and reporting anyone they do not immediately recognize—and the Germans are unparalleled at this."

Menzies lowered his voice as if he were concerned about being overheard. "We continue to monitor our contact with Admiral Canaris, Mr. Prime Minister. If there is a chance we might be able to get assistance from the admiral, obviously we will do so."

"I wouldn't bank on it, General," Churchill said. "By all means, continue to work on him, but I am increasingly convinced that the rumors of his disaffection with Hitler and Nazism are little more than a counterintelligence operation designed to get us to chase ghosts. They don't call him the Genius for nothing."

"Mr. Prime Minister," Fleming said, "Canaris may have a weak spot. A beautiful young lady who works for Jan Karski."

"Karski? The Polish agent?"

"Yes, sir."

Churchill nodded approvingly. "Can we use her, Commander?"

"We will certainly try, sir."

"We also have access to a number of Austrians and Germans trained by Donovan's OSS, but they are for assisting with extraction, not in turning Canaris. Nonetheless, I would not bank on anything positive from Canaris. He's outwitted us several times before. I'll be damned if he does so again." Churchill slapped his hand on the table. "You'll forgive me, gentlemen, but I have other matters to which I must attend. I will speak with Roosevelt presently. The rest of the details you may provide as necessary."

Menzies and Fleming rose to leave.

"Oh, yes," Churchill added. "Who do you propose to accompany Canidy and Fulmar?"

"McDermott, sir," Fleming replied.

"Wasn't he shot up last time?"

"Indeed, sir. His arm does seem to flop about a bit. But he insists he is just as lethal with the other arm and he does have experience with the Americans. Besides, he understands that, as he put it, if the mission doesn't succeed, Germany may rule the world."

"Hell with all that world-domination drivel," Churchill retorted. "We simply can't afford to make a bad showing in front of the Americans."

CHAPTER 26

"Back to Poland again?" Canidy asked. "Let me tell you, I had my fill the last time. The place is rotten with Germans."

William Donovan nodded. "No argument there. It will be far more challenging than last time. Not only because you will insert into German-occupied territory, but because you will go to Germany itself."

"Say again?"

"You, Fulmar, and McDermott will insert into Poland by way of the Baltic, make contact with the Home Army, who will guide you to German territory, where you will be met by an associate of Jan Karski by the name of Krupa. He and whomever he enlists to assist will take you within a kilometer of the Tirpitzufer. From there, you will be essentially on your own."

"A suicide mission," Canidy said flatly.

"If you choose it to be, it certainly will be so," Donovan said. "Dick, we have far more resources and support than we did last time. Your previous operation was among the first of its kind, not merely intelligence but intelligence combined with special military operations—or, if you will, commando tactics. We still have our fair share of gadgets and spycraft; but now with more blood, sweat, and guts. As the war evolves, the OSS has evolved. That includes a vast number of collaborators in both Germany and Poland. We've developed an extensive network of partners and collaborators in both countries and we have a little more experience than we had then. We've gone from being amateurs to highly sophisticated professionals. And that description includes you and Fulmar."

"Sir, not to be flip or insubordinate, but I've found during the course of this war that flattery often precedes an impossible assignment. I've seen more than my fair share of friends never return from doomsday assignments."

"No argument there," Donovan conceded. "But that's what OSS is all about. Fulmar and McDermott will accompany you, but as opposed to last time, you'll have plentiful and rather sophisticated support—Poles, Czechs, and Austrians who are positioned in the singular goal of acquiring the Kapsky document."

Canidy winced almost imperceptibly upon mention of the name. Ever since Donovan first contacted him about the operation several hours ago he wrestled with the feeling of acute embarrassment bordering on humiliation. *The Kapsky document.* He'd been charged with rescuing the professor but had found him dead. The notebook recovered from Kapsky was still being analyzed, but thus far the scientists charged with deciphering it had concluded that portions of it were, in fact, *indecipherable*, or, perhaps, just plain gibberish. Now it appeared the Germans had somehow acquired another critical document authored by Kapsky. Canidy couldn't help wondering if he'd somehow missed the document when searching Kapsky's body. He'd assumed the Germans had gotten to Kapsky first, but what if they hadn't? What if they'd encountered Kapsky's body after Canidy but had conducted a far more exhaustive search of the remains and found the document? The question had nagged him since Donovan first contacted him. He was determined to rectify the matter.

"Where do we insert, sir?"

"Same place as last time. No sense changing what works."

"*How* do we insert?"

"Again, the same as last time."

"By boat? It wouldn't by any chance be skippered by . . ."

". . . a six-foot Viking goddess." Donovan chuckled. "With her twin as first mate."

Canidy grinned. "One hell of a way to die, sir."

"You'll meet McDermott in Gotland as before. Then cross the Baltic to Poland. As you know, there'll be Messerschmitts everywhere."

"When do we leave?"

"Now. The Germans have had the scroll for some time. Although the most recent intelligence from Bauer indicates that they've yet to decipher the document, it's only a matter of time. When they do, they'll have a head start on us that may be insuperable. So it's imperative that we get it to our analysts immediately, or . . . die trying."

CHAPTER 27

Katthammarsvik, Gotland
1501, 12 August 1943

The broad smile through what appeared to be the world's thickest mustache revealed impressively white, if misaligned, teeth.

For a man who was about to embark on an operation that would subject him to a high probability of death, dismemberment, or capture, McDermott appeared remarkably carefree and jovial. He was standing in the same spot and dressed in the same civilian clothes as he'd been when Canidy and Fulmar had first met him. Only, this time he was alone.

Canidy and Fulmar approached him across the tarmac, hands extended. McDermott grasped their hands in turn and shook each vigorously. "I had a suspicion I hadn't seen the last of you two. When Commander Fleming told me about this operation, I thought that if the Yanks were going to send anyone, it would be one or both of you."

"Hell, Conor," Canidy said, "how did you draw the short straw again?"

"I didn't," McDermott said. "When Commander Fleming told me about it, I volunteered before he could even make the request or issue an order. Sounds like it could be a spot of fun, don't you agree?"

"You certainly have a perverse notion of fun, my friend."

McDermott cocked his head. "*I* have a perverse notion of fun? As I recall, on the last suicide mission we had the pleasure of sharing you two seemed absolutely giddy, like a couple of chaps on holiday."

Fulmar laughed. "That was due in large part to our cruise ship captain."

"And now her twin." McDermott laughed. "Those two look like they descended directly from Asgard. A bit—what's the expression you Yanks use?—'out of my league.'"

McDermott's expression sobered slightly. "I must say, however, that when Commander Fleming described the purpose of the operation, I felt almost compelled to volunteer. I feel somewhat responsible for the Gerries getting that document."

Canidy nodded, glancing at Fulmar. "We had a similar reaction. We were *there*. Kapsky was right in front of us. Did we miss something? Was this document there but somehow we overlooked it?"

"I keep playing it over and over in my head," McDermott said absently. "It was a thorough search. Most likely, we just got there too late—after the Germans had already taken it."

"We didn't search body cavities," Canidy said cryptically.

"Who searches the body cavities of a cadaver in the field?" McDermott asked. "I'll tell you who: nobody."

"Except the thorough and precise Germans," Fulmar said.

"Don't pay any attention to him," Canidy advised. "He's half Kraut."

Fulmar examined his watch. "Time to go. We don't have time to waste."

The three got into the Studebaker on the tarmac, McDermott behind the wheel, Fulmar in the passenger seat, and Canidy in the rear. McDermott started the vehicle and drove as if they'd just robbed a bank.

"How's the arm?" Canidy shouted from the back.

"Not as bad as they'd first feared. It looks like a mess and it gets numb from shoulder to wrist at odd times, but it's pretty strong, and I can move it about pretty well. Weaker than the other arm, but not by much."

"Any problem handling weapons?" Fulmar asked.

"None to speak of. I need to concentrate more, but it's manageable."

Canidy could tell through the fabric of McDermott's shirt that the arm was atrophied in comparison to his left arm. Although it gave Canidy pause, he surmised the Brits wouldn't have sent McDermott on such a critical operation unless he was fully up to the task.

They passed the time driving to the coast talking about everything but the operation, as if to do so would jinx it. Although each was optimistic by nature, a light pall hung over them. None had any illusions about the task ahead. Each thought the likelihood that any of them would return alive, let alone retrieve the Kapsky document, was questionable.

But not one of them would give up the second chance for glory.

The boat sported a fresh coat of paint but otherwise was as they'd remembered it, including the Teutonic skipper wearing drab weather gear standing next to it on the dock. She appeared just as serious as Canidy remembered. But looked even better.

As they approached, Canidy asked, "You never thought you'd see us again, did you?"

"I didn't," Kristin Thorisdottir admitted. "But neither did I think it was impossible."

"Where is your sister? I was told she was going to be on board also. Katla?"

Kristin's twin appeared from belowdecks with a smile on her face. "You were told correctly."

"The gang's back together again," Canidy declared.

Kristin Thorisdottir didn't look much different to Canidy from the last time. Her hair was a bit longer and almost white from the sun. It fell in nearly impossible abundance to her waist. Her facial features continued to remind him of a mythical Nordic goddess, albeit one who appeared somewhat weary from tension.

"We will take essentially the same route but with a few pivots. The Germans are more vigilant and more aggressive than they were last time," she informed them as she scanned the horizon from the helm. "The patrols are more frequent. They have less patience. Admiral Dönitz's wolfpack has been losing lots of subs, but the Baltic is still dangerous. They will sink a vessel with little hesitation if they even suspect it may be working for the Allies, and the planes do strafing runs for fun. My advice is to remain belowdecks."

"Thanks," Canidy said, standing next to her as she steered. "Good advice, but I'd like to see what's coming to kill me."

"It won't matter," Kristin said fatalistically. "There is nothing you can do to avoid them. Once they select us as a target, they'll make as many passes as necessary to shred us to pieces. No mercy."

"Still, I don't want to be surprised in my last seconds on Earth. I want to know what's coming."

Kristin smiled. "So you can curse your killers? Damn them all to hell?"

"Never underestimate the martial power of profanity. The best warriors can deploy curses like weapons. Some are single .45-caliber rounds, others are 155-millimeter howitzers."

Kristin continued smiling, sending a charge through Canidy. "I'm told your General Patton downed a Messerschmitt with a well-placed curse between sips of brandy."

"That just *has* to be true."

Kristin turned to face Canidy, her expression clinical. "This trip of yours is more hazardous than the last one, Major Canidy. I don't think you'll be coming back."

"How could you possibly know how hazardous the mission is? You don't know anything about it other than where you're dropping us off and picking us up. Are you always this optimistic?"

Kristin continued looking in Canidy's direction. "I understand, but I'm a simple sailor whose charge is to convey you across the sea along a relatively challenging course. But the purpose of your mission is plain, and I'm sure the Germans are waiting for you, or someone like you."

"With due respect, Miss Thorisdottir," Canidy said with a mixture of curiosity and irritation. "How the hell would you know that? Why in the hell do you think the Germans are waiting for us? The only people on this entire planet who know we're here are the five souls on this boat, three in Britain, and two in the USA. That's it. And the five who aren't on this boat are in charge of making sure the Allies don't lose the war."

Kristin shook her head almost contemptuously. "Because they're not looking specifically for *you*, although if they were it wouldn't surprise me. They're looking for the Allies to send *someone* for the Kapsky material. Whether it's you or someone else, eventually the Allies need to send someone, and the Germans know it."

Candidy took half a step back and examined Kristin for several seconds. She shouldn't know anything about this matter and, in particular, about the Kapsky document. What the hell was going on?

Kristin, sensing his bewilderment, continued. "Don't worry. Your operation has not been compromised," she assured. "Understand that the tiniest bits of information relating to German capabilities and intention are treated like gold by nearly everyone on the entire continent, especially by the various Resistances. Nearly everyone seizes upon any information, no matter how ridiculous or irrelevant, pertaining to Nazi capabilities, movements, or intentions. Sometimes the rumors are mere fantasy, sometimes not. But because lives—sometimes one, sometimes one million—can depend on such information, it travels like lightning. Often your intelligence services and military leadership are the last to know."

"When did you hear about it? From whom?"

"I don't even remember." Kristin shrugged. "Katla heard something from one of Jan Karski's associates about an SS Obersturmführer who has become Admiral Canaris's fair-haired boy."

"What do you know of Karski?"

". . . Polish Resistance. Katla and I have worked with him and his people. Your people know him and his information intimately. It is probably why they initiated the mission, at least in part. Karski's network heard from the SS Obersturmführer's lady friends that he had been bragging about a promotion and his growing influence with the top people in the Abwehr. He did not say much more than that, obviously. You do not get promoted in the Abwehr by talking about intelligence with friends and lovers."

Canidy turned to Fulmar and McDermott, who were engaged in banter with Katla on the foredeck.

"Come here, you should hear this." All of them gathered about Canidy and Kristin.

Canidy said, "Kristin says we should expect a Nazi welcome party when we arrive. It seems the Abwehr has anticipated someone would come for the Kapsky document."

"You're bleedin' kidding me," McDermott said. "How in God's name could that be?"

"They don't know any specifics," Canidy assured. "They simply calculated the probabilities that something as important as the Kapsky document might start rumors and the logical reaction of the Allies would be to get our hands on it." Canidy pointed to Fulmar and McDermott. "They don't know *we're* the ones coming for the document; they don't know *where* we're coming from or *when*." Canidy looked at Kristin.

"That is correct," Kristin confirmed. "Rather, they are on alert. Gestapo probably has been briefed to be even more vigilant. SS is being ever more aggressive—Karski informs that the Oberst who obtained the document has been assigned the responsibility of protecting it. He has been tracking down Karski associates, and doing so rather effectively. He has developed something of a reputation. Not a pleasant individual."

"That doesn't change anything," Canidy said. "But it does mean that we have absolutely no margin for error. As impossible as this operation seemed before, it just got more impossible."

Fulmar and McDermott began chuckling, then broke out in

guffaws, prompting Canidy to do the same. Kristin and Katla looked on with a mixture of puzzlement and bemusement.

"We're both indispensable *and* expendable," Canidy explained between breaths. "We're supposed to save the world from eternal Nazi domination *and* we're on a suicide mission."

"Then I suggest you go below deck before you become prematurely expendable," Kristin said.

"What do you mean?" Canidy asked, chest still heaving.

Kristin pointed to the southwest sky. "German planes."

Everyone turned in the direction to which she was pointing. Low on the horizon approximately four to six kilometers away, four Messerschmitt Bf 109s were approaching.

"If they see five people on a boat this size, they will become suspicious and likely strafe us," Kristin said. "They may strafe us regardless, but there is no sense increasing the probability."

The three men reacted instantly and descended the stairs. Twenty seconds later they could hear the whine of the planes' engines as they flew over the boat, the din indicating that they were probably no more than seventy-five feet overhead. The trio relaxed as the whine receded, but tensed as the sound grew louder again, indicating the planes were spooling up and doubling back. Canidy reflexively gripped a handle on a storage locker. Fulmar and McDermott simply clenched their fists.

The whine grew louder and more piercing than it was on the first pass, indicating the planes were approaching faster and at a lower altitude. Canidy looked at Fulmar and McDermott, who were staring at the stairs leading to the deck. He couldn't summon any witticisms.

Each of them tensed as the whine reached an apex and then relaxed when the sound receded without any strafing fire.

"I don't mind saying that almost made me wet my britches," McDermott confessed. "We're sitting ducks out here."

"It pains me to say this," Canidy said, "but I think the Thorisdottir twins have bigger balls than we do."

"Hell yes," Fulmar agreed.

The three laughed, but ceased abruptly as the whine once again grew louder.

"Aw, hell," McDermott said. "Hell."

The menacing pitch of the whine signaled that the planes were coming in even lower than before. In his mind's eye Canidy saw them at an altitude of about forty feet, low enough that the Thorisdottirs would be able to make eye contact with the pilots before they fired their MG 17s, shredding the five of them with 7.92-millimeter rounds.

The noise grew loud enough to rattle the utensils in the galley and hurt their eardrums, close enough that they could distinguish each plane's engine. They winced, held their breaths, and braced.

Nothing.

Once again, the whine receded. This time it kept receding east until the noise was replaced by the sound of the sea slapping against the boat.

Canidy exhaled silently. "Well, if I had to guess, I'd say they were just trying to get a better look at the Thorisdottirs." He turned to McDermott. "Sorry to say, Mac, but I suspect this won't be the last time we wet our pants on this run. And let's just hope we spare our pants from anything more disgusting."

CHAPTER 28

"Please shut the door behind you, Bill." Donovan nodded to Harry Hopkins and Laurence Duggan as they left the Oval Office. Donovan was mildly surprised. The President rarely closed the door to the office, even when discussing sensitive matters. He was good at picking reliable people, trusted them, and relied on their discretion. The request meant that FDR planned to address a matter of unusual significance.

Donovan shut the door and took a seat in one of the two chairs opposite the President's desk. The CIC was holding his cigarette holder, but the cigarette was unlit.

"Don't look so worried, Bill. I just wanted to check on the status of our—what do you call it?—operation. Churchill's being his usual pain in the ass. His people haven't heard anything from their man. He seemingly expects that our fellows are in constant contact with us, informing us every time they pass wind."

Donovan shook his head. "Mr. President, our men have been

instructed that under no circumstance are they to attempt to contact us until they have acquired the Kapsky document, returned to their extraction point, and are well on their way back to Gotland—preferably not until they arrive at RAF East Moor. Indeed, save for a few underground contacts who will guide them, they are to remain silent. Churchill's inquiries to you are because their men have been instructed similarly."

FDR pursed his lips contemplatively. "And if they are in jeopardy?"

"They are on their own, Mr. President."

"In the middle of enemy territory," FDR noted. "A most thorough, efficient, and ruthless enemy."

"We selected them because they are resourceful and highly trained. And that's putting it mildly. Not just training in weapons and tactics, but physical training of a most grueling sort. Modeled, in fact, after the training of Mr. Churchill's most elite soldiers."

Roosevelt snorted. "Yes, he reminds me of it regularly." He lit his cigarette and drew deeply. "The man is Britain's best hope, but he is a prodigious pain in the ass."

Donovan's expression remained unchanged. He knew better than to agree with the President on that point. Roosevelt complained about Churchill incessantly, but he deeply respected, even admired, him. Donovan had long ago concluded that Roosevelt wouldn't look favorably on anyone who concurred with his frequent disparagement of the prime minister.

"I feel compelled to know who these men are, Bill."

"Their names are Dick Canidy and Eric Fulmar. The Brit is a man by the name of McDermott."

"And how long will it take to complete the operation, Bill?"

"If all goes well, Mr. President, they should be able to go to the

Abwehr, acquire the Kapsky document, and return to Gotland in less than a week," Donovan replied evenly. "As you know, nothing ever goes according to plan once an op begins. The probability that everything will go according to plan is near zero."

"The Germans are actively searching for them, I gather?"

Donovan nodded. "We presume so, Mr. President, given that they may be in territory currently occupied by their forces. Our preliminary assessment is that they have likely assigned the task to their man Otto Skorzeny."

"Obersturmbannführer Otto Skorzeny. I have heard of him. Quite a character, from what I understand. Considered perhaps the most proficient—Special Operator, I think they call it—in the world. Am I right?"

"Yes, Mr. President. 'Scarface.' Cunning, ruthless, deadly. Six feet four and quite athletic. Very bright. Based on our intelligence, he's never failed a mission.

"The other possible candidate, we believe, is an Obersturmführer Konrad Maurer, Waffen SS. He possesses all of Skorzeny's qualities, save the scar. And he's even taller."

The President waved his cigarette holder, irritated. "What is it with these damn Germans? Sometimes it seems they actually take this Aryan business seriously."

"Dick Canidy is every bit the equal of Skorzeny or Maurer, Mr. President. Tall, big-boned, athletic. Except he has dark hair, close-cropped. Not very Aryan in that regard. But he's versatile and fearless. From flying protection over the Burma Road to thwarting the Germans' use of chemical weapons. Good man. Our best."

"Coming from you, Bill, quite an endorsement. But why Canidy? Don't we already have some unit under Oppenheimer to do such things?"

"Are you referring to the component under the Manhattan Project, Mr. President?"

"Yes, the group assigned to get the information on the German atomic weapons program."

"Operation Alsos," Donovan confirmed. "Under Lieutenant Colonel Boris Pash. It won't become operational until late September and we must get to Kapsky *now*, before anyone else. Besides, Mr. President, Operation Alsos is an intelligence-gathering endeavor, not a rescue operation. Finding and extracting Kapsky could be very bloody; not your standard spy run. Nonetheless, we must make the effort. Heinrich Maier of the Austrian Resistance provided the OSS with drawings of the V-2. For those efforts dozens of others close to the Resistance were executed by the Gestapo.

"*This* is much bigger, far more advanced. Allen Dulles has obtained information from the Swiss that SS Obergruppenführer Hans Kammler has moved all superweapons production, including the V-2, underground. They have conscripted slave labor to work on rocket production. But most of them are idle for the moment."

"Idle? That doesn't sound like the Germans," Roosevelt said.

"They are reserving them, Mr. President, for production of weapons based on the Kapsky document."

"You're not suggesting that the Kapsky weapons, so to speak, are that much more important than the V-2?"

"Yes, sir. That's what I'm suggesting. Dulles believes Kapsky's formulae relate not just to one component, but to both an incendiary device and a rocket to deliver it."

"How is that different from the V-2?"

Donovan exhaled. "Sir, the Germans are struggling to get the V-2 to land in London, barely a thousand miles from the farthest launch site. Dulles says the Kapsky rocket could deliver payload across the Atlantic to the U.S."

Roosevelt froze. It was several seconds before he uttered the words "My God."

"I'm afraid it gets worse, Mr. President. Do you recall your instructions to Secretary Stimson regarding the Manhattan Project?"

"Of course," Roosevelt responded with both anticipation and trepidation.

"Under Operation Alsos we are to acquire as much information as possible about whether the Germans are also developing an atomic program."

"Operation Alsos wasn't to begin until September," Roosevelt said.

"Yes," Donovan said somberly. "Well, it may not need to go forward at all. The Soviets, by way of Dulles, say that the Kapsky information could permit the Germans to deliver an atomic payload."

A large glowing ash fell from the President's cigarette. He did not so much as flinch.

"Apocalyptic," Roosevelt concluded.

"In a manner of speaking."

Roosevelt sighed. "Stalin has been insisting on a conference, purportedly to discuss how to address the world landscape after the war."

"I'd say that's just a bit premature. The outcome of the war could go either way."

"Indeed," the President said. "That's why it's more likely the actual purpose for the conference is to place pressure on Britain and the U.S. to open a Western Front as soon as possible—yesterday, if Stalin had his way. The Red Army is admittedly engaged in titanic battles with the Nazis. The scale is nearly incomprehensible. He needs to alleviate the pressure immediately."

"Mr. President, where does he propose to conduct the meeting? I assume in the U.S., given the obvious."

Roosevelt chuckled amiably. "Given my obvious travel limitations?"

"Given the security implications of having the Big Three in one location at the same time."

"They have proposed Tehran, Iran," Roosevelt said.

"My Lord, Mr. President, that is ridiculous. What kind of security is that? Skorzeny would be salivating at such an opportunity."

"I have confidence in our people—the Brits and the Soviets included—and their ability to secure such a meeting."

"Needless risk, Mr. President."

Roosevelt shrugged indifferently. "The Kapsky document," he declared somewhat theatrically. "It sounds like a religious artifact, some piece of ancient parchment unearthed in the desert and transcribed with a prophecy of Armageddon."

Donovan exhaled uneasily. "Mr. President, that description may be more accurate than any of us care to admit."

CHAPTER 29

Gromov was bewildered by the speed with which he'd been conveyed to the Lubyanka. He'd been resting between assignments in the apartment of a female acquaintance when two NKVD thugs burst in and instructed him to accompany them by order of Aleksandr Belyanov. Gromov, ordinarily imperturbable, was a bit rattled.

Gromov became even more apprehensive when he was instructed to wait in one of the seemingly innumerable white-walled rooms on the lower level. These were not rooms intended for cordial conversations. They were rooms where various alleged enemies of the state were interrogated, often brutally. The macabre joke was that the walls were painted white so cleaning personnel could more easily spot the blood and other organic matter that often speckled the walls and floors. At least he wasn't in the basement, where limbs and intestines covered the floor in quantities sometimes dwarfing that of a slaughterhouse.

Gromov hadn't been seated more than a minute when he heard

the unhurried, staccato cadence of Belyanov's heels on the stone floor of the outer corridor. Seconds later the door opened and two soldiers brandishing PPSh-41 submachine guns entered, followed by the chief of the OKRNKVD.

Gromov stood as Belyanov approached to within a few feet, flanked by the two soldiers. Their presence, though not quite unnerving, was troubling to say the least.

Belyanov observed Gromov in silence for several seconds that passed like minutes. He took another step closer, then said, "Twice shy, Comrade Gromov. Twice shy."

Gromov's brow furrowed with incomprehension. "Pardon, sir?"

Belyanov took yet another step forward, again flanked by the two guards.

"You've failed twice."

Gromov grew even more puzzled. "Respectfully, sir, in what sense?"

"Sit."

Gromov hesitated for a moment, glanced at the two guards, then sat. Belyanov remained standing, looming menacingly over Gromov. "You were given an assignment some time ago to acquire Professor Sebastian Kapsky and return him to us. You failed to do so. That was your first failure. A most pronounced one."

Gromov hesitated to defend himself, but concluded that if he didn't the situation would deteriorate rapidly. "Sir, Kapsky was dead before I could get to him, before anyone else could acquire him."

"The objective, Comrade Gromov, was not to secure Kapsky's body. It was to secure what was in his brain. Recall what I told you when we first met: 'If we fail to find him, we may not just lose the war, we will lose the future.'"

Gromov struggled not to respond with the obvious. He'd been

dispatched to acquire the man too late. Kapsky had been dead for some time before Gromov had gotten to him. That wasn't Gromov's fault. It was the fault of those who had sent him on the mission in the first place.

"Sir, respectfully, I searched for and located Kapsky as fast as possible. He was dead before I arrived. He was dead before the Americans arrived . . ."

"You did not search the body," Belyanov hissed.

Gromov looked at him quizzically. "But I did, sir. There was nothing of any consequence. Nothing whatsoever."

Gromov could see Belyanov's jaws tighten and his eyes narrow. A recess of the assassin's brain imagined the scores of individuals for whom that image was the last they'd seen before oblivion.

"Nothing," Belyanov repeated. "Nothing?"

"Yes, sir."

"*Absolutely* nothing."

"Absolutely."

"You are certain? Unequivocally certain?"

Gromov felt a pinprick of anxiety just below the solar plexus. He'd searched Kapsky's body. He believed there'd been nothing on the corpse. Yet the tenor of Belyanov's questions obviously telegraphed that something was amiss. But how? Gromov decided it was better to confront the issue directly rather than be defensive.

"Sir, clearly you have information that is contrary to what I'm telling you. What I told you was accurate at the time I encountered Kapsky." Gromov nodded toward the two guards. "Respectfully, sir, no impertinence intended. Are these two permitted to hear this discussion?"

"They are part of my personal detail," Belyanov replied. "They hear everything, and they disclose only on pain of death."

"Then can you tell me what it is I allegedly missed?"

"There's no 'allegedly,' Gromov. I have told you before, we have very good sources. Especially in Washington. And they've informed us of a document's existence.

"You failed to retrieve a document that is now in the possession of the Germans. The Germans are deciphering the document at this moment. They are said to be ecstatic about the acquisition of such document. Indeed, the SS Obersturmführer who acquired the document has been promoted and is now Canaris's most trusted assistant." Belyanov paused. "Beria is furious."

At the mention of the name Gromov's pinprick of anxiety became a dagger. Thousands went to their deaths when Beria was merely irritated. Indeed, thousands perished even when Beria was content.

"Your malfeasance is not limited to failure to secure the Kapsky document," Belyanov continued. "You were instructed to eliminate the Americans. That was your second failure, a most egregious one, since our informants state that the very same Americans have been sent to acquire the document from the Germans."

Gromov refrained from stating that he'd eliminated three of the Americans' party, under impossible conditions, no less. To state such would merely provoke Belyanov.

"You are, however, most fortunate," Belyanov noted. "You will have what most others on this Earth seldom receive—a second chance. Although, under the circumstances, it may seem a punishment. Despite your manifest failures, Beria maintains that you are the best person to rectify the failure. Among other things, you are undoubtedly the most motivated."

Gromov managed to conceal his relief as his confidence returned. Indeed, he *hadn't* failed. He'd done as well as anyone could have under the circumstances. Better. He was an assassin without peer.

"You are commanded to finish the job you were originally given," Belyanov continued. "Get the Kapsky document, kill the Americans."

"Yes, Comrade Belyanov," Gromov said, invigorated.

"We have arranged transport to a small port on Kattegat Bay, Denmark. You will be provided all the details we have en route. We have contacts with the Danish Resistance there and they will provide assistance infiltrating into Germany. From there, you will be alone, but we have arranged a communication network with elements in both Denmark and Germany if we need to contact you. They will provide assistance when feasible and relay any information about the location of the Americans. But you will largely be on your own."

"I work best on my own."

Belyanov's tone became oddly sympathetic. "Gromov, the likelihood is that you'll be killed or captured, but we must do what we can to acquire that document. Beria thinks highly of you. I agree with Beria that you are the best option we have, so the unfortunate responsibility falls to you. But if you succeed, you will be venerated for decades to come."

"Thank you for the honor, sir."

Belyanov stepped back, as did the guards. "A transport is waiting for you."

Gromov rose to leave. Belyanov placed a hand on his shoulder and said, "Remember one thing. No one can know that it was you who killed the Americans. No one at all. Do you understand?"

Gromov nodded. He also understood that he would have to kill many more individuals than just the Americans to accomplish the objective.

CHAPTER 30

Canidy stood beside Kristin in the center cockpit as Katla, Fulmar, and McDermott sat on a bench astern, still chattering about the runs by the Messerschmitt 109s, McDermott insisting, and Fulmar disputing, that a single sustained burst from just one of the aircraft's MG 131 machine guns would have sunk the *Njord*. Canidy watched, bemused. It was painfully obvious that the dispute was for the purpose of impressing Katla, who gamefully entertained their arguments as if they knew what they were talking about. Kristin, on the other hand, remained all business. She wore the same fierce expression as the first time she'd piloted the vessel with Canidy's team on board. Canidy expected the expression might simply be due to her concentration on the task. Whatever the reason, Canidy found it exceptionally seductive.

Kristin pointed ahead a few degrees off the port bow. Although Canidy hadn't noticed, the shoreline was on the horizon. "There. Approximately twenty degrees. We should be at the canal very soon."

Canidy turned to the rear. "Get your rucks and check your weapons. We'll be ashore soon. There may be enemy nearby this time."

Fulmar and McDermott went belowdecks to retrieve their equipment.

"The liaison from SHAEF has supplied us with generous allotments of fuel, medical equipment, and provisions," Kristin said. "We can sail the Baltic almost indefinitely, remaining as near to the coastline as possible. We have a rather powerful RCA marine console radio—also supplied by SHAEF—that will allow us to pick up your signal when you near the extraction point. We should be able to synchronize our respective arrivals."

Canidy nodded. "All solved, then? It sounds pretty simple until something breaks down. We have a small radio from our Professor Moriarty. Very weak signal, however."

"You strike me as a resourceful man, Major. Katla and I are fairly resourceful also. We'll improvise," Kristin assured.

"I like your confidence and optimism. I'd like to think I share those qualities. But I'm realistic enough to concede that the odds we don't come back alive aren't insubstantial."

"Consider that the United States of America chose you out of millions of soldiers in its armed forces to execute the assignment," Kristin said. "Your country obviously believes you have the greatest probability of succeeding."

"On a relative basis, yes," Canidy agreed. "But on an absolute basis, it's likely we're a little more than condemned men going through exercises on our way to our fates."

A grin creased Kristin's face. "Trying to generate sympathy for yourself, Major?"

Canidy raised his eyebrows. "Not interested in granting a condemned man his final wish?"

Fulmar and McDermott emerged onto the deck carrying their supplies and weapons—a carbine and a handgun. Katla followed and scanned the shoreline. She pointed to a spot ten degrees off starboard bow. "There's the mouth of the canal. It appears more overgrown than the last time I saw it. Good cover. We will be there in minutes."

Canidy looked at McDermott. "Get the maps out. We'll need them right away."

"You're more anxious than last time," Kristin observed.

"Compared to this time, that was a walk in the park."

"Very fatalistic, Major Canidy."

"*Realistic*, Captain Thorisdottir." Canidy grinned, leaned close to Kristin, and whispered, "Maybe you'd re-reconsider granting a condemned man his last wish."

Kristin turned her face flush with Canidy and said softly, "I'll be here when you get back."

CHAPTER 31

To many, SS Standartenführer Konrad Maurer's stride appeared intimidating, even menacing. His powerful legs encased in highly
polished black boots moved like pistons on a locomotive that would
stop for nothing.

Maurer knew this. He wasn't trying to look intimidating or
menacing, but didn't mind that he did. He enjoyed being feared.
And he liked being treated with respect and deference. He was, after
all, an SS Standartenführer who reported directly to the Genius.
More than that, he was the person who had obtained and delivered
perhaps the most consequential intelligence find of the war. It was
likely that even the Führer was aware of that fact.

Maurer entered the antechamber to Vice Admiral Canaris's office and greeted the normally dour Oberstleutnant sitting at the
desk. Maurer's newly enhanced status prompted the officer to acknowledge him with a measure of respect given only the Rommels,

Guderians, and von Rundstedts. He pressed a buzzer, rose from his chair, and opened Canaris's office door.

Canaris stood next to a credenza adjacent to his desk with a sheaf of documents in his hands. He looked worried. Upon Maurer's entry, he placed the documents on the credenza, pointed to them, and said, "Problems, Maurer. Your great success spawns problems."

"I am afraid I do not understand, Herr Admiral."

Canaris moved to his desk chair and sat. He gestured for Maurer to sit in one of the high-backed leather chairs on the other side of the desk. After Maurer was seated, Canaris explained, "The Americans and the Russians know about the Kapsky document. They know we have it, and they are working to decipher it and employ it to the benefit of the Wehrmacht."

Maurer was somewhat surprised. "How do they know we have the document? And how do *we* know they know we have it?"

"The Americans, British, and Soviets all were searching for Kapsky as we were. All believed acquiring him held strategic significance. Naturally, their resistance networks would be alert to anything pertaining to Kapsky. We have intelligence leaks like any army in wartime."

"Yes, Herr Admiral. But how do we *know* they know?"

"Quite simply, because they have intelligence leaks also. It seems the Americans learned of the Kapsky document from a spy in Germany. In this building, perhaps. The Soviets appear to have a spy in the *American* government who relayed the information to the NKVD. And *we* have a spy within the NKVD who relayed all of this information to us."

Maurer shook his head. Canaris continued.

"The Americans and the Soviets have each dispatched teams to acquire the document. We must conclude they are on their respective paths here at this very moment."

Maurer's face bore an expression that was a mix of skepticism and arrogance. "A worthless endeavor. Futile. They will sacrifice soldiers to obtain something that is under impenetrable guard and cannot otherwise be produced? The document never leaves the room. Everyone who enters is searched both upon entry and departure and only the most trusted are permitted entry. They are observed the entire time they are in the room to ensure no copies are made and ingested. The document script is far too long and complex to be memorized and the mathematicians analyzing the document are under twenty-four-hour surveillance."

"All true," Canaris agreed. "A suicide mission. Nonetheless, they are making the attempt, which is an indication of the importance they attach to the document."

"A document they have never seen."

"Yes. But they know who produced it. That is sufficient."

"And the fact they would even make the attempt tells us they believe they have a chance of obtaining it, however slight."

Canaris leaned forward in his chair. "Stalin will sacrifice tens of thousands to achieve a low-probability outcome. Lives are meaningless to him. But the Americans and British would not sacrifice lives for a futility."

Maurer grasped Canaris's point. "You believe obtaining the document may *not* be impossible. Neither the Americans nor Soviets have assistance of which we are unaware . . ."

"Just as we know both the Americans and Soviets are attempting to acquire the document, *they* must know something about a security vulnerability relating to the document. They must be receiving assistance from within this building."

"And you would like me to investigate and eliminate such vulnerabilities, Herr Admiral?"

Canaris shook his head. "I have already directed Hauptman Fischer toward such task. He and his men are conducting a thorough review of all individuals who are even remotely aware of the document and the security surrounding it. What I would like you to do, Standartenführer Maurer, is to go on the offensive. Find and destroy the men sent by the Americans and Soviets to acquire the document."

Canaris detected a rare uncertainty in Maurer's expression. "Do not be concerned that you will be intruding on the purview of the Gestapo. Himmler is aware of this. The Führer has been briefed and concurs."

Maurer struggled to conceal his exhilaration. The *Führer* concurs. The Führer himself concurs that SS Standartenführer Maurer—not Himmler, not the Gestapo—should lead the effort to safeguard the Fatherland's most precious strategic document. A document Maurer himself had obtained.

"It shall be done, Herr Admiral," Maurer said boldly. "What additional intelligence do we have regarding the efforts of the Americans and Soviets?"

". . . Don't forget the British," Canaris admonished lightly. "I must remind myself not to do the same. Churchill is perhaps the greatest thorn in the Führer's side, but we—many of us—have a tendency to merely include the British with the Americans, as if they are one.

"The intelligence we have is sparing, Maurer, but useful," Canaris continued. "Our source in the Lubyanka relates that the American team consists of three extremely well-trained, highly resourceful individuals. Two are Americans, one is an Englishman. The Americans are Major Richard Canidy and Lieutenant Eric Fulmar. The Englishman is a Sergeant Conor McDermott."

"Just three men, Herr Admiral? Are they serious?"

"Very much so, Maurer. Their assignment comes from and was fashioned by the most proficient unconventional warfare strategists the British and Americans have." Canaris nodded. "It is, I grant you, difficult to believe that three men could be expected to penetrate behind our lines into this building, obtain the Kapsky document, and successfully return to safety. Yet our informant in the Lubyanka relates that the Soviets are attempting to do the same thing with just *one* man, Major Taras Gromov. By all accounts a prolific assassin. Quite deadly."

Maurer's warrior instincts bristled upon hearing the description. *Maurer* was extremely well trained. *Maurer* was quite deadly. "I will destroy them, Herr Admiral," Maurer assured confidently.

"But to destroy them we must locate them, isolate them. And, preferably, well before they approach this building. Certainly the American team will be entering Poland from the Baltic, near Danzig. We surmise that a relay of resistance fighters familiar with the area between there and here will guide them. We have cartographers plotting the most likely routes of approach. They will provide you with their estimates and I will provide you with any reports we receive from our informants among the relevant resistance groups."

"Americans are sloppy, Herr Admiral," Maurer said. "They can be clever, but they tend to be cavalier and sloppy."

"Perhaps, Maurer," Canaris said. "But their cleverness can overcome their imprecision. Admittedly, their task is a near impossibility. But you should treat them as you would a force far more formidable. That also pertains to Gromov. It says something about him that the Soviets deem it sufficient to send a single man."

"I shall destroy him also," Maurer assured with a hint of irritation in his voice. *He* was more dangerous, more formidable, more competent than any of these four men. He'd proven just how dangerous, formidable, competent he was by obtaining the Kapsky document.

Now he would demonstrate how ruthless he could be.

CHAPTER 32

Northern Poland
2051, 12 August 1943

Major Dick Canidy liked to play the percentages. Except this time the percentages were that the three of them would never set foot on the Thorisdottirs' boat again. Nonetheless, he remained determined to do so.

Kristin had conveyed them to the same spot as before, but the place looked unfamiliar. The foliage was even denser than before and the canal water was dirty and rancid from the detritus of war.

Armed with an OSS compass and a map, they began moving westward with a sinking feeling that they were embarking on an impossibility. But a short time into the journey, a phantom appeared out of the brush.

And each of them beamed with joy.

It was Emil, only a short time later no longer a boy, if he'd ever been one. He was almost as tall as Canidy, with broad shoulders and a serious face that was taciturn, almost hostile, until he broke out into a grin. "You men look lost, once again," he taunted. "Need some help?"

Canidy clapped him on the shoulder. "You Polack son of a bitch. Dammit, you look good. Looks like you had a growth spurt. How in the hell did you know that we'd be here?"

"I did not. Commander Matuszek sent me to the area. We all have areas. We are assigned to harass the enemy. An OSS contact told Matuszek to look for men to take into Germany. I have been in the area for several days and saw your boat as it approached the coastline. It looked familiar, and truthfully, I was tired so I watched for the next half hour until it came to the dock."

"It's damn good to see you." Canidy shook Emil's shoulder. "Damn good."

Fulmar and McDermott each clapped Emil on the back.

"You're still in the fight," Fulmar said. "I will admit I was worried when I left you. After what we went through to get back to the coast . . . Honestly, I thought you'd have a hard time getting back to Matuszek. A boy among panzers. Thought you were likely dead. Boy, was I wrong."

"Yes, but not by much," Emil said. "I think I lost count of the number of times I should have been dead. What is the expression Americans use? I believe I am living on borrowed time."

"We're on our way west," Canidy said. "Any advice?"

"Yes," Emil said emphatically. "Do *not* go west. You will die if you go west."

"Orders," Canidy explained.

Emil shook his head in disgust. "Your orders will get you killed. I will wager you last twelve hours, no more."

Fulmar smiled sardonically. "Your previous experience didn't inspire a whole lot of faith in us?"

Emil shook his head once more. "It has nothing to do with you. It has to do with reality. Hundreds of thousands have died between here and the German border. You likely will be among them—not because of anything you do or do not do. But because of the fury of the war."

Canidy shrugged. "You're probably right, but we're on our way."

Emil asked, "Do you have any idea where you're going? How you're going to get there?"

"We do," Canidy replied with a hint of sarcasm. "We have all the good stuff. Maps, compasses . . ."

"Guides? Transportation?"

"We have the names of contacts along the way. They'll assist with transportation," Canidy replied.

"No, they will not," Emil countered. "The ones who can be trusted and who know what they are doing are probably dead. Those that can be trusted but *don't* know what they are doing will *get* you dead. The rest cannot be trusted. And they, of course, will make *sure* you're dead."

"You're a real ray of sunshine, Emil," Canidy said, but there was a hint of concession in his voice. "Do you have any suggestions?"

"My suggestion is *do not go*. But if you must, get the best guide you can find. He may prolong your lives a day or two more than would otherwise be the case."

Canidy sighed. "Can you recommend anyone who fits that description? The best guide we can find?"

"Me," Emil said bluntly. "I'm the best. We will survive a day or two longer, then we will all die."

Canidy, Fulmar, and McDermott glanced at one another. Canidy nodded. "Okay, Emil. We vote to live another day or two. Hopefully, you're wrong."

Emil said, "I am not wrong. But before I can lead you I must speak to Commander Matuszek."

"Of course," Canidy said. "We understand. We don't want you to get in trouble. How long will it take to reach him?"

"He's not far from here. To the south. I should be able to get to his position and back before the end of the day."

"All right," Canidy said. "But we're going with you. We can't afford to wait in one place an entire day for you to get back."

Emil turned southward and began walking. "Follow me."

They advanced in a column. Emil, followed by Canidy, then McDermott, with Fulmar bringing up the rear. Emil moved cautiously but at a brisk pace. Canidy didn't recognize the terrain and surmised they were moving along a different path than they had last time. "What's the German presence like now?"

"Worse than before," Emil replied. "Because we have had a few successes now and then they have been retaliating quite viciously. They were never merciful, but now they allow no quarter whatsoever." Emil paused. "I believe the American saying is 'they take no prisoners.'"

They walked silently for no more than a quarter hour before they heard the rumble of heavy vehicles. Canidy, Fulmar, and McDermott simultaneously felt a spike of anxiety, recalling their encounter with a panzer column.

The four sensed a subtle vibration of the earth, Emil motioning for them to stop and lower themselves to the ground.

They lay flat amid the foliage as the vibrations increased and the rumbling grew louder. Less than thirty seconds later a German truck carrying approximately a dozen sullen but alert-looking German troops drove slowly past over uneven ground flattened somewhat by the tracks of previous heavy vehicles. The troops had the unmistakable appearance of the battle-hardened—a forward pitch to their torsos and a distant, almost vacant look to their eyes, one that conveyed both fatalism and determination.

The four remained prone for nearly a minute after the transport passed. Emil was the first to get up, but immediately sank back to the ground as the rumble of another approaching vehicle grew louder.

"At this rate," Canidy hissed, "we'll get to Tirpitzufer around 1950."

Moments later a Panzerkampfwagen IV appeared, moving at ten kilometers per hour with a soldier in its turret wearing headphones.

The four lay prone for nearly a minute after the panzer passed, waiting for another vehicle or patrol. None came. They rose in unison and continued southward at a brisk pace, Canidy walking alongside Emil.

"How have you folks in the *Armia* been faring?" Canidy asked. "You and Matuszek's men?"

"About as well as could be expected. We are outmanned and outgunned, but our spirits are good, considering," Emil replied. "The Germans, despite having every military advantage imaginable, are showing signs of fatigue and perhaps even hesitancy. We have, of course, heard about their setbacks in Stalingrad and now in Kursk. Yet we are doing self-defeating things."

They came to a clearing that revealed a mammoth abandoned facility that Canidy speculated had once been a metalworks plant of some kind. The ground surrounding the building was pocked with shallow depressions from mortar and artillery fire. The structures appeared lifeless until they approached to within fifty feet, whereupon they were surrounded by more than thirty men and women that seemed to materialize from the debris strewn throughout the site.

A small woman with one arm approached Emil. She held a To-karev in her remaining hand and scanned Canidy, Fulmar, and McDermott wearily. Emil said to them, "Stay here."

After a brief, hushed, but highly animated discussion, Emil returned and said, "We lost forty-three while I was gone—as I said, Germans are no longer taking prisoners, literally. She says Matuszek has taken some men on a retaliation patrol. He should be back shortly."

"Can you afford to lose that many?" Fulmar asked.

"We cannot afford to lose anyone," Emil replied matter-of-factly.

"How frequently does this happen?" Canidy asked.

"Recently, almost daily. A few days ago, my friend Roman was killed. Today, my closest friend Milo is among the dead."

Canidy scrutinized Emil's face for any traces of emotion. He detected none.

"Follow me," Emil said.

He led them through the skeletal remains and rubble of the enormous facility, to what appeared to have once been an office of some sort. Three of its walls remained intact. The fourth was riddled with holes from machine-gun fire. There were several chairs and a ten-by-four metal table covered in dust in the center of the room. A filing cabinet lay on its side in the corner.

"Wait here," Emil instructed. "I need to see if any of my other mates were killed while I was gone."

Emil disappeared and the three stood in the dusty office examining the surroundings.

"How long do you think you could put up with conditions like this?" Fulmar asked.

"It's his country," Canidy said. "I suspect he'll put up with it as long as it takes."

"Or as long as he can," McDermott added. "Emil's taller than the last time we saw him, but he's a lot thinner, too. Handsome lad, but I couldn't help notice the scars and fresh cuts on his neck and arms. He's had some scrapes since we last saw him."

An elderly man who couldn't have been more than five feet tall emerged from the gloom of the plant carrying an M29 between the crook of his right arm and his waist. He smiled—revealing only upper and lower molars—and motioned with his left hand to put down their weapons. The three hesitated for a moment until they understood. As soon as they placed their handguns on the dirt floor, Matuszek, surrounded by Emil and four other men carrying rifles, also emerged from the gloom.

Matuszek stopped a few feet from them and gazed upon them with an expression of disgust. "You look no different from the last time we met. I must say, I'm impressed by your bravery and absolutely astonished by your stupidity."

Matuszek thrust out his meaty right hand to be shaken first by Canidy, then Fulmar, and then McDermott. Then he withdrew two steps to look them up and down once more. "I suppose you will do," the hardened resistance commander said. "If someone has to be sacrificed, it may as well be three expendable idiots."

Canidy squinted. "What makes you think we're being sacrificed?"

"You're on a futile assignment and everyone knows you're on a futile assignment. You are doomed, my friends." Matuszek smiled as he predicted their demise.

Canidy, although pleased to see the grizzled resistance commander, became more irritated. "What the hell do you mean we're doomed?"

"You are in search of the worst-kept secret in all of Europe, my friends," Matuszek replied. He put up a hand to ward off the obvious question. "Understand, we do not know *specifically* the terms of your mission. We know that it has something to do with a certain highly critical item in possession of the Germans. We further suspect that you are to obtain such item. An item in the custody of Canaris."

The perplexed look worn by the three prompted Matuszek to add, "You cannot penetrate Germany to your target. No matter how determined and talented you may be. You will be captured, and if you are fortunate, you will be killed immediately rather than suffer interrogation by the Gestapo or SS."

The three stared blankly at Matuszek. After several seconds of silence, Canidy asked, "How in hell do you *think* you know what you are talking about?"

"There is no leak in your Office of Strategic Services, old friend," Matuszek assured. "Do not worry about that. It is simple deduction. General Donovan communicates with us, as necessary, through numerous levels of intermediaries. We have heard he needs logistical help with an extremely important operation, an operation into Germany itself. Something that—shall we say—audacious would necessarily involve something of extreme importance and would have to be executed by men daring to the point of suicidal idiocy in order to obtain—"

"No need for flattery," Canidy said.

"So, here you are," Matuszek continued. "My old dear dog, now deceased three years, could deduce why you are here and that you will not be successful. It is not an improbable mission. It is an impossible mission. But the item is of such critical importance that Mr. Donovan has convinced your President that an effort must be made to obtain it. Or, more accurately, Mr. Donovan, with the indispensable assistance of Mr. Churchill, has convinced your President that history demands the risk be taken."

"At least we're making history," Canidy said amiably.

"Yes. Although your names will be lost—nothing more than anonymous heroes about whom literature is written to inspire the next generation of cannon fodder."

Canidy smiled. "So you are saying Emil can help us commit suicide?"

Matuszek smiled in return. "If you choose to commit suicide, that is your affair. Emil can assist, if he wishes, but he has more important things to do than that. You may have noted that the Germans are trying to conquer the world, and are doing a passable impression of doing so." Matuszek glanced at his four men, who smiled. "I suspect you prefer not to enter Germany and be torn to pieces— as you undoubtedly would in short order—if there were another means by which to accomplish your objective."

Canidy, Fulmar, and McDermott exchanged intrigued looks.

"What are you talking about?" Canidy asked.

"I'm not suggesting you will, or ever could, accomplish your objective," Matuszek replied. "But I am suggesting, more accurately, *saying*, that there is another means by which you may accomplish your mission without embarking on the impossible task of entering Canaris's lair."

"I'm all ears," Canidy said. "But understand our skepticism. We're supposed to—as you indicated—obtain something located in Germany, but you tell us we can accomplish that without going to Germany?"

"Better. Not only do you not have to go to Germany, but you

can acquire what you need here in Poland. Still quite hazardous, but not certain death. And you may give the Allies a strategic advantage for decades to come."

Matuszek's response raised several obvious questions. But before Canidy could pose any of them, a piercing whistle preceded an explosion that catapulted all ten men several feet into the air and propelled them against the corrugated metal walls of the office.

Sztum, Poland

Daria Bacior appeared uniquely out of place in Nazi-occupied Poland. She had none of the outward manifestations of someone who had witnessed monstrous atrocities, suffered prolonged bouts of hunger and thirst, and had desperately hidden from the enemy in conditions that were best described as feral.

Somehow, years into the most horrific conflict in human history, Daria Bacior retained the appearance and bearing of a nineteenth-century czarina. She was tall, redheaded, and strikingly beautiful, with an intelligent, erudite-looking countenance unblemished by lines or scars. Her clothing was neat and clean, and she managed somehow to project an utter lack of consternation regarding the madness that surrounded her. She looked, in a word, innocent.

It was a façade.

Daria was, in fact, quite beautiful, but she was a cunning and determined agent of the Home Army. She had not killed any of the enemy, but her actions had resulted in the deaths of hundreds of German soldiers, the destruction of hundreds of metric tons of enemy equipment, and the obliteration of nearly a half-dozen enemy installations.

Daria's most notable contribution to the resistance effort was something to which, despite her intelligence and cunning, she had been entirely oblivious for weeks. Several weeks ago, she'd had the feeling she was being watched. Not by the Germans, but by someone else. A few times she thought she'd glimpsed someone watching her from behind a tree or edifice, but upon closer inspection saw no one there. Then she did see someone; tall, lanky, haggard, with worn clothing. He didn't look like a soldier or partisan. He didn't look like a shopkeeper or farmer.

He'd appear at odd times—just for a moment—before disappearing. Daria thought perhaps her imagination was playing tricks on her.

Then two weeks ago, the apparition appeared before her as she walked to the run-down barn just outside of Sztum, south of Danzig, where she'd often made contact with *Armia*.

The apparition said, "I need assistance getting to the coast."

His voice was low, neutral, and unthreatening. He looked intelligent and sincere. And worn to the bone.

Nonetheless, Daria kept walking. She hadn't survived this long in Nazi-occupied Poland by being naïve. Still, she felt a pang of remorse for not at least listening for an explanation. She told her *Armia* contact about the encounter, who waved it off as inconsequential.

The next day the apparition appeared again this time closer to the barn. He appeared calm, and once again, unthreatening.

"I need help and I believe you can provide it."

Daria continued to walk without varying her pace. If an informant was watching the encounter, it would appear natural.

"I do not know you."

"Yes," the apparition acknowledged. "That is a problem. I understand. All I can say to assure you is that I am not a collaborator or spy. I am a Pole in need of help."

"And I am a Pole with no resources," Daria said warily.

"I will be grateful for anything you could do to help me get to the coast. Anywhere on the coast."

Daria said nothing and kept walking at the same pace. The apparition followed silently several meters behind. They walked for another minute until Daria entered the barn. The apparition continued past the barn, walked for another minute, then doubled back, surveyed his surroundings, and ducked into the barn. Daria was waiting just inside, a man brandishing a Poln M29 at her side.

"Do not move or you will be shot where you stand," Daria said coldly. The apparition did as he was told. A second man approached the apparition from the rear and searched him for weapons. After a few seconds he withdrew.

"Will you help?" the apparition asked.

"Who are you?" Daria asked.

"I escaped Katyn some time ago."

"I asked who you are, not where you are from."

"My name is Sebastian Kapsky."

Daria stepped backward and examined the apparition's face. "Repeat yourself."

"My name is Sebastian Kapsky."

Daria stared at him for several seconds. "Professor Sebastian Kapsky?"

"That is correct."

"You are a liar. Professor Sebastian Kapsky is dead."

The apparition smiled wanly. "Believe me, I am very much relieved that you and others believe so. Were it otherwise, I would not have a prayer of getting to the coast."

"The Germans were looking for Kapsky for quite some time. An SS Obersturmführer ravaged much of our region, interrogating scores of people and murdering dozens in the process. He did not locate Kapsky, but the Home Army eventually did. Rather, they located his corpse. That was the end of it." Daria glanced at the man holding the rifle. "I do not know what your intentions are, but I do not trust you. At my command or at the slightest provocation, Markus will be pleased to kill you."

The apparition raised his hands, palms toward Daria. "I have absolutely no intention of doing you or anyone associated with you harm. I have been moving about for over three years attempting to evade capture after escaping Katyn. Home Army assisted me when they could—often at the cost of their lives. The German patrols near the coast have been so numerous that I've not been able to penetrate. But then, among the multitude of corpses strewn throughout my travels, there was one that presented an opportunity—a ghoulish one, but such is war. I estimate the poor soul had been dead no more than a few hours, for there was no discernible decomposition. And it looked enough like me that he could have been a brother if not a twin. So I devised a scheme whereby I dressed the corpse in my clothes and left telltales that I hoped would convince the Germans to conclude that the corpse *was* me. And, therefore, they would discontinue their active search. It appears to have been successful. The SS Obersturmführer who led the German effort to capture me, and his men, seem to have left the area."

Daria scrutinized the apparition's face for several moments before turning to Markus, who tilted his head and shrugged, signaling he thought the story at least plausible.

Daria's eyes narrowed. "If you are indeed Kapsky you must understand that many Poles—perhaps more than a hundred—have died because of you. The SS Obersturmführer—an animal—who led the search for you executed many Poles to extract information concerning your location. Many, many more were tortured and disfigured because of you." Daria bit off the end of the sentence and spat. "Including my younger brother, Karol. He can no longer see. His eyes were gouged out."

Tears welled in the apparition's eyes and his face contorted with anguish. Daria immediately regretted her statement but could not summon an apology.

The apparition cast his eyes to the straw on the floor. "Many have been sacrificed because of me. I know. I know that. More acutely than even you, I wager. Please believe me when I say to you that I have many times considered surrendering myself. But I made a calculation. Perhaps an erroneous one. Undoubtedly one with which you would vehemently disagree. The calculation was that many more Poles—perhaps millions—might perish if the Nazis captured me and forced me to help them. And not just Poles, millions upon millions of others as well."

The apparition composed himself and looked at Daria. "I have given thought to killing myself, but I cannot do it. I suppose if I were captured, I might do so, but as long as there is a chance I might escape, I do not have the capacity to take my own life. I am sorry."

Daria and Markus once again exchanged looks. This time Markus's gesture was more emphatic. The phantom's story seemed not just plausible, but probable. Who would make up such a story? And for what purpose?

Daria silently scrutinized the apparition, debating the merits and consequences of assisting him. If he was a Nazi agent, rendering assistance could expose the entire network of resistance agents and Home Army fighters to the Germans, resulting in their likely extermination. Were she just to ignore him—and if his story were true—she might be providing the Germans a significant tactical, if not strategic, advantage. She decided to assist him . . . cautiously.

"You may stay here—it is relatively safe—until I am able to find a more secure location for you. I will ensure that you are given provisions." Daria turned to Markus but continued to address the apparition. "Should you provide the slightest impetus for doing so, Markus is authorized to shoot you—in the foot or in the head—whatever he deems appropriate for the circumstances.

"I will send word to one of our more resourceful *Armia* commanders about your existence. If he concurs, and only if he concurs entirely, we will convey you to him. He may be able to get you to the coast and secure transfer for you." Daria shook her head and sighed. "You understand the risks to all of us with this course of action," Daria said. "You better merit such risk."

"I am grateful and owe you a debt," the apparition responded with a slight bow.

"Your gratitude is immaterial to me," Daria said coldly. "You better be worth it or we'll find and kill you."

CHAPTER 33

Northern Poland
2311, 12 August 1943

Candy lay on the floor of the office, desperately trying to suck air into his lungs. The explosion from the 7.5-centimeter KwK L/24 had created a temporary vacuum while also knocking the wind out of everyone in the room. Candy's eyes grew wide as he inhaled against the lack of oxygen, his body feeling as if he were entombed in concrete. When the first rush of air did enter his lungs, he then felt as if he were drowning. He stabilized his breathing within seconds, only to be overcome by a sensation suggesting nearly every bone in his body had been pulverized. Mercifully, the sensation lasted only seconds, after which he looked about to see what had happened to the others. They all appeared to be alive and grappling with the same sensations he was experiencing. He could see Matuszek's mouth moving but could hear nothing except a shrill ringing that seemed to come from within his skull.

Candy rose to one knee, fell and rose again, before bracing himself and struggling to his feet. As he stood, he heard Matuszek's voice pierce through the ringing.

"*Move now.* As fast as you're able." He pointed behind Canidy to where a moment earlier there had been a wall.

Canidy shouted at Fulmar and McDermott to move, but they were already sprinting to the cavity in the edifice toward the woods beyond. Matuszek and his men, save one, did the same. The one who didn't no longer had legs for locomotion.

A second explosion blew all of them off their feet and sprawling onto the soft carpet of pine needles blanketing the forest floor. Once again, Canidy and the rest fought to suck air into their lungs as their eyes darted about, struggling to regain their bearings and reacquire their weapons. A blanket of dirt and debris rained upon them as they once again secured their weapons and started running as hard and as fast as they could from the source of the mayhem.

A fraction of a second later yet another explosion staggered but did not upend them as they ran. A random burst of MG 34 machine-gun fire followed them, to no effect other than to cause them to run even harder and farther.

The next shell exploded forty meters and at a seventy-degree angle to their right—indicating that rather than aiming for them, the Germans were simply saturating the area with fire.

Still, they kept running.

They ran until the fire was well behind them.

"Infernal panzers everywhere," Matuszek said between gasps for air. "They fire because they can, not because they have a particular target in mind. They just want to destroy."

Canidy said, "I thought the Wehrmacht was under orders to conserve fuel and ammunition."

Matuszek shook his head dismissively. "No, that is just German precision. They still like to shoot things up as often as they can." Matuszek said to his men, "All but Emil return to camp." His men vanished into the woods in seconds.

They continued moving away from the fire for ten minutes, when Canidy stopped and turned to Matuszek.

"Finish telling me how we save the world without getting ourselves annihilated in the process."

"Frankly, my friend, almost anything has a higher probability of success than infiltrating Germany and absconding with a document in the highly protective custody of the SS. An insane task."

"Insane tasks are what we do."

"Perhaps, but at least give yourselves a possibility, if not a probability, of success."

"You have our attention," Canidy said as they continued to thread through the woods.

"The item you are seeking, the one in Canaris's possession, is a document obtained by the SS from a deceased Polish mathematician."

Canidy said nothing.

"You need not confirm," Matuszek continued. "It may, however, interest you that reports of the deceased Polish mathematician's demise may have been premature."

Canidy stopped walking, which caused the others to stop also. "What in hell do you mean, *'reports of the deceased mathematician's demise'*? You were there. You saw his rotting corpse. That corpse wasn't coming back to life in this world."

"Perhaps not that corpse, my friend," Matuszek conceded. "But did it occur to you that maybe we were all wrong and the corpse was not that of the mathematician?"

Canidy, Fulmar, and McDermott stared at Matuszek in silence.

"You took us to the corpse. We determined it was Professor Sebastian Kapsky. And evidently the Germans did, too," Canidy said.

"The document in Canaris's possession allegedly came from the corpse," Fulmar added.

"Yes," Matuszek acknowledged. "All true. Note that I said 'perhaps.'"

"Look," Canidy said, "'perhaps' doesn't cut it. We're on an assignment. From the little Donovan has chosen to tell us, it's a pretty damn important one; suicide missions usually aren't about something trivial.

"Now, believe me, I'd rather be on a mission that had a reasonable likelihood of success, while permitting me to get laid in the process. Unless you have something concrete, we're doing precisely what Donovan told us to do."

Matuszek shook his head again. "War is never about certainty. Success and survival depends upon choosing the most viable option. And having a spot of luck. I cannot guarantee anything, but I have been fighting for ages and have lost many men. I've lost fewer over time with the benefit of experience. That experience tells me that there is a way to actually accomplish your seemingly impossible task and survive the mission."

"Well, stop beating around the bush," Fulmar said. "What the hell are you talking about? What have you got?"

"Professor Sebastian Kapsky may not be dead after all."

The looks on the faces of Canidy, Fulmar, and McDermott were of derision. Canidy's also betrayed contempt.

"He was doing a pretty good imitation of being dead when we saw him," Canidy said.

"*Someone* was doing a pretty good imitation of being dead," Matuszek agreed. "But there is reason to suspect that person may not have been Kapsky."

"This is absolutely nuts," Fulmar said. "Everyone saw him. We saw him. You saw him. And your troops saw him. Apparently, the Germans saw him and came to the same conclusion. *One* case of mistaken identity I get. But *everyone* making the same mistake reduces the probability that it is, in fact, a mistake to near zero."

"Besides," Canidy said, "the clincher is the document. Our intelligence sources maintain it was retrieved by the SS from *inside* one of Kapsky's body cavities. Apparently, the vaunted SS discipline couldn't prevent someone from squawking about it. On top of that, the genius Canaris and the rest of the infallible *Übermenschen* are sure as hell acting like they discovered Kapsky's Holy Grail."

"Misjudgments, errors, mistakes—they are all inescapable components of war," Matuszek said. "I have made more than my share, regretfully. And scores have paid the price for my missteps. Many have died because of my mistakes. I live with it only because I know I used all of my faculties to make the best judgments I could possibly make."

Canidy stopped walking and turned to face Matuszek. The others stopped also. "Look. *You* live with *your* mistakes. Don't expect us to make mistakes of our own. Hell, we don't even know what the hell you're talking about."

Matuszek pointed ahead. "Keep walking. The last thing you need is another panzer surprise."

"We're on our way to Germany, pal," Canidy said. "We'd be immensely grateful if you loaned us Emil to help us get there. The guy is a damn genius. Donovan gave us a task and we're gonna execute it or die trying."

"You will die trying. That's almost a certainty." Matuszek pointed in a southeasterly direction. "Keep moving while I tell you a brief story. Then if you like, you can take Emil—if he volunteers. I will not order it but will allow it." Matuszek halted abruptly, causing everyone to freeze in their tracks. They listened for a full minute before Matuszek resumed walking and the others followed suit.

"A short time ago one of our most reliable operatives had an encounter with an individual with a rather peculiar story. This individual had been observing our person for some time and apparently concluded she was neither careless nor a collaborator. She, in turn, judged him to be sober and truthful."

"Skip the background," Canidy said curtly. "Get to the point."

"The individual identified himself as Dr. Sebastian Kapsky."

Canidy stopped walking again and faced Matuszek. "You've really disappointed me. Everything about you to this point said 'tough, sober, competent.' Now you're telling us ghost stories." Canidy shook his head and resumed walking. "Telling ghost stories or stories you want us to believe. Stories *you* want to believe."

Matuszek nodded. "Skepticism and cynicism are good qualities in a commander, in a leader. It's more likely to keep you and those in your command alive."

"Damn right," Canidy concurred. "And it keeps you in the good graces of the man who gave you an assignment. In our case, a *very* serious man who has earned just about every citation known to a fighting man. Not someone to be trifled with. He gives you an assignment. You execute it. That simple."

Matuszek seized Canidy by the arm, startling him.

"Do not be an idiot, Major. I know of Donovan and his reputation. It's well earned. And I know how Donovan and men of his caliber think." Matuszek dropped Canidy's arm and closed to within inches of Canidy's face—their chests nearly bumping. With his jaw jutting forward, the resistance commander vaguely resembled Donovan himself. "Donovan chose you because he *expects* you will not blindly follow orders, but, rather, use your judgment; to improvise and change direction when the occasion demands." Matuszek poked Canidy hard in the chest for emphasis. "*Think*. That's why you are on this mission. *Think*."

Canidy swatted Matuszek's finger away. "I *think* you're nuts. Look, we have a short time frame to get this done. The longer the mission lasts, the greater chance it fails, that we end up dead or in a German POW camp." Canidy pointed to the rear. "Hell, we nearly got our butts blasted less than twenty minutes ago. We don't have the time or luxury to improvise. We have time to take one route, into Germany and to the Abwehr. We don't have time to go anywhere else. We have to commit to one destination and one destination only."

Fulmar came to within a few feet of the two. "Dick, my vote is to find the guy claiming to be Kapsky."

Canidy stepped back from Matuszek and examined his friend quizzically. "What the hell are you talking about?"

"Pretty simple, really. If we go into Germany, we're not getting the document, we're getting dead. Plain and simple. Sure, we can make a valiant effort, but in the end we're dead and no document.

"If we go to wherever the guy claiming to be Kapsky is, we may still get killed. But we have a better chance of staying alive."

Canidy looked incredulous. "We *may* have a better chance of staying alive, but no document. And we go back to Donovan empty-handed, telling him we went in the *opposite* direction from his instructions?"

Fulmar shook his head. "Matuszek's right. Donovan is the king of improvisation and adaptability. He *expects* that from *us*. Think about it, Dick: What's better, a document allegedly prepared by Kapsky, or the man himself?"

"Presuming he's Kapsky. Whom everyone has seen dead."

"I'm afraid I'm with Eric," McDermott said. "I'm not trying to avoid going to Tirpitzufer, although I have no desire to commit suicide. It seems to me, however, that the very implausibility of Kapsky being alive makes it that much more likely this bloke who claims to be Kapsky is, in fact, Kapsky. What benefit would anyone gain from claiming to be a math professor who everyone thinks is dead? And by everyone, I mean the tiny handful of people who even know who he is. Rather odd, wouldn't you say?"

Fulmar nodded emphatically. "McDermott's got a point, Dick. A guy who needs help doesn't say, 'Hey, my name is Kapsky. You don't know me, but I'm dead and I do math. Can you help?'"

A faint smile crossed Canidy's face and he turned to Emil. "Okay. Let's go. Lead the way."

Puzzled, Fulmar asked, "What?"

"We're going to find the guy who claims to be Kapsky," Canidy said.

"You changed your mind that quickly?"

"What can I say? You guys are very persuasive," Canidy explained.

A look of realization crossed Fulmar's face. "You just wanted buy-in from the rest of us, didn't you?" Fulmar said. It was a conclusion, not a question.

"Damn right. If we're going to disobey Wild Bill Donovan's orders, I sure as hell don't want anyone to say it was *my* idea."

CHAPTER 34

Kattegat Bay, Denmark
2351, 12 August 1943

There were Germans everywhere. Dour, uncompromising faces. The lamps along the pier illuminated their forms. They looked as if they would kill without provocation.

They were stationed at equidistant points along the pier and along the dock, rifles slung over their shoulders. In disciplined German fashion, they looked straight ahead. Unflinching.

But Gromov knew they were alert and could see everything. At least everything that was illuminated. He quietly slid off the dinghy and into the water nearly fifty meters from shore. He swam slowly toward the underside of the pier, careful not to make a sound. Once there, he grasped one of the struts supporting the boardwalk and waited in the gloom.

Less than ten minutes later he saw a shadow under the pier approximately thirty meters to the left. Its outline was that of a man, but beyond that he could discern nothing. It remained stationary for about a minute, as if observing him, before it began closing the distance between them. It took nearly a minute, the figure's pace slow, to minimize the possibility of any splashes or other noises.

When the figure drew to within three meters, he stopped, grasping a strut for support. Even in the gloom Gromov discerned the figure was a large, heavy man with thick, short blond hair. A Norseman.

"Magnus Nielsen," the Norseman whispered.

"Gromov."

Nielsen pointed behind Gromov, where the pier extended for another one hundred twenty meters. "Go there," Nielsen whispered.

They proceeded under the boardwalk, pulling themselves slowly from strut to strut to minimize splashes. It took several minutes to reach the end of the pier, where a small black raft sat, a middle-aged woman in the bow. Nielsen slowly and quietly hoisted himself onto the raft, followed by Gromov.

"Bridgette," the woman said.

"Gromov."

Bridgette began paddling slowly away from the pier. Gromov was certain they'd be detected by one of the German sentries, but they were facing toward the sea, oblivious to the raft's presence behind them. A minute later Nielsen grabbed another oar and began paddling also, quickening their pace. They proceeded at a forty-five-degree angle away from the pier and toward the rocky shoreline, saying nothing the entire time.

When they reached the shore, Nielsen secured the raft by looping a rope around one of the rocks and all three scrambled off the raft and into the adjacent woods. Nielsen led them to a small clearing with an abandoned, crumbling water well.

Nielsen stopped and turned to Gromov. "I have excellent news for you, Gromov," he said. "Your suicide mission is aborted. You have new orders."

Gromov blinked at Nielsen uncomprehendingly.

"You need not continue to Tirpitzufer," Nielsen continued. "Not that you had any realistic hope of getting there anyway. An associate of Jan Kubis forwarded a communique earlier this morning. You are being redirected to Poland."

Gromov frowned. "I have orders, Nielsen. You are to escort me to Forst Grunewald next to Tirpitzufer. This is an assignment of paramount importance." Gromov placed his hand on the rubberized holster containing his Tokarev TT-33. The gesture wasn't lost on Nielsen, who raised his hands to his chest, palms outward.

"What I'm telling you is that your orders have changed, Gromov. As have mine. Good fortune for us both."

"Who changed the order?"

Nielsen looked perplexed. "I do not know *who* changed them. I only know that they were changed."

"Who *gave* them?"

"Belyanov," Bridgette said.

Gromov looked at Bridgette. Her face was difficult to make out in the dark. Gromov reached into a waterproof pouch hanging from his belt, produced a book of matches, struck one on the box, and held it near Bridgette's face. She could tell that Gromov was surprised by her appearance.

"I was considered fairly pretty twenty years ago, Gromov."

Gromov didn't respond. Although she had a few lines across her forehead and around the corners of her eyes, Bridgette was astonishingly attractive. Indeed, Gromov found that the age lines added to her appeal.

"I am the leader of our cell," Bridgette explained. "We received a communication that originated from Czech Resistance only a few hours ago that you are not to go to Tirpitzufer."

"And these orders came from Belyanov?"

Bridgette shrugged. "That is what we were told. I do not know Belyanov. I only know that Belyanov, whoever he is, gave the order. The order was conveyed through Czech Resistance mere hours ago."

Gromov was both irritated and perplexed. He had made this journey to occupied Denmark to execute a mission that, if successful, would both vindicate and glorify him. He had no illusions about its difficulty. But as Belyanov had stated, a successful execution would nearly beatify him.

"What is this of Poland?" Gromov asked, his voice dripping with skepticism. "What am I to do there?"

"You are to execute your mission, Gromov," Bridgette replied matter-of-factly.

"My mission is to obtain a certain document in the Abwehr," Gromov said, not disclosing the additional instructions to kill the Americans. "I cannot obtain a document located in Berlin by going to Poland."

"I am merely the messenger." Bridgette shrugged. "Holger Danske was informed by UVOD by way of an *Armia* fighter by the name of Markus Zuchowski that a gentleman who calls himself Kapsky is under their protection."

Gromov stood silently, arms slack at his sides for several moments. "Dr. Sebastian Kapsky is dead."

Bridgette shrugged once more, indifferent. "Perhaps so. But apparently your Belyanov suspects he is alive and instructs that you locate and secure this Kapsky. As soon as possible. Apparently, Belyanov believes others are, or soon will be, searching for Kapsky also.

He also instructs that the remainder of your orders, whatever those might be, remain unchanged."

Gromov stood contemplatively for several moments. "Did Belyanov by any chance state precisely how I am to get to Poland and locate Kapsky? I haven't the slightest idea how to get there. I did not plan for this." Frustrated, Gromov waved toward Nielsen. "Is Magnus supposed to guide me there? Did Belyanov provide any guidance whatsoever?"

Bridgette smiled sympathetically. "Magnus is big and beautiful," she noted. "But he has his limitations. I will take you to Markus Zuchowski. From there you may execute your mission."

Gromov's jaw tightened. "It must be at least a thousand kilometers from here."

"Approximately," Bridgette conceded. "Thus, I suspect you should want to get on your way without a moment to waste." She observed the look of consternation on Gromov's face. "You should be pleased, Mr. Gromov. Your original mission was a death sentence. Now, at the very least, you have a prospect of survival." Bridgette drew closer to Gromov and inspected his face. "But mere survival, though welcome, is not sufficient for you, is it, Mr. Gromov? You have the look of someone who wishes to be a hero. Not that you aren't already. But you wish to be spoken about in worshipful tones. In awe. Preferably on national holidays. Am I correct?"

The killer Gromov, whose face was normally rigid and taciturn, looked down at Bridgette and, despite his best efforts, grinned. She'd accurately taken the measure of the assassin within mere minutes of meeting him.

"I am Russian," he said and shrugged.

"You need men to respect you and women to crave you," she said in a mockingly seductive voice. "You want martial hymns to be written about you, sung reverently on national holidays."

The assassin concluded that he liked this woman. Although she was Danish and more than a decade older than he, she seemed to understand him almost immediately, intuitively. Oddly, as opposed to every other woman he'd known, she didn't seem intimidated by him. Neither was she afraid. He sensed she was a kindred spirit; a killer like he, though by circumstance and necessity rather than nature and preference.

Bridgette, eyes still holding Gromov's, said, "Magnus, go back to the shore and send the signal."

For a big man, Magnus moved with surprising speed and agility. He was out of sight within mere moments.

"We've already arranged for a Kriegsmarine Schnellboot to take us to a location off the coast of Poland."

Gromov raised his eyebrows. "A Schnellboot?"

"Yes. It even flies a Reichskriegsflagge."

"How did you manage that?"

Bridgette smiled. "We stole it."

"You stole a vessel with six-thousand-horsepower Daimler-Benz engines? Were the Germans deaf?"

"Ours is a bit smaller, but it can travel over forty knots per hour. We had assistance from the Office of Strategic Services."

"Americans."

"Yes." Bridgette nodded. "They are quite resourceful."

"I have heard."

"The Schnellboot will take us to a location off the Polish coast. From there we will travel inland to Markus's location. We have documents that show we are Sanitätsdienst Heer, so if we encounter

Wehrmacht patrols we should be given passage, although we should avoid them at all costs. It should not take much time at all."

"Unless we encounter the Gestapo," Gromov said. "I doubt they will be fooled by your papers."

"We're unlikely to encounter Gestapo south of Danzig, where we are going," Bridgette said with another smile. "Besides, if we do, you look like you can handle the situation, Mr. Gromov."

Bridgette turned and began walking toward the coastline. "Come with me. Let's get started."

Gromov inspected Bridgette's figure approvingly as he followed. He was going from an apparent suicide mission to one that might merit the Order of Lenin, and present other intriguing possibilities.

CHAPTER 35

Berlin, Germany
0230, 13 August 1943

A single low-wattage lamp illuminated Standartenführer Maurer's desk as he sat with fists clenched and read the Eastern Front intelligence summary. The report, in typical Germanic tradition, was precise and exhaustive. The bulk of the summary pertained to the mammoth battle of Kursk, but three-quarters of the way through was an obscure reference to something that had been resolved some time ago. A Polish collaborator located approximately fifty kilometers south of Danzig had noted a drunken *Armia*'s casual reference to a ghost—a lunatic, really—who had the ability to change the world. The ghost claimed that he was thought to be dead and fervently wished to remain so. Supposedly, he was under the protection of the *Armia*.

No location was attached to the ghost/lunatic. Indeed, there was no other information in the report except for the lunatic's last name: Kapsky.

Maurer reread the passage. Then he stared at it, thinking. He'd verified Kapsky's death some time ago. More important, he'd retrieved a document from the corpse. The question wasn't whether Kapsky was dead. That was inarguable. The question was why would a drunken partisan—presumably some illiterate farmer—claim that Kapsky was alive? What benefit would possibly be derived from the claim? How would he even know who Kapsky was? Neither he nor whomever he was bragging to would have any idea who Kapsky was.

Maurer rose from his desk and walked to the map table at the center of the room. The area from which the report came was not far from the location where Kapsky's corpse had been found. Though navigating the area was treacherous, it was no more so than any war zone and, for the enemy, considerably less than an attempt to enter Germany.

Maurer placed an index finger at a point approximately thirty kilometers south of Danzig and traced it upward toward the Baltic near Danzig. Then he traced a line from Danzig to Tirpitzufer. He stared pensively at the map for a full minute.

Canaris had charged him with seeking and destroying the elements the Americans and Soviets had dispatched to acquire the Kapsky document. Toward that end, Maurer had been reviewing all Gestapo and Wehrmacht reports for any suspected Allied forays into Germany. There were precious few, most of which were from the west. Maurer suspected any intrusions would likely come from Denmark and perhaps western Poland, the former originating in the North Sea and the latter in the Baltic. He'd already dispatched one team to Danzig and another to Copenhagen in anticipation of such Allied forays. Indeed, he was slated to join his Danzig team the day after next.

SS Standartenführer Konrad Maurer slowly paced the length of his office, turned and paced in the other direction. He repeated the trek several times before deciding to play a hunch, something the regimented officer rarely did.

Napoleon played hunches, Frederick the Great played hunches. And when they did so, they conquered entire continents. Konrad Maurer would play a hunch.

He picked up the receiver of the heavy black telephone on his desk and began speaking without salutations to the Unterscharführer who had immediately picked up.

"Expedite all arrangements for Danzig. I will leave immediately."

CHAPTER 36

North Poland
0512, 13 August 1943

They walked quietly yet briskly through the woods, Emil on point, followed by Matuszek, Canidy, Fulmar, and McDermott. The accidental brush with the panzers only hours ago still had each of them on edge, keeping them alert despite creeping fatigue. Emil had informed them at the outset that they were approximately forty kilometers from Daria Bacior's location. Canidy estimated they'd already traveled nearly ten. At their present pace, with a few rest stops, they could arrive in a day or so. Canidy caught glimpses of gray through the canopy of leaves. Although the forest remained dark, the sun would be up soon. Canidy was uncertain whether he preferred darkness or light. The former made it easier to conceal themselves but also increased the risk they'd stumble upon a German patrol. The latter increased the probability they'd be seen, but improved their odds of sighting Germans.

Barely two seconds after that thought sparked across the synapses of his brain, he emphatically concluded he preferred neither.

The furious fusillade of machine-gun fire that ripped the bark off the trees adjacent to their column demonstrated that they'd both failed to conceal themselves and failed to avoid a German patrol.

All five dove to the forest floor as the fire continued to strafe and denude surrounding trees and saplings. Canidy scanned the area immediately around him and determined that none of them had been shot. They were spread in a fifteen-foot semicircle, Emil at the top of the arc, with Canidy and Fulmar to his left and Matuszek and McDermott to his right. Approximately forty meters in front of them he could see the fire from the weapon but nothing else.

"How many?" Canidy shouted above the din.

Matuszek said, "MG 42 machine-gun fire. I cannot see them, but an MG 42 means an eight- to ten-man *gruppe*."

Matuszek was drowned out by another furious spray of rounds barely three feet off the ground. *These guys sure aren't rookies*, Canidy thought.

Canidy was startled to see Emil stand and sprint in a crouch, looping to the right until he disappeared into the trees and darkness. Instinctively, Canidy rose and sprinted to the left. As he did so, Matuszek, Fulmar, and McDermott laid down suppressing fire, which was met with not just MG 42 fire, but scores of rounds from enemy rifles, one of which seared a shallow but painful gash into the same arm McDermott had wounded on the previous operation.

"Fire discipline!" Fulmar shouted. "That buzzsaw's got more rounds than we do."

"Hell, I can't shoot what I can't see," McDermott said, ignoring the sting in his arm.

Canidy hurdled logs and dodged saplings as he sprinted around the enemy's right flank to their rear. He prayed the din from the machine-gun fire drowned the noise of the snapped twigs and brush in his wake. He caught a flash of muzzle fire to his right and determined he was now approximately forty meters to the right and ten meters behind the enemy's position. He slowed to a walk and crept toward the fire spitting from the MG 42. When he drew to within twenty meters he dropped to the moist ground and began crawling toward the MG 42 placement as fire from Matuszek, Fulmar, and McDermott sliced the air overhead.

Just as Canidy sighted the Unteroffizier next to the MG 42, Emil flew from the brush at the opposite end of the German fire line, rifle slung across his back and an FS blade in his extended right hand. Before the Germans even knew he was upon them, Emil raked the knife across the trachea of the Gefreiter manning the MG 42 with such fury he nearly decapitated him. Canidy sighted the first German who had begun to react to Emil's attack and sent a .40-06 round through the German's right temple at the same time Emil thrust the FS into the abdomen of the soldier to the Gefreiter's left.

Canidy shifted his sight slightly to the left and fired two rounds at a bespectacled German who was just beginning to seize the MG 42 from his fallen compatriot. The first round missed, but the second round turned his face into a sickening mass of pulverized bone, blood, and brain tissue. With another slight shift to the left with his M1911, Canidy smoothly sighted and fired two rounds at a young German who appeared to be paralyzed by the ferocity of Emil's attack. Both rounds struck the young soldier squarely in the chest, propelling him backward as his Kar98k flew from his grasp.

Canidy rapidly searched for the remaining German troops. Two were lying facedown in the loamy soil behind a rotting log, apparently shot by some combination of Matuszek, Fulmar, and McDermott. The last German Canidy sighted was on his knees, Emil standing behind him with his left arm around the German's skull, holding the FS raised high overhead. Emil plunged the blade deep into the German's thoracic cavity, prompting a geyser of blood to erupt from the wound.

Canidy noted the look on Emil's face: Disciplined, stoic. Another day at the office.

The echoes of gunfire were quickly absorbed by the forest. Canidy lay still, listening for any signs of German reinforcements, a task made difficult by the ringing in his ears. After a few moments, he rose and moved swiftly toward Emil and the carnage surrounding him. Matuszek, Fulmar, and McDermott arrived seconds later, weapons at low-ready.

Matuszek poked and prodded the corpses, turning one over on its back. He pointed the rifle at the insignia on the corpse's uniform. "Waffen SS. Not regular army. Himmler's assassins."

Canidy said, "Well, we made quite a racket. They probably heard it all the way back in Berchtesgaden. Let's get out of here before their friends come looking for them."

"Hell, which way should we go?" Fulmar asked. "These guys were in our path. There are probably more in that direction."

"Well, we'll shift slightly eastward, then continue to proceed south," Emil said in the tone of someone who had just come from a tedious meeting. "These troops were likely attached to the Totenkopf regiment outside Tczew." He rubbed a trickle of German blood from his cheek. "They were probably off their assigned patrol and decided to bivouac here for the night."

Canidy massaged the back of his neck with his free hand. "I

hope you're right, Emil. And you probably are. But after getting a shot of adrenaline like that, I can't help but wonder why the SS is wandering around a backwoods place like this."

"Hell, Dick, it's war," McDermott said. "They could say the same thing about us."

"Right," Canidy said. "That's exactly right. We *are* wandering around the backwoods. But we've got a very specific reason for doing so."

"What's *their* reason?"

CHAPTER 37

Northern Poland
1209, 13 August 1943

Taras Gromov had a feeling of growing urgency.

Gromov detested feelings of urgency. He rarely had them. Gromov was usually the one who sparked anxiety, fear, and terror in others. The closest he came to feeling anything akin to urgency was a feeling of irritation.

Belyanov, by way of Czech Resistance and Bridgette, had conveyed that others were searching for Kapsky. Presumably, those "others" were the same individuals who had searched for Kapsky before—the ones Gromov was to eliminate. Belyanov didn't say where such individuals were or from where they had begun their mission. But since Belyanov knew they were already searching for Kapsky when he conveyed the message to Bridgette, those individuals already had a head start. Moreover, Gromov had first been going in a direction that took him *away* from Kapsky. Whereas the Americans, presumably, had been heading toward Kapsky from the very start.

Thankfully, they were making swift progress, primarily because of Bridgette's prodigious knowledge and talent. They'd traversed the Baltic to the Polish north coast without encountering a single German vessel. When she pointed out their expected landfall on a map, he'd protested, stating that it wasn't anywhere near Danzig, requiring them to make too much of the journey by land, thus vastly increasing the probabilities of an encounter with German troops. But so far, they'd avoided any such contact.

Gromov was thankful for Bridgette's proficiency. Without her, it would have been difficult if not impossible for him to even remotely make the progress he was making. He liked her. And he was attracted to her. Her attractiveness was not merely a consequence of intelligence and proficiency. Nor was it her face, which was the first feature he'd noticed. Though her clothing was rather utilitarian, he was able to discern that her face and intelligence were not the only impressive assets she possessed.

Her personality also suited him, another fact that made him struggle with his calculation that he most likely would have to kill her. He considered all of the reasons why he wouldn't have to do so, but thus far hadn't been able to persuade himself that there was an alternative. Nonetheless, he didn't have to kill her yet, and there was still time for circumstances to change. Besides, killing her would make navigating Poland very difficult.

Bridgette led him swiftly past several hamlets, all of which bore some scars of war. They remained on the outskirts, reducing the likelihood of encountering Germans or meddlesome villagers. At one point they rode, unbeknownst to the driver, in the bed of a rickety vegetable truck.

"You cannot tell who is friend or foe most of the time," she said.

"Best to stay out of range and, as much as possible, avoid 'interactions.'"

"Forgive me for asking," Gromov said. "But how do you know where you are going?"

"Czechs, Poles, Danes . . . The resistance network necessarily has scores of people like me—couriers, guides, informants, and even spies and saboteurs. We are not confined to one country. We travel throughout occupied Europe. I've traveled here several times since September 1, 1939. I've had the privilege of meeting Władysław Sikorski, premier in exile. Women are better at this than men. Men are conspicuous. Men are suspicious. The Germans trust no one, but sometimes women can pass where men cannot."

They walked cautiously along a dry creekbed in a sparsely populated area southwest of Danzig. They were careful not to stumble upon the unexploded ordnance strewn throughout the fields. Trees denuded of leaves, and in some cases bark, were evidence of what not long ago had been a seemingly limitless battlefield.

"Do you have an estimate of how much farther?" Gromov asked.

"Impossible to say. Much depends on whether we must make detours and whether and by how much we must change our route to avoid Germans. If we stay on this route, we should reach Markus's general location in somewhat under forty-eight hours."

"Unacceptable," Gromov said.

"Irrelevant," Bridgette said. "It is what it is. Who are you going to complain to?"

"There must be some way to speed our journey."

"Not without considerable risk," Bridgette informed. "We would need to rely on strangers and the happenstance of a passing vehicle. The Germans are devilishly clever. They send ordinary vehicles about the countryside driven by SS in civilian clothing. We have heard reports of resistance agents seeking rides from these vehicles, only to be executed by the drivers."

"So we walk?"

"So we walk," Bridgette confirmed. "Unless you see your mother driving a Kubuś down the road, and even then, I would insist that you hold your pistol to her temple as she drove." Bridgette touched her index finger to his left temple. Gromov seized her wrist reflexively and bent her hand away from him. He immediately released his grip, embarrassed by his reaction.

Bridgette stood mere inches from him and examined his face. "Gromov, I pity your station in life. It is clear that you are an assassin, a killer, and I suspect a very good one. Otherwise you would not have been sent by someone such as Belyanov. Because you are a very good assassin, that is all that you will do for as long as you live. Killers do not become cobblers, except in absurdly long Russian stories."

Gromov scanned Bridgette's face in turn. He detected no artifice, only despair for him.

They were startled by the sound of an approaching motorcycle somewhere beyond the curve of the nearby dirt road. They flattened themselves into the creekbed just as they heard the vehicle—a BMW with sidecar—shift and come to an idle a mere five meters above their position. Her face buried in the loose red dirt of the creekbed, Bridgette shifted her head to see two German soldiers scanning the area. They appeared not to have yet seen Bridgette or Gromov.

Before Bridgette could take her next breath, she watched as Gromov charged furiously up the slope and slammed his body against the rider and passenger, causing both to fly off the vehicle onto the road, with Gromov falling atop the passenger.

Gromov validated Bridgette's assessment of him with a display of savagery exceeding anything she'd witnessed in three years of war. Gromov thrust the three middle fingers of his right hand into the passenger's throat, crushing his trachea, then with both hands immediately grasped the driver's head and twisted it so forcefully that Bridgette could hear the vertebrae snap.

Without a pause, Gromov turned back to the passenger, whose desperate gasps for air could be heard even over the idling motorcycle engine. Using the edge of his fist as a bludgeon, Gromov brutally pounded the passenger's face for what seemed to Bridgette to be nearly half a minute.

The elapsed time between the vehicle stopping above the canal bed and the last breath of the passenger was no more than forty-five seconds. Even before Bridgette began walking up the slope, Gromov was dragging the motorcycle off the road and down to the canal bed. Within a few seconds, he'd done the same with the two bodies.

Gromov then turned to her. "We must move quickly—and not use the canal bed. We cannot lose more time." He turned and began walking briskly toward an adjacent tree line half a kilometer from the canal bed.

Bridgette followed, disturbed that she was unable to suppress an overwhelming swell of desire toward the assassin.

CHAPTER 38

Northern Poland
1312, 13 August 1943

For several hours Canidy's team moved swiftly but warily over the countryside toward Sztum before stopping in a cornfield near a small farmhouse to reorient.

"How much farther, Emil?"

"Ten, fifteen kilometers. Just a little east of Sztum."

"We'll stop here for a few minutes," Canidy said. "Get our bearings, think." He rattled his small rucksack and looked hopefully at Matuszek. "Any chance the farmer can spare any decent food?"

"None of them can," Matuszek replied, "but they will. We must be careful. The Germans will kill them if they find out . . ."

"Also," Emil added, "these farmers are very suspicious. The Germans have killed a number of them; torched their crops if they assist *Armia*. Sometimes the Germans send troops dressed like civilians to see how the farmers react. I do not know how often this happens, but it doesn't have to be very frequent. If the farmer provides assistance, the Nazis will make a not-very-pleasant example of him.

If he is fortunate, maybe a chicken or two is taken. Sometimes something much worse happens. A very effective method of keeping people in line. The uncertainty of retribution is much worse than certainty."

"Do they know you?" Canidy asked Matuszek.

He shook his head. "They may know of me, or the rumor of me, but it is unlikely that they've ever seen me." He pointed to Emil. "I would not be surprised, however, if they know of this fellow."

Canidy looked at Emil and grinned. "That's obvious. Based on what I saw back there, I suspect his legend has spread far and wide throughout the countryside."

Emil's expression remained taciturn, but Matuszek smiled. "In fact, that is not much of an exaggeration. I myself have heard tales told by old men and young women. In desperate times, people need heroes. Regrettably, heroes do not survive long in this theater," Matuszek said. "If the SS find him, they will execute him, most likely in a village square, where attendance is mandatory."

"Do they know who he is?" Fulmar asked.

"They are Germans," Matuszek said. "They have extraordinarily detailed files on much of the *Armia*."

Canidy said, "We need rations. We're low as it is, and we've got a way to go. We shouldn't arrive hungry, if we're fortunate enough to arrive at all. If it *is* Kapsky, we're going to have to move him quickly before we draw a crowd and the Germans are alerted."

"I will go," Emil volunteered.

"We'll all go," Canidy said. "But you make the contact. We'll stay out of sight so as not to alarm the farmer." Canidy pulled up his M1911. "Let's go." The five threaded through the cornfield to remain unobserved until they came to within thirty meters of the farmhouse. It was the size of a small cottage. Through the window closest to them they could see the kitchen. They watched for a full minute but saw no movement.

"I am going in," Emil said. He crossed to the front porch with his rifle at the ready. The door appeared to be ajar, so he pushed it open with his right foot, raised the rifle to his shoulder, and proceeded inside. The rest of the team waited for a signal that they could enter. They waited for more than thirty seconds before Canidy decided to go in. He was followed by the rest, each brandishing their weapons at the ready.

The first thing Canidy noticed was the smell—something akin to rotting meat. It took only a few seconds for him to discover the source: a man's torso lying atop dried blood on the kitchen floor. No head, no legs, just arms spread at odd angles. From the maggots visible at the neckline, Canidy surmised the remains were several days old.

Emil appeared from a hallway that led to a small dining area. "Two more bodies are back there," he informed while cocking his head over his right shoulder. "I cannot tell if they are male or female. They appear, however, to have been adults."

Canidy's face was drawn into something between a scowl and a grimace. To no one in particular, he asked, "What do you think? Interrogation? Retribution? Making an example?"

"Probably all three," Matuszek replied.

Canidy shook his head, partly from disgust and partly in anger. "What does this have to do with war? These are civilians. There's no sign they were combatants."

"I wish I were carrying a camera right now instead of this rifle," McDermott said.

"Cameras can't kill Germans," Matuszek said.

Fulmar blinked several times as if trying to recall something. Then he placed his M1 on a nearby table, reached into his left front pocket, and pulled out a cigar cylinder. The others watched as he unscrewed the cylinder and pulled out not a cigar, but another cylindrical object slightly larger than his index finger.

"Peculiar time for a smoke, lad," McDermott said.

Fulmar pulled both ends of the cylinder, which extended another two inches, revealing a rectangular lens at the center. "I'm disappointed you don't have one of these," Fulmar said to McDermott. "I would have expected that your man Fleming would have insisted you carry one. He's big into gadgets, isn't he?"

"What is that supposed to be?" McDermott asked.

Canidy laughed as if remembering a joke from the past. "It's a camera," he informed. "It supposedly can take a photograph at close range. At least, that's what Donovan told us. We haven't tried it." Canidy patted his breast pocket. "I have one, too, but completely forgot about it. Donovan had some technicians at the Office gin these up. I think the idea was we could at least take a photograph of the Kapsky document if for some reason we couldn't actually abscond with it or if the document was later destroyed. I don't think any of us actually thought it could work."

"What good is a photograph of a massacred farm family?" Emil asked.

"Accountability," Canidy replied. "To have a record of what happened. The Office is compiling evidence for after the war."

"I do not understand," Emil said.

"I can't say I do, either," Canidy conceded. "But Donovan sees things five to ten years ahead of most. He insists it's important to have a record of events."

"He is a historian, this Donovan?"

"He's a lot of things, including being twelve steps ahead of almost everybody else."

"Where is the . . . flashbulb?" Matuszek asked. "It is so small it does not appear capable of producing a photograph. Where is the film?"

Canidy shrugged. "Hell if I know. They give this stuff to us, show us how to use it, and we don't ask questions. It either works or it doesn't. We'll find out eventually."

Fulmar manipulated a metal lever on the right end of the cylinder, aimed the lens at the remains on the floor, and then flipped it downward. He waited, as if expecting something to happen. Nothing did.

"When does it take the photograph?" Emil asked.

Fulmar smiled sheepishly and returned the device to his pocket. "I think it just did, but I don't really know."

"Let's look for some food," Canidy said. "Something we can take with us."

"I saw a basket of bread on a shelf next to the stove in the next room," McDermott said. "I'll go get it."

The rest rummaged around the small edifice but found little. They gathered next to the front door and took inventory: at most a day's worth of stale bread for the five and a roll of hard sausage. Canidy shrugged. "It is what it is. Let's get out of here."

They ate as they walked, rifles slung over their shoulders. Although it wasn't much, the food was enough fuel for the day—buoyed by the prospect of a more substantial meal once they reached their destination.

They were grateful that most of their path was relatively desolate. It was evident that most of whatever meager population had once inhabited the area had evacuated or been destroyed during Barbarossa. Hamlets and farmland were covered with craters, scorch marks, and makeshift cemeteries. Emil deftly guided them around a minefield, a detour that added another hour to their journey. After a few hours, the topography changed from plains to low, rolling hills but remained relatively desolate. Canidy could see a road a half kilometer to the east. There appeared to be a dry creek or canal bed parallel to the road.

"Does that take us where we need to go?" he asked Emil.

"Generally speaking," Emil acknowledged. "I know what you're thinking. Why not walk along there? Riverbeds are usually good for cover and navigation. But not one like that. It's too exposed to traffic on the road above. Better to stay amid the fields. Slower progress, but better coverage."

"Time," whispered Canidy, "is not our friend."

CHAPTER 39

Northern Poland
1441, 13 August 1943

Maurer had replicated the scene numerous times over the last few years. It had proven highly effective: Petrify the citizenry to elicit information. Break their will. Make even the toughest cower and submit.

Five SS Panzer IVs sat in a precise line in front of a small fountain in the village square, where Maurer sat imperiously in the rear seat of his Horch Kfz, its top down. His visor was drawn low over his forehead, just above his sunglasses. He sat motionless the entire time it took his troops to roust the residents from their dwellings and herd them into the square, where they first gawked at the panzers and then at the menacing figure in the car.

The crowd consisted of women, old men, and children of all ages. As in most such villages, most of the older boys and men were either dead or fighting somewhere. Any men or teenage boys that did remain were the first to be placed in the center of the square. They would be made to kneel with their hands clasped behind their backs. Those that were slow to do so or who outright refused would be shot at the first refusal. Thereafter, obedience was almost always universal. The men knelt for nearly an hour as the SS searched the village and rounded up the remainder. Spouses and children saw husbands, fathers, uncles, and brothers added to the queue. All remained absolutely silent, as if any noise, any utterances, might prompt violence from the SS guards.

The longer they knelt, the more some began to falter. One of the older men fell onto his face. An SS guard strode quickly to his position and struck him in the back of the head with the butt of his rifle. When the man righted himself, his face was smeared with blood from his broken nose. He appeared more dazed than frightened. An Unterfeldwebel faced the semicircle of assembled villagers grasping a Walther P38 in his right hand, which hung at his side. He spoke casually, without raising his voice.

"We are seeking Sebastian Kapsky. He is somewhere in this village. We know that. We know someone is harboring him. We do not wish to visit any harm on any of you or your village. We seek only Kapsky."

Maurer sat quietly and comfortably in his command car, allowing his subordinates to conduct the investigation and interrogation. He understood that his silence made his presence that much more ominous.

The Unterfeldwebel strode behind the line of kneeling men for several seconds, saying nothing. Then he stopped behind a middle-aged man, the left side of whose face was disfigured. Maurer watched the Unterfeldwebel lean forward, whisper something into the man's ear, and discharge his Walther P38 inches from the man's head. Screams and cries erupted from the crowd as the man winced from the weapon's sharp report.

The Unterfeldwebel walked to the end of the line and repeated the maneuver with a boy of twelve. More screams and cries from the crowd. The boy, however, refused to flinch and continued to gaze forward with a look of defiance. A moment later the Unterfeldwebel discharged the weapon into the back of the boy's skull, the round causing his face to explode outward. The body fell forward to the horrified shrieks of his mother and three younger siblings.

Maurer remained expressionless and motionless. Through his sunglasses he could see the villagers with pleading expressions, willing him to put an end to the nightmare. They understood the Unterfeldwebel was operating at the will of the Standartenführer and could do nothing without his approval.

The Unterfeldwebel moved behind an old man kneeling next in line. "Kapsky," the Unterfeldwebel said to the crowd, "he is here among you. Deliver Professor Sebastian Kapsky now." A gurgle of cries and whimpers issued from the crowd. Not of protest, but of resignation. Maurer could hear nothing intelligible. The Unterfeldwebel placed the muzzle of the weapon against the base of the old man's skull. The man closed his eyes; an oddly serene look covered his face.

"The mathematician Kapsky," the Unterfeldwebel said, standing with his free hand on his hip. "Give him to me." He waited no more than two seconds before discharging his weapon. A single, piercing shriek came from somewhere in the crowd. The man fell forward. Maurer remained motionless, though behind his sunglasses his eyes scanned the villagers' faces for reaction, anything that might betray knowledge of Kapsky's whereabouts. All he saw was anguish. All he heard was sobbing.

The Unterfeldwebel took a step to the right, free hand still on his hip, and placed the muzzle of his Walther to the back of another grandfatherly-looking man. Wails of desperation rose from the crowd.

"Kapsky. Produce him."

Maurer rose to his feet and slowly stood erect in the back of the command car, giving the crowd a look at his impressive physical presence. The crowd fell silent and the Unterfeldwebel let the Walther fall to his side.

An Unteroffizier opened the rear door of the vehicle in anticipation. Maurer stood for several moments, his hands clasped behind his back, expressionless. Then he descended onto the square and strode casually—chin tilted upward and black boots gleaming—to the line of kneeling men, stopping within five feet of the man at the center.

There wasn't a sound. There wasn't a person whose eyes weren't riveted to the SS Standartenführer.

Maurer scanned the crowd. He addressed them in a conversational voice, several leaning forward, straining to hear.

"Perhaps Kapsky is not here. Perhaps he was not here. That is immaterial." Maurer paused and again scanned the crowd. He could sense their tension. "Whether Kapsky is here, whether he *was* here, does not concern me," he repeated. "Unterfeldwebel Dietz has demanded production. We know that if he is not here, he is nearby. And we know that someone here knows his location. *Armia* knows his location. Therefore, someone in this village knows his location. Or knows who can produce him.

"Tell me now and no one else will be harmed." Maurer paused and surveyed the assemblage as if assessing whom to execute. "Fail to tell me and be assured, starting in sixty seconds, we will execute one of you every thirty seconds until Kapsky's location or his presentment is secured."

Maurer looked up to each of the machine gunners in the row of five panzers. Almost in unison they pulled the bolts on their MG 34 machine guns. Then he nodded almost imperceptibly to Unterfeldwebel Dietz, who snapped to rigid attention, awaiting Maurer's signal to blow the grandfather's brain tissue through the front of his skull.

A teenage girl fell to her knees wailing. She was joined by a chorus of other women, a few of whom shouted "Please" to the gathered to confess anything they might know about a Sebastian Kapsky's whereabouts. The kneeling grandfather began shouting curses, entreaties, and obscenities at Unterfeldwebel Dietz, alternately pleading for his life and daring him to shoot.

The bedlam continued for nearly a full minute before a tall, middle-aged woman with striking red hair raised her hands above her head to attract the attention of the crowd, which became silent. She turned to Maurer and asked, "Is this Kapsky a tall man with green eyes and a bolt of thick black hair at his forehead?"

Maurer eyed the woman for a moment and replied, "He is."

"He was near Sztum a week ago."

A hint of a smile, something resembling gratitude, covered Maurer's face. "Splendid," he said softly. Then he turned to Dietz and nodded once. Dietz discharged his weapon into the neck of the grandfather kneeling before him, cleanly severing his skull from his spine.

The villagers erupted in a cacophony of horror. A frail elderly woman collapsed to the ground. Maurer pointed at the fresh corpse. "This is what happens when you withhold information, even for a second. The rest of you have been spared only because information ultimately was provided." Maurer faced the redheaded woman. "But be assured, if the information is false or even merely flawed, I will back."

Maurer returned to the rear seat of his vehicle and commanded the driver to proceed to Sztum. The five panzers roared to life and followed in a single line, leaving the grieving villagers huddled over the dead bodies, praying that Kapsky was indeed in Sztum. The woman with the striking red hair watched as the Germans receded into the distance. Then she turned to the villagers and waved her arms over her head to get their attention. It didn't take long. After several seconds they grew quiet and focused on her in anticipation.

"Andrej?" she called loudly.

A short, stocky bald man with a scarred face and pronounced limp separated from the crowd. "Here."

"Get on your motorcycle and go as fast as you can to Malbork. Tell my sister Daria that the SS devil is on his way to Sztum in search of Kapsky. It is only a matter of time before he learns Kapsky is not there and the devil will then kill as many as necessary to learn that Kapsky is with Daria in Malbork. She must move. She will know what to do."

Andrej disappeared into a nearby alley and within seconds the crowd heard the roar of a motorcycle and saw a cloud of dust waft from the alleyway. After a moment, their heads turned back to the redhead in anticipation. She addressed them in a powerful, commanding voice.

"We must all leave at once," she instructed. "Gather only necessities for a day's journey and then disperse. It is best to go east, but whatever direction you choose go *now*. I pray you have good fortune."

"But we are doomed," a woman cried. "We cannot outrun the SS. It is useless."

The redhead shook her head firmly. "You are not doomed. Unless you remain here. Once you have placed some distance between yourself and this place, they will not know where you are from. They won't remember your individual faces. But if you remain here, they will return and they will execute every last one of those they find."

CHAPTER 40

"Not much farther," Emil said, pointing to a narrow pass between two wooded hills. "Just a couple of kilometers beyond that gap."

Emil's comment spurred them to pick up their pace.

"Hell, if Kapsky's not there we're really screwed," Canidy reminded them. "We must be hundreds of miles from where we're supposed to be."

Fulmar said, "We'll know soon enough. Fingers crossed. If we chose right, we'll get a medal and maybe a pat on the back from Donovan. If we chose wrong, the consequences—"

"Better not to think about it," Canidy interjected. He pointed to the hill on the right. "Emil, can we see the town from the top of that hill?"

"Much of it," Emil replied, anticipating Canidy's question. "If there are any Germans there, we should be able to spot them."

Minutes later Canidy determined Emil was right. Kneeling at

the crest of the hill, they had an excellent view of most of the edifices and roads in the town. Better yet, there was no evidence of German soldiers.

"Where's your *Armia* contact?" Canidy asked Matuszek.

Matuszek turned to Emil. "Same place as before?"

Emil nodded and pointed to one of the larger structures on the western perimeter of the town. "Markus likes that barn over there."

Canidy pointed to the trees to their right. "The trees go all the way to the back of the barn. If we stay just inside the tree line, we'll be able to reach the back door without being seen. I don't see anybody, but if we encounter any Germans, we need to kill them as quietly as possible, find Kapsky, and get the hell out of here as fast as humanly possible."

Canidy rose and began descending the hill, followed by Fulmar, Matuszek, McDermott, and Emil. Staying within the tree line, they were at the back door three minutes later. Canidy listened for any sign the structure was occupied.

Hearing nothing, he nodded to the others, who were holding their weapons at low-ready, and pushed the door open slowly. He expected a creak, but it was silent. Matuszek placed a hand on Canidy's shoulder and moved in front of him. "Better I go first."

Matuszek stood outside and called softly, "Markus? Markus Zuchowski, you lazy sack of shit. Are you asleep?"

The door opened wide to reveal a beaming Markus Zuchowski. Matuszek clapped him on the shoulder and gazed toward Canidy, Fulmar, and McDermott. "Don't shoot them. They're Americans and a Brit. We're here for Kapsky."

Markus frowned. "Daria took him. We received word just a short time ago from her sister that an SS Standartenführer is searching for him. *Seriously* searching for him. Daria had recently moved him to just south of Malbork. Now they'll have to move again shortly."

"Where did you say?" Canidy asked.

"Malbork. The Pomerelia region. The biggest castle in the world is there." Markus pointed to what appeared to be radio equipment in the loft. "She also sent word of her destination to the OSS contact stationed in the Baltic."

Matuszek pointed to Canidy and Fulmar. "These men are OSS."

"That was fast," Markus said and whistled.

"We were dispatched days ago," Canidy explained. "You sure it's Kapsky?"

Markus shrugged. "He claims to be a mathematician everyone is searching for. I do not know. He seems intelligent. Unusual green eyes."

Canidy exhaled audibly. "Kapsky. At least it looks like we made the right choice not going to Germany," he said. "For now."

"By any chance, is the SS officer you mentioned Konrad Maurer?" Matuszek asked.

Markus nodded. "It sounded like his methods."

"How far to Malbork?" Canidy asked.

"Fifteen, twenty kilometers north," Matuszek said. "Not far, but not easy." He turned to Markus. "I recall there is a house we kept there . . ."

"That's where she is headed," Markus affirmed.

"We are—how you say—in business," Matuszek told Canidy. "It is SS Totenkopf area. Very treacherous. But we have smart, tough fighters there."

Canidy looked at Fulmar and punched him on the shoulder. "Odds are we still get killed, but if we make it at least there, probably won't be a court-martial."

CHAPTER 41

Donovan and Stimson waited for the President in the Map Room, Donovan with a scowl and Stimson with a faint patrician air of disapproval. Neither approved of the Map Room for a meeting such as this. It was too large and airy. The acoustics were not suited for a highly sensitive discussion, but FDR hated being confined to the Oval Office and insisted on a change of scenery.

The President entered the room, assisted by Laurence Duggan, who stationed him at the head of the long map table, both Donovan and Stimson to his right.

FDR had a mischievous look in his eyes.

"I've discovered a nearly foolproof way of winning the war and winning it quickly," the President said. "It is quite simple, really. Keep Georgie Patton thinking he is about to be relieved of command. Every time he gets in trouble with Ike or Marshall, or *thinks* he's in trouble with Ike or Marshall, he commits himself to proving to the world—no, not just to the world, but to posterity, to the scribes who will write the history of this epic engagement—that he is the greatest fighting general that this country has ever produced." The President leaned forward as if disclosing a confidence. "And frankly, though I abhor his politics, he *is* the finest fighter we've ever produced. Would that we had two more like him. One more in the European theater and one in the Pacific—though I would expect there would be a titanic clash of egos with Doug MacArthur." The President chuckled at the prospect. "Wager as to which ego will prevail?" He examined the two men before him. "And here we have the two most humorless men who have ever provided counsel to an American President in time of war."

The President removed his cigarette holder from the corner of his mouth. "By God, gentlemen, lighten up. We only have a world-wide war to win. It's not as if we must structure myriad Potemkin villages to confront an economic crisis. War, after all, is something one can understand and address in a rational manner."

Stimson and Donovan remained still.

"All right, gentlemen, we shall remain dour in accordance with your wishes," Roosevelt conceded. "Now, what is it that demands that two men of your elevated status convey information to the commander in chief? Only bad news, am I right? A debacle?" There was a gleam in the President's eyes. He enjoyed projecting flippancy at serious moments.

"Mr. President," the secretary of war said. "There appears to be good news regarding the Kapsky operation. He is in the protective custody of the *Armia* somewhere in northern Poland."

Roosevelt looked exuberant. "Outstanding. He was thought to be deceased, was he not? A remarkable, unexpected development. But what is the likelihood he will remain secure?"

"We understand he is being guarded by several *Armia* troops, and the Germans are completely unaware of his whereabouts in an area east or southeast of Sztum."

FDR laughed and slapped his leg. "War is a cascade of the unexpected. And sometimes it's even good news. We certainly can use it." He paused thoughtfully, then asked, "What of our men who we sent to retrieve the Kapsky document in Germany? I was given to understand the likelihood of their success was nearly nil, as was the likelihood of survival."

Donovan shook his head. "We did not expect to hear from them unless and until the operation had been executed, Mr. President. The assumption must be that they are now somewhere in Germany . . ."

"Or captured. Or dead," Roosevelt concluded.

"There is a good probability of either, yes, sir," Donovan said. "There has been no update regarding their status from our contacts among the resistance groups."

"Are your British counterparts aware of this development?"

"Not to our knowledge, Mr. President," Donovan replied. "We wanted, of course, to inform you first."

"Yes. I will inform the prime minister," Roosevelt said. "He will insist, I'm sure, upon a joint extraction effort." Roosevelt tilted his head back and gazed at the ceiling for a moment. "Is one even feasible?"

Donovan's face assumed a look of bulldog determination. "Mr. President, the Office has many capabilities. We are designed for innovation."

"You are saying, Bill, that you will do your best. I understand. What about our various resistance contacts?"

"They're quite admirable, Mr. President. They can provide assistance, of course. But an extraction operation would be an enormous challenge. Our best bet would be a joint American/Brit operation with the help of local resistance intelligence."

Laurence Duggan appeared at the entrance to the room. The three looked at him expectantly.

"Mr. President, excuse me. Mr. Hopkins asked that I remind you of the meeting with the speaker. He's waiting outside the Oval Office. Shall I send him here instead?"

Roosevelt appeared irritated. "Yes, please do. In five minutes."

Duggan retreated and Roosevelt looked to Stimson and Donovan. "Gentlemen, domestic policy matters await. Thank you both for the smashing news of Kapsky." Stimson and Donovan took this as their signal to depart and stood. "I trust your judgment regarding this extraction. Your best estimate as to how long that may take?"

Stimson looked at Donovan and then back to the President. "Ten to fourteen days, sir."

"I understand you're starting from scratch again, Bill," Roosevelt said. "I won't hold you to it. I know that you and your people will do their best." Roosevelt looked down for a moment and then back up. "Any hope for the men we sent to retrieve the document?"

Donovan wore his usual look of determination.

"They were extremely resourceful men. That's precisely why they were selected for this operation."

Donovan's use of tense was not lost on the President.

CHAPTER 42

The five ate voraciously.

Markus had taken up a collection of food from the locals. He didn't tell them the purpose; they assumed it was for the Resistance and gave what they could. Individually, they could spare little, but cumulatively it amounted to a feast for Canidy and his men.

"What the hell is this stuff?" Fulmar asked, pointing to the object in his hand. "It's incredible."

"Pierogies," Matuszek answered. He pointed to a large pot in the middle of their semicircle. "And that's bigos. Don't ask what's in it. But it will give you energy for the next few days."

"Meats, vegetables, and kraut," Emil informed them, dipping a hard roll into the stew. "Very cheap but very filling."

"Hell yes," Canidy mumbled, nodding in agreement as he chewed ravenously. "A pot of this and we can march on Berlin." Canidy pointed to the pierogies. "Everybody, grab as many handfuls as you can and put them in your rucks. We don't know when we'll eat next." Canidy turned to Markus. "You say fifteen to twenty kilometers to Malbork?"

"Closer to twenty. Somewhat wooded. Fairly flat."

Canidy then looked to Emil. "Do you know how to get us there?"

Emil, chewing vigorously, nodded until he was able to swallow. "I've not been there before, but I know how to get there."

"Do I have your permission to take him?" Canidy asked Matuszek.

"I am coming also," Matuszek said. "My men are in capable hands in my absence. It is best to have an old peasant along to communicate with the locals."

"The more the merrier. As long as we can stay out of sight of the Wehrmacht," Canidy said. "Emil, any estimate on how long it will take?"

"Provided we are not delayed by the Germans, less than a day by foot."

Canidy washed down the bigos with a long drink of water. "Okay. Markus, how secure is this place?"

"No place is secure, but we have used it since the invasion with no problem."

"Good. We haven't slept or rested in a long time. Don't know the next time we can. We'll get a few hours' sleep here and then push on. If we do find Kapsky it will likely be another push to the coast without rest." Canidy looked about the barn. "Find your spot. I'll take first watch. Then Fulmar, McDermott, Matuszek, and Emil."

Markus shook his head. "All of you rest. I will stand watch."

"Outstanding," Canidy said. "Thanks. Okay, get some rest. We move when I wake up."

CHAPTER 43

The large office on the fourth floor of the Lubyanka was utterly silent. No footsteps of aides hurrying to discharge commands, no chattering of typewriters producing reports and orders. When the large oak door leading to Aleksandr Belyanov's office was closed, it was understood he demanded not necessarily silence, but quiet.

The door, however, had been shut for nearly an hour, and before he'd closed it Belyanov had appeared uneasy, even apprehensive. No one dared disturb him.

Belyanov sat rigidly at the desk staring at the decrypted message and assessing how to convey the contents to Beria. Beria was precise. Beria was exacting. Beria punished mistakes, however slight.

This was a massive mistake.

Contrary to what Belyanov had told Beria, the Americans were not oblivious to the possibility that Kapsky was alive. In fact, his likely survival was known to the highest levels of American government. Belyanov had previously informed Beria that the Americans were unaware of Kapsky's existence, that they'd futilely directed their efforts at acquiring a Kapsky *document* in the custody of the Abwehr. In fact, they now were focused on acquiring *Kapsky*.

Belyanov had assumed Gromov had a head start, that the Danish Resistance had turned Gromov in the right direction. Belyanov had conveyed that assumption to Beria, who had been pleased. Now Belyanov had to inform Beria that, at the very least, the Americans were aware Kapsky was alive and were, or soon would be, sending a team to secure him. Beria famously did not like corrections or amendments to previous reports. He expected reports to be right the first time.

The last Belyanov had heard from the Danes was that they'd made contact with Gromov. Since then, nothing. Gromov could be dead or wounded. He could be detained. Gromov didn't realize he was in a race against the Americans. The last he knew, the Americans believed Kapsky was dead.

Belyanov rose from his chair to give Beria the news, hesitated, then sat back down. He stared straight ahead as he tapped his index finger on his desk, thinking. He desperately did not want to tell Beria that they'd made a mistake, that the Americans were aware Kapsky was alive and they would try to rescue him. He wanted to present Beria a report of a spectacular accomplishment. Why tell Beria of a mere *assumption* that might not yield negative consequences? Why not wait to see how it plays out? After all, Gromov still had a head start on the Americans, and Gromov was exceptionally proficient.

Belyanov continued to tap the desk with his index finger. He concluded, quite rationally, that there was no need to inform Beria that the Americans would be dispatching someone to acquire Kapsky. That was a contingency, not a result. Instead, Belyanov would send a communique to the Danes to relay a message to the woman guiding Gromov: Tell Gromov the Americans were coming for Kapsky. Expedite the operation to acquire Kapsky. And all other orders, including those pertaining to the competition, remained unchanged.

No need to trouble Beria with a minor wrinkle. No need to aggravate him with every contingency. Belyanov was determined to present the boss with only one report: success. And he was determined not to share the fate of the untold masses who entered the Lubyanka in the morning, never to be seen alive again.

Maurer sat patiently in the rear of the command car as it drove over the pockmarked dirt road, a light coating of dust covering his clothing and sunglasses. The engines of the trailing panzers masked the sound of the BMW motorcycle with sidecar that approached from behind until it pulled parallel with his door. The Oberschütze in the sidecar saluted and tendered a folded piece of paper. Maurer retrieved the document, returned the salute, and opened the message; it stated that Soviet NKVD has been informed that the Americans believe that Dr. Sebastian Kapsky was alive and in the custody of the Home Army in Poland. They were dispatching soldiers to acquire him.

Maurer folded the message, tore it into small strips, and let it flutter from his hand into the wind. So it was now a race among the Germans, Soviets, and Americans. No doubt the British were somewhere in the mix. No matter. The race was being run on German-occupied land. And the German entrant in the race had five SS panzers with two MG 34 machine guns and a 75-millimeter cannon. More important, the German entrant was SS Standartenführer Konrad Maurer.

CHAPTER 44

Northern Poland
1835, 13 August 1943

They'd seen the dust in the distance, kilometers away. To be seen from a distance, the volume of dust must have been generated by large vehicles. They were moving slowly. But not as slowly as Gromov.

Gromov liked Bridgette. She was intelligent, capable, and attractive. But she was slowing him down, and that aggravated him.

Nonetheless, he needed her. She had contacts and resources that were helpful. Had it not been for her, Gromov would probably still be in Germany on a futile mission that likely would have ended in his death. So he was grateful. But in Gromov's world, gratitude had limits. It did not supplant duty or efficiency.

"You are tired and hungry," Gromov said.

"You are not?"

"That is irrelevant."

"Not so, my dear Major Gromov. We must execute the assignment. We need your strength and wits. I am merely your guide."

"A rather exceptional one," Gromov said, despite his irritation with their pace. He was sincere. Absent Bridgette's knowledge of the area—the terrain, distances, and locations of German forces—Gromov wouldn't have made nearly the progress he had.

There was even a fair probability that he would've been killed or captured by now. Nonetheless, they needed to move faster.

"You're tired and hungry," Gromov repeated. "Perhaps a short rest is in order. I can forage to replenish our provisions."

Bridgette dismissed the suggestion with a curt shake of her head. "I can walk faster, Major Gromov. I do not mean to slow you down." She pointed to low hills approximately two kilometers to the southeast. "Besides, just beyond those hills should be our destination. Czech Resistance informs that there are partisans there who are quartering Sebastian Kapsky. The partisans likely can provide some food, and far more quickly than if we forage."

Gromov felt a spark of anticipation. Throughout their journey he'd been anxious that someone would get to Kapsky before he did. The anxiety wore on him. He needed to *see* his objective, know that he could discharge the mission. Especially since Belyanov had judged that he'd been "twice shy."

He would not get a third chance.

He noticed that despite being tired and hungry, Bridgette had picked up her pace. In fact, to his surprise, he'd fallen several steps behind. He accelerated to draw abreast. "You are quite a good soldier," he said sincerely. "Many Russian women make fine troops . . ."

". . . but Western women do not?" Bridgette finished.

"I suspect they do," Gromov said. "I've not had occasion to observe it until now. You are exceptionally resourceful and dutiful. Thank you."

Bridgette smiled and nodded. "I do my best." She pointed northeast. "But thanks may be premature." Gromov looked where she was pointing. The dust cloud was approaching far more rapidly than either of them had calculated. Though obscured by the dust, Gromov determined that the cloud was produced by at least half a dozen vehicles.

"It is somewhat difficult to tell from here, but I suspect they are several armored vehicles," Bridgette opined. "Panzers, with a motorcycle at the rear."

The spark of anticipation Gromov had felt reverted to anxiety. He was not a believer in happenstance. The competition for Kapsky was about to become pitched.

The Germans were on their way.

They moved almost at double time, Emil in the lead and Canidy nearly abreast. They'd slept far less than any of them had anticipated, nervous energy compelling them to get to Kapsky as quickly as possible.

"I haven't seen much evidence of German occupation in this area," Canidy said to Emil.

Emil shook his head. "We must not be complacent. We are skirting the western edge of the Reichskommissariat Ostland. A few kilometers farther west is an SS nightmare. I am taking a slightly longer route to avoid the area with densest German occupation."

"Hell of a childhood you've had there, Emil."

"The SS Totenkopf are present throughout this area. The Einsatzkommandos are notorious; frankly, merciless. They have slaughtered thousands upon thousands of innocents. The very fact that there is resistance in the face of such terror is extraordinary."

"It would be normal, even natural, to capitulate, hoping one day to be liberated," Canidy agreed. "In the meantime, just keep your head down."

"Some, out of terror, desperation, or calculation, do capitulate. They inform, collaborate. But relatively few, given the circumstances. Poles do not bend to tyranny. But all it takes is a few."

"With Russians on one side and Germans on another, you've plenty of experience with tyranny."

"That is—how you say?—an understatement." Emil pointed north. "There is a camp near Stutthof, only a few kilometers from here. It is difficult to get near because of the dense SS presence. Also, it is surrounded by electrified barbed-wire fences.

"There are dozens of barracks there housing government officials, religious leaders, scholars—but mainly Jews, Jews of every kind: shopkeepers, farmers, teachers, craftsmen. Ordinary people who have committed no offense.

"It is a place of evil."

"Evil? That's not a distinguishing feature in a war zone, Emil," Canidy noted.

"It is in this case. The prisoners there are not combatants. They are not soldiers. They are mere civilians—men, women, and children. Innocents. They are being slaughtered in great numbers."

"We've heard about camps like that. Count Raczyński gave a speech to the League of Nations about them. But without actually seeing them, lots of people just have a hard time believing anyone could do that—even the Nazis."

"Believe it. The SS has constructed chambers that emit gases, poisonous gases. Hundreds at a time are herded into these chambers. The victims are gassed to death and then placed in a large crematorium and incinerated. Some say the stench can be smelled over ten kilometers away.

"Those not immediately gassed upon their arrival at the camp eventually die of starvation or disease. I have not seen this with my own eyes, but my compatriot Milo, the one who was killed yesterday, saw the camp and described it to me. I have heard whispers from others, also."

"We understand there are at least half a dozen such places."

"More. There are at least half a dozen much smaller related or— what is the term?—*satellite* camps in the Danzig area. Larger ones are scattered throughout Poland. Evil."

"If we make it out of this place, first thing we do is let OSS know the location, although something like that—if it's even remotely as you describe, well, *it must* be known to the Allies."

Emil pointed west. "We are getting close to Malbork. It is a short distance in that direction. Remain alert. There are numerous hamlets between here and there. More populated than where we have been traveling. There are probably a few checkpoints. We will try to remain within cover of forest where possible, but we will be exposed from time to time."

"How much longer?" Fulmar asked.

"I have not gone to that location before. But I estimate just a few more hours if we are not forced to make large detours."

Fulmar made a snorting noise. Canidy turned to see what prompted it. "What?"

"Just thinking about our orders."

Canidy nodded acknowledgment. "Right now we'd be on a wild-goose chase in Germany looking for some damn piece of paper."

Fulmar shook his head. "No, we'd be dead. Now we may be

within a few miles of Kapsky himself. If we can come back with Kapsky . . ."

"Let's not get ahead of ourselves. We're on the most dangerous territory on the planet." Canidy smiled. "But, hell yes, if we come back with Kapsky, Donovan will owe us drinks until doomsday."

CHAPTER 45

Northern Poland
1919, 13 August 1943

Bridgette pointed to a small white barn as they stood on the hill overlooking the village.

"That must be it. Kapsky's location. It appears deserted."

She fell silent as she and Gromov watched the cloud of dust approach the outskirts of the village. A car followed by five panzers.

"It appears we are not Kapsky's only visitors," Gromov said.

"What should we do?"

"We have only one option. Get Kapsky before the Germans," Gromov replied. "Let us hope they do not know Kapsky is in the barn. While they search for him it presents an opportunity for us to retrieve him and escape—hopefully unnoticed."

Bridgette pointed toward the vehicles. "We should do it now. It appears they are rounding up villagers for interrogation. It is only a matter of time before someone talks."

"Do they know about Kapsky?"

"I do not think so. Our contact and her assistant should be the only ones. But we cannot be certain no one else has seen a stranger in the area."

"The SS will suspect any stranger might be Kapsky," Gromov said.

"They must."

"Let's go," Gromov said abruptly.

"Where?"

"We have no choice. We cannot wait. We must get to the barn and get Kapsky before they do."

They descended the hill at a brisk pace, losing sight of the German column as they did so. They wove among the trees at a trot until coming to within fifty meters of the barn.

"What is your contact's name?"

"Daria," Bridgette replied. "Only she and her assistant Markus should be in the barn."

Gromov advanced rapidly, Tokarev at the ready and Bridgette trailing a few meters behind. Opening a side entrance, he blinked to adjust to the gloom and scanned the barn, locating a man he assumed was Markus in a loft-like area next to radio equipment. Upon seeing Gromov, the man's face registered alarm and he began to lunge for his rifle resting against a wooden beam. Before he could reach it, Bridgette yelled, "Markus, I am Danish Resistance. Bridgette."

Markus seized the rifle but remained still save for the rapid blinking of his eyes.

"Danish Resistance," Bridgette repeated. She pointed to Gromov. "Major Taras Gromov. Red Army. We are here for Kapsky. We are here to help. We are here to get him to safety."

Markus held his rifle on the pair as he descended the stairs. Gromov held his pistol over his head.

"Markus," Gromov said. "A column of panzers just arrived. They are in the square. They are surely looking for Kapsky. He must leave immediately. We can escort him to safety."

Markus continued to hold his weapon on the pair as he approached. "A column of panzers arrives in the village at the same time you enter my barn," Markus said slowly.

Gromov nodded. "Yes. We concede. Too coincidental. You are right to be suspicious. Any soldier would." He gestured toward Bridgette. "Bridgette is Danish Resistance. Your people, as I understand it, have communicated with her before. We are here to secure Dr. Sebastian Kapsky. You have no time to waste before the Germans smash through the door with their panzers."

Markus stared at Bridgette. "You received the message."

"Yes."

Markus lowered his weapon. "Kapsky is not here. We received word that the Germans were on their way so Daria took him elsewhere."

"My job is to get him out of occupied Poland, Markus. I can do that, but I need to know where he is."

"There is no need," Markus replied.

"There certainly is," Gromov said. "You know their methods. They will come in here and extract the information from you no matter how much you resist. Painfully. They will get Kapsky."

Markus shook his head. "What I mean is a team of Americans, *Armia*, and a British soldier were here. They are already on their way to collect Kapsky and remove him from Nazi-occupied territory. They left some time ago on foot. Provided they've not been intercepted, they are probably within a few hours of Malbork."

Gromov became rigid and bit the inside of his lower lip to keep from cursing. The Americans. They were supposed to have gone to Germany. They were ahead of him.

"That is excellent news," Gromov lied. "How long of a journey on foot?"

Markus shrugged. "It depends on how many Germans they must avoid. The area is saturated with SS. But they have an outstanding guide."

"An estimate?" Gromov asked.

"Not far. A few hours from here. They left a couple of hours ago."

Gromov struggled not to show his frustration. He turned to Bridgette. "Do you know how to get to Malbork?"

"Are you thinking of going there? For what purpose?"

"They may not get there. Or, if they do, they may need assistance. Our orders are to get Kapsky out of harm's way. I cannot tell my superiors I deferred to the Americans and British, that I heard from a man I never met before that the Americans were on their way. What if they are not successful? What if they do not even get to Malbork?"

"You heard Markus. They are far ahead of you. They will be gone by the time you get there."

Markus said, "Stay adjacent to the paved road that leads you north. It is in that general direction."

"We cannot go on the road."

"Yes, but you can stay near it."

"It is futile," Bridgette said. "You cannot catch up. You are only imperiling yourself."

Gromov stared at the straw on the floor for several seconds and then looked up. "Thank you for your help, Markus. You must leave *now*. When the Germans find you with the equipment upstairs, you will be dead." He turned to Bridgette. "We also must leave now."

"Where are you going?"

"South of Malbork."

Bridgette rolled her eyes. "Impossible."

Gromov grasped her right arm with his free hand, pulled her toward the barn door, and peered outside. No Germans.

"I'm going to be moving quickly and quietly. You must run as fast as you possibly can to follow me."

Without uttering another word, Gromov bolted from the door toward the tree line forty meters away. Then he paused to allow Bridgette to join him. He put his finger to his lips and then began moving rapidly through the trees and brush for several minutes, navigating in the direction of the village square. Bridgette followed close behind.

As they drew near the square, their pace slowed and they moved quietly and cautiously. They halted just within the tree line and watched as German soldiers herded dozens of villagers into the east side of the square at gunpoint.

On the opposite side of the square an imposing figure stood in the rear of a Horch command car. Arrayed behind the car was a row of five panzers, their MG 34 machine guns trained on the villagers. Behind the line of panzers sat a Zündapp KS 750, a driver and passenger seated in their respective seats.

Gromov assessed the scene for scant seconds before telling Bridgette, "Watch me and act appropriately."

Then he inserted his sidearm into his belt, withdrew his NR-40, and sprinted from behind toward the motorcycle. Both driver and rider were oblivious to his presence until he wrapped his free arm around first the driver and then the passenger and sliced their necks to the bone. He pulled each of their bodies from their respective seats, dragged them to the ground, and mounted the motorcycle.

He waited no more than a heartbeat as Bridgette climbed into the sidecar. Then he kick-started the vehicle and sped from the square onto the northbound road recommended by Markus.

Startled, the German troops in the square took several seconds to realize that the motorcycle was being stolen. By then, the vehicle was nearly two hundred meters down the road and obscured by thick clouds of dust. They began firing haphazardly to no affect until a disgusted Maurer ordered them to cease.

Gromov didn't throttle down until they were more than a kilometer from the village. Even then, he stayed at more than sixty kilometers per hour.

Bridgette's chest was still heaving from exertion and exhilaration.

"What will you do if we encounter a German patrol?" she shouted over the din.

"Drive past them as if there is nothing wrong and hope for the best."

"What if they try to stop us?"

"Then I will kill them, too."

CHAPTER 46

Northern Poland
0617, 14 August 1943

It was more a small cluster of dwellings—barely two dozen—than a village or town.

The house in which Kapsky purportedly was hiding was as described by Markus: a small one-story wood-and-brick affair consisting of, at most, four rooms situated at the north edge of the village.

The last two kilometers of the journey had become increasingly treacherous. Emil was right. The SS seemed to be everywhere. Whoever had decided to move Kapsky here, Canidy thought, had made a mistake. There had to be a better place than this to hide. Or maybe it was sheer genius. Very few would suspect someone wanted by the SS would pick a place crawling with them in which to hide.

The five observed the house from inside the ruins of what appeared to have been a general store that had been struck by a mortar some time ago. The shattered piles of bricks, blocks, and mortar provided outstanding cover. They had not spied any sign of civilian activity since they'd arrived a quarter of an hour ago, but a Totenkopf squad had patrolled within seventy-five meters of their position, eventually passing out of sight.

"I'm going in with Matuszek. Daria knows him," Canidy said. "The rest of you remain here and provide cover and keep watch." He pointed to a window on the right. "Watch that window. If Kapsky's there, I'll signal and you be ready to move."

"Then what?" Emil asked.

"Simple. Then we bring him out and we make our way back to the canal."

"What if a patrol stumbles upon us?"

Canidy shrugged. "Use your head. Avoid them if you can. Kill them if you must. But *quietly*."

Canidy looked about before he and Matuszek rose from the rubble and jogged to the front of the dwelling. For a moment Canidy felt foolish. What was he supposed to do, knock on the door and then ask for Sebastian Kapsky? Absurd. But after a short deliberation, that's precisely what he did: two quick raps at the door, his free hand gripping the pistol at his waist. The door opened immediately and a redheaded woman pulled them inside and shut the door. She embraced Matuszek heartily.

"Roch, it is good to see you," she said, grasping his wrists.

Startled by how swiftly the woman had opened the door, Canidy asked, "How did you know who was at the door? There are Germans everywhere."

"I have been watching you for several minutes. You really are not very good at concealing yourselves." She pointed out the window. "See for yourself."

Canidy peered out the window and was appalled to find that he could see the scalps of Fulmar, Emil, and McDermott above the rubble. He had to look very closely, but they were visible none-theless.

Matuszek wasted no time. "Daria, is Dr. Sebastian Kapsky here with you? We are here to get him to safety."

Daria hesitated, examining Canidy.

"This is Major Canidy of the United States Office of Strategic Services. He has been dispatched by the highest levels of the United States government to secure a document from Dr. Kapsky. I was able to convince him he might be able to secure Dr. Kapsky himself. I trust him."

"SS are everywhere," Daria said.

"Yes, we know."

"I received a message from my sister Ilsa to move Dr. Kapsky immediately," Daria continued. "An SS officer is searching for Dr. Kapsky. His name is Maurer. He has something of a reputation. He was on his way to our previous location, so we came here, a place we've used before—but that was before the Germans seemed to triple in number. Especially Totenkopf. I am afraid it is only a matter of time before Maurer arrives or we are discovered by the Totenkopf. So we will need to move him once again. Clearly, Dr. Kapsky is a priority for them."

"He's a priority for us, too," Canidy said. "Is he here?"

"He is in the cellar," Daria replied.

"No, I'm right behind you," Kapsky said.

Canidy saw a tall, thin man with intelligent green eyes and a shock of black hair across his forehead. He looked like the descriptions Donovan had given him. He looked haggard and ill.

"Dr. Kapsky, I'm Major Canidy. This is Commander Matuszek. We are here to escort you to safety."

"How, may I ask?"

"By any means necessary."

Kapsky, though worn, appeared amused. "I assume you are singularly capable of doing so, otherwise your government wouldn't have chosen you from literally millions of candidates to conduct this operation."

"Capable or expendable, it's unclear which."

Kapsky asked, "You two are to perform this task? Again, how, if I may ask?"

"Before I answer that, answer this: Our original assignment was to retrieve or find you. We did. At least we found your corpse. Along with a notebook containing indecipherable equations. Apparently, the equations are so complex and advanced that it's taking forever to understand. Our next assignment was to retrieve another document created by you: yet more mathematical equations, which document is in the possession of the Abwehr. Two questions: How are you here and what's on that document?"

"You need to verify that I am Dr. Sebastian Kapsky?"

"The last one was dead."

"The corpse you encountered was a decoy. I had subtly spread information of my whereabouts. Then I found a corpse—unfortunately not a difficult task in Poland these days—and placed it where you found it. I had the rather macabre good fortune of finding a corpse roughly my dimensions and appearance. I dressed him in my clothing. But I could not be certain, of course, that those searching for me would necessarily conclude it was me as opposed to some other unfortunate. So for good measure, I crafted both a notebook and a document—a scroll—containing an encrypted series of equations that related to matters the scientific establishment, and, therefore, intelligence services, knew I was working on. The notebook, I estimated, was sure to be found. But the addition of the scroll was in order to be certain to convince the finder they'd found something of extraordinary value. I inserted the scroll into the corpse's mouth to give the appearance that I was trying to destroy it—to keep it out of hostile hands—before I was killed, to convey the impression it was of utmost importance."

"Perhaps too clever," Matuszek said. "We did not see it. It seems you may have shoved it too far down the corpse's throat. Not to worry, however, the meticulous Germans found it and have it in their possession."

"And both you and the Germans abandoned the search for me. You see, I needed the *certainty* that the Germans would cease looking. Both the scroll and notebook contain very complex but ultimately counterfeit equations that scientists would initially conclude pertain to an advanced rocket propulsion as well as a crude atomic device. I expressed the equations in code to slow them down, so it would take considerable time to determine that the equations are infeasible. I would, therefore, have sufficient time before they concluded the same—sufficient to make my escape."

"I do, however, have a notebook with genuine work in it," Kapsky said, patting the right side of his shirt. "Right here. It contains the salient corpus of my work. Taped to my side. Be sure to take it if I do not survive."

"You can bet on it." Canidy walked to the side of the window and waved, alerting the rest. "Dr. Kapsky, it's time to move. If you have anything else that's essential, get it now. I suggest it weigh no more than five to ten pounds total."

"I have no possessions."

"Good." Canidy turned to Daria. "Ma'am, you're welcome to come, but I can't guarantee your safety. My priority is Dr. Kapsky."

"I will remain here. I am a Pole. I will be all right." She grinned.

"I have outwitted and bedeviled the Nazis for several years. Why stop now?"

Kapsky kissed Daria on the cheek. "Thank you for everything. Good luck to you. I will see you after the war."

All of them fell silent upon hearing the rumble of a motor vehicle. Canidy stood to one side of the window and looked out. A truck carrying six German soldiers in its open bed passed slowly in front of the house and out of view. The rumble continued for another thirty seconds before fading.

Canidy eyed Kapsky and Matuszek. "On three."

Matuszek and Kapsky both asked, "What?"

Canidy smiled. "We move out after I count to three. Fast."

Before he could begin counting, a German foot patrol emerged from the direction in which the truck had disappeared. From his spot next to the window, Canidy counted eight. He felt the hairs on his arms stand on end as the patrol moved slowly past the rubble where the others were hiding. Canidy signaled to Matuszek to be ready to move, but by the time Matuszek moved to the other side of the window the patrol was receding to the east. Within a minute they were out of sight.

Canidy didn't move. Matuszek frowned. "Dick? Let's go."

Canidy held up a hand. "This isn't going to work."

Puzzled, Matuszek asked, "What do you mean 'This isn't going to work'?"

"Just that. There are far too many Germans in the area. Too high a risk."

"What are you saying?" Kapsky asked. "That we stay here?"

"No," Canidy replied, thinking as he spoke. "*I* am staying here. *You* are leaving. With Matuszek."

Matuszek looked bewildered. "What?"

"There are too many Germans. We don't stand a prayer of avoiding them much longer. My job is to deliver Kapsky from this hellhole safely. The best way of doing that is to make the Germans think Kapsky is alive and here."

Matuszek and Daria looked perplexed. Kapsky smiled, anticipating what Canidy was about to say. "A live decoy instead of a dead one."

"Precisely," Canidy said. "Matuszek, you and Dr. Kapsky are going to join the rest of our group and get the hell out of here. Get him to the canal and Kristin's boat. From now on, I am Dr. Sebastian Kapsky, although immeasurably better looking."

Matuszek and Daria stared at Canidy, perplexed. Kapsky continued to smile.

"Pretty simple, really. If a dead decoy could keep Dr. Kapsky alive for so long, a live, moving decoy should do the trick even better. The Germans will be looking for me, a moving target. More specifically, a target moving in a different direction than the real Kapsky."

"You cannot survive," Matuszek said somberly, with a hint of anger. "You do not know the area. You will be caught or killed. Perhaps both."

"We'll see," Canidy said cavalierly. "If Daria just points me in the right direction, I'll take them on a hell of a wild-goose chase and take some pressure off you guys." He extended his hand, shaking first Kapsky's and then Matuszek's. "Now go."

Matuszek glanced out the window. "Clear. Follow me."

Matuszek opened the door and ran toward the rubble, Kapsky just a few feet behind.

Fulmar, McDermott, and Emil provided cover. Upon reaching the rubble Matuszek squatted next to Fulmar. "He's not coming. He's acting as a decoy for Dr. Kapsky here." Kapsky nodded his introduction to Fulmar.

"That's so . . ." Fulmar restrained himself. This was, after all, Dick Canidy. *Nothing* was unexpected. Without a pause, he extended his hand toward Kapsky. "Dr. Kapsky, Eric Fulmar. By order of the President of the United States of America, we are taking you to safety."

Standing next to the window, Canidy watched as Emil led them out of sight.

"You must have a large meal before you go," Daria said. "You do not know when you will eat again. I have latkes already made."

"Thanks. I'll take them with me, if you don't mind."

Daria went into the small kitchen and began wrapping latkes in wax paper. Canidy asked, "How did you know to move Kapsky?"

"My sister Ilsa sent word that the SS was searching for him and were on their way to Sztum."

"What about Markus? We met him in the barn there. Why didn't he go with you?"

"Markus is originally from there."

"If the SS locates him, he's dead."

Daria nodded solemnly. "Yes." A moment later she smiled mischievously. "Markus is quite resourceful, however."

"As is Kapsky," Canidy observed.

Daria placed the wax paper–wrapped latkes in a cloth bag and handed it to Canidy. "Quite resourceful," she agreed. "He escaped from Katyn using his wits."

"Katyn? The place the Nazi's chief liar, Reichsminister Joseph Goebbels, claims the Red Army supposedly executed thousands of Polish officials and intellectuals?"

"We in the *Armia* heard stories," Daria explained. "More than stories, we saw thousands upon thousands of intelligentsia—doctors, academics, administrators—rounded up by the Red Army and sent to Katyn Forest, where we suspected something terrible was occurring. The Soviets, of course, denied they were executed. But Dr. Kapsky was there. He *saw* it, the executions. And now he's escaped."

Canidy stared at her. "So the Red Army—the Soviets actually did this? It's not just Nazi propaganda? The *Soviets* killed Poles?"

Daria nodded. "Kapsky confirmed it. Bodies stacked in shallow graves. He saw it himself. A credible witness. Not a Nazi propagandist or Soviet *propagandist*. Thousands, maybe tens of thousands, executed. Most of them, he says, by one man with a handgun."

Canidy rubbed the back of his neck and exhaled. He doubted OSS—or any Allied service—had actual verification of this information. Canidy knew little of diplomacy or the compromises Allies made, the fictions that were tolerated, to forge and sustain coalitions. But he knew intuitively that what he'd just heard from Daria, if accurate, had the potential to significantly disrupt the relationship between the U.S. and the USSR, as well as the conduct of the war. The Katyn fiction would be blown wide open.

"Daria, is this common knowledge among Home Army? Among Poles in general?"

She shook her head. "In war one hears lots of things and lots of people hear things. But the only person who was *there* is Dr. Kapsky. He is the only live witness who is not Red Army. Be assured, if anyone had actual proof of it, *Armia* would have known. The knowledge would have spread like wildfire."

Canidy sat on a wooden stool and pondered the implications. He understood instinctively he now had two missions: draw the Germans away from Kapsky, and get home alive in case the first objective wasn't met. *Someone* had to convey the Katyn Forest information to the Allies.

Daria scrutinized Canidy's face and understood. "You didn't believe you were going to evade the SS, did you? You were only planning to distract them for a while so that Dr. Kapsky could escape."

Canidy shook his head distractedly. "I'm not sure what I was thinking."

"But now you cannot simply sacrifice yourself because you must convey the Katyn information to your superiors, correct?"

Canidy exhaled. "Something like that."

"Sacrificing yourself for a worthy objective is noble, but sometimes much easier than ensuring that an objective is actually met. The former is heroic, but the latter is responsible. It is easier to be a heroic martyr than a responsible one."

Canidy chuckled wryly. "A responsible martyr would have been sure to have a guide get him back to the boat. I just dispatched mine. I have a general idea how to get there, but now I have to be *sure* to get back."

"Where do you need to go?"

"All I know is it's a canal on the Baltic near Danzig."

Daria said, "I can guide you to Danzig. It will be quite hazardous. But I do not believe I am familiar with this canal. Where near Danzig is it located?"

Canidy chuckled again. "I suppose I should have paid closer attention. I depended upon McDermott and Emil. I have a decent recollection, but I can't ask you to do this. It's tantamount to a death sentence."

"Be assured, I'm aware of the risk. Living in Poland under the Nazis is nearly—" Daria stopped abruptly and looked at the window. A German patrol was approaching the house. As she quickly proceeded to the kitchen, she looked over her shoulder at Canidy and said, "Come with me. *Now.*"

CHAPTER 47

Northern Poland
0801, 14 August 1943

Gromov pulled the motorcycle off the road and into a dense grove of pear trees. They had encountered no German patrols, but he didn't want to press their luck. According to Markus's directions they were nearing Malbork and the likelihood of running into Germans increased every minute.

Bridgette pointed to a depression several meters into the grove. Gromov wordlessly guided the vehicle into it and cut off the engine. They dismounted, stepped back, examined the area from the road, and satisfied themselves that the bike was invisible.

They could hear the rumble of heavy vehicles to the north, in the direction Markus had given them. Both felt pinpricks of nervousness. Both assumed the Germans in Sztum had radioed ahead that someone—likely *Armia*—had killed two of their men and escaped northward.

"This area is not familiar to me," Bridgette said. "I've never been here."

Gromov chuckled. "As difficult as it may be to believe, I didn't expect you to know all of Europe."

"I'm afraid I will just slow you down."

"I could move a lot more quickly on my own," Gromov conceded. "But after acquiring Kapsky I need help getting him to safety. My original instructions were to acquire the Kapsky document and return to Kattegat, where your people would ensure that I get back to Soviet territory."

"I can help you there," Bridgette said. "We will proceed in a northwesterly direction until we near the coast. We'll have vessels near Mikoszewo and Krynica Morska that can take us to Kattegat. Not Schnellboots, but serviceable. I have used one before. We may have to wait for them, but they are reliable."

"Please tell me again how my original assignment was a death sentence as opposed to this one."

They proceeded quietly but briskly through the woods for nearly a quarter hour, the rumbling of the heavy equipment to the northwest gradually growing louder. Both were startled by a prolonged burst of machine-gun fire to the rear. Instantly, they dropped to the ground and remained silent. Another short burst of fire sounded. Then nothing except the rumbling to the north.

"Someone found the motorcycle," Gromov concluded.

"That was too fast," Bridgette said. "This area must be saturated with Germans."

"They're taking precautions. They don't know precisely when the motorcycle was abandoned, so they are strafing the area just in case."

"Do you mean they know the motorcycle was stolen?"

"That's exactly what I mean. That wasn't random. A patrol—or patrols—is searching for us."

They remained prone for a minute, listening for signs of nearby German presence, before rising and continuing northward. The woods quickly began thinning and the rumbling grew louder. They could see glimpses of movement approximately half a kilometer north.

Gromov stopped and dropped to a knee, Bridgette coming alongside and doing the same. A German armored column was proceeding from west to east. Panzers and troop carriers. Gromov could see neither the head nor the rear of the column.

Bridgette pointed toward the vehicles. "I see rooftops down that slope on the other side of the column. That must be where Kapsky is."

Gromov's jaws clenched. "A stupid place to hide. Germans everywhere."

"Perhaps not so stupid. Who would think to look for him in a place like this? Anyone would expect he would hide in a place where there would *not* be Germans."

"Stupid," Gromov insisted.

"Not stupid. Difficult," Bridgette said. "For us."

Gromov said nothing.

The cellar Daria had directed him to was small, dank, and dark, with a musty smell. No lights.

Canidy had caught a glimpse of some small wooden shelves lined with jars before Daria had shut the trapdoor behind him after he'd descended a short ladder. He heard something scurrying about the dirt floor around him. Too small to be rats, he convinced himself. Likely mice. He balled his fists and bit his lower lip.

He heard a voice overhead, guttural, imperative, unmistakably

German. Then he heard Daria's voice, even and calm. Although he didn't understand what was being said, he knew the issue: "Have you seen someone named Sebastian Kapsky? I do not know such a man. Have you seen anyone more recently? No. Is there anyone else here? No."

Footfalls heavier than Daria's traversed the floor above. Not many. The house was small, not much to search, not many places to hide. Canidy estimated three men above. Maybe more waiting outside.

He withdrew his M1911 and aimed at the cellar door, his grip tight. There was another German imperative sentence followed by a three-word question. He could hear no response and assumed Daria shook her head either yes or no. Then silence.

He sensed something small run over his right boot, yet somehow resisted the urge to shake his foot. Only good trigger discipline prevented him from involuntarily discharging his firearm.

The voices above became somewhat indistinct. He strained to listen, but was unable to discern what was being said. The inflection of the German soldier's voice was that of a question. Canidy couldn't discern Daria's reply, but the tone of the German's voice became skeptical, then insistent, then urgent. There were a few seconds of silence, then the German's voice became loud enough to startle a swarm of small, unseen creatures whose scurrying movements Canidy could hear around him. The grip on his pistol remained steady as he bit harder on his lip in an effort not to be distracted. He could hear himself breathing: short, ragged, and shallow. He strained to hear any sounds whatsoever from above for the next thirty seconds. Nothing. Not movement, not voices. Then he heard the sound of heels moving rapidly and purposely on wood. He held his breath, but the noise was *receding*. The Germans were leaving.

Canidy continued to train his pistol on the trapdoor. He heard nothing for nearly a minute, then the sound of light footsteps, the steps of someone small.

Then silence for nearly three minutes that seemed to Canidy far longer.

The cellar door opened and Daria's face appeared from above. Canidy lowered his weapon slowly, then looked about the floor of the cellar for whatever had been scurrying about, but they had disappeared. There appeared to be a transmitter in the corner on the opposite wall. Other than that, he saw nothing but dirt and dust. Not even small tools. He looked back up at Daria, who appeared calm and relaxed.

"They are gone. For now," she informed him. "I think I persuaded them that I know nothing about a Sebastian Kapsky."

Canidy lowered the M1911 and began to ascend the short ladder to the kitchen. He got no farther than the first rung when he heard a rap on the front door and saw Daria's eyes grow wide. Canidy froze for a moment before descending again, brandishing his pistol at low-ready. *A return visit is never a good sign*, he thought.

Daria's face disappeared as she lowered the trapdoor. Canidy heard her cross to the door, then silence. *The Germans were not convinced*, he thought. *They're on to her.* He must have made a noise when the unseen creatures caused him to flinch.

Canidy backed into the corner farthest from the trapdoor and dropped to a knee, the weapon held steady on the trapdoor. He strained to hear the muffled voices from above, prepared to hear commands, shouts. But he heard nothing for several maddening seconds. The next sound Canidy heard was indistinct, but it was not Daria's voice. Though he didn't understand German, he strained to discern what he could from the voice's inflection and tone. It was, however, too low. So low that Canidy could hear the pronounced pulse of blood in his ears.

He thought he heard movement from above, but it was so subtle it may have been his imagination. Then he heard the sound of a door closing. It, however, was distinct. It wasn't his imagination. The footsteps, heavier than Daria's, drew closer to the trapdoor, then stopped.

Canidy glanced about the gloom of the tiny cellar for anything behind which he could conceal himself. There was nothing of use. He determined he'd simply empty his weapon when the trapdoor opened.

He dropped to one knee to get a better angle on the opening. He was a sitting duck, but he'd take as many as he could with him. *A cellar in Poland*, he thought. *A damn rodent-infested cellar in Poland.*

He sensed the presence of someone directly overhead and restrained himself from firing through the trapdoor. There was a confusing mix of heavy footfalls and light. Then silence.

The next sound he heard was Daria's voice posing a question. He strained but couldn't discern what she was saying. After a pause, she spoke again, too soft to comprehend.

Move out of the way, Daria, Canidy thought. *Get out of the line of fire.*

Daria spoke again but was interrupted by a male voice—strong, confident, and commanding. He recognized the voice.

The trapdoor opened slowly. Canidy blinked at the light streaming from above, the dust wafting upward toward the opening. He braced for the target to appear. Instead he heard a voice say, "Do not fire your weapon. It is I, Emil."

Canidy exhaled and lowered the weapon, perplexed but relieved. Light streamed into the cellar as the trapdoor opened slowly. Though his gaze was riveted on the aperture, his peripheral vision nonethe-less registered that whatever creatures had scurried about him on the floor remained hidden.

Emil's face and torso appeared overhead, Daria behind him over his left shoulder. Canidy exhaled forcefully, relieved yet perplexed. Before he could ask why Emil had returned, a loud knock on the front door caused the young warrior to leap to the cellar floor, Daria closing the trapdoor behind him.

CHAPTER 48

Standartenführer Konrad Maurer's command car proceeded along the same northwest road Gromov and Bridgette had traveled hours earlier. The five panzers trailed close behind, now with far less machine-gun ammunition, a significant amount of which had been expended in Sztum.

No matter. They were in German-held territory. Besides, they would soon replenish their supply at the depots at their destination.

Nonetheless, Maurer was frustrated, even anxious. Despite his having executed dozens of their compatriots, the peasants in Sztum refused to disclose any information pertaining to Dr. Sebastian Kapsky. They were either uncommonly brave or, more likely, remarkably stupid. Either way, they steadfastly refused to cooperate. Maurer was fortunate to stumble upon the partisan in the barn on the outskirts of the village. He, too, had been obstinate—impressively so—refusing to speak despite the methodical excision of each of his fingers and all but two of his toes. The peasant had nearly bled to death without yielding any information regarding Kapsky before one of Maurer's men discovered notes next to a radio in the loft. They were a handwritten transcription, a confirmation from someone that he or she had arrived safely in Malbork with "the ghost." Maurer felt blessed to have adversaries who were such simpletons.

Despite his frustration, Maurer remained confident. Although he suspected the theft of the motorcycle might be attributable to one of his opponents in the contest for Kapsky, he was still in control.

The entire area was controlled by the Wehrmacht. Even if the Americans and Soviets acquired Kapsky, they would still have to navigate through scores of kilometers of territory over which the Germans held dominion. Maurer would ultimately win the race to secure Kapsky. He was more talented than his adversaries. Because of his prowess, Maurer had come to the attention of the Führer himself. He was *that* talented. He would succeed. He had to succeed.

Canidy and Emil squatted in the recess of the cellar farthest from the trapdoor and listened intently to the sounds upstairs. Daria had opened the front door to a German who identified himself as SS Untersturmführer Lange. His voice sounded gruff and impatient.

Canidy whispered to Emil, "Can you make out what he's saying?"

"Something about whether she's seen any strangers in the area. He says one of his men reports he saw someone come to the door a few minutes ago. Daria says no. He sounds skeptical."

Both Canidy and Emil strained to hear the conversation, which was obscured by the rumble of a lorry passing nearby. For several moments they heard no voices and hoped that the Untersturmführer had satisfied his curiosity and departed. Each of their chests tightened, however, upon hearing what sounded like a door closing and the tap of boots walking slowly across the floor above.

Canidy cursed quietly, motioned for Emil to stay where he was, and moved to the ladder. He paused at its base and listened for what seemed like a minute before he heard the SS officer give a command in German that ended in the only word Canidy recognized: *Keller.*

Canidy cursed again to himself, stuck his pistol in his waistband, and quickly, but quietly, ascended the ladder to just below the trapdoor. As he did the door began to open, with the SS officer leaning forward, preparing to peer inside.

Canidy thrust his right hand upward, seized the officer's service tunic, and pulled downward as hard as he could. The German crashed on top of the American to the cellar floor, Canidy maintaining his grip on the tunic with his right hand while viciously punching the officer with his left. Blood from the German's mouth and nose splattered across Canidy's face, getting into his eyes, but he continued to rain blows down on the man's head. Desperate, the German bucked violently upward, throwing Canidy off him. Emil, however, leapt on him immediately, driving him back to the earth floor and giving Canidy a second to recover and wrap his right arm around the German's head, twisting it viciously clockwise and then counterclockwise. The crack of the man's cervical vertebrae was loud enough to startle Emil, who stared in wonderment as the man's hands maintained a stubborn grip on Canidy's shirt. Canidy withdrew his trench knife from under his shirt and thrust it into the left temple of the German, whose arms and torso twitched for several seconds before ceasing altogether.

Canidy, chest heaving from the exertion, forcefully pulled away the man's hands, which maintained a grip on Canidy's shirt. He then pulled the knife from the man's skull and wiped the blood onto the man's trousers. Noticing a shadow on the cellar's floor, Canidy looked up to see Daria peering down with a rueful look on her face. He understood what she was thinking: How to dispose of the corpse of an SS officer in densely occupied territory and explain to inquiring Nazis what happened to such officer, who was last seen approaching her door.

Canidy rose to one knee, his heart pounding more from adrenaline than exertion. As he caught his breath, Emil, reading his mind, said, "He appears to be about seventy-five kilograms. That is enough dead weight to make disposing of the corpse difficult, but manageable. But that is the easy part. Daria is in trouble."

Canidy stood erect, still breathing hard. "First things first. Why the hell did you come back?"

"Fulmar, through Commander Matuszek, directed that I return to guide you, to assist you both in being a decoy and in evading the Germans. Almost immediately after we left here they concluded that since you don't know the country as I do, your career as a decoy would be a rather short one, resulting in your certain death and Kapsky's eventual capture."

Canidy smiled wryly. "Yeah, that's probably right. Didn't give that as much thought as I should have. I sometimes tend to . . ."

". . . have a great deal of—how do you Americans say it?—hubris? Is that the right word?"

Canidy pursed his lips. "Yeah, that's as good as any. Now, back to matters at hand. You go upstairs and check to see what is going on outside. Let me know if there are any Germans nearby. Then I'll carry this guy upstairs . . ."

"Forgive me, Major Canidy, but I fear you may be, once again, engaging in a bit of hubris. I'll give you a hand taking him upstairs when I get back from checking outside."

Emil scaled the ladder and disappeared. Canidy bent over and grasped the corpse by his belt buckle and collar. Then he bent his knees and hoisted him over his right shoulder. *Hubris.*

Emil returned and peered down from the kitchen. "There are no patrols in sight. Daria suggests we bury the body in the thicket behind the house. I agree. It's about ten meters from the back. We will not be seen from the street." Emil pointed to the body over Canidy's shoulder. "Wait, I'll help you."

"Get back. There's not enough room. It's easier if I do it. Keep watching out the window. We can't afford any surprises."

Emil's face disappeared from overhead as Canidy tested the first rung of the ladder to see if it could bear his weight combined with that of the corpse. He then proceeded tentatively up the next seven steps, until the corpse was level with the floor above, and dumped the body onto the floor. He disciplined himself to take shallow breaths so Emil wouldn't notice his exhaustion.

Daria pointed to the kitchen door leading to the back of the house. "The thicket is about ten to fifteen meters to the rear. There are picks and shovels in the little shed on the left side of the door."

Emil returned from the front room and grasped the corpse's ankles. "No activity out front. We can move the body now."

Canidy gripped the corpse's armpits as Daria held the door open. After Canidy and Emil dumped the body among the shrubs, they used the implements in the shed to dig a grave in the soft earth of the thicket.

Although Daria kept watch out the front window, they paused every thirty seconds or so to listen for any sounds of Germans approaching. Barely fifteen minutes later they lowered the body into the ground, and covered it with earth overlaid with branches and leaves arranged as naturally as possible.

They returned inside and met Daria in the kitchen.

"Emil's going to guide me on my wild-goose chase," Canidy informed. "You need to come with us."

Daria smiled but shook her head. "I understand the risks," she said. "An SS officer goes missing, so they will search every house. Soon they will determine that he was last seen approaching this one. So I will receive special attention. But I have gotten this far by my wits. I will remain here."

"Your wits won't save you this time, Daria," Canidy replied. "Not when they see the earth behind the house."

"A risk, to be sure," Daria conceded. "But if I go with you, you will appear more conspicuous, and I will slow you down."

"Maybe, but not by much," Canidy said. "Come with us."

Daria shook her head with finality. "I am afraid not. The two of you need to be as nimble as possible so you can distract the Germans long enough for Kapsky to get to safety. Once they capture you, the charade is over."

"Then at least leave on your own."

"A Polish woman on her own in a Totenkopf zone? I stand a better chance here."

Canidy and Emil were reluctant to leave her behind, but they didn't argue. They knew she was right.

Daria said, "Go out the back door and through the thicket. The woods clear a half kilometer from here and you will see a gravel road in front of an old coal plant. That road will eventually turn into a larger one bordered most of the way by woodlands, and that will eventually take you to Danzig—at least the general direction of Danzig. I will wait a suitable period after you have left and seek a

German officer, resort to my well-worn acting skills, and inform him I saw someone bearing a strong resemblance to their description of 'Dr. Kapstein' proceeding along the road. That," Daria emphasized, "will be where your wild-goose chase begins in earnest."

Daria gave each of them a brief hug. "Remember," she added, "I will be giving the Germans a fairly accurate description of both of you. In the process, I may also gain some credibility, thereby diverting attention from my backyard."

Canidy nodded. "You *have* to give them a good description in order for the charade to be successful."

". . . Therefore, do not travel on the road, otherwise they will capture you too readily. Stay in the woods next to the road. You must prolong the chase, divert them from your friends and the real Dr. Kapsky."

"That's the plan. He escapes, we escape, and you're 'left alone.'"

As they said their goodbyes, Canidy suspected that at least two prongs of the plan would never be met.

CHAPTER 49

Gromov and Bridgette lay on a bluff overlooking the village. One house matched the description that the man in the barn had given them for Kapsky's hiding spot. As they watched, a redheaded woman emerged. She walked unhurriedly less than a kilometer to a store that appeared to have been converted to temporary German Army headquarters. The roof of the store supported a large antennae array and numerous telephone lines, presumably for dispatching orders to the many German Kampfgruppen in the region.

Gromov pointed to the house. "Watch the house for any sign of activity," he instructed Bridgette. "I will watch the headquarters."

Mere minutes after the redhead had entered the headquarters, three Kübelwagens carrying approximately a dozen troops sped in a northwesterly direction from the adjacent lot. A Panzerwagen ADGZ trailed them.

Barely a minute later the redhead left the building and proceeded back toward the house. Gromov believed he detected a spring in her step.

Gromov surveyed the immediate area for the best path toward the Kapsky house. There were no good ones. He told Bridgette, "We will proceed west along the ridge until we are perpendicular to the house." He pointed to the piles of rubble near the home. "Then we'll go down the ridge to those ruins. From the ruins across to the house. That should give us adequate concealment eighty-five percent of the way."

"Then?" Bridgette asked.

"Then we take Kapsky to safety."

"Obviously," Bridgette said. "But by what path? Your original orders were to acquire the Kapsky document and return it to the Soviet Union. But we are now in Poland. I do not know how to guide you to the Soviet Union from here."

"As long as we can get around the German-Russian front, we should be able to get to the Soviet Union."

Gromov rose and proceeded along the ridge with Bridgette behind him. There were no German troops visible in the area. Within minutes, they were crouching in the rubble across from the Kapsky house. They could see movement behind the curtain of the front window. It appeared to be only one person.

Gromov scanned the area for any German presence before he and Bridgette crossed quickly over to the house. Gromov rapped on the door, watching the surrounding area nervously.

Daria opened the door within seconds with a quizzical expression on her face. If anyone, she had been expecting Germans.

Gromov wasted no time. "I am Major Taras Gromov, Red Army. I understand from your man in Sztum that Dr. Sebastian Kapsky is hiding here. I am here to take him to safety."

Daria's face registered caution, then both mirth and confusion. After a second she said, "Come in. Quickly."

Gromov and Bridgette stepped inside and Daria closed the door. Bridgette introduced herself. "I am Bridgette Nørgaard. Danish Resistance. I am assisting Major Gromov."

Daria smiled, shaking her head in wonderment. "This has been a most eventful day. Bridgette, I am Daria. We have spoken at least once before, by radio. And we have exchanged messages. It's good to finally meet you."

Bridgette gave Daria a brief hug, then stepped back. "Markus told us you were here with Dr. Kapsky. He also mentioned that a team of Americans, assisted by a British soldier and *Armia*, were on their way here also."

Daria said nothing.

"So, is Dr. Kapsky here?" Gromov asked.

Daria inspected the two visitors. "Dr. Kapsky is not here."

"Where is he?" Bridgette asked. "Is he with the Americans?"

Daria took several seconds to answer. "I do not know."

"*Was* he here?" Gromov asked.

Daria said nothing.

"Daria," Bridgette said, her voice sympathetic. "Major Gromov and I can get him to safety, but we need to know where he is. I understand you need to be careful. But time is critical."

Daria rubbed her hands against her sides nervously. "He is safe," she replied.

"Where?" Gromov asked. "Is he with the Americans?"

"We can help," Bridgette added.

"I should not say," Daria said. "You are Resistance. You know how it is. The more people who know, the greater the risk."

"But we can *help*," Gromov restated. "Even if he is with the Americans."

Daria said nothing.

"He is with the Americans, then," Gromov said. "Yes?"

"Please," Daria said. "He is safe. That is all I can say."

Gromov's face tightened. "My orders are to ensure Dr. Kapsky's safety, including providing assistance to the Americans," he lied. "We—Soviets, Poles, and Americans—we have a common enemy. The area is controlled by the Germans. Kapsky—and the Americans—need all the help they can get."

Bridgette touched Daria's shoulder gently. "Please. Help Dr. Kapsky. Help us."

Daria exhaled sharply. "The fewer people with knowledge, the less the risk," she said, as if reciting a mantra. "That is the discipline. Again, Bridgette, as Resistance, you know that."

"Yes, but not always. Sometimes we must exercise our best judgment," Bridgette replied. "Under the present circumstances, the best judgment is to do that which provides Dr. Kapsky the most resources, the best opportunity to escape." Bridgette grasped Daria's hands. "The odds for Dr. Kapsky were poor to begin with. We are deep in Nazi-occupied territory. They are formidable and they are vicious. They also are thorough and leave absolutely nothing to chance. Dr. Kapsky's chances improved only slightly with *Armia* assistance. Major Gromov can improve it much more. I have seen him perform. He is an exceptional soldier. He can provide the difference between Dr. Kapsky escaping and his being caught or killed. Please help."

Daria's eyes began to water as she rubbed her sides more vigorously. Gromov stepped closer and put his left hand gently on her shoulder. Daria looked up and held his eyes, which conveyed patience and sympathy. She nodded and then looked down at the floor. After several seconds she said softly, "I cannot."

Gromov emitted what sounded to Bridgette like something between a growl and a roar before his right fist crashed squarely against Daria's face, catapulting her backward more than five feet and onto the floor. Blood gushed from her mouth and nose, which was flattened nearly flush against the rest of her face.

Frozen in horror, Bridgette watched as Gromov leapt on top of Daria and struck her two more times on her right cheek, causing her eyes to roll about in their sockets.

Gromov seized a handful of Daria's hair and slammed the back of her head against the wooden floor. Then he placed his face inches from hers and hissed, "Where is Kapsky? Where are the Americans? Tell me or I will rip your lungs out of your chest."

Bridgette seized Gromov's shoulder from behind and tried to pull him off Daria, to no effect. She then wrapped her arm around his neck and yanked backward, prompting Gromov to spin about and push her with such force that she was propelled back against the front door nearly ten feet away, the breath knocked from her lungs.

Gromov withdrew his NR-40 from his waistband and placed the tip against Daria's left cheek, just below the eye socket. The sensation prompted her to regain her senses and become rigid with terror. He placed his face inches from hers. "Now you are no longer pretty, Daria, but at least you can still function. Tell me where Kapsky went. Tell me his path or I will first cut out your left eye, and then your right."

Bridgette, air knocked out of her lungs, tried to regain her bearings. Seeing Gromov draw the blade toward Daria's eye, she attempted to scream, but nothing emerged.

Daria coughed up drops of blood and spoke softly, the words indistinct. Gromov placed his ear closer but couldn't make out the words. Daria paused to catch her breath, then spoke again. Once more, too low and garbled for Gromov to discern.

As he bent closer, Gromov felt his pistol being withdrawn from his waistband from the rear but was unable to react in time to prevent Bridgette from leveling the weapon dead on his torso. He rose from his crouch and turned to face Bridgette, who appeared both stunned and frightened. She began to speak, but before she uttered even a syllable, Gromov slashed her trachea to the spine with a powerful backhanded swing of his knife, causing her to involuntarily discharge a 7.62-millimeter round that grazed the right side of his rib cage.

Bridgette collapsed to the floor as if she were a marionette whose strings had been cut. She convulsed once as blood gurgled from her throat and pooled about her head. Then she lay still, lifeless eyes locked on her executioner.

Gromov knelt next to Daria, who was attempting to speak but was struggling to get enough air to do so. He put his ear close to her mouth. She spoke, but he couldn't make out any of the words. She paused to gather her strength, took a deep breath, and in a strangled voice told Gromov the precise direction that Kapsky had taken, as well as what time he'd left, and that he was escorted—guarded—by Fulmar, Matuszek, and McDermott. She took a last breath, said something barely intelligible, and then became rigid.

Gromov rose and moved toward Bridgette's body to retrieve his sidearm. Before he could do so the front door burst open and an Obergefreiter and two Soldaten entered with weapons trained on him.

"*Hände hoch!*"

With a look of resignation, Gromov complied by placing his hands on top of his head. As the soldiers approached to restrain him Gromov reached into a leather sheath sewn into the back collar of his shirt and pulled out a serrated dagger. He shifted his wrist and swung the dagger forward over his head as if chopping wood. Gromov impaled the German's forehead, penetrating through the cranium and into the soldier's left eye socket. A jet of warm blood burst from the socket as Gromov pulled the dagger from the soldier's skull and he collapsed to his knees. Gromov squatted and plunged the blade into the second soldier's inner left thigh, slicing a deep gash upward from the soldier's knee to his groin, severing the femoral artery.

The third soldier reflexively squeezed the trigger of his weapon, trained on the spot where Gromov had been standing a fraction of a second earlier. The bullet discharged nearly a foot over the kneeling assassin's head and slammed without effect into the wall behind him.

Gromov catapulted himself forward from his crouch and hurled himself, dagger extended, toward the remaining German. The blade drove into the soldier's throat just beneath the Adam's apple, penetrating under his chin, through the floor of his mouth, and impaling his tongue against his palate. The soldier fell to the floor next to the other two, twitching briefly before becoming still.

Gromov exhaled and composed himself. He took a momentary mental inventory of the state of affairs. He needed to leave immediately. But he felt a spark of excitement coupled with optimism. Finally, Kapsky was within reach. It was a matter of catching up to him and disposing of his escorts, a task Gromov could discharge as effectively as he'd disposed of the Germans now lying on the floor.

Gromov went to the door and surveyed the perimeter of the house for German troops. For the moment it was clear. He began walking northwest, consistent with the splendid directions Daria had just given him.

They were precisely the same misdirections she had provided the Germans who had sped away from headquarters in the three Kübelwagens twenty minutes ago.

CHAPTER 50

Canidy saw the ghostly headlights in the distance before Emil. They were moving slowly, too slowly for a mere transport. Both almost immediately concluded that whoever was behind the lights was looking for them.

They had traveled mostly on the sides of the road, near the brush. The area was predominately rural, and vehicular traffic was nearly nonexistent. Whenever they'd get a hint that a vehicle was approaching, they would resume their practice of traveling inside the tree line, out of sight.

"They are about three kilometers away," Emil estimated. "Moving very slowly. It is very hard to estimate from this distance, but I would say they are moving at no more than fifteen kilometers an hour."

Canidy kept watching the lights. "No doubt, they're looking for us," he said. "More accurately, they're looking for Kapsky. No other reason to be out here. Daria's little misdirection worked."

"For now," Emil said. "We need to string them along somehow. The longer we can do so, the more likely the real Kapsky can get to the boat. I wager those headlights belong to Kübelwagens. They have decent speed and maneuverability. And they usually carry about three, four troops each."

Canidy squinted in the direction of the vehicles. "What's that last one?"

Emil stopped walking and stared at the convoy for several seconds. "Again, if I had to wager, I'd say a panzer. Light."

Canidy spat, exasperated. "What's with these Germans and their damn panzers? Don't they ever go anywhere without them?" Canidy stopped and gauged the distance to the lights. "They'll overtake us in no more than ten minutes. Probably a good idea for us to start walking in the woods again, just in case."

"At some point, if they do not find us, will they not conclude they should search elsewhere?" Emil asked.

"Maybe. Let's hope that we can string them along for a while. Long enough for Fulmar to put more distance between us."

"How do you plan to, as you say, 'string them along'?"

Canidy smiled sardonically. "Very carefully. But we may have to take overt action so they don't become discouraged or suspicious and start looking in areas where the *real* Kapsky happens to be."

"Overt action?"

"What kind of weaponry do you think our friends back there are carrying?"

"Kübelwagens are for transport. They typically do not have mounted weapons, although on occasion one may have a mounted MG 34. The troops will have standard-issue Karabiners."

"And the panzer?"

Emil stopped again to look back at the procession in the distance. "As I say, it looks rather on the small side. Likely a Panzer ADGZ."

"Flamethrowers?"

Emil smiled slyly. "You did not enjoy your previous encounter with panzers?"

"I've had better days than that."

"Panzer ADGZs are light. They have MG 13s."

"Not my favorites," Canidy said. "But okay. If they get close enough, we can hit them with harassing fire. Let them know we're here. Keep them interested."

"Somewhat risky," Emil said without a hint of trepidation.

"That's why they pay us the big bucks, son."

Emil looked a bit confused, but understood Canidy was using an American colloquialism. He pointed back to the vehicle lights.

Canidy watched as the vehicles drew closer. "Yep. They're picking up speed. Let's get into the woods."

The pair stepped off the road and waded into the bordering vegetation a few feet into the tree line, deep enough to be invisible. They lay on the ground, peering through the vegetation, with their weapons trained on the road.

They watched in silence as the vehicles came down the road toward their position. "When they get close enough, take a few harassing shots to cause them to track us. Shoot two to three rounds and keep your head down to avoid return fire. Then move laterally and back—left and backward—to get out of here."

Emil nodded, then noticing movement behind the Kübelwagens, pointed, and said, "Look there. Your favorite German vehicles."

Approximately one-half kilometer behind the Kübelwagens and

Panzer ADGZ was the outline of a car trailed by several larger armored vehicles. They were closing rapidly.

"Panzer IVs. The real thing," Emil observed.

"Machine guns and flamethrowers?"

"Yes. Just like our previous panzer encounter."

"And, all things considered, I was having a pretty good day until now."

As the procession drew nearer, Canidy discerned what appeared to be a Horch 108 command car trailed by the five massive panzers. The same configuration Canidy had observed on the first expedition.

"Let's move back farther into the woods. That's a lot of firepower coming toward us. Don't shoot unless I do."

Canidy and Emil rose and retreated at a slight incline another forty meters into the woods, then dropped to the ground.

"I do not have a clear line of sight," Emil informed him. "Too many trees in front."

"We don't need to hit them," Canidy said. "We just need to get their attention. Daria told them Dr. Kapsky went in this direction. We want to make them think that maybe they're getting close."

"I'm afraid we will only convince them we are idiots. Why would Kapsky—or his escorts—fire on a *panzer* column. Will they not think it is a diversion?"

"Nobody thinks while under fire, not even armored troops. They react. The natural reaction is to think the guy they're looking for is the guy shooting at them. And the beauty of that is that they won't fire back because they need Kapsky alive."

"Very well," Emil replied. "Although I'm not completely convinced."

Canidy chuckled wryly. "Tell you the truth, neither am I."

The rattle of the vehicles grew louder and Canidy could feel the earth vibrate. When the procession was parallel with Canidy and Emil's position it came to a halt. Three Kübelwagens, five panzers, and a German command car.

Emil turned to Canidy with a look of concern. "They could not have seen us down the road, could they?"

Canidy didn't respond. His gaze was fixed on the figure in the rear seat of the car. He—more accurately, his silhouette—was recognizable even in twilight.

Emil examined the figure. "It is he," he said to himself.

Konrad Maurer rose slowly from his seat, stood in the rear of the vehicle, and scanned the woods where Canidy and Emil lay with their pistols extended before them. Although in the gloom they couldn't see Maurer's face, the slow, deliberate turn of his head conveyed prescience—a sense that something or someone was concealed in the forest.

Maurer got out of the car and paced the perimeter of the road, seemingly staring directly at Canidy and Emil. He raised a gloved hand over his head and brought it forward, signaling all gunners to aim at the woods.

Canidy's chest seized with terror as the panzer turrets instantly swiveled in unison ninety degrees.

"Feuer!"

Both Canidy and Emil dug their heads into the soil as five MG 34 machine guns sprayed a prolonged burst of 7.92-millimeter rounds into the forest, causing a blizzard of leaves, branches, and pine needles to fall atop the two. The forest quickly absorbed the roar of the guns. Maurer stood silent and immobile, listening. He raised his hand again and again ordered the guns to fire. More debris rained down on Canidy and Emil, but they were unharmed.

Maurer stepped closer to the perimeter of the woods and peered in Canidy's direction. Canidy, M1911 before him, prepared to fire. The probabilities indicated they would not survive another burst. At least he would take Maurer out of the equation.

Maurer stepped back slowly and returned to his vehicle. He took a last look in Canidy's direction before climbing into the backseat and motioning for the procession to continue forward.

Canidy and Emil waited until the caravan was half a kilometer down the road before rising from the ground.

"Panzers," Canidy spat. "Never ran into them flying P-40Bs. Wouldn't bother me if I never ran into them again. If it weren't for all of that firepower, that SS sonuvabitch would have a bullet in his big Prussian forehead right now."

Emil brushed soil from the front of his trousers. "You should be happy. Your—how you say?—wild-goose chase is working. They are searching for us, not Dr. Kapsky. Commander Matuszek should get him to the boat soon."

"I'm not so sure," Canidy said. "I don't know why they were firing in this direction, but it couldn't be because they thought Kapsky was here. They don't want to kill Kapsky, so they wouldn't fire if they had a realistic expectation that Kapsky might get hit."

Canidy and Emil turned and walked into the woods, the American vowing to put as much distance as possible between himself and motorized armor.

CHAPTER 51

Northern Poland
0517, 15 August 1943

They proceeded two abreast. Fulmar and Matuszek in front, Kapsky and McDermott to the rear. They remained, as usual, within the tree line adjacent to the single-lane road.

Fulmar was pleased with their progress and good fortune in not encountering any patrols. The countryside was bleak, riddled with artillery craters and damaged abandoned buildings. There were, however, a fair number of tiny hamlets with small clusters of undamaged buildings. Matuszek made sure they circumvented them and remained out of sight, explaining that they were nearing an area in which a large percentage of the residents were ethnic Germans. More precisely, Prussians, whose allegiances weren't necessarily certain.

They'd consumed most of the latkes, but Fulmar wasn't concerned about the food supply. Even the abandoned or nonworking farms had patches of crops that insisted on growing regardless of neglect.

Fulmar's primary concern was his watch. They had approximately twelve hours to get to the canal and the Thorisdottirs' boat. Fulmar calculated that at their present pace they should be able to get there on time, but barely. They couldn't afford slowdowns or delays. Matuszek seemed to know every road, village, and German outpost in northern Poland—but he was concerned whether Kapsky could keep up this pace.

Kapsky had shown no signs of fatigue in the first hours after they'd left Daria's house. Indeed, Fulmar nearly completely forgot that the professor purportedly had some type of illness or condition. Fulmar hadn't asked about it and Kapsky hadn't talked about it. In Fulmar's estimation, the professor looked pretty good—especially for an academic. Fulmar had assumed that sitting behind a desk or in a laboratory or wherever professors sat, Kapsky would be physically frail and somewhat hunched—the stereotype of an intellectual with little regard for his physique. Kapsky, however, had an athlete's build. Lean and sinewy, likely due—at least in part—to having been constantly on the move for the last forty months. He was a good-looking guy with an interesting face, especially his eyes—intelligent and peculiarly green.

But in the last couple of hours, Fulmar sensed that Kapsky was struggling to keep up. He hadn't faltered—in fact, he'd kept up with the rest. But his strides were shorter and he was breathing through his mouth, a sign that he was challenged by their pace.

Fulmar couldn't afford to stop the team for any appreciable period to rest. Although they were making good time, they had to anticipate and account for contingencies such as German patrols or roadblocks. Fulmar was reluctant to test the radio in his ruck. It was another contraption minted by the OSS lab. Although it seemed to work when they tested it before they'd embarked on the operation,

Fulmar remained skeptical about its effectiveness in the field. More important, Fulmar was concerned that if he used it, the Germans might be able to detect it. Although they'd been assured by the lab boys that detection was unlikely, he didn't want to risk it. The lab boys were in the lab; he was in the field—an unforgiving field. So he determined that he'd reserve use of the radio until they were within a few kilometers of the dock. He'd keep it off until then, hoping that Kristin and Katla weren't trying to reach him with important information—such as the dock was swarming with SS.

Matuszek drew next to Fulmar and nudged him with an elbow. He quietly asked, "Do you think he can keep this pace?"

"He doesn't have a choice."

Matuszek nodded. "We should move a little more quickly so we will have—how do you Americans say—a cushion. So far, he's kept up well, but he appears quite fatigued."

"He's a tough son of a bitch for a professor. Hell, all that time evading Nazis probably made him as hard as your best Home Army troops. But Canidy and I were told he could be ill. They were concerned he might even die before he could provide whatever information he possesses. Don't know what it may be. Hell, they briefed us on everything—even speculative stuff—but I'm not sure how much longer he can go at this pace, let alone a faster one."

As if to punctuate Fulmar's statement, Kapsky began coughing— a strained sound unlike a mere cough produced by dust or other ambient cause.

"You okay, Professor?" Fulmar asked over his shoulder.

"I am fine."

"You sure as hell don't sound like it. Look, tell me when you need a break, okay? You're the reason we're on this excursion through the delightful war-torn fields of Poland. We want to keep you in good shape, so say the word and we'll take five."

"Thank you. But that will not be necessary."

Fulmar detected the faint rumble of a motor vehicle somewhere on the road behind them. To this point the only traffic they'd encountered was an iron-and-wood cart driven by an old man and pulled by two oxen.

Fulmar signaled for the team to move farther within the tree line. He knelt and the others did the same. Thirty seconds later they spotted a flat-nosed truck pulling a twelve-foot trailer with a canvas tarp covering the bed. It was moving at about thirty kilometers an hour. Some type of farm vehicle, Fulmar thought, one of only three vehicles they'd encountered on the trip. Not Wehrmacht. Nonetheless, they would remain concealed until it passed before resuming their journey.

Matuszek had other plans. He rose and was at the tree line and in the middle of the road before Fulmar could register a protest. Alarmed, Fulmar whispered, "What the hell is he doing?"

Matuszek raised his rifle with both hands over his head and the truck slowed and came to a halt fifteen feet in front of him. Matuszek walked to the driver's side of the cab. Fulmar and McDermott watched with weapons trained on the front windshield. The look on the driver's face appeared to range from fear to concern to delight.

"Commander! Is it you? Commander Matuszek, no? I recognize you from the posters in Tczew Square. It is you, yes?"

Fulmar and McDermott looked at each other with expressions of disbelief. Fulmar shook his head. "Unbelievable. We're traveling with Clark Gable."

"Yes, it is I, *kolega*," Matuszek confirmed. "Are you traveling much farther down the road?"

"You call this a road? I'm sure to break an axle on this horrible excuse for a road. The Germans have ruined it with their heavy transports."

Matuszek tilted his head toward the trailer. "What are you hauling back there?"

"What else? Potatoes. That is all that I can grow anymore. And I am lucky to be able to grow that."

"How much farther are you going?"

"Another twenty kilometers, if my axles don't break and the motor does not stop. To Borkowo. Just south of Danzig. Do you know it?"

Matuszek shook his head. "I do not think so."

"I do not like going there. Lots of German troops. They sometimes give you a hard time. And the people in the region—they were Poles before the war, now they claim to be Germans."

"Not many," Matuszek said.

"Perhaps not. But still, *too* many."

Matuszek inspected the trailer. "I would like to ask a favor, *kolega*."

"Of course. Anything I can do for Commander Matuszek. Wait until I tell the old goats back in Czarlin. What can I do?"

"I need a ride. Not all the way to Borkowo, but as close as we can get."

The smile on the driver's face turned to apprehension.

"It is a risk, I understand," Matuszek conceded. "But it is most important. I have an appointment, a deadline to meet nearby Borkowo. At foot speed I may make it or I may not. But I cannot be late under any circumstances."

The driver appeared contrite. "Commander, please understand. I do not want to appear reluctant, but I am just a farmer. I am not Home Army. I am not trained. If the Germans stop us—if they see me with you—we will be shot dead. My children will be without their father. They are already without their mother."

"Yes. We have all lost loved ones," Matuszek acknowledged. "I am sorry about your wife. I ask for this favor because I have no other options and it is a matter of great importance that I get there."

The driver rubbed his bald pate and exhaled. "Obviously, I cannot refuse a request for help from Commander Matuszek. Please do not misunderstand. I am not brave, but neither am I a coward. I am just worried for my children. If the Nazis learn I have helped you, they may kill my children also."

"That is a risk," Matuszek acknowledged.

The driver nodded vigorously, part in agreement and part to steel his resolve. "My children will be proud when I tell them I assisted Commander Matuszek. They will look upon me as a *hero*."

Matuszek smiled. "Perhaps you should not tell them for a while."

"Yes. Of course. That would be foolish." The driver waved toward the other side of the cab. "Please, Commander, get in."

"Perhaps I should ride in the back, under the tarpaulin, out of sight."

The driver looked momentarily surprised, then relieved. "Yes, of course. If you do not mind. That would be most shrewd, Commander Matuszek. Very smart. But a bit uncomfortable. The potatoes are fresh. Hard as rocks."

"No matter," Matuszek replied. "My friends and I are used to tough conditions."

The driver frowned, confused.

Matuszek pointed to Fulmar, McDermott, and Kapsky, who

had emerged from the woods. "These are my traveling companions . . . What is your name, *kolega*?"

"Mikołaj."

"These men are very important friends, Mikołaj. I tell you that because I trust you and because it is true. I cannot tell you their names. It is that important. It is not because I do not respect you. It is to protect your life. The less you know, the less risk for you, us, and your children." Matuszek could see Mikołaj's grip tighten on the steering wheel. Matuszek understood. This was a potentially fatal undertaking for the driver, one that also could have consequences for his family. But this was Nazi-occupied Poland. Ordinary people were forced to make life-and-death decisions regularly, often by the hour.

The driver loosened his grip on the wheel and smiled genuinely, without bravado. "This will be an adventure that I will tell my grandchildren about. I drove Commander Matuszek and other very important people past the Nazis."

Mikołaj got out of the vehicle and looked down each end of the road before untying the tarp, revealing a mound of brown potatoes, more than Fulmar had ever seen in his life.

Mikołaj said to Matuszek, "You are welcome to ride on top. Just climb on top of the baseboard. I am afraid it will be most uncomfortable. I will put the cover over you when you are settled."

"Thanks," Fulmar said.

Mikołaj turned toward Fulmar, startled. "You are American?" he asked in English.

Fulmar said nothing.

Mikołaj stroked his chin. He turned to Matuszek and spoke in Polish. "Clearly, this is something extraordinary, is it not? I *truly* am helping something important."

"When this is all done, we'll send you a postcard," Fulmar said.

Fulmar stepped onto the rear bumper and climbed on top of the mound of potatoes, which rolled and shifted beneath him. He gained his balance and thrust out his hand to assist Kapsky aboard, followed by McDermott and Matuszek. Each staked out a corner of the truck bed and dug into the surface of the load to secure themselves.

Matuszek checked to see if everyone was secure and then said to Mikołaj, "You can pull the cover over us. We're ready to go anytime you are. Just before we get to Borkowo, stop and let us know."

The driver did as requested, climbed back into the cab, and slowly eased the truck forward so as not to upend his new passengers, each of whom were trying to maintain a balance among the oblong-shaped vegetables.

Fulmar resigned himself to an uncomfortable journey, but at least Kapsky didn't have to walk and, barring any mishaps, they'd arrive at the dock on time. But mishaps, Fulmar knew, were the currency of war.

A quarter-kilometer north, Frederick Hahn watched with curiosity and anticipation. The farmer had survived the war, indeed thrived, by conveying useful information to those that presently controlled the country. He had waved amiably toward the group before they'd boarded the truck. Trying to convey nonchalance, they'd waved back.

CHAPTER 52

Northern Poland
0652, 15 August 1943

Canidy and Emil continued to walk north through the woods. Canidy muttering curses about panzers from time to time. He was a pilot. A damn good one. One that had bedeviled the Japanese along the Burma Road. He should be destroying panzers from above, he told himself, not acting as their target on the ground.

Not long after the encounter with the panzers, the woods began to thin.

"Emil, are my instincts right? We're no longer going northwest but moving due north?"

"That is correct. Toward Danzig."

They crested a shallow slope, and through the thinning trees could see below the glimpses of civilization: dozens of houses, stores, at least two warehouses, and a small plant of some kind.

And on the west side of the plant, lined up north to south, was a precise row of Kübelwagens, a precise row of panzers, and a command car.

Canidy cursed loudly.

"I did not expect this," Emil said somberly. "They were moving away from us and away from Kapsky in a westerly direction. They must have turned north somewhere and looped around. I confess my knowledge of this area is lacking."

"Don't worry about it," Canidy said. "Not your fault. They're the ones who screwed up. Based on what they know, they should have kept going west." Canidy stopped and squinted at the command car in the distance. "Got to give that giant son of a bitch credit. He's very thorough. And he's no dummy."

"He is still not on Fulmar's trail, however, Fulmar's group is moving northwest."

"True. But now the big Nazi's not heading *away* from them, either." Canidy pointed to the scores of villagers who were being herded into a lot on the south end of the village. "We've seen this play before. Let's hope none of those poor folks down there happened to see Fulmar's team on their way to Danzig, because that SS SOB will sure get it out of them."

Emil said, "In order to avoid them, we will need to skirt the perimeter of the town, staying in the woods. That will add two or three kilometers, at least another hour, to our trip to the canal. We will need to move very fast to get there in time."

Canidy eyed the scene unfolding in the factory lot. He estimated more than a hundred villagers were already gathered, with more streaming in at gunpoint.

"Emil," Canidy said somberly, "give me your best estimate as to whether we have enough time to get to the boat if we go around the village. Don't sugarcoat it."

Emil sighed heavily. "We can get there, but everything must fall in our favor. No detours, no delays from trying to avoid or hide from German troops."

"So fifty-fifty?"

"More likely, forty-sixty," Emil replied.

Candidy peered at the scene in the parking lot. Dozens of adult males were being forced to line up on their knees. The big SOB with the gleaming boots had disembarked from his command car and was striding slowly down the line with his hands clasped behind his back. "That's not quite the odds I was hoping for. But it actually makes things much clearer, much easier."

Emil grinned. "It certainly does, doesn't it."

"If it's unlikely I'm going to get to the boat even under the best of circumstances, I may as well increase the chances Fulmar's team gets there. After all, my job is to get Kapsky out of Poland, not necessarily get *myself* out of Poland. I'll have to figure that out later. If I get a chance."

Candidy reached into his ruck and withdrew what looked like a black baseball. "They're going to start executing people down there any minute. We have to assume someone saw something or knows something and is going to talk. I'm going to see if I can buy Fulmar a little more time."

Candidy moved cautiously down the slope, closer to the factory. Emil followed. The trees and brush continued to thin the closer they got to the factory, but were replaced with tall grass that provided good cover, permitting them to approach undetected to within fifty meters of the factory lot. Candidy stopped, knelt, and motioned for Emil to do the same.

Candidy observed the interrogation of the men kneeling in the lot for a minute before turning to Emil and whispering, "Emil, I'm going to distract these guys with some harassing fire. Maybe they'll even chase us. Obviously, they've got a fair amount of firepower. Even if they can't see us, they can saturate the area with those MG 34s on top of the panzers. We got lucky once before—"

Emil interrupted, "How you say—'I am in.'"

Candy suppressed a chuckle. It struck him that he was kneeling next to probably the toughest adolescent on the planet.

"Seriously, Emil, I knew you'd say that. But you've done your job and more. Spectacularly well. We've provided the misdirection Fulmar's team needed. Since it's unlikely I can get to the boat, I don't need your guidance anymore. There's nothing more for you to do but accept my thanks and that of Wild Bill Donovan for a job well done. So get the hell out of here."

"No."

"Emil . . ."

"I report to Commander Matuszek. He ordered me to guide you to the boat. I will do as he ordered."

Candy shook his head. "I don't—"

Emil interrupted, pointing to the black baseball. "What is that?"

"A toy from Professor Moriarty and the boys in Donovan's lab. It's a T-13. Affectionately called a Beano. I've got three of them. It's a wonder one of them hasn't gone off already."

"A bomb?"

"Something like that." Candy took another Beano from his ruck and handed it to Emil. "When I say 'Go,' throw that thing at the Germans farthest from the villagers. Preferably near those Kübelwagens. Then move laterally with me to the left. Fast, so we're not where they'll probably return fire, especially those panzers. When we've moved about one hundred yards—meters—we'll hit them with some harassing fire. It's harder for them to tell where that's coming from. Let's keep drawing them away from a northwesterly direction. Give Fulmar's team more of a cushion to get to the boat."

When Canidy returned his attention to the factory lot he saw that the big SS officer with the gleaming boots had a Walther P38 in his right hand. Someone was about to be shot. Canidy nudged Emil. "No time to waste. Pick your spot now. Ready?"

Emil nodded.

"Go."

Canidy rose from a crouch and threw the Beano at the closest Kübelwagen. Emil then threw his at the German troops farthest from the line of kneeling villagers. Canidy's Beano exploded against the passenger door of the vehicle, propelling it a foot in the air and causing it to burst into flames. Emil's Beano fell a few feet in front of the line of panzers without effect. A dud.

Canidy and Emil sprinted to their left, the tall grass providing cover. Within seconds, hundreds of rounds of machine-gun fire were shredding all vegetation within a hundred-foot radius of the spot the two had just left.

The roar of the machine-gun fire caused them to sprint even harder. A second later the fire was replaced by several deafening explosions caused by the shells from the panzers' cannons.

The machine-gun fire resumed, but this time tracking westward and closing behind them, contrary to Canidy's expectations. Canidy dove to the ground followed by Emil a scant second before scores of 7.92-millimeter rounds caught up with their position and scythed the grass a mere foot over their heads. They remained prone as the fire tracked in front of their position, then returned back to their original position. As it did so the pair rose and began sprinting west through the tall grass once again.

The sound of machine-gun fire was replaced by the shouts of German soldiers. Although Canidy didn't understand precisely *what* they were saying, he could tell the shouts weren't *receding*. The Germans were giving chase.

Canidy cursed. He'd hoped to draw the Germans away from the direction Fulmar's team was proceeding, but not to be so close on Canidy's heels. The pair had no options other than to keep running and hope to elude their pursuers.

Canidy's legs quickly grew heavy from the strain of sprinting against the tall grass. Though younger, Emil was feeling the same. Another half kilometer and they wouldn't be able to go much farther.

Canidy broke to his left—southward—and back up the slope toward the forest. Emil followed. Their chests heaved, trying to inhale as much oxygen as possible as they struggled up the slope against the tall grass.

As they moved farther up the slope, the shouts of the Germans began to fade. Canidy slipped on the incline and fell, followed by Emil. Both popped up immediately and resumed climbing toward the sanctuary of the forest only a hundred meters away, the shouts of the pursuing Germans falling yet farther behind.

The fading shouts, however, were replaced by the growing din from a panzer that was moving across the lot to join the uphill pursuit. The sound of the infernal machine caused Canidy to momentarily forget the pain in his legs and lungs. He and Emil mowed rapidly through the grass to the crest of the slope and continued running into the forest, slowing only after they were more than two hundred meters within. Only then did Canidy slow enough to turn and look behind them. Although the foliage partially obscured his view, he could see no movement.

Canidy came to a halt, listening. No shouts, no snap of branches or twigs broken underfoot. He asked Emil standing next to him, trying to catch his breath, "See anything? Hear anything?"

Panting, Emil simply shook his head.

Canidy took several more breaths before speaking again. "Well, that sure didn't accomplish anything. Amateur hour. The idea was to continue to misdirect them from Fulmar."

Emil shook his head. "No, sir. As you said, the idea was to give Fulmar's team more of a cushion. I think you've done that. Even if they figure out which direction Fulmar's team is actually going, they've been delayed."

". . . But almost got ourselves killed in the process," Canidy said. "Even if we've given Fulmar a cushion, I've probably aggravated the big Nazi with the shiny boots enough that he's going to take it out on the poor SOBs from the town."

"He was going to do that anyway. You know that."

Canidy stood erect and stared at the young soldier. "How old are you *really*, Emil?"

Emil smiled and pointed westward.

CHAPTER 53

When Gromov first heard the explosions and gunfire he ducked from the road into the woods and waited. The sounds were coming from the general direction in which the redheaded woman said Kapsky was going. It didn't seem to be very far away, so he remained still for several minutes, trying to glean more information from the noise.

When the noise abated, he resumed moving in Kapsky's direction. Through the trees in the distance he caught a glimpse of a figure he thought he'd seen before. One of the Americans; one of the Americans he was commanded to kill. He couldn't be certain, but it made sense. The Americans were escorting Kapsky. A person unknown to Gromov was with the American, but Kapsky was nowhere to be seen.

The two figures disappeared from view, concealed by trees and distance. Gromov moved stealthily in pursuit, a task made difficult by the underbrush that both slowed him and made noise when he passed. But Gromov was encouraged. He was on the right path and not far from his target.

Colonel Yevgeni Goncharov cursed several times under his breath. He wasn't one for the wilderness. He much preferred operating in urban environments, as would any civilized person—even assassins.

His shoes were caked with mud, his clothes were torn by thorns, and he sported welts from numerous insect bites. It had not been a pleasant trek. Nonetheless, he remained well within range of his assignment. Gromov had impressed him with his brutality and efficiency. He had little doubt Gromov would discharge his orders. Based on what Goncharov had witnessed thus far, the Americans didn't have a chance. Unfortunately for Gromov, neither did he.

CHAPTER 54

Northern Poland
0800, 15 August 1943

The ride was loud and uncomfortable. Fulmar felt nearly every bump acutely, and there was an uncommonly large number of bumps. Each bump was accompanied by a shifting of the load of potatoes on which they rode, creating a sensation akin to an amusement park ride. Nonetheless, Fulmar was pleased. They were moving far faster than they would be had they remained on foot, and Kapsky didn't have to exhaust himself trying to get to the boat.

The tarp covering the bed of the truck was moldy and smelled accordingly, and Fulmar could feel bugs crawling over him. Annoying, but inconsequential as far as he was concerned.

Fulmar sensed the truck slowing and presently heard the squeaking of brakes. The truck sputtered and came to an abrupt halt. They weren't anywhere near the canal, Fulmar thought. They hadn't been traveling long enough. Maybe a stubborn farm animal in the road? A fallen limb?

Fulmar became rigid and held his breath when he heard the unmistakable inflection of a German imperative sentence. Then a question, accusatory in tone.

Fulmar remained still and tried to listen to the specific words being spoken. At the same time he slowly withdrew his M1911 and held it in his right hand. Although he couldn't see the rest of the team beneath the darkness of the tarp, he suspected they were doing something similar.

Fulmar strained to hear an exchange between the driver and the German speaker. The only discernible word was the German word for potato: *"Kartoffel."* Then he could hear nothing until a bayonet pierced the tarp inches from his face, then withdrew. Then another thrust that narrowly missed his right shoulder. Followed by another and another. Fulmar strained against the urge to fire his weapon. He feared the others might not resist doing the same. He didn't have to fear long. Thankfully, the bayoneting ceased within seconds.

More unintelligible chatter from outside. Then he heard the ignition of the engine and felt the stutter of the truck as the clutch was being released, followed by a slow acceleration.

Fulmar was just beginning to exhale when the truck stopped abruptly, causing the potatoes to shift beneath him. He strained to hear what was happening outside, but it was unintelligible before falling silent. Fulmar surmised the Germans remained suspicious— second-guessing themselves. He prepared to fire at the first figure he saw when the tarp was pulled back.

Suddenly Fulmar heard shouting, Polish mixed with German. Angry, impatient, profane.

Fulmar was astonished. It was Mikołaj berating the Germans. Though Fulmar could understand only the German, he easily concluded that Mikołaj was feigning outrage at being stopped not once, but twice, for reasons unworthy of his time. These frivolous, moronic guards were keeping him from business. *Real* business, not the make-believe plays these idiots were engaged in. Little boys playing soldier. No, he had real work to do and these marionettes were keeping him from doing it.

Fulmar expected the tirade to cease with the sound of a gunshot to the driver's chest. Instead, he heard the sound of contrition. After a few utterances in an apologetic tone, the truck lurched forward again and slowly began to pick up speed.

Only then did Fulmar notice a spider crawling on his chin toward his mouth. He started, nearly discharging his pistol, the trigger of which he had begun to squeeze. He swiped the spider from his face and exhaled.

Fulmar estimated that the truck had traveled nearly ten kilometers.

The noise from the engines was moderating when he heard an anguished groan a couple of feet from him. Although he couldn't see him, Fulmar knew it must have come from McDermott, who was the closest to him.

"McDermott, can you hear me?"

"Yes. They got my arm. Again."

"With the bayonet?"

"Yes. My bad arm. The forearm. I need to tie it off."

Fulmar could hear the strain in his voice. "Can you wait a few minutes?"

"Do I have any options?"

"Just wait enough time so we're pretty sure we're clear of the checkpoint."

"I'll have to manage . . ."

"Hell, I don't know how to let our driver know until we come to a stop. We're trapped back here."

"Not to worry, it feels no worse than when it was shot."

Fulmar ground his teeth. He respected McDermott's stoicism, but if the wound was remotely like the previous one, it needed to be dressed immediately or McDermott wouldn't last long.

Fulmar needed the driver to stop the truck, but first he needed to get the driver's attention. He couldn't see or hear whether there were Germans nearby. Riding in the bed of a noisy truck covered by a tarp left him with few options. He held his breath, hoped for the best, and fired his pistol once. The truck kept moving. He fired again and the truck began to slow and came to a halt moments later.

From outside, Fulmar heard Mikołaj shout a question.

"What is the problem?"

"Are we clear?" Fulmar asked.

"We better be, otherwise we're all dead. We are between Pszczółki and Borkowo. We are in a wooded area."

"One of my men needs help," Fulmar said. "He was stabbed with a bayonet."

"One moment."

Mikołaj untied the ropes that secured the tarp and pulled it back. Fulmar blinked against the light, looked about, and saw the others do the same. McDermott was doing his best not to grimace, but the strain was evident on his face.

All four descended awkwardly from the load of potatoes and gathered at the side of the road. McDermott's right arm dangled limply and blood was dripping off his hand and onto the ground.

Fulmar said, "Let's get off the road and go into the trees in case someone comes down the road." He turned to Mikołaj. "Thanks for the lift. We've made outstanding progress."

Mikołaj looked confused. "What do you mean? You are leaving? But I will drive you as far as you need to go."

"You've already taken a hell of a risk," Fulmar said.

"That is nothing." Mikołaj nodded toward McDermott. "He is tough. But he is in tremendous pain. He is also . . ."

"Conspicuous?" Fulmar added.

"Conspicuous, yes. Blood everywhere. Also"—Mikołaj pointed to Kapsky—"he does not look well. I am uncertain he can get to the canal."

Fulmar examined Kapsky in the light of day. Mikołaj was right. Kapsky's face was colorless and he appeared exhausted. The ride atop the potatoes surely hadn't done him any favors, but Fulmar wasn't sure Kapsky had the strength to walk—and if necessary run—the remaining distance to the dock.

"Okay," Fulmar said. "We ride as far as we can. But first, let's patch up McDermott."

Mikołaj waited in the cab of the truck as Fulmar, McDermott, Kapsky, and Matuszek proceeded to the woods bordering the road. Movement appeared to increase the blood flow from McDermott's wound, so Fulmar guided him toward the nearest fallen tree and had him sit. Fulmar knelt next to McDermott and gently peeled back the Scot's sleeve to reveal a gash in the forearm deep enough to see glimpses of ulnar bone. "We need to tie this off or he's going to start getting light-headed fast, maybe pass out. Especially if he has to exert himself."

Matuszek handed Fulmar strips of cotton and iodine from his rucksack. "Here, use these. God knows where that bayonet's been."

Fulmar applied the iodine and addressed the wound as well as he could. McDermott grimaced but remained silent throughout.

"I'm not going to be of much use from here on," McDermott

said. "Dead weight. The smart thing for you to do is cut me loose at the first sign of me slowing you down, because I'm not going to get any better between here and the boat. If I do get back, this time they *will* put me to pasture. The arm's done."

"Shut the hell up," Fulmar snapped. "You might not make it back, but the rest of us might not, either. I don't want to hear any of this heroic self-sacrifice crap from you, McDermott. We're dragging you across the finish line, no matter how much you bitch about it. You can take your sweet time dying later."

Fulmar secured the wrap around McDermott's arm. The Scot flexed the arm painfully and nodded appreciation. The wrap was fully soaked with blood within seconds.

"Commander, what's your best estimate for how much longer it will take before we get to the boat?"

"We're approaching Danzig. This area has one of the highest concentrations of Germans in Poland. Depending on how far our potato farmer can drive us and assuming we do not have to make excessive detours around Germans, we should get to the boat in between fourteen hundred and fifteen hundred hours."

Fulmar shifted to Kapsky. "Professor, no disrespect, but you look like crap. How are you feeling?"

Kapsky smiled gamely. "Your assessment is correct. I look and feel like crap. But I've been evading the Germans without an escort for more than three years. I can do so for another couple of hours."

"What about Canidy?" McDermott asked.

"We will have to play it by ear." Fulmar shrugged. "He's somewhere out there. Likely well behind us. Knowing Dick, he's probably making things as difficult for the Germans as possible, which means he's probably *really* far behind us."

"If he's alive, Emil will get him to the boat," Matuszek said firmly.

"I have no doubt, Commander," Fulmar agreed. "But my first responsibility is to make sure that Dr. Kapsky gets out of Poland safely. My orders couldn't be clearer. Everything, *everything*, else is secondary. And if you know my boss, you'd know that *everything* is to be sacrificed to that objective."

"I do not wish to burden all of you, cause you to make such sacrifices," Kapsky said quietly. "I did not expect a party to come to my rescue."

"We weren't responding to your request, Professor," Fulmar said. "We're executing my boss's command. So don't worry about it." Fulmar rose. "All right, we're wasting time. We have a load of potatoes waiting for us."

McDermott rose and the others turned and walked back to the truck.

Fulmar stopped instantly and signaled for the others to do the same just as the driver issued a shrill whistle from the road.

CHAPTER 55

Belyanov was adept at intimidation. The mere fact of being chief of OKRNKVD was sufficient to intimidate all but a handful of individuals in the entire Soviet Union. But he was about to enter a meeting with the two individuals whose titles and reputations were more fearsome than his own: head of People's Commissariat for Internal Affairs Lavrentiy Beria and. . . . premier of the Union of Soviet Socialist Republics, Joseph Vissarionovich Stalin himself.

Like most in the Soviet Union, Belyanov had spent a good portion of his lifetime developing a thick skin, a veneer of stoicism. He conveyed toughness and confidence to nearly all. Stalin and Beria, however, were the two most frightening people in the Soviet Union, and Belyanov was suitably anxious about meeting with them.

The aide opened the large, highly polished oak double doors to the room. Stalin was seated at the end of a long marble table, Beria to his immediate left. They were illuminated by bright rays of sunshine beaming through the tall windows to Belyanov's right. The rays sparkled off a mammoth chandelier hanging over the center of the table.

Belyanov felt his chest tighten and his throat constrict. He stood awkwardly for what seemed to be a full minute, but in reality was no more than five seconds, during which Stalin and Beria inspected him like a laboratory specimen.

"Enter, Belyanov," Beria commanded. "Sit."

Belyanov hesitated, unsure whether to sit at the end of the table opposite Stalin, or move closer, perhaps next to Beria. He decided to do neither and took a seat across from Beria and to Stalin's right.

Stalin and Beria stared at Belyanov, the only sound in the room the ticking of an ornate grandfather clock near the entrance. He sat rigidly with his hands folded in his lap like a schoolboy waiting to be scolded by his teacher. He was relieved when Beria finally spoke.

"What is the status of the Kapsky matter, Belyanov?"

"Major Gromov remains in pursuit. The last information we received is that he is closing on Professor Kapsky southeast of Danzig."

"When does he expect to acquire Kapsky?"

"Unknown. My information does not come from Gromov but from Colonel Goncharov."

"Goncharov, I assume, is to ensure that there are no witnesses to Gromov acquiring Kapsky or any matters ancillary thereto?"

"Correct."

"Goncharov reports a high probability of success?"

"Yes."

"What percentage?"

A charge of anxiety coursed through Belyanov. Goncharov hadn't provided any probability.

"Ninety percent," he lied.

Beria's eyes seemed to bore through him as if he could mine Belyanov's brain for details and accuracy. Belyanov dared not glance at Stalin.

"Under ordinary circumstances, Belyanov, ninety percent would be sufficient. These are not ordinary circumstances," Beria informed. "The acquisition of Professor Kapsky was originally an imperative for our own short- and long-term strategic interests. Those interests, although of extreme importance, are joined by another interest of equal importance. An interest that must be met urgently.

"As you know, Dr. Kapsky escaped from Katyn Forest. Do you appreciate the significance of that fact, Belyanov?"

Belyanov nodded. "Should the Americans and British acquire Kapsky, and thus acquire *proof* of Katyn Forest, it will complicate matters with the Western Allies, particularly Mr. Roosevelt."

"The Germans only discovered the graves barely four months ago. They have been trying to propagandize it to drive a wedge between the Western Allies and the Motherland. To this point the story seems so fantastical that neither the Americans nor the British believe it. After all, it comes from the Nazis, from Hitler. But if a credible source, someone other than the Nazis, were to confirm the story, that might cause the Americans and British to rethink opening a Western Front against Hitler, a front the Motherland desperately needs. Katyn Forest is the difference between fighting a Hitler whose energies are fully directed at the Motherland or fighting a Hitler who must be concerned with two fronts. We have been encouraging, persuading, whipping, and prodding Churchill and Roosevelt to open a Western Front against the Wehrmacht for quite some time. Churchill presently demurs that he is barely surviving the Battle of Britain and Roosevelt is occupied with the Japanese. They make pleasant noises about opening a Western Front and we believe they will do so—but if the reality of Katyn Forest was ever confirmed it would complicate things drastically. We cannot permit such complications, Belyanov."

In his periphery, Belyanov watched Stalin's expression. Nothing. Only an intensity that caused Belyanov's stomach to burn. His decision not to inform Beria that the Americans had taken custody of Kapsky would prove fatal if they escaped. But if Belyanov informed them now, they'd be outraged at being kept in the dark. He rationalized that it didn't matter; they'd be outraged that the Americans had Kapsky, regardless of when he informed them of such.

"Gromov is proficient. He will acquire Kapsky," Belyanov assured.

Stalin shifted in his seat to face Belyanov, whose throat and jaw tightened. Both Belyanov *and* Beria sat frozen.

"Belyanov, Kapsky must be acquired," Stalin said coldly. "You understand me, yes?"

Belyanov nodded and consciously tried to sound confident. "Yes."

"However, as you know, that is insufficient. Nothing whatsoever must be left to chance. Anyone with whom Kapsky may have had contact—specifically, the Americans—cannot be permitted to survive. I assume Gromov understands that?"

"He does."

Stalin leveled his gaze directly at Belyanov's eyes. "Good. Is there anything that I should know?"

Belyanov's chest constricted. "No. I shall report immediately upon the mission's conclusion."

"No, you will not, Belyanov," Stalin corrected. "You will report on the mission's *successful* conclusion. Which, I expect, is imminent?"

"It is and I will."

Stalin sat utterly motionless and stared at Belyanov. The chief of

OKRNKVD had an unblemished record. He'd served loyally and well. He'd received nothing but accolades over the course of his career. And he understood his life had absolutely no value to the men staring at him as though he were a worm underfoot.

"Leave us," Beria said. "Report to me the successful conclusion of the operation."

Belyanov rose and awkwardly walked the length of the room to the large oak doors.

CHAPTER 56

The quartet lay silently among the brush at the edge of the woods and watched a dozen German troops surrounding the potato truck as an Oberfeldwebel questioned Mikołaj, who repeated his act of appearing irritated that he'd been stopped. The act had worked at the previous checkpoint, but this Oberfeldwebel didn't appear to be impressed with the performance. Indeed, to Fulmar's ear the tone of the Oberfeldwebel's question was between skeptical and hostile.

One German was lying on the ground inspecting the truck's undercarriage. One was rifling through the truck's cab. And two were climbing onto the truck's bed, half of which remained covered by the tarpaulin.

The two on the bed repeated the checkpoint guard's maneuver of stabbing the tarp and the uncovered potatoes with the bayonets. Mikołaj protested vehemently. Part of it was an act, but part was genuine: his crop was being destroyed.

The Oberfeldwebel's questioning grew in intensity. Whatever Mikołaj was saying, it wasn't satisfactory.

"Let's hope those guys on the bed don't notice the blood from McDermott's wound on any of the potatoes," Fulmar whispered to Matuszek.

"This isn't routine or happenstance. The Germans must have been alerted to something, perhaps by that farmer we saw in the distance. He keeps asking about passengers. Mikołaj insists the only passengers are his potatoes, which the troops are destroying."

"They've gone over the truck thoroughly," Fulmar said. "But they're not leaving."

Matuszek agreed. "The Oberfeldwebel doesn't seem to be in a hurry to be on his way. He's waiting for something to happen."

"How much farther to the canal?"

"You mean by foot?"

Fulmar nodded.

"If we leave in the next ten minutes, between eight to ten hours, depending upon how much evasive action we need to take."

"That's cutting it really close. Too close. I don't think our ride will leave us—at least not right away. But we need to get going right away to be sure."

The Oberfeldwebel was walking casually around the truck, inspecting it for the third time. His men were now arrayed in front of the truck, blocking the roadway. Fulmar could see no other vehicles up or down the road. "This isn't good," Fulmar said. "They're in no hurry to leave and we need to get moving—whether or not that's by truck or on foot." Fulmar glanced at Kapsky, who was lying just behind them. "Also, the professor's not looking any better. I'm not sure he can travel very far by foot. We may have to force the issue."

"We only have two guns," Matuszek replied. "McDermott may have the will, but his arm is useless."

"Believe me, I prefer not to have to engage. But we're fast running out of options."

"Taking on that many Germans isn't much of an option."

"I can take two or three before they can react. I'm sure you can do the same. Plus, it'll take the remainder several seconds to even figure out where the fire's coming from."

Matuszek shook his head. "I am used to being outnumbered and outgunned, but these are not favorable odds. Let's wait a few more minutes."

Fulmar examined the scene in front of him. He counted the number of German troops again to be sure. Twelve, including the Oberfeldwebel. All but the Oberfeldwebel carried Karabiners. Half were now in front of the truck with the Oberfeldwebel and the driver. The remainder were walking about the truck, continuing to inspect.

Fulmar glanced back at Kapsky again. The professor wasn't even watching the scene. His head was resting on his folded arms, eyes closed, as if trying to conserve strength. McDermott was watching the scene in front of them with his jaw clenched, grimacing in pain.

"They have more rifles," Matuszek whispered, driving his argument home.

"No good options," Fulmar agreed. "But we're being forced into taking one. These guys look like they're in no hurry to leave, like they're just passing the time waiting for something to happen. But we can't afford to wait."

"They have a big firepower advantage. If we engage them now, they will probably win. Even if *we* win, how long will the fight last? What if one or two get away and alert others?"

Fulmar withdrew his M1911 and extended it before him, sighting the Oberfeldwebel. He held the sight for two seconds before moving to the soldier to the Oberfeldwebel's immediate right and then to his left. At least three of the soldiers were hidden from view on the opposite side of the truck bed. He calculated that he would be able to hit two or three before the rest could get to cover.

Fulmar expelled a lungful of air, cursed, and rested the butt of the pistol on the ground. "We need that truck," he concluded.

"They've checked the truck already," Matuszek observed, perplexed. "What are they doing? What are they waiting for?"

Fulmar nodded to the road behind the truck. "Maybe that."

Matuszek followed Fulmar's line of vision to see several vehicles engulfed in a swirl of dust approaching rapidly from the rear. Within moments, a command car and four Kübelwagens came to a halt immediately behind the truck. The passenger in the rear of the command car got out and strode imperiously toward the Oberfeldwebel and the truck driver. Fulmar recognized his bearing in an instant. Six foot five, at least 250 pounds, gleaming black boots, the hair exposed under his peaked visor cap so blond it was almost white. The monster who terrorized villagers into confessing. The one who executed women and children to coerce cooperation. For once he was without his precious panzers.

Konrad Maurer ignored the salutes from the soldiers surrounding the truck and walked slowly toward the driver until he was barely two feet away. The Oberfeldwebel moved deferentially several steps back.

Maurer towered over the driver in silence. Then he craned his neck about, slowly scanning the surrounding countryside before staring down at the driver once more.

"Where are they?" he asked quietly.

The driver blinked several times, a confused expression on his face. "What do you mean?"

Before the driver's mouth had even closed, Maurer's gloved right hand struck the man on the right side of his head with enough force to cause his legs to quake.

"Do not waste my time or I will have you disemboweled. They are nearby. I will ask only once more. Where are they?"

Staggered, the driver tested his jaw with his right hand before vomiting, barely missing Maurer's gleaming boots. Fulmar could see a sneer of disgust cross Maurer's face as he withdrew his Walther from his holster and placed it against the driver's temple.

"You were conveying four men in this wretched piece of machinery. I know that, so do not try to be clever. Polish potato farmers are not clever.

"I assume you do not know these men. Indeed, you could *not* know, having only just encountered them. They mean nothing to you. You provide assistance to them only out of your hatred for us Germans. To be frank, I care nothing about them, either. I care only for the one among them who is a professor."

Maurer pressed the barrel of the pistol against the driver's temple. "Do you know this professor? No. But you know who I am, correct? You have heard of me? Perhaps even seen me. You know how I proceed with such matters. So save yourself. Where did you drop your passengers? Tell me where and you can be on your way with your precious potatoes. In fact, I will *purchase* them from you at double—no, triple—your standard price."

The driver looked terrified but said nothing. Maurer waited several more seconds.

"You are an old fool," Maurer said resignedly. "It appears you prefer to die. Is it because you believe it is the honorable thing to do? Where is the honor in dying for men you do not even know? They would not do the same for you, believe me. You are just a potato farmer. A stupid Polish potato farmer. You will provide them with precious transportation and, in return, they let you die."

Maurer turned the barrel of the weapon so that it was parallel to the driver's temple. The SS Standartenführer tilted his head upward and shouted, "Professor Kapsky! You are nearby. I know it. You do not want any more to die because of you. This man *will* die if you do not come out and surrender. Should you surrender, this man will be treated well, extremely well, because you are extremely valuable to the Reich. You will have every comfort provided, every need fulfilled. You will become wealthy. You will be celebrated.

"Now you are exhausted. Already, many have died because of you. *This man* will die because of you if you do not surrender."

Maurer fell silent and scanned the woods where the quartet remained prone. Then he discharged the pistol next to Mikołaj's temple, the muzzle flash scorching the skin, and the shock collapsing him to his knees.

Fulmar flinched but restrained himself from firing. He glimpsed Kapsky, who had an anguished look on his face, tears pouring from his eyes. Fulmar put a finger to his lips and shook his head sharply.

"Son of a bitch," Fulmar whispered to Matuszek. "Kapsky can't take much more of this. He's going to break. Crawl back there and put a hand over his mouth. Don't let him make a *sound*."

Matuszek did just that. Kapsky nodded that he understood, but Matuszek's hand remained clamped firmly across Kapsky's mouth.

Maurer reached down, pulled Mikołaj upright by the back of his collar, and steadied him on his feet. "We shall repeat the performance, Professor Kapsky," Maurer shouted, "but this time the bullet will enter your friend's temple and exit out the other side of his skull, taking large amounts of brain matter along with it. Think about that for a moment, Professor. That image will be seared into your brain for the remainder of your life." Maurer paused and again scanned the woods, listening for a response.

Fulmar braced for the SS officer to fire his weapon, looking behind him to be sure that Matuszek had a firm grip over Kapsky's mouth. Then he cursed furiously.

Standing over Matuszek and Kapsky, mere feet behind, were four black-clad German troops, Karabiners trained on Fulmar, McDermott, Matuszek, and Kapsky.

"*Hände hoch,*" one of the Germans ordered.

McDermott swore loudly, the volume magnified by the pain in his arm.

Fulmar, McDermott, and Matuszek each complied, McDermott with a continuing string of profanities. The Obergefreiter motioned with his rifle for the four to stand. "Hands over your heads." He motioned with his rifle in Maurer's direction. "Move."

The four complied, walking slowly through the woods toward the road, Fulmar grinding his teeth and McDermott continuing to issue profanities.

When Fulmar emerged onto the road he saw a smile of superiority on Maurer's face.

"So," the Standartenführer said smugly. "My performance so riveted you fools that my men could approach undetected. A simple ruse and you idiots are mesmerized. Just as I'd expected. Only Americans could be so stupid."

"I'm British," McDermott growled through the arm pain.

"Nearly as bad," Maurer said dismissively. He examined Matuszek's face. "Am I mistaken or is this Commander Matuszek himself? Hero of the *Armia*?" Maurer grinned expansively. "Kapsky and Matuszek; Canaris will be pleased. The *Führer* will be pleased." Maurer examined Kapsky. "Professor Kapsky. It is a pleasure to finally meet you. Much of my time these last three years has been occupied trying to find you. I must say, you do not appear to be well. Do not be concerned. You will receive the finest care and sustenance as soon as we convey you to our post in Danzig. That will not be long. We will convey you there presently and then, after treatment and all the food you can eat, to Seventy-six Tirpitzufer." Maurer scrutinized the twelve soldiers and the Kübelwagens. "Oberfeldwebel, take your men and tell them we have Kapsky and to prepare for treatment."

Maurer watched as they departed. He then gestured toward Mikołaj. "I am certain you observed from your place in the woods that this man, despite being threatened with his life, refused to disclose your whereabouts. A mere potato farmer. Most courageous, especially given that he does not appear to have any connection to you. Motivated, perhaps, out of patriotism. In a sense, quite admirable."

Maurer raised his Walther and shot Mikołaj twice in the face. Kapsky emitted a strangulated wail.

"Admirable," Maurer continued, "but ultimately useless. The rest of you will not be shot, at least not by me. You shall be prisoners and interrogated. Again, not by me, but by experts in extracting information. This, of course, does not apply to Professor Kapsky, who shall have only exemplary treatment as long as he cooperates."

Maurer stopped speaking and stared at Fulmar, whose expression had gone from anger and consternation to amusement. Maurer took several steps toward him until he was at arm's length.

"You have quite a curious look on your face for someone who has just been captured by enemy forces and has just witnessed someone executed. Do you find your predicament amusing?"

Fulmar broke into a grin. "I find *you* amusing."

Maurer cocked his head back slightly, perplexed. No one, especially prisoners, found him amusing. Intimidating or frightening, perhaps. But he was anything but amusing. Amusing suggested that he might be an object of ridicule. Maurer was nothing of the sort. He fired several rounds into the engine of the potato truck.

"How am I amusing . . . Fulmar, is it not?"

Although Fulmar was taken aback by Maurer's knowledge of his name, he betrayed no emotion. "You're obviously impressed with yourself. In my experience, individuals with such high regard for themselves usually crash and burn spectacularly, because they're oblivious to their deficiencies and don't make provision for them."

Maurer stood ramrod straight and made a show of looking down on Fulmar. "Deficiencies, Fulmar? It strikes me as ironic—no, humorous—that a prisoner in custody would remark about the deficiencies of his captor. After all, *your* manifest deficiencies resulted in your team being captured by me. I dispatched soldiers to circle behind your position well before I arrived on the scene and you were so riveted by my little performance with the idiot potato farmer that you were oblivious to their presence. A mere schoolboy ruse was sufficient to capture you."

Fulmar shrugged. "I'll concede that. But your deficiencies will ultimately lead to your defeat."

Maurer smirked. "Precisely which deficiencies are those?"

"Lack of self-awareness."

"A tautology. Would you care to be more specific?"

"Not really." A jocular smile crossed Fulmar's face. "I don't want to give you any clues as to how we're going to beat you."

Maurer threw his head back and laughed uproariously. "You're quite the comedian, Fulmar. I shall enjoy your interrogation."

"I will say this," Fulmar offered. "You do have an utter lack of irony."

Maurer raised his eyebrows. "Really? How so?"

"You're pretty impressed, obviously, with your cleverness, your wits. You outsmarted us. But it's always the guy that thinks he's so smart that gets outsmarted in the end."

Maurer laughed again and drew closer. "Did it occur to you that in this play, *you* are the character that gets outsmarted in the end?"

Maurer turned abruptly and addressed the officer who had halted Mikołaj's truck. "Leutnant, take your men back up the road and conduct a thorough sweep of the area between here and the factory. There is another American somewhere in the vicinity. He is to be found and captured. Kill him only if you have no option." The officer immediately directed his men into their vehicles and departed, dust in their wake.

Fulmar remained composed despite his bewilderment that Maurer seemed to have infallible intelligence. Intelligence that suggested the highest levels of the U.S. government may have been compromised.

Maurer turned back to Fulmar with a self-satisfied smirk. "Throughout this war I have been baffled by the ineptitude of you Americans. You have an abundance of resources and a sizable population. One would think you could produce a more effective opposition. Perhaps, in the end, there is no remedy for stupidity."

Maurer stepped back from Fulmar and addressed Kapsky. "Professor, it is my privilege to convey you to Berlin, where I'm sure you will thoroughly enjoy the comforts and privileges afforded you there. But first, we will take care of your immediate needs: food, medical care, rest. There is a factory not far from here that we have converted into a fine medical facility. We will convey you there, where you will receive the necessary medical attention and sustenance. Once the medical personnel declare you fit for travel, you will be taken to Tirpitzufer, Berlin—most likely by rail, but perhaps by air. There is an airstrip east of Danzig."

Maurer stopped and looked at Fulmar, who was shaking his head. "Do you have commentary, Lieutenant Fulmar?"

"No, but I have a wager."

"I rather enjoy gambling. What is your wager?"

"You won't get to Tirpitzufer," Fulmar said. "There is a man in Washington, D.C., who will make sure of it."

"Would that be your head of Office of Strategic Services?" Maurer asked with a smirk. "I rather doubt it."

Fulmar, concealing his astonishment, said nothing.

Maurer motioned to the Kübelwagens. "Get into the vehicles, please. We are done wasting time."

Maurer stepped into his car and signaled for his driver to proceed. The driver looped around the Kübelwagens and proceeded to the front. Maurer's troops directed Fulmar and McDermott into the vehicle directly behind Maurer's; Kapsky and Matuszek were directed to the third vehicle in the caravan. The remainder followed in the fourth vehicle.

Maurer signaled his driver, who led the caravan back in the direction of the factory. Fulmar's mind was racing, evaluating options for escape. They had no viable means to do so while moving. Perhaps if they came to a stop he could overpower the driver, but the other troops would easily assume control merely by brandishing their weapons. Fulmar was reluctant to concede that they had few, if any, options. But he was also a realist. An opportunity might present itself at some point. He had to be prepared to seize it immediately. Even so, he couldn't rely on McDermott for assistance. The man's right arm was useless and he was in extreme pain. Matuszek was the only person on whom he could plausibly rely, and he was in another vehicle. Coordination would be impossible. Any escape attempt would likely result in one of them—and perhaps everyone but Kapsky—being killed.

Waiting until they arrived at the factory was not much more satisfactory. Presumably there would be a greater troop presence there, and Maurer—if he hadn't done so already in anticipation of capturing Kapsky—would likely order the construction of a field prison or convert part of the facility into one.

No good options. The worst option, however, was to do nothing. Kapsky would be in the custody of the SS and Fulmar had no illusions that they wouldn't gain his "cooperation." That would have potentially catastrophic implications.

Fulmar concluded that under no circumstances could Kapsky remain in German custody. He glanced back at the vehicle in which Kapsky and Matuszek were riding, the soldier in the front passenger seat giving Fulmar a disapproving look. Kapsky's appearance remained the same—weak and distraught—maybe too weak to exert enough energy to flee even if they could engineer an escape.

Matuszek, on the other hand, wore a determined, defiant look that telegraphed willingness to take on the Germans at the best opportunity. Matuszek knew the odds as well or better than anybody. But, Fulmar surmised, Matuszek calculated that this might be his last opportunity to strike a blow against the enemy.

Fulmar turned and faced forward again, looking at Maurer sitting almost regally in his command car: the conquering hero of the Reich, and, Fulmar conceded, justifiably so. The acquisition of Kapsky and the knowledge he possessed purportedly had world-changing implications, and so it would have momentous implications for Maurer's career. The soulless bastard needed killing, and Fulmar tried his best to conjure a way to do so.

As he did, he noticed Maurer barking at his driver as he pointed forward. Fulmar looked past the lead vehicle and saw what appeared to be a small cloud of black smoke approximately a kilometer ahead. The lead vehicle slowed as the convoy approached the source of the smoke, which to Fulmar appeared to have the heaviness and thickness of an oil fire. From a distance it seemed to shroud the entire width of the road and extend into the woods on each side.

The convoy slowed as it got closer. Fulmar could smell the heavy odor of hot oil. Nothing beyond the curtain of black smoke, which rose to at least twenty feet, was visible, and the stench was nearly overwhelming.

When they came to within fifty meters of the smoke curtain, Fulmar could make out the source of the smoke—an overturned Kübelwagen that had caught fire. Fulmar couldn't discern any passengers, but concluded they had to be seriously injured or dead.

Fulmar saw Maurer stand in the rear of his car, surveying the scene, his head moving from right to left. There was no room on either side of the vehicle for the convoy to pass. The fire would have to be extinguished and the obstruction removed for the convoy to pass.

Maurer stepped from the rear of his car and onto the dirt road to inspect the obstruction more closely. The soldiers on the passenger side of each of the Kübelwagens also got out in anticipation of executing whatever command Maurer was about to issue. As they did so, the top of his driver's skull was sheared off by a round coming from somewhere in the woods to Fulmar's right. Before the driver's body slumped limply against the door, Fulmar felt warm blood spray across his face from the head of *his* driver, who also fell against the driver's-side door.

Fulmar reacted instantly, lunging toward the German in the

front passenger seat, who was stunned by what he had just seen. Fulmar grasped the side of the German's head and jacked it backward over the rear of his seat with such force that the snap of his cervical vertebrae could be heard by McDermott, who had already relieved the man of his Karabiner 19 and was beginning to sight the German in the passenger seat in the rear vehicle. Before McDermott, face contorted in pain, could acquire the target and squeeze the trigger, the German's body shuddered twice from two shots to his torso, and fell against the vehicle's driver, who was being strangled from behind by Matuszek, whose face remained beet red from exertion even after the driver collapsed limply against the rear of his seat.

Fulmar reached forward instantly and seized the sidearm of the passenger-side German and began to train it on SS Standartenführer Maurer standing along the edge of the woods. But Maurer was not alone.

Fulmar smiled, then laughed, then hooted. Standing behind Maurer was Major Richard Canidy, USAAF, with his combat knife against Maurer's trachea and a vicious look on his face.

Fulmar scrambled out of the Kübelwagen and approached Canidy and Maurer. On the other side of the road, Emil emerged from the woods carrying his rifle. He looked, as usual, calm—as if he'd been on a butterfly expedition in the woods.

As Fulmar drew within a few meters of Canidy, he could hear him interrogating Maurer, who shook his head—carefully, to avoid slicing his neck on the blade.

"Are there any more checkpoints heading northwest along the road? Have they been alerted to us?" Canidy asked.

"Surely you don't expect a response."

"Surely I do."

"You'll not get one," Maurer said coolly. "You have no recourse."

"My recourse is to slit your throat and watch your face as the blood drains from your body."

"If you were a Russian, that might persuade me," Maurer said, keeping his head and neck as still as possible, "but you are an American. You cannot and will not do anything even remotely approaching that threat."

Candidy's jaws tightened. "No one, other than the men you see here, will know." Candidy tilted his head toward Commander Matuszek. "You see that man over there? You know who he is? You know precisely what he's capable of and what he'd love to do to you. Scores of his troops are dead or mutilated because of you. Scores more Polish civilians. I'll just hand the blade over to him."

Maurer forced a relatively convincing chuckle. "You are not dealing with an ignorant foot soldier. I know a bit about the American military and its strictures. You cannot avoid accountability by simply looking away while another performs a violation of one of your codes."

Candidy began to respond when Kapsky rushed toward Maurer and struck him in the face with his open hand, drawing a bead of blood from the German's left nostril.

"Professor Kapsky is uniquely motivated to elicit the information from you," Candidy said. "And he's a civilian. I'll defer to him."

Maurer swallowed carefully so his Adam's apple wouldn't make contact with the blade. "Be my guest. Place the burden on a poor civilian. A pathetic display, Major Candidy. I was given to understand that you were somewhat of—what do you Americans refer to it as?—a cowboy. That is why you were selected for this extraordinarily challenging mission. Your superiors believed you had the talent and courage to do it. Clearly you have neither."

Canidy's wrist tensed involuntarily, and the blade nicked the underside of Maurer's chin, a smear of blood oozing from the incision. Fulmar's eyes locked on Canidy and he shook his head sharply once.

Everyone's head but Maurer's turned upon hearing the sound of an engine somewhere behind the curtain of black smoke. A vehicle was approaching at high speed.

Canidy heard the vehicle brake and skid to a halt. Emil immediately raised his rifle to his shoulder and aimed toward the curtain. Fulmar bent down, withdrew the sidearm of the driver of one of the Kübelwagens, and also raised it toward the smoke. There was silence for at least ten seconds and then Canidy heard shouts in German from behind the curtain. In a low voice Matuszek said, "They are asking Maurer if he's here and if he can hear them."

The shouting continued for a few more seconds. Canidy's team remained utterly still. Seconds ticked by in silence. Suddenly, Maurer erupted with shouts for help. Canidy reflexively dragged the blade of the knife across Maurer's trachea, slicing nearly to his spine.

Canidy stepped back from the gush of blood, dropping Maurer's lifeless body to the ground as shouts came from the other side of the curtain. Without hesitation Emil sprinted into the woods with his rifle held low. Less than a minute later Canidy's team heard a series of shots, a slight pause, and another series. Then silence.

Moments later there was a rustle in the woods and Emil appeared, a passive expression on his face. Yet another day at the office. Canidy, Fulmar, Matuszek, and McDermott all nodded their appreciation toward the young soldier.

Fulmar said, "Okay. We've handled the immediate problem, but we've got a ways to go. An unknown number of checkpoints, and the possibility that we won't get to the canal on the Thorisdottirs' timetable." He looked at Sebastian Kapsky, whose face was drawn and sallow. "Professor, we need to move now. Can you walk?"

"I will have to."

"That won't work," Canidy said. "Our job is to get you out alive. Due respect, Professor, you look like hell."

Kapsky nodded. "I've heard that before. I feel worse."

Fulmar stated what was obvious to everyone: "No way can we walk, evade Germans, and get to the boat on time—or even within a reasonable proximity of the Thorisdottirs' window."

"Give it to me straight, no bull, Professor. We need to go fifteen to twenty kilometers to the canal in about five hours. The good news is the terrain from here to the Baltic is mostly pretty flat. The bad news is we need to be prepared to run if we encounter un-friendlies. Now, can you do that?"

Kapsky straightened and said, "I think—"

"Sorry," Canidy interrupted. "I don't care what the hell you think. Can you *do* it? Yes or no?"

"I do not know."

"Honest answer," Canidy said.

"Dick," Fulmar said. "Let's at least start moving. We'll know whether or not the professor can get to the canal when we do or don't get there. In the meantime, we're wasting precious minutes."

Canidy's face tensed with frustration. "Hell, you're right. Let's get moving. We don't have any options. We either get there or we don't. But we can't stand around here playing Hamlet."

Canidy put his hand on Kapsky's shoulder. "Professor, this is your last and only opportunity to get the hell out of here. You've evaded the Germans longer than anyone could have expected. You can do it again. One last push. One last push, then freedom."

Kapsky nodded. "Thank you. Thanks to all of you. I will do my best in honor of those who have perished to protect me or simply because of me. I owe all of you my best effort." Kapsky shuddered as if chilled. "But I must eat soon. I need fuel."

"We all do," Canidy acknowledged. "Anybody got any crumbs in their rucks?"

"All out," McDermott said.

The rest grumbled and shook their heads.

"Okay. Let's get moving, then. First order of business is rustling up something edible. We'll all need some calories if we're going to hump fifteen kilometers."

McDermott, jaws clenched from pain, piped up. "There were some blackberry bushes where we were lying in the woods"—he pointed to Maurer's corpse—"watching that SOB. It's on our way. There's probably some other fruits in the woods along the way."

"And don't forget," Matuszek added, "there's a whole truckload of potatoes back there, too."

Canidy stared blankly at Matuszek as he stuffed the Walther in his waistband. "Yum."

"We better get going," Fulmar said. "We can discuss our options on the way. Walk."

They turned and began walking back down the road. Canidy stopped abruptly. "No," he said sharply. "We'll ride."

The rest looked at him, confused.

"We'll ride," he repeated.

"What the hell are you talking about?" McDermott asked. "Ride *what* exactly? The potato truck again? Under the tarp? You, Fulmar, and I don't speak Polish and our sweet little SS Standartenführer shot the truck up, if you recall. It won't operate."

Canidy shook his head and pointed to Maurer's command car. "Would be a shame to waste an exquisite specimen such as that."

Everyone looked at the car and then back to Canidy. Fulmar said, "Dick, you don't look like you're suffering from battle fatigue or anything, but all due respect, you're nuts. We might as well put a siren on it with flashing lights, drive right to the nearest German field headquarters, and turn ourselves in."

Canidy squinted as he pondered the command vehicle. "I'll grant you it's not without risk, but we might just be able to pull it off with a bit of discipline."

Canidy walked toward the vehicle, the others following.

"Dick," McDermott said. "Do I need to point out that if we come to a checkpoint and they see us in this we'll get machine-gunned before we even have a chance to brake or stop?"

"No one would dare impede, let alone machine-gun, an SS Standartenführer and his staff," Canidy replied.

Fulmar shook his head. "I don't believe this. We're going to play Halloween?"

"Damn right. We're going to change clothes with these guys and drive as far as we can." Canidy patted Kapsky on the shoulder. "This guy's game, and I respect that. But the odds of us getting him to the boat on foot aren't good. He can barely walk now. And"—Canidy faced Kapsky—"to be honest and respectful, the wear and tear may be too much for you, too, right?"

Kapsky said nothing.

"We have no good options, gentlemen," Canidy said. "But this is the better one."

Thumbing his shirt, Fulmar noted what the others were thinking. "Even if we do this, we can't ride in an open command car looking like this . . ."

"Exactly right," Canidy acknowledged. "So start getting undressed."

"Whoa." Fulmar put a hand up. "Hold it, Dick. You're actually serious? We're supposed to . . . ?"

"Getting a little squeamish, Eric? I'll grant you, I'm not a big fan of wearing a dead man's clothes, but we can't very well ride around in a topless SS command car looking like Home Army rejects."

"There's blood on some of them," McDermott said. "Bullet holes."

"What do you expect? We're getting them at no charge." Canidy pointed to Maurer's corpse. "That's mine. I think I can pull off SS Standartenführer."

Canidy bent down and began removing Maurer's uniform. The others reluctantly chose subjects similar in size and began doing the same. Matuszek said, "We are six. The car can fit six, but it will appear peculiar."

Canidy asked, "What do you suggest?"

"It will look more natural if two ride in front and three in back," Matuszek replied. "I suggest I sit in the front passenger seat, since I'm most familiar with the area and the route to the canal. Fulmar drives, since he speaks German and is most likely to have to speak if we are stopped, although I doubt anyone would dare stop a car conveying an SS Standartenführer.

"Major, you obviously should sit in the rear center seat flanked on the right by your loyal adjutant McDermott so that his wounded arm is better concealed against the door, and to the left by the professor"—Matuszek glanced at Kapsky—"who appears to have assumed the rank of Stabsgefreiter."

Matuszek came over to Emil. "You have performed well, son. Your services will no longer be needed here. Report back to Porucznik Kutylowski. Tell him I said you shall be promoted upon my return and you deserve a leave."

Emil slung his rifle over his shoulder, straightened, and saluted Matuszek, who returned the salute. Canidy, Fulmar, and McDermott did the same. Canidy began clapping, and Fulmar and McDermott followed suit.

"See you in hell, Emil," Canidy said with a grin.

Emil laughed. "See you in hell, Major." Then he waded into the woods and disappeared.

"I hope to see him again one day," Canidy said.

"I hope you do, too," Matuszek said as he pulled the trousers from a German corpse. "The probabilities, however, are not good."

Canidy removed his shirt and dabbed at the fresh blood from the throat wound on the collar of Maurer's shirt. Thankfully, it blended sufficiently with the shirt collar that it would be visible only from a short distance.

Although Maurer was a bigger man, his clothes fit Canidy surprisingly well. Canidy struggled, however, to pull the boots on, never having worn footgear that rose above the knee. Canidy checked Maurer's Walther and made sure he had spare ammunition. He saved the visor cap for last, letting it sit low on his brow. When he was done dressing, he examined himself in the car's sideview mirror.

He looked the part.

Fulmar, McDermott, and Matuszek didn't look bad, either. The clothing was a bit loose on each, but not noticeably so. Kapsky's uniform, however, was visibly ill-fitting. The sleeves were too short and the pants and shirt were baggy. Canidy hoped that the mismatch wouldn't be visible while seated in the vehicle.

They placed most of their own clothing they'd removed in the trunk of the vehicle. Fulmar fingered the bullet hole in the shoulder of his uniform. "What do we do about these?"

Canidy shrugged. "If we get stopped, we say nothing. What

checkpoint guard is going to question the staff of an SS Standartenführer?"

"A petrified Soldat who wants to appear alert and thorough in
the eyes of such Standartenführer," Fulmar responded.

"You say what should be obvious. We were in a fight," Canidy
said to Fulmar. "Then I'll act impatient and ask the Soldat what the
hell does he *think* happened?"

"But you don't speak German."

"Even better. I'll let you, my subordinate, do the talking for me.
Just be sure to act highly offended."

CHAPTER 57

Washington, D.C.
1207, 15 August 1943

Donovan sat at the end of the bar at the Old Ebbitt Grill farthest
from the 15th Street NW entrance, sipping Macallan. The restau-
rant and bar, usually filled with White House and Treasury staffers,
was sparsely populated. He recognized an assistant secretary of state
sitting with a woman not his wife at a table on the other side of the
room. Secretary of the Interior Harold Ickes and Secretary of Labor
Frances Perkins were engaged in conversation at the other end of
the room. When Henry Stimson walked in the door, they rose to
greet him. After short salutations, Stimson came to the bar and sat
next to Donovan.

"Hell, Bill," Stimson said. "I know you're not a big fan of their
politics, but for goodness' sakes, you could at least acknowledge
them."

"I don't see them going out of their way to acknowledge me,"
Donovan said dismissively.

"Of course not. You scare the hell out of them. They think you eat small children for breakfast."

Donovan took a sip of Macallan. "Not this morning."

"What do you hear from Commander Fleming?"

Donovan took another sip of whisky and shook his head. "They haven't heard a thing since the operation began, either. None of their contacts have sighted Canidy, Fulmar, or McDermott anywhere in Germany. We know from the boat captain that they were dropped off as scheduled at the designated spot near Danzig, but after that it's been radio silence."

"They have a radio?"

"Figure of speech. But, as a matter of fact, yes. A tiny contraption put together by our mad scientists. Not much range. Doubt it even works."

Donovan stopped talking as the bartender approached.

"Water, Mr. Secretary?"

"Thank you, Bert."

"Christ's sake," Donovan said as the bartender retreated. "At least order something with some flavor."

"What conclusions, if any, do you draw from the silence?" Stimson asked.

Donovan shook his head. "The logical one. These men were sent to perform a near impossible task. In Germany."

Stimson clapped Donovan on the back. "You can't blame yourself over this, Bill. Everyone knew what was at stake. Everyone knew the risks. Those men had absolutely no illusions about what they volunteered to do."

"They didn't volunteer."

"Of course they did, Bill. No one ordered them to go."

Donovan took another sip of Macallan and looked at Stimson.

"Come on, Henry. The head of the Office of Strategic Services asks you to go on an operation of extreme importance to the Allied effort, an operation that few beyond Roosevelt and Churchill have been briefed on. Seriously, that's an order. No one would refuse that."

"And they didn't." The bartender placed a glass of water before Stimson and retreated. "Did Fleming say *anything* whatsoever about the operation?"

"The last time they heard from their man was when he was in Gotland. Shortly thereafter, he was to meet Canidy and Fulmar and they were all to cross the Baltic into Poland. The Brits are as much in the dark as we are. None of their resistance contacts reported seeing Canidy, Fulmar, or McDermott. We don't know if they even made it into Germany. They disappeared shortly after making landfall."

"I expect you assume the worst."

Donovan pinched the bridge of his nose. "There's nothing else to expect, logically. Canidy and Fulmar are the best. I assume if Churchill sent him, McDermott was their best, or at least one of their best."

"What are our options, Bill?"

"We have no option other than pray that the Nazis can't figure out what the Kapsky document is about. And if they do figure out what it's all about, pray some more."

CHAPTER 58

Northern Poland
1312, 15 August 1943

Gromov was growing increasingly anxious.

Despite moving through the countryside at a trot, he feared he was getting no closer to the Americans and Kapsky. Worse, he believed that for a considerable period of time he had been moving in the wrong direction.

The redheaded woman had misled him, causing him to pursue the Americans at nearly a forty-five-degree angle from what he now believed was their actual path. Thankfully, he had heard the gunfire through the forest and followed his instincts, threading through the woods until coming upon some type of factory in a valley where German troops were guarding civilians. The smell of gunpowder was still in the air, and from his vantage point atop the hill he could see rapidly moving vehicles in the distance.

He knew he had to take a chance. He circumnavigated the factory and followed the path of the vehicles. More anxiety. Even assuming he was now following the right path, he couldn't make up the distance on foot. He had no visual contact with the Americans.

Thankfully, he encountered a boy of about twelve riding a bicycle on the same road taken by the vehicles. Gromov flagged the boy, who, upon discerning Gromov was armed, prudently turned around and began pedaling in the opposite direction.

Gromov surprised himself by not shooting him. Instead he sprinted after him, overtaking the frightened adolescent and pulling him to a halt. Then he tendered twenty *złoty* for the bicycle, which the relieved boy happily exchanged.

Gromov pedaled at a brisk pace for more than an hour, encountering only a farmer driving an empty ox-drawn cart. Yet more anxiety.

Then he heard gunfire again. Hopeful, he began pedaling faster, only to have the bike's chain snap, rendering it useless. The assassin cursed to himself repeatedly as he dismounted and began jogging down the road until he heard another round of gunfire, this time much closer. Above the treetops there appeared to be a plume of black smoke.

He ducked into the adjacent woods and proceeded quietly and cautiously toward the sound of the gunfire, silently praying that his instincts would be confirmed. With each moment, the window of opportunity for acquiring Kapsky was closing, and he'd yet to even *see* the man.

He paused to orient himself, to listen for more sounds, when there was a sound of movement—subtle, barely audible. Perhaps an animal.

Perhaps not. He dropped to the ground and lay still.

Less than a half minute later Gromov saw the tall young scout he had seen leading the Americans previously. He was weaving expertly through the trees, making hardly any noise.

Gromov's tension eased and was replaced by anticipation. This wasn't coincidence. The appearance of the scout meant the Americans—and Kapsky—were nearby. But where?

Gromov remained still, tracking the scout until he vanished amid the foliage. The scout was moving in the wrong direction— the direction of the factory—and no one was following. The gunfire Gromov had heard a short time ago had come from the opposite direction—northwest. Northwest was where the Americans would go to get out of the country.

The assassin counted slowly to one hundred. He wanted to rise, but disciplined himself to keep still for another count of one hundred. Then he rose and continued in the direction from which he'd heard the gunfire. He moved slowly and quietly, looking behind him every few seconds to ensure the scout hadn't doubled back.

It took only a few minutes. He could see breaks of light between the trees, indicating he was coming to a clearing, maybe a road. He slowed his pace yet further, moving from tree to tree, pausing for a moment before proceeding onward.

He saw a dirt road twenty meters ahead. He crouched with his weapon at the ready and crept toward the edge of the woods. He saw nothing to the right—southeast. But approximately a quarter kilometer to the left—northwest—was the unmistakable scene of combat. There were bodies on the ground, vehicles strewn haphazardly. Maybe an ambush. He observed the scene for a moment before approaching. He saw no movement. Whoever was responsible had moved on.

A peculiar scene. Kübelwagens, dead bodies stripped of their outer garments, a few random civilian garments strewn about nearby.

One body appeared familiar. The assassin took a closer look. The corpse was that of a large, tall man, throat cut to the bone. The hair was so blond it was almost white.

Not an ambush, Gromov thought. If it had been an ambush it would be more likely that the SS officer would have been shot.

Gromov inspected the immediate vicinity for clues. The most obvious was the absence of a command car. An SS Standartenführer did not travel in a Kübelwagen with the troops. The tire tracks in the dirt showed that a vehicle had turned about and headed northwest.

Gromov reflected as his mind's eye re-created the events that resulted in the macabre scene. The Americans had overpowered the Germans, stripped them, donned their uniforms, and departed in the command car.

It wouldn't work. The Germans would identify them as impostors and kill them at the next checkpoint. And if Kapsky was also wearing a German uniform, it would be unlikely German soldiers would know his importance, and would kill him, too.

They had a head start, but not by much. Gromov inspected the remaining Kübelwagen. The keys were in the ignition. He got in, started the engine, and drove as fast as it would go after the Americans.

CHAPTER 59

Northern Poland
1325, 15 August 1943

The sense of optimism bordering on exhilaration the team had felt when they drove off in the German vehicle lasted no more than twenty minutes. They'd traveled primarily through countryside dotted with a farm or two until they came to a nameless cluster of dwellings near Suchy Dąb, where they were compelled to come to a halt because of the seemingly endless procession of panzers crossing the road.

A large, empty, open-bed truck was in front of them, so the procession and the Gefreiter directing traffic at least fifteen meters away were not close enough to afford close inspection.

"Dick," Fulmar said. "Just remember, look smug and arrogant. In other words, be yourself. If one of these jackboots has the nerve to come over, I'll do all the talking."

Canidy thought he could see the tail of the procession less than a quarter of a kilometer to their right. But on closer inspection determined the procession was endless.

The Gefreiter directing traffic finally seemed to take interest in the car, glancing over every few seconds with a puzzled look on his face. He was short, stocky, with a pug face, and looked like a busybody. He waved over a Soldat standing on the other side of the convoy to take over for him and began walking past the truck toward the command car with a curious, somewhat irritated expression on his face.

Everyone in the command car except Canidy tensed upon his approach. The Gefreiter didn't appear cowed or intimidated by the presence of an SS Standartenführer.

Fulmar, speaking High German, changed that in an instant.

"You have the temerity to leave your post when this convoy is crawling along at a timid pace in the midst of a combat zone? What kind of incompetent fool are you to both slow the progression of a fighting column as well as that of SS Standartenführer Maurer?"

Stunned, the portly Gefreiter stopped abruptly.

"Come here, you incompetent idiot," Fulmar shouted. "Now!"

The Gefreiter obeyed instantly, if reluctantly, the attitude of his body shifting from dominance to almost canine submission.

"What are you waiting for?" Fulmar hissed.

The Gefreiter looked horrified, unsure of what to do.

"Name and unit. Commanding officer," Fulmar demanded.

The Gefreiter stuttered before beginning to respond. Fulmar cut him off. "Where is your salute? You have the audacity to address the Standartenführer without a salute? Particularly after this incompetent display?"

The Gefreiter began to salute, stopped abruptly, then stood at attention and began to salute again. Fulmar cut him off.

"Get out of here."

The Gefreiter spun abruptly and began to retreat.

"Wait. What is your company commander's name?"

The Gefreiter spun about to face Fulmar. "Hauptmann Hans Meyer."

"He will hear directly from Admiral Canaris and will be made to account for your incompetence and impudence. Now, expedite that column. *Move.*"

The Gefreiter saluted and spun on his heels, scrambling toward his previous post. A trail vehicle and convoy came into view over the northern horizon. Each of the car's occupants cursed silently. It would be some time before they could move.

"That came way too naturally for you," Canidy observed of Fulmar's performance, adding, "That's our one free pass. We're lucky we encountered the one blithering idiot in all the Wehrmacht. That won't happen again."

"With any luck, it shouldn't," Matuszek said, pointing northwest to wisps of smoke in the distance. "That's Danzig ahead. We should go on for a bit more, then proceed the rest of the way by foot."

"This doesn't look familiar," Canidy said.

"That's because, if you recall, the first time we were here we proceeded from the canal in a more westerly direction before turning south," McDermott explained in a strained voice.

Canidy turned and looked closely at McDermott, whose face was crimson with pain. His eyes were shot red and he was perspiring heavily. The sleeve covering his wounded arm was soaked with blood.

"McDermott, how are you hanging in there?" Canidy asked.

Instead of an oral response, McDermott nodded, causing Canidy to conclude that, in fact, the Scot was barely hanging in there.

Canidy looked to the right. The trail vehicle seemed barely

closer over the horizon. Each of the car's occupants silently cursed. It would be some time before they could move. Canidy hoped the idiot traffic cop wouldn't suddenly have an epiphany regarding Mc-Dermott's appearance. If he did, he was probably too intimidated to say anything. But it would be a while before they could move. Maybe enough time for him to begin thinking straight and summon the courage to say something.

Canidy passed the time performing mental calculations on how long it would take to get to the canal, but conceded to himself that without more precise knowledge of their whereabouts, any such calculations were little more than wild guesses. He hesitated to ask Matuszek, whose estimate would be far more accurate but, he feared, much longer.

Not one of the passengers spoke the entire time it took the column to pass. McDermott's breathing was becoming more audible and ragged. When the final vehicle passed before them, every occupant of the command car moved his feet as if engaging the clutch to put the vehicle into gear.

No more than a minute after they had begun moving again, Canidy couldn't wait any longer. "Commander, what's your estimate of when we'll reach the canal?"

"Close. But the roads are poor. Slow. With no delays we should arrive in the next two hours. We will drive for another twenty minutes. The remainder of the trip will be by foot."

Canidy refrained from glancing at McDermott. Everyone in the vehicle, McDermott included, wondered whether McDermott could possibly walk a half hour, a portion of which would no doubt be through dense forest and over challenging terrain.

"How long before we need to ditch the car and go on foot?" Canidy asked.

"At this pace, twenty minutes at the most."

Canidy pursed his lips, thinking. "Maybe we should've ditched our clothes back there instead of bringing them with us. We'll look conspicuous walking in civilian clothes."

"Hell, we'd be conspicuous no matter what," Fulmar said. "Roll with the punches."

Canidy exhaled. "Exactly right. Fourth quarter, ninth inning, championship round. We've made it this far, miraculously. Time to close the deal."

Canidy reached under his seat for the potatoes they'd taken from Mikołaj's truck along the way. He handed one to each of the passengers and was about to take a bite when he noted the potato was covered with numerous, almost microscopic, white grubs.

A torrent of Polish profanities from Matuszek confirmed that Canidy's potato wasn't an anomaly. They'd have to hump on empty stomachs.

CHAPTER 60

Northern Poland
1335, 15 August 1943

The Americans were a little more than a kilometer ahead and oblivious to his presence. Gromov had seen them stop in front of a lengthy German convoy. He'd been a bit surprised to see them so soon—he'd estimated they were at minimum several kilometers ahead of him. The convoy, however, had permitted him to gain significant ground and the ability to calibrate the distance between their vehicle and his.

He was but one against five. More accurately, for combat purposes, four—since Kapsky was not a combatant. Their numerical advantage was offset by their ignorance of his proximity. And by his martial superiority.

Gromov assessed that only three of them posed a challenge. Kapsky clearly was not. And Gromov detected something amiss with the one seated in the rear to the right. The pitch and attitude of his body was that of a wounded man. Of this Gromov was fairly confident, as he'd wounded more than he could recall and could assess the dispositions of the wounded well enough that he could tell even from a distance.

One of them appeared older than the rest, at least from a distance. Probably brave and experienced. War was for the young and strong; which meant middle-aged men who were still in the field were tough and savvy, but they had invariably lost a step. He most likely was an honorable soldier, but no match for Gromov's speed and ferocity.

Gromov concentrated on the driver and the tall one sitting in the middle rear. The latter was the leader. Gromov had observed him the last time. A proficient warrior, although not in Gromov's class. Still, uncommonly talented. Gromov needed to kill him first.

Fulmar slowed the vehicle as the road became increasingly pockmarked and the ride bumpy. Matuszek, as if in response, assured, "Not much farther."

Canidy felt Kapsky jostle against his shoulder and then slump forward. Alarmed, Canidy grasped Kapsky's collar and pulled him upright, his head lolling against the backrest.

"Slow down. We've got a serious problem," Canidy informed. "The professor is unconscious."

Fulmar immediately reduced the vehicle's speed and craned his head around to see for himself. Kapsky's eyes were half closed and appeared vacant, lifeless. "Check his pulse. He looks worse than just unconscious."

Canidy placed two fingers against Kapsky's neck, just beneath the jaw. After several seconds Canidy said, "I can't tell if his heart is even beating."

He quickly grasped Kapsky's left wrist, placing the same two fingers just below the base of the thumb. Canidy clenched his teeth and cursed. "He's barely got a pulse. Stop the car."

Fulmar took his foot off the accelerator and coasted to a halt. Both he and Matuszek turned in their seats to see Kapsky's head slump forward. Canidy placed his hand under Kapsky's nostrils for ten seconds. "Weak, damn it. I can hardly feel a damn thing."

"Slap him," Matuszek instructed. "Listen to me! Slap him hard."

Canidy slapped Kapsky twice across each cheek and immediately checked for a pulse in his right wrist. He cursed again. Then froze. "Wait, I think I have something. It's just that it's weak. Barely there." Canidy's eyes darted about the interior of the vehicle. "Everybody look for something. A field box. A first-aid kit . . ."

"What do you hope to find?" Matuszek asked.

"Hell if I know. Something."

Fulmar waved his hand underneath the driver's seat. Matuszek opened the compartment in the console separating the driver and passenger seats. Both said, "Nothing" simultaneously, but kept running their hands against the dashboard, side door pockets, and under the seats.

Canidy gently propped the professor up against the backrest and kept him upright with his left hand while running his right hand over the back of the front seat. Again, nothing.

"What do you have?" he asked the others. "What do you have?"

Fulmar and Matuszek continued to search. "Still nothing."

Canidy began slapping Kapsky's face several times, but there was no visible response.

"Here!" Fulmar shouted. "Here!"

A canteen in the bottom of the console. He pulled it out, unscrewed the top, and thrust it toward Canidy. "It's full. Throw some water on his face and then get him to drink the rest. It's all we've got."

Canidy tilted Kapsky's head back with his left hand, seized the canteen from Fulmar, and placed the nozzle to the professor's mouth.

"Be sure he doesn't choke," Fulmar cautioned.

Canidy ignored him and poured nearly half the contents of the container into Kapsky's mouth. Then he doused the professor's face with the remainder, drawing his head back from the pungent odor wafting toward him.

Shocked, Canidy said, "Crap."

"What?" Fulmar asked.

Canidy didn't respond. A moment later Kapsky's eyes snapped open and he retched violently, chest heaving.

Canidy continued to hold the professor upright as he hacked and wheezed for a full minute, his eyes darting about wildly.

"Professor, can you make it?" Canidy asked. "How do you feel? Are you able to keep going?"

Kapsky's eyes darted about wildly. Canidy patted his cheek repeatedly. "Professor? Are you with us? Can you hear me?"

Kapsky nodded, a startled expression making him appear frightened but alert. He continued hacking for another minute, then took several deep breaths, trying to compose himself.

Canidy withdrew his left hand from Kapsky's chest. "Listen to me. Do you think you're okay?"

Kapsky nodded vigorously and continued to gasp for air. Canidy looked at Fulmar and Matuszek, whose expressions continued to convey concern. "Based on the evidence," Canidy said, "it appears the previous operator of this vehicle had a fondness for rye."

Fulmar and Matuszek exhaled simultaneously. Kapsky placed a hand on Canidy's shoulder, a gesture of gratitude and assurance. "I am weak. I am very weak. But I will not let you down."

"That's what I want to hear," Canidy said resolutely. "All we need to do is hold out until we get to the boat. There will be food, water, and medicine on board. Just hang on."

"Dick," Fulmar said, "look at McDermott."

Canidy turned to see the Scot slumping against the door, barely conscious. The entire right side of his shirt was soaked with blood.

Canidy winced but said nothing. McDermott's face was drained of color. His eyelids fluttered, but his eyes were motionless and vacant.

Canidy shook his head. "This bandage isn't doing the trick, even for a tough bastard like him," he said as he bent down, seized the cuff of his left pant leg, and began tearing the fabric. "Got to put a tourniquet on the upper arm or we may lose him."

Canidy placed the strip of cloth from his pant leg around McDermott's upper arm just below the shoulder socket, pulled it as tight as he could, and tied it with a double knot. McDermott remained slumped against the car door.

Canidy shook the canteen and listened. A few dregs left. "I think he might appreciate this more than our good professor." He placed the canteen to McDermott's lips and simply poured. The Scot stirred a bit, and his eyes opened a bit wider.

Fulmar said, "We need to get going or we'll miss the boat, literally."

Canidy nodded and asked Matuszek, "How much farther?"

"We'll need to leave the car in less than a couple kilometers and go by foot the rest of the way."

"How long will it take?"

"Not long. Shorter than last time, because we've traveled farther west before turning northward than when Emil guided you previously."

Canidy examined his watch and then looked at Fulmar. "What time do you have?"

"Fifteen hundred hours. Almost on the dot."

"That's what I show also." Canidy nodded. "Commander, our boat is already at the dock. The Thorisdottirs will give us as much leeway as they can, but our window will close at about seventeen hundred hours. Can you get us there?"

Matuszek looked at Kapsky, and then McDermott. "I do not know."

CHAPTER 61

Northern Poland
1501, 15 August 1943

The anxiety had returned.

More than mere anxiety, something close to panic. The road had veered west, but there had been a northward split several kilometers after the convoy. Gromov was uncertain which road the Americans had taken. Both roads, he knew, passed within the woodland areas near Danzig that led to the sea. One went northward, while the other went farther to the west. They might have taken either. The northward road was safer. They'd have to disembark and travel a bit farther by foot to the sea, but the area was more heavily wooded, providing better coverage. The westward road was faster but more treacherous. It was closer to Danzig, and, as such, concentrations of German troops. The probability of encountering those troops was far greater.

Gromov chose to go westward. If it were his decision, that's what he would do. The tall one seemed to share many of Gromov's qualities. So that's likely what he would do.

Matuszek squinted and pointed to a thicket on the right side of the road. "There."

Fulmar veered off the road and slowed as he drove on the grass and into a grove of apple trees. The car pitched and bounced as he guided it as deep into the woods as it would go, obscuring it from anyone who might pass on the road.

Canidy looked to Kapsky. "Can you walk?"

"I do not know."

"Can you stand?"

"I will try."

Canidy looked at McDermott. "How about you?"

"I *will* walk."

Fulmar got out of the car, went to the rear, and assisted Kapsky. McDermott got out of his side of the vehicle, stood, and tested his legs. He slapped his right thigh and looked at Canidy. "Good enough."

Canidy was the last to get out of the car. He went to the rear and opened the trunk. "All right, everybody. We need to change back into our civilian clothes." He thumbed Maurer's shirt. "If the Thorisdottirs see us approaching in these things, they'll either shoot us or leave. Probably both. Besides, I doubt there are any SS Standartenführers strolling through the woods around here."

They were changed within minutes.

"We're going to have to hump. They'll wait, but not long. If the radio works as advertised, we might be able to let them know our expected arrival time and to wait, but we shouldn't count on it. Anyway, I think we need to get closer." He pointed at Kapsky and McDermott. "Can you go?"

Both nodded.

"Don't be heroes. If you need help, let us know. Hell, I'd put McDermott over my shoulder if he didn't smell so bad." Canidy patted Matuszek on the back. "Commander, your show. Lead the way and make it quick, please."

They began walking up a slight grade into the woods.

"Hold it," Canidy said. "Eric, let's give the radio a shot right now, see if Moriarty's contraption really works."

Fulmar dug into his ruck and retrieved a leather case no more than six inches in length, eight inches in width, and two inches thick. The others looked on in curiosity as he unzipped it and pulled out a device matching the dimensions of the case.

"*That* is a radio?" Matuszek asked. "It cannot possibly work."

"It's got no W/T transmitter box and doesn't use Morse code, but let's try it," Fulmar said. He pressed a small black button on the right side of the device and it came to life, static crackling softly. Fulmar pressed another button and spoke into the front grid of the device.

"Saint Paul to *Njord*. Come in. Saint Paul to *Njord*."

Fulmar released the button and the soft static returned. All five men listened intently.

Fulmar pressed the button again. "Saint Paul to *Njord*. Come in. Saint Paul to *Njord*." Fulmar released the button again and the static returned. They listened for another ten seconds before Fulmar repeated the exercise. Once again, nothing.

"I don't know if that means Moriarty's contraption doesn't work or the Thorisdottirs aren't there," Canidy said. "But we can't waste time standing around here. Just our luck the damn Nazis are picking it up. Clever bastards. Let's move before they locate us."

CHAPTER 62

Northern Poland
1557, 15 August 1943

Gromov grew increasingly concerned as he continued to drive westward. He'd contemplated doubling back and taking the northerly route but calculated he was already past the point of no return. He drove as fast as the vehicle would go along the bumpy road, feeling slightly nauseated from the persistent jostling. Thankfully, the road was beginning to smooth out a bit. With one hand on the steering wheel, he reached into his ruck on the seat next to him, rummaged about, and pulled out a hard roll. Bread helped settle his stomach, but it did nothing for his nerves. He took a large bite of the roll but stopped chewing almost immediately and slowed the vehicle. He squinted at a spot approximately a kilometer ahead on the right side of the road. Two . . . three . . . four . . . eight German soldiers were gathered near a grove, their evident attention on something they appeared to have found.

Gromov slowed and drove only a bit farther before stopping to focus on the scene ahead. He confirmed; one, two, three, four . . .

eight soldiers milling about something he was unable to discern until one of them moved a bit.

Gromov exhaled. It was the command car, somewhat obscured by the trees in the grove. He'd guessed right. They couldn't be too far ahead, but he'd have to move quickly before they reached the sea. He should be able to overtake them: one man could move faster than five.

Gromov drove forward slowly, assessing the scene, judging angles and distances. When he neared to within two hundred meters, the soldiers began gesturing toward the woods. After a few seconds, Gromov could see them nodding in unison and gesturing toward the forest. Seconds later they disappeared into the brush.

Competition, thought Gromov. *They may not know they're pursuing Americans, let alone Kapsky, but they are pursuing something suspicious.*

He got out of the vehicle, placed his Tokarev in his belt, and carried his rifle at low-ready. He walked briskly into the woods—moving northward along a parallel path fifty meters west of the Germans.

Gromov could hear the sounds of the Germans moving through the woods. In reaction, he stepped lightly so as not to reveal his presence. He winced upon hearing a dried twig snap underfoot and paused to see if there was any reaction from the Germans. There was none. Gromov sensed a subtle change in the air quality, the scent of salt water. He estimated the sea was no more than thirty minutes away.

He had less than that to acquire Kapsky.

CHAPTER 63

Northern Poland
1632, 15 August 1943

Canidy looked at his watch for the fourth time since abandoning the command car in the grove. The Thorisdottirs were probably well into the second hour of waiting for them at the dock. He pictured Kristin standing impatiently at the bow with her fists on her hips, listening intently for signs of their approach. She would not leave precisely at 17:00 hours, but neither would she wait longer than she deemed prudent. Canidy didn't know how long that would be, but he didn't want to test it. She made it clear that the German patrol boats along the coast dictated her timing. And Canidy couldn't argue with that. Katla might implore her to wait five or ten minutes longer for them to appear, but that would be the most Kristin would wait. And Canidy couldn't argue with that, either. He'd do the same.

The rest of the team appeared to share Canidy's sense of urgency. Matuszek, guiding them at the point, was advancing at near double time. Behind him McDermott gamely kept pace despite being visibly in pain and demonstrably weakened from loss of blood. Fulmar followed, looking a bit exhausted but otherwise fit and moving well. The professor trailed Fulmar by several meters, struggling to keep up. His breathing was labored and raspy, and his legs were unsteady; Canidy placed an arm around him every thirty to forty meters to keep him upright and moving. It was obvious that if they did make it to the boat, he'd need immediate and intensive medical attention. Canidy admired his grit.

The area was beginning to look familiar to Canidy, but he knew that the woods could play tricks with one's perception. He didn't want to risk going in any but the most optimal direction to get to the boat, but neither did he want to slow down.

Nonetheless, Canidy stage-whispered to Fulmar, "Eric, ask Matuszek to stop for a second." Fulmar, in turn, stage-whispered the request to Matuszek, who halted. All four huddled around Canidy.

"McDermott, you look like crap. You still in the fight?"

Irritated, McDermott said, "I told you, don't worry about me. You worry about yourself, you big shit."

Canidy looked at Matuszek. "Commander, how are we doing on time? Is this the best route?"

"We're closer. This is the direct route. We should see the terminus of the canal any moment. From there, perhaps another fifteen, twenty minutes to the dock."

"Good," Canidy replied. "Because that's all the time we've got." Canidy turned to Kapsky. "Twenty minutes more, Professor. Let me know if you can't go on your own power and we'll carry you. Got it?"

Kapsky nodded.

"How do you feel?"

"I cannot say. My legs and feet are numb."

"I'm not sure what he means," Canidy conceded. "But it's not good. We *have* to get past the next twenty to thirty minutes. You'll be okay if we get to the boat. All right?"

Kapsky, breathing heavily, said, "Let's move."

Immediately, Kapsky stumbled and fell. Canidy helped him up and stooped in front of him. "Get on my back, Professor. Piggyback, like when you were a kid." Kapsky nodded and climbed aboard Canidy's back, wrapping his arms around Canidy's neck and his legs around his waist. Canidy was grateful that he was lighter than he looked.

Mere moments later Matuszek pointed ahead to a canal. Canidy felt a charge.

"Almost there, Professor," Canidy informed. "Keep your fingers crossed."

The sight of the waterway prompted them to move faster despite the fact that the ground was becoming softer and, in some places, muddy. Canidy strained to keep pace with Matuszek and Fulmar. McDermott had fallen slightly behind Canidy but was buoyed by the sight of the water.

The sound of their movement remained minimal—primarily a muted crunch of leaves, even more so because of the soft ground. As a result, the snap of a branch behind them immediately caused Canidy, with Kapsky fastened to his back, to spin around and scrutinize the woods behind them. He remained still, looking from left to right.

Then another sound of indeterminate origin. He dropped Kapsky to his feet. The others also stopped and turned around. They remained still for several seconds without hearing another noise. Canidy turned and signaled to the others to advance. "Professor, I need you to do your best to walk on your own power just in case I need to make a fast move."

Kapsky blinked acknowledgment and followed the others. Canidy brought up the rear.

Gromov moved smoothly and silently through the forest, listening intently for noises made by the German troops.

Gromov was more experienced and was more disciplined. He discerned the subtlest of movements—the crack of a twig, the soft crunch of rotted leaves. He couldn't see through the foliage, but he gauged their presence approximately seventy to eighty meters west of him. They were a complication he didn't need. Given that the Americans were moving northward toward the Baltic, he knew his window would close soon—perhaps in less than twenty minutes. Their escape route was the sea. A boat would rendezvous with them or was already waiting for them. They would have to time their exit to avoid the infernal German maritime patrols, but they would be leaving soon.

Gromov evaluated his options as he threaded through the woods. He concluded he had few. The most methodical option, the one that most reduced his risk of death, was to kill the Germans first, then kill those escorting Kapsky. But he had no effective or timely means by which to kill the Germans without alerting the Americans to his presence. On the other hand, killing Kapsky's escorts first would require him to secure Kapsky and fight the Germans—all while preventing Kapsky from escaping.

He decided to keep moving and simply let the circumstances unfold.

———

Canidy grew more anxious the closer they got to the dock. He'd heard no suspicious sounds in the last few minutes, but every sound his own team made seemed magnified with each step closer to the dock. He walked with his head turned at nearly a ninety-degree angle to his right so as to see as far to their rear as possible without losing momentum. Were it not for Kapsky, he wouldn't resist the urge to break into a near sprint for the dock.

In front of him Kapsky was slowing. His strides grew shorter and unsteady and his arms were swinging in an exaggerated manner to afford more locomotion than his legs could generate on their own. His labored breathing was the loudest sound in the forest, but nothing could be done about it. He had to keep moving. If the sound gave them away, they'd just have to handle the consequences.

Gromov changed his opinion of the Germans somewhere to his left. Though he had judged them undisciplined, it seemed that was merely a matter of orienting themselves. For the last couple minutes, he heard no sounds whatsoever coming from their direction. They're *concentrating*, he thought. Focusing on their prey as they closed in for the kill.

He stopped for a moment, hoping to catch a telltale sound.
Nothing.

Though anxious to continue his pursuit, he waited a few seconds longer: nothing but the ambient rustle of leaves.

Gromov stared in the direction where the Germans should be, hoping to get a glimpse of fabric or maybe even exposed skin moving between gaps in the leaves and trees.

Still nothing.

He cursed under his breath as the anxiety rose once again.

"I must stop a moment," Kapsky said to Canidy as he sat on the rotting trunk of a fallen tree. "I am sorry. I cannot move as fast as the rest of you. After all of this time evading Germans, I thought I could. But, no."

"Take a blow, Professor," Canidy said, patting him on the shoulder. "But just for a minute. We have no options. We have to make our window, and it's closing quickly."

"Just for a moment," Kapsky repeated between labored breaths.

"Hold up," Canidy stage-whispered to the rest. "Hold up."

The others stopped and turned with sympathetic expressions, save for Fulmar.

"No," Fulmar said sharply, pointing at his wristwatch. "No way. Sorry. We've got to move. Now. *Right* now. We can rest later, on the boat. If there still *is* a boat."

Kapsky nodded and placed his hands on his thighs to lever himself upright. Canidy grasped him under his left armpit to assist, but Kapsky sat back down.

"Let's give it another shot," Canidy said. "We're out of time."

Once again assisted by Canidy, Kapsky catapulted himself up, this time successfully, although unsteadily.

"Eric," Canidy said. "Try Moriarty's radio again."

"That thing's a piece of shit," Eric replied. "Besides, no time. They're either there or they're not. Let's go."

"Try it," Canidy insisted.

Fulmar flashed an aggravated look, but pulled off his ruck, retrieved the device, and tried to transmit. All five men listened intently for a response. There was none. Fulmar shoved the device back in his ruck and said, "Okay. Let's go."

"Now we know if they leave without us, we'll have no means to get them to come back," Canidy said. He placed his hands under Kapsky's arms and lifted. "That's it, Professor, this is the home stretch. You didn't spend three years on the run only to fail ten minutes from the end."

Kapsky exhaled sharply, his jaw tensing with determination. "I will do my best not to slow you down anymore."

"Just a few more minutes, Professor. Just a little farther."

Gromov heard something he couldn't quite discern except that it wasn't indigenous to the forest. And it came from somewhere ahead of him. Somewhere close. He paused again and scanned the sur-roundings. Another sound. This time distinctly that of footsteps on litterfall. From somewhere ahead of him but very close. *If I can hear them, they can hear me*, he thought. But he had an advantage over the Germans and Americans. He *knew* someone was close. They did not.

Gromov dropped to one knee and focused on the spot from which the sounds had come. Almost immediately he heard another sound and locked his eyes on the point of origin. Only two heartbeats later he glimpsed a movement of leaves, then branches, then a flash of metal.

Good. Within striking distance. A bit closer and I have them.

Canidy had his right arm around Kapsky's waist, holding him up-right as they proceeded at a brisk pace along the canal. Fulmar, at the point, had quickened the pace.

Canidy wasn't sure, but the area seemed to be getting more familiar. He refrained from raising his hopes, but the area appeared to be recognizable. He permitted himself to do the mental calculations he'd avoided earlier. Five, no more than ten minutes, he estimated. Although the banks of the canal had no benchmarks and the docks were nowhere in sight, the air's scent and humidity signaled they were getting much closer to the sea.

"A few more minutes, Professor," he guessed. "We'll be at the dock and on the boat. Then England. Hang in there. You've just about made it."

Gromov's stealth yielded to speed. He feared he'd fallen dangerously behind the Americans and needed to close the gap.

He could easily hear the movement in the forest in front of him now, close enough that he couldn't lose them. The Germans, on the other hand, seemed to have gone off track. Amateurs. He had heard no sounds whatsoever coming from his left flank for several minutes.

Good. Fewer complications. He'd kill the American team, get Kapsky, and proceed eastward out of the woods.

Canidy released his arm from Kapsky's waist and spun around. M1911 held at shoulder level.

The sound was clear. Something or someone was moving behind them. Canidy bet it was the latter. He signaled to Kapsky to get the attention of the rest. Not hearing any footsteps behind him, McDermott had already stopped. He whispered to Fulmar—who whispered to Matuszek—to halt. All faced toward the rear, weapons ready.

For a fraction of a second, Canidy thought he saw movement. He signaled for everyone to drop to the ground, but after everyone complied, they saw nothing. Nonetheless, each remained still, waiting.

Gromov crested a low rise and was stunned. The Germans, backs toward him, were forty meters *in front*. He'd misjudged them. They'd moved even more swiftly than he. They were advancing rapidly, as if anticipating acquiring their target.

Gromov's jaw jutted with anger and determination. He wasn't going to let a few Germans thwart his victory.

Canidy held his breath so the sound of his breathing wouldn't interfere with his detection of movement. He heard nothing. He saw nothing.

Fulmar crawled next to him. "What do you see?"

"Nothing. I think something's back there, but whatever it is I can't see it, and we can't wait. We need to force the issue. We're close. The rest of you take Kapsky and go to the boat as fast as you can move. Matuszek, too. On my signal, sprint. Don't worry about making noise. Just run your asses off. Don't stop or look back, whatever you hear. I'll cover you until I think you've separated enough and then I'll follow. Since Kapsky and McDermott can't move very well, I should be able to get to the boat about the same time as you do."

"If it's there."

"If it's there," Canidy conceded. "If it isn't, we're all screwed anyway. But if it is, and I'm not right on your tail, don't wait for me.

Tell the Thorisdottirs to get the hell out of there and into the open water. I'll find my own way back, somehow."

Fulmar said nothing.

"Go."

Fulmar crawled toward the others. "Listen to me. We think someone's behind us. When I say 'Go,' we all get up and run like hell to the boat. Canidy will cover. I don't know exactly how far, but the boat's close. Regardless, run harder than you've ever run. Hold nothing back.

"Professor, this is your Olympics. Give it everything you've got."

Fulmar turned back to Canidy, who was lying on the ground with his left hand raised, and said, "Get ready."

Canidy dropped his arm. Fulmar said, "Go" and the forest erupted in gunfire.

Gromov was alarmed. The Americans and Germans were exchanging fire and Kapsky was somewhere in the midst of it.

Gromov could hear the air snapping from bullets streaking over him. Leaves and branches were fluttering from the impact of stray rounds.

This was madness. Kapsky would be killed.

Eight Germans armed with Karabiners were charging toward Canidy with astonishing speed. He sighted the one in front and squeezed the trigger of his M1911. The round struck the lead German squarely in the chest and he dropped to the ground as if a trapdoor had opened beneath him. The others kept charging without a pause, firing as they ran.

Canidy fired four rounds to give himself cover, rose from the ground, and ran in the direction of the dock. The air snapped around him as the Germans fired a volley of rounds after him. Canidy broke through a bank of thornbushes into a clearing and saw Fulmar, Kapsky, Matuszek, and McDermott no more than seventy-five meters in front of him along the bank of the canal. Fifty meters north of them sat the *Njord*, the Thorisdottir twins standing on deck, fists on hips.

Canidy spun and fired three more rounds at the pursuing Germans, dropping one of them on his face. The other six stopped, aimed, and fired several rounds. One grazed Canidy's left shoulder, spinning him sixty degrees to the left. He grimaced, gathered himself, and fired a round that went wide but caused the pursuing Germans to dive to the ground.

Canidy catapulted himself off the ground and sprinted toward the dock, zigzagging as he went. He could see Fulmar, Matuszek, McDermott, and Kapsky at the dock beginning to board the boat and Kristin raising her Gevarm to her shoulder. Seeing a weapon raised in his direction, Canidy immediately dove to the ground as Kristin fired several blind rounds at the Germans, causing them to drop to the ground for cover once again.

Canidy instantly popped back up and resumed sprinting, the effort producing a piercing sensation in his wounded shoulder. He heard the air snap inches from his right ear and a millisecond later saw Matuszek pitch forward and disappear onto the deck of the *Njord*. Canidy turned, fired toward the Germans, striking one in the throat, but without slowing the charge of the remainder. He emptied his weapon firing at the five remaining Germans, turned, and resumed running toward the dock.

Again, the air snapped above him and his eyes locked on the dock and the boat, where Fulmar and McDermott were struggling to assist an exhausted professor onto the vessel—all three presenting prime targets to the Germans.

Canidy shouted, "Move! Move! Move!" and leapt onto the dock and turned just in time to see the five Germans slow to a halt forty meters from the dock. For Canidy, the next ten seconds seemed to grind almost to a standstill and unfold over minutes rather than seconds. As Fulmar and McDermott lifted Kapsky onto the deck, the Germans trained their rifles at the boat. Everyone but Matuszek and Katla Thorisdottir was exposed on either the dock or the deck. Kapsky, being held upright on the deck of the boat by Fulmar and McDermott, displayed his back to the Germans as if it were a bull's-eye.

Even as Canidy thrust himself toward Kapsky to knock him to the ground he knew it was too late. He and Kapsky, along with Fulmar and McDermott, would be shredded by Karabiner rounds.

As he drove himself against Kapsky, Canidy heard a rapid succession of gunshots. Crashing into Kapsky, Fulmar, and McDermott, he braced for the sickening impact of the rounds. All three fell to the deck of the *Njord* as Katla drove the boat away from the dock up the canal.

But there was no pain. No blood. Not even a moan.

Canidy and Fulmar, lying together on the foredeck of the boat, stared at each other in astonishment, astonishment that they were both alive, astonishment that Kapsky, though debilitated, was unharmed.

They remained prone on the deck waiting for another volley of shots. None came.

———

Major Taras Gromov emerged from the brush, lowered his rifle, and surveyed the scene fifty meters in front of him. Five German soldiers lay on the mossy banks of the canal. One hundred meters beyond them, the stern of the *Njord* was rapidly disappearing around a shallow bend in the canal.

Kapsky was on the boat with the Americans. They would reach the Baltic within minutes, and from there—if Gromov's intelligence was as accurate as it had been throughout this operation— they would proceed toward Gotland. They needed to avoid U-boats and Messerschmitts, of course, but from Gotland the Americans would take Kapsky to RAF East Moor Field in Britain. Most likely Kapsky would remain there for a few days while British physicians nursed him back to health. Then he would be flown to Gander, Newfoundland, on his way to Princeton, New Jersey, by way of New York.

After a short period of rest, Kapsky would be debriefed by scientific luminaries. Kapsky would be giving the West what would seem to be an insuperable advantage over Germany and any other rivals that might challenge them after the war. An edge that could exist for decades.

Gromov pulled a cigar from his breast pocket, lit it, and took his time stoking it. It was Turkish, not pure tobacco, but he savored it nonetheless, sitting on a smooth boulder next to the canal as he puffed.

When he'd seen the Americans scrambling to get Kapsky aboard the boat, it was clear that the Germans had no idea who Kapsky was. They were simply shooting at an enemy who they'd tracked through the forest to a boat on the canal. Thorough, efficient, and perhaps expecting commendations, they would have killed Kapsky, oblivious to who he was. Under the circumstances, Gromov made the only decision he could and killed every single one of the German soldiers before they killed Kapsky.

Belyanov, of course, would be furious. The Americans had won. Gromov hadn't killed them and they had Kapsky. Not only would Kapsky provide the science for superweapons, but he would tell them about Katyn Forest. Stalin now would have to somehow convince the Western Allies that despite Kapsky's allegations, the Wehrmacht, not the NKVD, was responsible for the massacre. But, after all, how difficult would it be to convince the Americans and British that the *Nazis* had committed atrocities? Besides, Churchill was already pressing Roosevelt to open a Western Front against Hitler. Churchill needed it as much as Stalin did. And it was becoming increasingly clear to Roosevelt that it was imperative for the United States to do it. Beyond that, Belyanov would have his own problems. As Gromov looked at Goncharov's corpse, he imagined how Stalin would react upon hearing that the assassin Belyanov had sent after Gromov interfered in his attempt to capture Kapsky, thereby letting the scientist escape.

Gromov permitted himself a faint smile. He would still receive the Order of Lenin, perhaps awarded by Joseph Vissarionovich himself.

He stabbed the cigar into the soil, rose, and began walking back toward the vehicle he'd left on the edge of the forest. He proceeded at a leisurely pace, stopping after approximately one hundred meters to squat and yank his NR-40 from Colonel Yevgeni Goncharov's still-warm corpse. The dead man had been a respectable assassin—talented—but had stepped on one twig too many. Gromov wished he could be present when Belyanov would be forced to explain to

Beria why his favorite assassin had himself been marked for assassination by Goncharov.

Gromov wiped the blade against his right thigh before returning it to the sheath in the back of his collar. Then he trod cautiously back through the forest. He paused after a few steps, thought for a moment, and walked back to the corpses of the Germans lying along the canal. He chose one that most closely approximated his size and removed his clothing. Then Gromov undressed and donned the German uniform.

A careful assassin is a live assassin.

CHAPTER 64

The galley of the *Njord* in some ways resembled a field hospital, except everyone's spirits were high.

Katla was dressing Matuszek's wound with iodine, adhesive tape, and gauze. McDermott was resting on a floor mat, his back propped against the hull. Despite having suffered the most—and most severe—wounds, he was smiling broadly, having consumed the missing half of the bottle of Mortlach cradled in his lap. By comparison, Canidy's and Fulmar's wounds were minor, but their grins were nearly as broad, courtesy of healthy gulps of the Luksusowa vodka that had once inhabited the empty bottle on the galley floor.

Kapsky was in a deep sleep on a cot. Kristin and Katla recognized that in addition to suffering from extreme exhaustion, he appeared dehydrated. They'd fed him copious amounts of herring and bread that he'd consumed with generous amounts of beer and water. Before he fell asleep, he lifted his shirt and gently peeled from his left side the tape holding his notebook and handed it to Canidy, who handed it to Kristin and said, "Please keep this in the most secure compartment on the vessel until we disembark."

None of the passengers gave any thought to a possible encounter with U-boats or Messerschmitts. They were too elated or too exhausted and had the fatalism of transient victors. Canidy and Fulmar in particular looked both contemplative and elated.

"Don't worry, Commander," Canidy said to Matuszek, who was complaining, albeit good-naturedly, about being away from the battlefield. "After Gotland, we'll get you to Britain, patch you up, and you can return to the fight."

Matuszek's eyes lit up. "Do you think that perhaps I might even meet Sikorski?"

Canidy grinned. "Hell, Commander, I'll bet he'll insist on meeting *you*."

Fulmar said to Canidy, "Can't wait until we see Donovan. I bet he gave us no more than a ten percent chance of coming back alive, let alone coming back alive with Kapsky."

"The minute we get to the London OSS office, this will be legendary. Dulles will inform Donovan; Donovan will inform Roosevelt and Stimson. As long as we're in London, we won't have to buy a drink. And for at least the first week after we get back to the United States, too."

Canidy rose to his feet and began ascending the steps to the deck.

"What are you doing?" Fulmar asked.

Canidy winked. "Gonna extend our gratitude to the captain."

He found Kristin standing on the bow, chin held high, scanning the northern horizon. The sky to the west was a mixture of crimson, gold, and violet as the sun's corona sank into the sea. The evening air had a chill, but Canidy was insulated by success and alcohol.

Without turning, Kristin sensed his presence. "Congratulations, Major."

Canidy came beside her. "How long did you wait?" Canidy asked.

"Longer than I promised myself."

Canidy smiled.

"You should know, Major, that we will reach Gotland in approximately three hours, but your plane to Britain will not be arriving for approximately twenty-four hours thereafter due to weather off the North Sea."

"How disappointing," Canidy said with mock earnestness.

"There is, however, an outpost in Gotland that will tend to your wounds and provide food and lodging. You should be quite comfortable. All of your immediate needs will be met."

"And where will you go?"

"Katla and I are to be debriefed in Gotland and will depart when your flight arrives."

Canidy drew closer. "Enough time to teach me how to fish?"

Kristin turned. Her lips brushed lightly against his cheek.

"Not nearly enough, I'm afraid."

Canidy turned at the sound of Katla coming onto the deck.

"All is secure below," she reported.

"It's been a challenging last couple of days," Canidy said. "If you don't mind, I need to get some rest before we arrive in Gotland."

Kristin smiled. Electric. "Of course."

Kristin and Katla watched as Canidy disappeared down the steps to the lower deck. Kristin said, "Keep an eye on the steps. This should only take a minute."

Katla stationed herself at the top of the stairs to the galley as

Kristin locked the wheel and proceeded to the bow, where she removed the tarp from a three-by-five maple cabinet. She opened the double doors, flipped the transmitter on the RCA radio, and placed the microphone close to her mouth.

Gromov proceeded east along a desolate dirt road. He encountered no German patrols or checkpoints, although he'd seen Wehrmacht vehicles in the distance. He'd determined not, however, to press his luck. Even though he had the cover of the German uniform and the Kübelwagen, and he spoke German well, remaining on the roadways was a risk. The vehicle made him visible, and in this environment visibility, however camouflaged, was a risk.

He heard a raspy sound and immediately slowed and came to a stop on the side of the road. The sound erupted again and he reached into his bag on the seat next to him and pulled out a gray metal box the size of a large dictionary. A headset with earphones and microphone were attached.

Freed from the bag, the noise, while still raspy, became intelligible. It was a voice speaking in Russian.

Gromov arranged the earphones over his head and the raspiness disappeared.

"*Njord* to Bulba."

Gromov adjusted the microphone in front of his mouth and responded. "Bulba, *Njord*. Go."

"We have obtained the notebook."

"Repeat."

"We have obtained the notebook. And we have its author, who is likely to acquire a terminal illness and probably will not survive the journey. All is well."

Gromov nodded to himself in satisfaction. "Received. Good work. Proceed as planned. Bulba out."

Gromov got out, bashed the radio against the door of the vehicle until it was inoperable, and threw it into the brush alongside the road. Then he threw his bag over his shoulder and began walking east.

With her dying breath the redheaded woman had provided at least one piece of truthful information. And that information had secured Gromov's victory.

A look of satisfaction covered his face as he began the long journey back to the front.